THE COUNCIL

By L. M. Peralta

THE ELEMENTALS TRILOGY

The Elementals
The Council
The Creator

THE ARCADIAN STEEL SEQUENCE

The Wings of Heaven and Hell
The Seven Archangels of Heaven
The Seven Princes of Hell

United Trace

THE COUNCIL

BOOK TWO OF THE ELEMENTALS

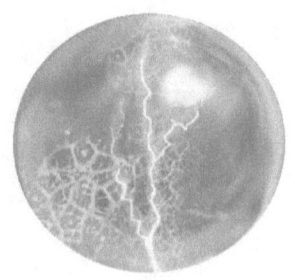

L. M. PERALTA

First Paperback Edition: April 2014

Summary: After the battle against Hephaestus, Sara's life becomes routine until Farah reveals that the Element Spheres have gone missing.

ISBN: 978-0-9888448-2-7

On a dark day, the spheres were created;

Set in glass houses reflecting the light,
Every element was bound and fated
To be wielded as nature's stolen right.

It was promised to the willing keepers
That the elements now bound could not rage,
But they were told falsely by the reaper;
Nature's elements they could not cage.

Yet still the elements were absorbed
By those whose origin determined it;
The reaper, skin eaten-away, teeth barbed
Lived not to see the day, retired to the pit.

And the long-wished peace the keepers await
Never came as they entered the gate.

PROLOGUE: THE KEEPERS OF THE SPHERES

Five hundred years ago . . .

NIGHT cloaked the city like a well-worn shawl, draping over it like something familiar and comforting. The dark sky loomed above, full of stars and far off satellites. The sky rail sped travelers to the bars and night clubs that kept the city well-lit and alive under the darkness.

Lamp posts lined the streets like watchful sentinels, and power lines connected all in a web of surging energy. Life could be heard in the roar of the engines, the buzz of the city lights, and the static drone of the monitors that hung atop the highest buildings of the city.

"Omega City ranks number one among Mirmina's safest cities. According to public opinion . . ." the monitor hummed. The news reporter's pixelated image dotted the screen.

Lina and Destan sat at a night café, waiting as the sky darkened. Fingers typed and drummed on the screens that lit the faces of the people.

"Do you have to go?" Lina asked. "Street racing is illegal."

"Either I do this," Destan said, "or I become the subject of Styx's pride for a lifetime. He'll feed off that for weeks until the whole underground is talking about it, and then he'll sit digesting it as it embeds in everyone's memories."

Lina folded her arms and leaned back in her chair. "You're exaggerating. Nothing Styx could throw at you is worth being thrown in jail for weeks."

"You don't know Styx as well as I do. He'd eat his own kids before he'd let me live this down. Besides, who says I'm getting caught?"

"Our trackers." Lina held up her arm. A blue chip glowed under her skin below the wrist. The chip tracked her location from anywhere in the city.

"That's why we wear these." Destan tapped on his metal armband. The armband covered his wrist to his elbow. "It blocks the signal. The sentinels won't know how fast I'm going with this on."

"I'm coming with you."

"Seriously? You hate the races."

Lina nodded. "I'm going with you. I didn't say I was cheering you on."

Destan pressed a code into his communicator, and his motorcycle sped from around the corner to the curb not far from where they sat.

He got onto the motorcycle. "You coming?"

Lina sat behind him and wrapped her arms around his waist. Destan put on his helmet, and they sped down the street bright with lights.

*   *   *

PEOPLE from the underground crowded the street. As Destan and Lina neared the crowd, a young woman approached them. Destan removed his helmet.

"You're late," Erina said.

Another motorcycle and its driver were positioned at the starting line.

"I'm sorry. Traffic," Destan said.

"Who's this?" Erina asked.

"Lina, my girlfriend."

Lina got off the motorcycle and extended her hand to Erina. "Pleasure."

Erina kept her arms folded.

"You two play nice," Destan said. He pulled up to the other motorcyclist, and the crowd hooted.

The other driver refused to look over at Destan.

"Styx, how you holding up?"

Styx had a black eye. He stared forward at the dark pavement stretching out in front of them, imagining that he was bashing Destan's face into it.

"Trying to be funny?" Styx snapped the visor of his helmet over his eyes.

"No. Trying to be nice. I don't want you to give me a black eye to match the one I gave you. It's starting to swell really bad."

"Don't worry, we won't match," Styx said, "not after I smash one side of your body in with my bike."

"I just smiled at her." Destan put on his helmet and pulled down his visor.

The driver waited for Erina to wave the flag. Destan made a show of smiling at Erina, and Styx released a guttural groan and squeezed his handle bars.

Erina raised the flag over her head and brought it down.

The motorcycles roared and zoomed down the well-lit street.

Styx reared ahead with Destan trailing him. They rounded the bend and drove onto the bridge. Destan sped up until his motorcycle was in line with Styx's.

Styx veered left and smashed his motorcycle into Destan's. Destan's motorcycle hit the side of the bridge and sent up sparks as it scraped the concrete wall.

Destan glanced down at the scratched paint and sighed. Styx slammed into his bike again, forced it against the concrete barrier of the bridge, and pinned it there.

"What are you doing?" Destan yelled over the roar of the bikes and the scraping of metal on concrete. "I thought this was a race?"

Styx had his bike against Destan's, hugging it to the barrier. Styx leaned in further until the concrete scraped Destan's arm. His metal arm band protected his flesh from the same scraping the paint on his bike was getting.

They neared the end of the bridge. Destan's arm band sent sparks that bounced off his helmet.

Destan pushed back against Styx's motorcycle. He gave himself enough room to zoom ahead. His armband cracked and fell off in pieces. The chip under Destan's skin glowed red.

AT the control station, the patrol guard snacked on chips. His eyes drifted over the monitors, and his headset hugged his head. He hadn't had any crimes to report for several nights.

The alarm sounded. Someone's tracker was moving fast through the city, beyond any legal speed limit. A red dot beeped across the monitor.

The patrol guard wiped the oily crumbs off on his shirt, and jabbed the keys on his keypad.

"Report."

"Sir, send a sentinel downtown. There's a citizen driving above the speed limit on Core Street."

Destan sped up to Styx. "My tracker's red," Destan shouted. "The sentinels will be on their way."

"Let them come." Styx laughed and clapped Destan on the shoulder as he rode alongside him.

"Friends again?"

"After you lose to me, and I get to bash your face in for trying to steal my girl."

"It was just a smile."

Destan and Styx turned the corner when the flashing lights and sirens accosted their eyes and ears.

"You weren't kidding," Styx shouted. "Do you think we can finish this race before they catch up with us?"

"We'll see." Destan sped up ahead of Styx.

Two sentinels riding motorcycles chased them as they hugged the curved corners and ignored the stop lights.

"Pull over," one of the sentinels demanded over his speaker.

Destan flew down the street. He wished he could remove his helmet so the cool air could hit his face and dry the sweat on his brow. This would be his last race. He sighed. Lina would be angry. He calculated in his head how much time he would get for this.

A street racing charge, first time caught, so first offense would be about a month and a fine plus community service. Probably probation and a revoked license. But then there is resisting arrest, which is likely what this amounts to. That would be up to a year and a hefty fine. Lina won't like this at all.

"Pull over."

Destan rounded the next corner. Styx neared the cliff. Omega City was built in the center of a mountain, bordering the sea. Signs warned drivers to drive a maximum of twenty miles per hour when rounding the bend. Any faster and a driver would risk falling into the chasm below. Drivers had fallen, and their vehicles and bodies were never recovered. No one knew how far down the chasm went. No one was that anxious to find out.

Destan reduced his speed, but Styx maintained his.

"What are you doing?" Destan shouted. "Slow down!"

But Styx increased his speed.

Destan stepped onto his accelerator and sped to Styx's side. He pushed against Styx's motorcycle and forced the vehicle away from the cliff. Both their bikes skidded across the street, and the drivers landed on the ground. Destan and Styx stood. The landing scraped Destan's arm.

Destan removed his helmet and dropped it to the ground. "What the hell, man?"

But Styx looked past him. A shadow darker than the night covered the street. Destan turned. A wave hovered over the city. The roar deafened the sirens.

Both drivers ran to their motorcycles. But Styx grabbed the closest one: Destan's.

"You son of a . . ." Destan rushed down the street and got on Styx's bike.

When he lifted the motorcycle, it faced the direction from which they had started the race. With no time to turn around, Destan sped down the street in that direction, trying to speed past the wave's massive shadow as it grew over the city.

Destan passed the sentinels. The bright, blinking lights on their motorcycles assaulted his eyes. But the sirens were not as deafening as the roar of the wave.

"Pull over!"

"Turn around!" he shouted.

The crash of the wave echoed through the city as it flooded the streets at locomotive speed.

Destan sped over the bridge and back to the finish line.

The people glanced around and murmured.

"What are you doing?" Erina said. "You came around the wrong way."

Destan searched the street. "Lina?"

"I'm here!" Lina came out from among the crowd.

"Get on!" Destan shouted.

"What's wrong?" Lina asked.

"No time to explain. Just get on the bike!"

Lina got on the back of the motorcycle.

"What's going on?" Erina asked.

"You have to get out of here," Destan said.

"I don't understand. Where's Styx?"

"Just go! Just drive out of the city now! As fast as you can!" He slammed on the accelerator, and Lina clung on before the force knocked her off the bike.

As the wave grew, people ran only to be swept up by the deadly waters. Buildings toppled as the wave's force ripped them from their foundations.

Lina cried, and she loosened her grasp on Destan's waist.

"I need you to hold on," Destan shouted over the roar of the wave tearing through the city.

"Dad, mom, Kath. What if they don't get out?"

"You have to worry about *you* right now."

Vehicles crowded the streets, and Destan had to maneuverer around them.

"I don't want to go, not without them," Lina said.

"I need you to hold on and be quiet!" Destan blinked the sweat from his eyes as it trailed off his forehead.

As Destan entered Omega Circle, he dodged an oncoming vehicle. Lina was thrown from the bike.

Destan was light-headed, and he couldn't swallow the lump that had formed in his throat. He slammed on the brakes and ran over to where Lina lay. Blood spilled down the curb.

Lina rested with her eyes open, staring up at the sky. Blood pooled around her head, which Destan cradled in his hands.

Destan shook his head.

Lina's eyes were glassy and unmoving.

He placed her head down and held her hand in his. Her fingers hung limp.

Destan rubbed the tears from his face and sprinted back to his motorcycle. He pressed down on the accelerator until the engine roared. He left the city behind him.

He stopped on a cliff above the city. The wave rushed through the streets, knocked the lights from their posts, forced cars against buildings, and swept the citizens up in its wake. The lights of the city blinked out as the wave moved inland and engulfed the city in water and darkness.

He kneeled on the rocky ledge and sobbed until his chest ached. Lina's blood painted his hands, and the chill that ran through his body as he grasped her lifeless hand had stayed with him.

DESTAN traveled the long road from Omega City to Vella. He had been to the neighboring city once, which was a two-hour journey by vehicle. But his motorcycle was running out of gas. On foot, the journey might take more than a day, and that was without sleep.

His motorcycle sputtered to a stop. He abandoned it. No light guided him across the plain. He looked up at the dark sky. He checked his communicator. It had no signal because all the towers had been toppled, but the time was eight in the morning.

Destan shook his head. Where was the sun?

His tracker glowed red. He pressed on it. It shifted under his skin.

"What are you doing, young man?" a voice arose from the darkness.

"Who's there?"

A light flickered, and an old man appeared from amidst the darkness. His face was weathered and wrinkled, and, in places, his flesh was eaten away revealing the muscle beneath.

The light was in full illumination, glowing in the old man's hand from an unknown source.

"Who are you?" Destan asked. "Can you help me?" He tried not to stare at the old man's decaying face.

"You came from there?" The old man pointed in the direction of Omega City.

"Yes. A wave hit. It flushed the city. I don't know if anyone made it out."

"*You* made it out."

"Yeah." Destan hung his head.

"My name is Erebus, and I can help you."

"Anything. Food. Water. Directions. If you have another flashlight that would be great."

Erebus reached inside his cloak and removed a clear orb.

"What is it?"

"A sphere."

Destan furrowed his brow. *How could that help?* He needed food, shelter, civilization, not a glass ball.

"You have seen great destruction, young man, the power of Water. Others have seen such destruction: the power of Wind, Frost, Earth, Lightning, Fire, and Darkness. The world needs someone who has seen the destruction of Water."

"Why?"

"So we can become gods."

"I don't know what you're talking about." Destan tried to move past the old man, but Erebus grabbed his arm.

When Destan seized the old man's hand in attempt to loosen his grasp, the skin on Erebus's hand was pulled away, revealing the sinews underneath.

"Don't you want to live a life without tragedy?" Erebus hissed, ignoring the flesh that had been ripped from his hand. "Elements that cause such destruction can be contained. Water can be contained. It can be ruled by human hands."

Destan tried to shake the old man's hand away, but Erebus was stronger than his fragile body appeared.

"You're crazy."

"This isn't a flashlight, boy!" Erebus held out his hand. The flame hovered above his deteriorating flesh. The flame disappeared and lightning flashed, vines grew from the old man's palm and down his hand, curling around his fingers.

Destan escaped the man's grasp and backed away. A gust of wind knocked him off his feet.

Destan scrambled backward across the ground, got on his feet, and turned to run.

"Don't run away, young man. What do you have left? Wouldn't you like to shape the world with your hands? Or do you want to feel helpless in the face of it?"

Destan stopped. Lina was dying, bleeding on the concrete as the wave rushed in.

"You can know such power, but you must be willing."

Erebus approached him and held out the sphere.

Destan took it. It was cold and light, devoid of life. But as he held it, the sphere became warm like a summer stream and grew heavy like a stone on the riverbank.

Destan withered. His skin became pale and wrinkled as power gathered within the sphere.

A single droplet fell from the sky and landed on Destan's face below his left eye. The liquid burned like acid.

He clenched the glass sphere and felt powerless to let go despite the energy it drained from him. Water swirled inside the sphere, and Destan fell to his knees.

1

DREAMS

SARA danced on the surface of the lake, surrounded by crystals. Ripples danced through the clear water as she twirled upon its surface. She delighted in the cool lightness beneath her feet as the water wavered like silk in the breeze.

This moment was long forgotten. Sara stopped when she felt a hand upon her shoulder. Arms hugged her and blond hair brushed against her cheek.

"I missed you," she whispered.

His arms loosened their grasp, and the scene faded. As wakefulness pulled Sara from the dream, two voices sounded.

The first was Talon's: "Your story is not over."

And the second . . . "You're not alone."

Sara woke. She closed her eyes and tried to return, but her body was refreshed and sleep would not come back to her.

She pushed her light brown hair from her face. She combed through her hair with her fingers and got out of bed.

She went to the window. The sun peeked over the mountains, and the training field was deserted. But soon, the apprentices would have their breakfast and meet their trainers on the field. Fewer apprentices attended Element than in the years previous.

Element's lack of apprentices was the fault of Morica Council. The Council had gone into hiding when Hephaestus gained power. They hurt many Elementals, including Sara's mother. They blamed Elementals for the imbalances of nature, the thirst for power, and the destruction.

Parents refused to send their children to Element for fear that the Council meant to do something more than political containment. Many trainers had left as well to join the Resistance, hoping to get into the graces of the Council.

The Resistance was now the Council's military strong arm. Both claimed to be devoted to the protection of Mirmina and its people. Most of their influence remained in Lumina, but the Council was spreading its ideals to the out-lying regions.

Sara looked across the field to the lake. For three years, no one had danced there. The water was still, sleeping. Not even the branches of the low-hanging tree disturbed its surface.

Now that Brina was gone, Sara took on her duties: making sure Element was well-maintained, keeping the schedule, and waiting, waiting for someone like Talon to disturb her waters.

Sara sat in Brina's library when a knock came to the heavy oak door of Element.

She went into the entrance hall, and opened the door. A girl stood outside. Her canary yellow hair was piled atop her head. Her skin was tan.

A little bird perched upon her shoulder. Green feathers surrounded her small, black eyes. The bird chirped.

"Farah!"

Farah grinned.

*   *   *

SARA led her into Brina's library where they sat in large armchairs.

Farah sank deep into the armchair with plenty of room on either side of her. "Ah, comfort," Farah said. "You wouldn't believe the things I've had to sit on in the last few weeks."

Farah's boots were well-worn.

"Have you been traveling? I thought you were still in Breeze."

"I couldn't stay in that steel prison for another minute. All my dad wants to do is talk about politics and how we all should get on Morica's good side. From what I've heard, those no-good cowards ran at the first sight of danger."

"How is your father doing otherwise?"

"He's been off on *business*. Wouldn't say what kind. So, at the first sight of a clear opening, Thatch, Shift, and I took off."

"Shift went with you?" Sara remembered how unwilling Shift had been to disobey his father.

"Shift's not so bad. He just needs the right kind of guidance. Besides, Dad made him really mad when he told someone else to manage the city while he is away. After all, it is Shift's birthright."

"Why would Tag do that?"

"Shift hasn't been right since the battle in Omega Ray. He's having trouble calling Wind."

"Oh." Sara could sympathize. Since Fero's destruction of the Water Sphere, she had not been able to call Water.

"I have so much to tell you, but first, do you want to say hello to the guys?"

"Sure. Where are they?"

"Well, Thatch couldn't land in the city."

"Land? You mean the dome?" Sara recalled the large metal contraption that rested on the back of Thermal.

"Not exactly. Thatch's new toy is much bigger than the dome."

*   *   *

SARA followed Farah through the streets of Elementa. No Elementals performed in the market or outside the alleyways. They followed the trail up to the mountains. Beyond the cliff, on the beach, Thermal dug his long claws into the sand. Thermal raised his ashy gray beak and cawed. Attached to his back was a harness, and a wagon-like structure four times as large as the dome trailed behind him.

The structure had wheels like a giant carriage. Where the driver would sit, holding the reins, a glass covering tilted downward.

"What is it?" Sara asked.

"Thatch calls it our Flying Chariot," Farah said.

As they approached, the hatch door opened and a ramp unfolded.

Sara looked up.

"Don't worry," Farah said. "It's completely safe. A lot safer than the dome."

That's not saying much, Sara thought.

She led Sara up the ramp and into the carriage. Inside the large structure, various metal contraptions spun on axels, and gears moved in circles.

"This is the engine room," Farah said. "Wait until you see the rest."

They walked to the elevator in the center of the structure, which brought them to the upper floor.

"Thatch worked hard to get this thing together. He's been working on it for years, gathering materials from the ruined streets of Breeze."

The elevator doors slid open to the control room. Machines lined the walls. Steps led to the cockpit. Three seats faced the big glass panels overlooking Thermal's head. At one seat was a blue monitor streaming with little white words falling across its face. In the middle was a wheel to navigate the structure. Pipes and wires lined the right side of the room. Monitors clustered against the opposite wall.

Sheets of metal covered the floors, walls, and ceiling, which curved up.

"Hey." Thatch spun in his seat at the blue monitor. "It's been a long time."

Shift sat in the driver's seat. He turned to look at Sara as she approached.

"What do you think?" Thatch asked.

"I've never seen anything like this," Sara said.

"I hope not. It's an original design. Shift's the pilot. That wheel controls Thermal's direction. It pulls the reins connected to Thermal's harness. I'm the navigator. These numbers on the screen here—they're coordinates."

"Coordinates?"

"A map of Mirmina. Like in the books I've studied. The books from the old world. Up there," Thatch pointed to the sky, "there are structures that can pinpoint any location. This machine can communicate with them to create a map."

"Tell her what you do," Shift said.

"Me?" Farah asked. "I sit at the window over there and point when I see something interesting and say: 'Oh, oh, land there!'"

"Yep, that about sums up what she does."

"Hey, I do more than that!" Farah said. "I handle negotiations."

"What negotiations?" Shift asked.

"Like when I talked to Lord Fletzi about allowing Thermal to land in Lumina Port. For a price, of course."

Orka chirped.

Shift shook his head and turned back to the windows.

"So," Sara said, "if Thermal flies the Chariot, what are the machines for?"

"Well," Thatch said, "the ones up here are location-trackers. They find places, things, people."

"People?"

"Well, provided they have a tracking device on them."

"Oh," Sara said.

"And," Thatch said, "the ones you noticed downstairs are engines. They not only run the locators, but they also power the Chariot, to a certain degree, which is a lot less strain for Thermal. I wish I could get them strong enough to power the whole structure, but that may take some time and a huge jolt of energy."

"Where's Stan?" Farah looked at the cluster of computers and the empty seat in front of them.

"Yeah," Shift said, "I was wondering where that little buzz-can got off to myself."

Thatch held down a button on the arm of his chair and spoke: "Stannum, report to the control room."

Buzzing and crashing echoed from the back of the room.

The sliding door opened and an oversized metal beetle with skinny steel arms flew into the room. Sara ducked as it zoomed past her. In the center of the room it stopped and shook itself until something rattled inside its head.

Its metallic body gleamed in the light, but its skinny arms showed signs of rust. An orange light blinked in the center of its body as it hovered in the air.

"You called?" The floating machine's voice was monotone and high-pitched.

"I wanted you to introduce yourself to Sara," Thatch said.

"Hello, Sara." Stannum floated over to her and extended one small steel hand. "I am Stannum. It is nice to meet you."

"And you as well." Sara shook its hand.

Stannum's eye turned deep orange. He tilted his eye up and down until the light scanned Sara from head to toe. Stannum's glowing eye projected a small holographic image of Sara. "Lady Sara, former Water Elemental. Three years ago, she spearheaded the group of Elemental fighters that waged a battle against Hephaestus, a Fire Elemental and tyrant. His tyrannical reign lasted approximately twenty-four years before the battle, where he then perished."

Shift sighed.

"Excuse me?" Stannum said.

"Shift, why did you have to start?" Thatch asked.

"Start?" Shift turned to face the room. "I didn't say anything."

"You never appreciated me," Stannum buzzed.

"Appreciate you? You're a metallic piece of junk."

"You are an organic piece of junk who will not admit that I am superior in every way."

"Shift, it's just a machine," Thatch said.

"With an attitude, which you gave it," Shift said. "I wish I would have never built it. Why did you feel the need to finish putting together this heap of junk?"

"Heap of junk?" Stannum buzzed. "I will be ticking long after you are gone."

"We'll see about that." Shift made a move to get out of his seat.

"Please," Thatch said, "we need Stannum. He's a machine and a helpful one at that. But his thoughts, feelings, and reactions are programmed, and you made him that way, not me."

Stannum's glowing eye turned a pale shade of orange, and his arms hung at his sides.

"Shift made Stannum when we were kids," Thatch said. "But he failed to make the right connections in Stannum's brain network. Stannum went haywire and destroyed some very valuable prototypes Uncle Tag had been working on. Shift got in trouble for it. He was frustrated with Stannum so he locked him up. One day, I found Stannum, half-smashed in a supply cabinet, and I salvaged him. It took years for me to fix him, but now he works fine."

Stannum zoomed over to the blue-screened machines and pressed buttons, his long arms stretching over the control panels, allowing his skinny steel fingers to reach the keys.

"Stannum analyses objects we find on the locator. He's working on a link right now.

"A few nights ago, we picked up a reading on the locator. A strange landmass appeared far out to sea, but as we got closer to it, it blinked on and off the map until it disappeared. It was strange. Something that big coming in and out like that. We couldn't find it again.

"Stannum is scanning and analyzing every map from Lumina's library. We hope we can send him to scan the maps in Element."

"We asked around," Farah said. "No one's heard of an island that far out. Neither Caleena nor Lumina Port has ever shipped there."

"I don't think it will come up again," Shift said. "Probably a mishap with the locator. I think all this map scanning is a waste of time."

"Don't say that," Farah said. "We'll find it. I know we will."

"Why?" Sara asked. "You think it could be the Insula?"

2

Unexpected Journey

SHIFT leaned back in his seat. "The Insula Somnia Perpetua—everyone's favorite fairy tale. Don't fill her head with nonsense," Shift said. "It's cruel."

"It isn't nonsense," Farah said. "It could be the same place Bolton talked about."

"Just because he spread the fairy tale doesn't make it true," Shift said. "And it doesn't mean that the landmass we think we saw is the Insula. Everyone knows that story."

Farah shook her head. "You don't know anything."

"No," Sara said, "your brother is right. It's a story for children."

"Shift is never right," Farah said.

"Thanks," Shift said.

"There's a chance." Farah looked at the monitors lining the wall.

"Maybe," Sara said.

"You should come with us," Farah said.

"But what are the chances we'll find the landmass again," Sara said, "and besides I have a life here now. I've been taking over where Brina left off. I can't just leave."

"That's not what you would have said three years ago."

"It was different then. I was young. I have responsibilities now."

"Just give me a week," Farah said. "In three years, have you had one vacation? Come on, a week and we'll take you back."

Sara hesitated. "What if we run into trouble? I wouldn't be able to help." Not only could she not call Water, but Sara hadn't been able to manipulate water since the battle in Omega Ray.

"Thatch might have found a way around that." Farah glanced over at Thatch. "Show her."

"I'm not sure it will work," Thatch said.

"We haven't tried it on someone without an element," Farah said. "We should at least try."

Thatch nodded and got up from his seat. "We'll have to go to the roof. This might get a little dangerous."

THE elevator brought them to the roof. Elementa stretched out before them. The rolling hills were like the back of a large cat. The marketplace was clustered in the center of the town. The people, small from a distance, crawled through the streets and alleys like tunnels in an ant farm.

The roof rose above Thermal's head. It was flat in the middle and sloped at the edges. A railing ran all the way around the roof. The railing stood about three and a half feet high. The roof was paneled with sheet metal starting from the back of the Chariot and stopping mid-way from the center. The rest was glass.

Thatch held out an arm bracer. It was steel, and soft cloth padded the inside. At the top, the metal curved up, creating a semi-circle, and to complete the circle, the object was hollowed out, making a second semi-circle. In the center of the circle, filling it almost completely was a small, gel-like substance. It changed colors as it quivered inside the circle.

"An Aether?" Sara asked.

Thatch nodded. He strapped the bracer around Sara's right arm and tied the bindings. "Okay, when I tell you, grip your hand into a fist and release," he said. "Pretend you're calling Water. The Aether will react to the movement. They're influenced by sensory suggestion. But don't get your hopes up. I've tested it repeatedly. The Aether doesn't respond to Elementals. We haven't tested it on regular people."

Sara nodded. She didn't like the way Thatch put her in the same category as regular people. She was ashamed at the thought. It was pridefulness she didn't know she had.

"Aim at the sky, grip your hand into a fist and release."

Sara took a deep breath. *This won't work*, she thought.

She did as Thatch instructed. The arm bracer jolted back as a bolt of energy zoomed through the sky.

Farah gasped, and Orka hid in her nest-like hair.

"Lightning," Sara whispered.

"Were you thinking about Lightning just then?" Thatch asked.

"I don't think so," Sara said. "But seeing you all again. I couldn't help but think about Bolton too."

Thatch scratched his head.

"How did you know to make this?" Sara gazed at the Aether.

"I have books on the subject," Thatch said. "Not much is known about Aethers, but they have similarities with Elementals."

"I didn't ask it to send Lightning," Sara said. "It was like the Aether could sense what I wanted, but it chose of its own accord. Perhaps because of my thoughts, but I didn't command it. If it chooses what element it wants, how can I trust that it will choose the one we need?"

"Maybe you can't," Thatch said, "which is why there's a backup plan. When all else fails . . ." Thatch handed her a dagger like the one Farah carried.

"A weapon of steel."

"There's no shame," Farah said.

Sara nodded. "Of course not. Talon carried a weapon of steel." Talon had wielded a long, curved sword. When the Resistance delivered Talon's body for burial, they had failed to recover the sword. It was the sword forged from his father's teachings and the sword that ended his life.

SARA walked with Thatch and Farah back to Element. Stannum floated alongside them. Sara packed a few things, including paper, charcoal, and the handheld mirror Bolton gave her.

Stannum and Thatch scanned the maps in the library.

Farah was out in the field showing off to the new apprentices. They watched as she called Wind to sweep the fallen leaves into a funnel.

Sara watched from the window. Farah would make a good teacher, she thought, if she could stay in one place long enough to train her apprentices. Unless her apprentices could follow her.

After Sara informed the head trainer she was taking some time off, she boarded the Chariot and was given her own earpiece and tracker.

"Any data on the landmass?" Thatch asked.

"No," Stannum buzzed. "Still analyzing. I am putting the maps from the library in Element into my database, but I still cannot find any record of our Chariot ever passing over a landmass in the sea. It is as if our files were wiped clean or stopped recording when we passed over. Strange."

"Keep looking," Thatch said. "Maybe the file is buried."

"I do not think so. My brain computes instantly."

"How long will it take?" Sara asked.

"No way of telling," Thatch said. "Stannum may not have enough information, but we won't know until he has completed his work. In the meantime, we can travel. Is there anywhere our new crew member would like to go?"

"I haven't seen Spire in some time," Sara said.

Thatch nodded.

Shift pulled the steering wheel towards him, and the Chariot lifted from the ground. It hovered as the wheels retracted into its body. The dust rose, and the thunderous sound of steel settling echoed through the Chariot.

Thermal cawed and kicked off the ground, a whirlwind of sand and dust billowing around him as his massive wings swept the beach. He gained momentum, and the Chariot tore through the sky.

WHILE Farah pointed out things on the ground, and Thatch, Shift, and Stannum were at their respective posts, Sara explored the Chariot.

She boarded the elevator. Numbered buttons indicated the four floors. The first floor was the engine room and entrance into the Chariot, the second floor was the control room, and the fourth floor was the roof, but she hadn't been to the third floor.

"Nothing exciting there," Farah had said. "That's just where we sleep."

Sara pressed the number three. The elevator brought her to the third floor and opened to a short, steel-paneled hallway.

At the end of the hall, the door slid open. Stools ran along the edge of a bar. A loft lined with beds rose above the bar. Glass made up the ceiling and walls of the loft. The sun shined through the glass and lit up the room.

Clouds moved past as the Chariot soared through the air.

Sara walked up the stairs to the loft.

Beside one of the beds was a perch for Orka. On top of the bed something gleamed in the light.

Sara moved closer to it.

It couldn't be.

She picked up the medallion. A fissure ran through the middle, and the medal was tarnished. The element symbols rested one atop the other to form an intricate pattern. The chain from which the medallion hung was broken. A link was missing.

Sara sat on the bed and stared at the medallion. Her finger traced the fissure.

"Shift said we shouldn't disappoint you with it." Farah walked up to the bed and sat beside Sara. Orka flew onto her perch.

"He said it would only make you unhappy."

"Where did you find this?" Sara asked.

"By the Water Sphere sanctum."

"The cave?"

Farah nodded.

Sara looked down at the medallion. "I don't understand how it got there."

"Why?" Farah asked.

"He left this. I remember the first time I saw he wasn't wearing it. I asked him about it."

"Maybe that's where he left it. By the cave."

Sara shook her head. "No, that's impossible. He got rid of it before that. He wasn't wearing it after we left Tosia."

"It's been three years," Farah said. "He would have come to you. The best thing we can do is to find the Insula."

Sara nodded.

"Come on," Farah said, "Let's go up to the roof while the Chariot is still in the air. It's amazing. It feels like you're flying."

"Is that safe?"

"Yeah. Come on," Farah said. "Orka, you stay here."

Orka chirped, but remained on her perch beside Farah's bed.

Sara followed Farah. Farah pressed a button in the wall beside the elevator, and the hatch door opened. The wind rushed along the Chariot's surface.

The sunlight streamed in, lighting the stairway up to the roof.

"Stay low," Farah said. "The wind will knock you off balance."

They climbed the short staircase to the roof. As they got closer to the surface, they stooped to avoid catching the wind, which roared in their ears.

They sat on the cool metal surface as the clouds, white and misty, sashayed across the sky.

Sara gazed at the clouds and where the water embraced the sky. The pull was unbearable. Her power was gone and yet still real, like the phantom feel of a limb long detached.

Farah put her arms out as if she was a bird. She was quiet in that moment. Sara couldn't remember a time when Farah had simply sat in silence.

Something buzzed in her ear. Thatch spoke through the earpiece: "We're about to land. Everyone, report back to the control room."

THE Chariot hovered over the forest near Caleena.

Sara climbed with Farah through the trees.

"Are Shift and Thatch coming?" Sara asked.

"No," Farah said. "Thatch doesn't trust Thermal to behave himself." Farah climbed through the underbrush, and Sara followed her.

Things had changed in Caleena. The banners were replaced with flags of blue-violet and silver that displayed a wheel with six spokes. Guards in blue and silver uniforms patrolled the wharfs.

"Arrogant Blue Jays," Farah said.

Orka chirruped.

"Who are they?" Sara asked.

"Morica guards. They strut around like big birds squawking orders."

They walked along the wharfs until they met a tall and muscular man with dark, auburn hair. His skin was tan, making his white teeth even brighter.

"Decca," Sara said.

"Hey." Decca set down the large crate he was carrying. "Spire will be surprised. What are you two doing in Caleena?"

"Visiting," Farah said.

"She will be very happy to see you. Maybe I can catch up with you after I move these crates. I'm excited about the new arrival." Decca picked up the crate and hurried down the wharf.

"New arrival?"

"A package or something?" Farah shrugged.

Seeing Decca after so many months made Sara feel guilty. She had wanted to come visit but had gotten caught up in her routine. She was glad Farah had woken her up.

Spire and Decca's hut was on the second level of wharfs above the venders. The second-floor wharfs were on columns of wood.

They took the stairs leading up to the second level and stopped outside a hut with a curtained doorway.

Orka chirped.

Sara knocked on the doorframe.

"Come in."

They entered. The hut was spacious, and Spire sat on a sofa in the back of the room. Her narrow, deep set eyes hung below dark, angled brows. She no longer wore her black garb, but had a bright, almond-colored dress with beading decorating the hem and neckline. Her curly, dark hair flowed freely down her back, and some locks settled over her shoulders.

"Sit. Make yourselves comfortable." Spire gestured to the chairs across from her. "I was worried about you."

"I meant to visit," Sara said. "I just got caught up."

"We ran into Decca," Farah said. "He was excited about something. He said something about a new arrival."

"I could have sent a message, I know, but I wanted to tell you in person once I was further along." Spire placed her hand over her belly. "Decca is too anxious not to slip. He knows I wanted to tell you myself."

"A baby!" Farah said.

"Yes." Spire stood. "Let's walk. I need the fresh air. Decca thinks pregnant women need to rest all day. He's been doing everything for me. I can count on my fingers how many times I've been up from this sofa in the last week. It's unbearable."

They walked to the wharf ends where they fought the first battle of their journey three years ago. The tide's shadow hovered over the village. *Sara, stop the wave!*

"Sara? Sara, are you alright?"

Sara emerged from the memory. "What?"

"I asked if you were enjoying your journey so far?" Spire asked.

"Oh. Yes. It's great traveling with Farah. It was so fast getting here in the Chariot."

"The Chariot?" Spire asked.

"It's like the Dome," Sara said, "but better."

"Decca was talking as fast as an auctioneer when we ran into him," Farah said.

"He's nervous," Spire said. "His father died as a Resistance fighter. His mother struggled with his older brother to raise them both. His brother left to join the Resistance a few years later and never came home. He never had a father figure growing up."

"But Decca would make a great dad," Farah said.

Orka cheeped.

"I know," Spire said. "I wish he knew that."

One of the guards in blue and silver passed by and eyed them.

"What are Morica guards doing here?" Farah asked.

"A disturbance on Cal Hill," Spire said. "I think it might have something to do with the chapel. Villagers are saying a man witnessed something strange there, but Morica is keeping it all secret. They won't say who they suspect is responsible, but they don't trust Elementals. Seems like an old-fashioned power struggle to me."

"Can we get access to the chapel?" Sara asked.

"They're guarding it," Spire said. "They've closed the gates and only let blue suits through. But a few villagers are still up there. They were praying to the Creator when the guards blocked the entrance. They're probably keeping the villagers up there because they know too much."

"Spire!" It was Decca. He ran down to the wharf ends and took Spire by the arm. "Don't you know pregnant women should be safe at home and not wandering around the wharf ends?"

"Normally, I wouldn't let him win, but I am getting tired." Spire walked with Decca as he led her away from the docks.

After Decca and Spire left, Farah's eyes lit up. "Want to find out what's going on at the Fire Sphere Sanctum?"

3

UPON CAL HILL

SARA and Farah walked to the gates that barred the entrance to Cal Hill. A blockade of guards in blue and silver stood before a mob of shouting villagers.

"We want to see our families!"

"My son is up there!"

"Let them leave!"

A young girl approached Sara. "I remember you. You're the lady who saved the village. Please, I need your help. My mom sent my older brother up to the chapel to pray to the Creator. Now my brother is trapped there without food. Please, bring him home, please."

"We'll try," Sara said, "but I'm afraid they won't let us in either."

"High Councilor Veil will be here any minute. He'll help us," someone in the crowd shouted.

"Who is High Councilor Veil?" Sara asked.

Farah shrugged.

"He's a new high councilor for Morica," the little girl said. "My mom says he's a good man, but I don't trust him. I don't know why. I just don't. But I can help you get through the gates."

"How?" Sara asked.

"Around this time every day, a few of the Blue Suits go out for lunch and are replaced by more Blue Suits. They must open the gates to let them out and let the others in. If you hurry, I can distract them, and you can sneak in."

"There must be another way," Sara said. "We wouldn't want you to get into any trouble."

"I'll do this for my brother. Please, you have to help him."

SARA and Farah edged around the crowd and neared the gates. The little girl took her post in front of the crowd where the guards held back the mob.

The bamboo gates cracked open as the guards performed the exchange. The girl dodged the first set of guards and stood in front of the guards about to be relieved.

"Stop that girl!"

The guards chased after the girl as she side-stepped them, and the crowd pushed forward, making the exchange more hectic.

While chaos ensued, Sara and Farah slipped in and hid among the wild brush.

"Close the gates!" the gatekeeper shouted.

The guards had not changed stations. The guards to be relieved made it through the gates, but the guards who were to take up their posts had been so busy trying to catch the girl and repel the crowd that they hadn't made it through to the other side.

"Come on," Farah whispered, "they're probably waiting until the crowd quiets. Then they'll send more guards. We might have the upper hand."

They tiptoed along the edge of the gates and into the forest and stayed away from the path leading to the chapel in case guards lined it.

When they were half way to the chapel, they stopped to catch their breath, lost half through exhaustion and half through nerves.

Farah looked around. Trees and foliage surrounded them. "That wasn't so bad."

Orka squeaked.

"Orka, shush!" Farah whispered. "Wait, do you hear that?"

"What?" Sara asked.

"Something's rustling in the trees. We're being followed."

"What should we do?" Sara asked.

"Hey, who's there?"

"We're almost to the chapel," Sara said. "Maybe you shouldn't shout."

"I'm warning you," Farah said.

Someone dropped behind them from the trees.

Sara and Farah turned around.

Farah held out her hands. Wind blasted the assailant to the ground.

She was a young woman with long dark hair. Her straight black brows hung low above dark brown eyes. She wore a dark gray belted tunic with black pants. She had a black band around her arm. Once the assault was over, she stood and brushed the grass from her pants. A curved sword hung at her side.

"I know you," Sara said.

"Rai?" Farah asked. "From the Lake de Somnia?"

"Sorry for walking in your shadows," Rai said, "but I've been trying to find out what's been going on here for days." She took a swig of water from her canteen. "You two need to work on your defenses."

"Hey," Farah said, "wasn't I the one who knocked *you* down?"

"After you allowed me to get this close to you." Rai glanced at the dagger sheathed at Sara's side. "And next time, I suggest you get that dagger out and point it at your attacker."

"I haven't trained with it yet," Sara said.

"You're lucky we're a little rusty," Farah said. "Three years ago, you would have had more than the wind knocked out of you."

Rai smirked. "I thought maybe you could use my help." Her voice still held that same toughness, but the confidence was hidden beneath the surface. "What do you say? Can I join you?"

Sara nodded.

"Alright." Farah frowned. "Welcome to the team." The enthusiasm left her voice.

Farah turned.

Rai placed a hand on her shoulder. "From the trees, I could see guards lining the steps of the chapel. If you want to get in, they seem impossible to avoid."

"Well, let's go as far as we can without alerting the guards," Sara said. "If we must, we'll threaten them and demand they let the villagers go."

"Bold," Rai said. "But there are more than twenty guards posted. I doubt they'll be in the mood for threats or negotiations."

"They don't know who they're dealing with," Farah said.

Orka chirped.

"I also doubt having Breeze's princess in our company is going to win us any friends," Rai said.

"You have a sword, don't you?" Farah said. "And you're a Fire Elemental, if I remember correctly. Maybe it's time you learn to use your gifts if you want to join us."

"I've had plenty of chances to use my gifts," Rai said, "but I only use them when it's necessary. I don't want to get killed.

Listen, if we climb through the trees, there's less of a chance the guards will see us as we near the chapel. I'm not saying we can avoid the guards completely, but we should give it a shot, especially because you're rusty."

They climbed through the trees instead of taking the stairway. As Rai predicted, they avoided all but one set of guards at the entrance to the chapel.

"Who are you?" the guards asked as they approached.

Villagers were grouped up against the sides of the platform outside the chapel entrance. The flames glowing atop the chapel columns flared with a strange blue fire.

"We're here for the villagers," Farah said.

"You're not allowed up here," the guard said. "Step down!"

"At least he's being polite," Rai, said.

"We're not leaving," Sara said.

The guards laughed and unsheathed their black batons. "We'll see about that."

Sara pointed her wrist gun at the guards, Farah unsheathed her dagger, and Rai held her long curved sword, the edge of which flared with Fire as she called it.

The guards staggered back.

"Elementals," one of them whispered.

"Now," Sara said, "we're going into the chapel, and once we fix whatever is going on inside, we want you to let these people go."

The lead guard looked toward the guards sentineling the stairs below, but Rai put her sword up to his neck. He could feel the heat of the flames rising to his face.

"Move aside," Rai said.

The guards backed up.

Rai continued to hold her sword up to the neck of the lead guard until his back was against the wall of the chapel.

Sara, Rai, and Farah ran into the chapel and down the tunnel to the sphere room. Rai lit the way as they walked down the long tunnel.

"I hope they do what we say," Sara said, "and let those people go home."

"Doubtful," Rai said. "I've seen how these guards operate. They only take orders from six men known as the High Councilors."

"What are they up to?" Farah asked.

"Nothing good."

As they descended, the glow of the light from the door increased.

"It's open." Farah approached the door.

"Careful," Sara said.

Farah stepped across the chapel floor. "So far so good. No Sphere Protector."

Sara and Rai followed her to the sphere room.

The door to the small room that housed the Fire Sphere was also open. The pedestal which rose from the marble floor was bare.

"The sphere," Sara said, "it's gone."

The ground thundered behind them. The floor of the sphere sanctum cracked. The crack widened. The Sphere Protector emerged from the abyss. Its massive goat-bull head hosted curved black horns. Bronze adorned its hooved feet, and blue flames surrounded its dark, thick fur.

From the floor, tiny, glowing worms emerged and spread across the marble on all sides.

They backed up, drawing their weapons.

"Please," Sara shouted, "don't make us do this. We didn't come to hurt you."

The Protector roared, and flames issued from its bronze coated mouth.

"I don't think it's listening," Rai said.

Farah reached into her bag and pulled out two razor-edged disks and threw the disks at the Protector, but the disks went through the massive beast without harming it. The disks embedded themselves into the wall behind the monster.

"How's that possible?" Sara said.

"Hologram?" Farah asked.

The Protector threw flames, and they dodged the fire. Rai felt the heat of the flames. "That seemed real enough to me."

"We should leave," Sara said.

As the beast threw more flames, they ran to the glowing doorway. They stood behind the door and pushed.

"Heave!" Rai shouted.

The door eased closed as the Protector continued to throw blue flames toward them. They used the door as a shield to block the flames, until it closed with a clapping boom.

They leaned against the door. Farah slumped to the ground. "What in Mirmina was *that* all about?"

"Rogue Protector," Rai said.

"But the sphere is missing," Farah said. "That Sphere Protector should be dust."

"Did you write the almanac on Sphere Protectors?" Rai asked.

"You only removed one sphere, right?" Farah said. "Well, we've removed four. The Sphere Protectors. They turned to dust every time."

Sara stood. "We should go."

When they came through the chapel doors, Morica guards and Resistance fighters surrounded them.

"I told you two this wasn't going to work," Rai said.

"What are we going to do now?" Farah asked.

"Pray," Rai said.

"We were sent by High Councilor Veil," Sara announced.

Rai looked back at her and mouthed, "Really?"

Sara stepped forward. "The High Councilor sent us because we are the finest warriors in all Mirmina. He wanted to keep it discreet. We've contained the problem."

"That's one way to put it," Rai said.

"Now, he asks you to release the villagers back to their homes."

The guards laughed. The Resistance fighters tried to keep their composure, but a few of them smirked as well.

"A High Councilor in league with Elementals?" the lead guard asked.

"Yes," came a voice from beyond the crowd of guards and warriors.

The crowd moved aside to let the newcomer pass.

He was a tall, thin man dressed in blue-violet robes. His hair was light gray, silver in the sunlight, although he was young, in his late twenties. His black brows swept just above his eyes which held a look of intensity. His nose was narrow and long, contrasting with his sharp and pronounced jawline. His footsteps were graceful, but firm.

He stopped in front of Sara. "The very finest of warriors. I could only send the best to quell this disruption. Did everything go well?"

"We have contained the problem." Sara continued to play her part.

"Good," Veil said. "You have done well. We'll take it from here. Men, stand down and let these people go back to their homes."

"But High Councilor . . ." the lead guard said.

"Do you know who this lady is?" Veil's tone was even, calm yet commanding.

"No, High Councilor."

"This young woman saved all of Mirmina. We owe her a great debt, yet she is still helping us." As he said this, he never took his eyes off Sara.

"I'm sorry, High Councilor. I was not aware."

"Apologize to her, not to me."

"I'm sorry, my lady. I did not recognize you." With that, the guard left to aid the others in escorting the villagers back to their homes.

Only the High Councilor and the two men attending him remained.

"Thank you," Sara said.

"Releasing these people was the reason I came," Veil said. "But meeting you has been a pleasure. I hope that we meet again, Lady Sara."

4

SPHERE SIGNALS

"WHO was that guy?" Farah asked.

They walked back to the village where the families reunited. The guards returned to their posts to keep the villagers away from the chapel.

"Veil came to save us," a man rejoiced as he walked past them through the gates.

"Hey," Farah said, "what about us!"

"Farah," Sara stopped her.

"I don't know who he is," Farah said, "but I don't trust the guy. Morica hates Elementals, and he's just their poster boy. They're trying to put a good face on it, but it's all an act."

"Veil is the youngest of the High Councilors," Rai said. "He took the position when his father died suddenly. I was there during his confirmation in Vella City."

"Vella City?" Sara asked. "But I thought Vella City was deserted."

"Not anymore."

"Why aren't you at the Lake de Somnia?" Farah asked.

"Business at the Lake is slower than ever," Rai said. "Now with my father gone, it's lonely up there. I've been traveling. Keeps my mind off things."

"I'm sorry," Sara said.

"Don't be sorry," Rai said. "He was in pain every day. It wasn't right for him to hold on for me any longer."

"You could come with us," Sara said. "We could use your help. We need to find out what happened to the Fire Sphere."

Before Rai could answer, Farah chimed in. "I don't know if that's such a good idea. We travel by air, and for someone who's not used to it . . ."

Rai nodded. "I work better alone."

"How are you both doing down there?" A voice sounded.

Rai drew her sword.

"Don't worry," Farah said. "It's just my cousin, Thatch. He's speaking through our earpieces."

"The Fire Sphere is missing," Sara said.

"I heard," Thatch's voice buzzed. "It sounded like things got intense in the chapel. That Veil guy. He sounded a lot like you."

"Me?" Sara asked.

"Yeah, it seemed he was there to help those people. If he was acting, he was very convincing."

"Do I have to knock some sense into you?" Farah shouted.

"Well, first," Thatch buzzed, "there's something you might want to see on the locator."

Rai turned to leave.

"Wait." Sara turned to Rai. "Why don't we all go to the Chariot to see what Thatch found? The least we could do is give you a ride to Lumina Port."

Rai sheathed her sword. "Alright. But only because I'm tired of traveling by boat."

Farah pouted, and Orka rustled her feathers.

"First, we must warn Spire about the Sphere Protector," Sara said.

They walked up the wooden steps to Spire's hut and lifted the curtain. Spire sat on her cushioned couch. "If it isn't the Lady of the Lake."

"We've come to warn you," Rai said.

"Warn me?" Spire asked. "Of what?"

"The Sphere Protector," Sara said. "The sphere is missing, but the Protector is very much alive."

"Missing?"

Farah nodded. "Just gone." Orka scratched her head with her foot.

"It's not safe here," Sara said. "You and Decca should come with us."

Spire raised her hand. "We have built our life here. If the Protector goes rogue, we'll be on the first ship to Lumina."

"The Protector *has* gone rogue," Rai said. "It's only a matter of time before it descends upon the village."

"I forgot," Spire said. "You are the expert on Sphere Protectors. Decca and I will be fine. We're warriors."

"But you're pregnant," Farah said.

"If my baby is an Elemental, he will only make me stronger."

THERMAL cawed as he hovered above the forest. His wing span shaded the trees.

Thatch pointed at his screen. "It's a map of Mirmina. And look, large pulses of energy. Here, here, and here. The sphere sanctums."

"What could that mean?" Sara asked.

"Judging from what went on back in the chapel in Caleena, I would guess that all the spheres are missing."

"Wait," Shift said from his seat, "I thought the Resistance returned the spheres to their sanctums."

"That must mean someone else took them," Farah said.

"We have to find answers," Sara said, "a lead to get us going."

"That's why I think we should go to Lumina," Thatch said. "The gossip there can deafen ears."

"But much of it isn't true," Rai said.

"We might be able to sift through the sand to find a diamond though. It's a start."

"Watch out for that Veil guy," Shift said. "His ship is bound to reach Lumina Port by morning."

"You three should get some rest," Thatch said. "We'll be in Lumina before dawn."

SARA gazed up at the stars as she lay in bed. Farah, Rai and Orka were asleep, but Sara couldn't sleep. She couldn't stop thinking about the spheres. *The battle was over, wasn't it? Hadn't they won?*

Battles end, wars don't. Power would always exist, and if one could acquire more, wars would not end. Bolton had told her three years ago that the world didn't want her to martyr herself, but it did.

"Can't sleep?" a voice buzzed.

"Stannum?"

Stannum's orange eye glowed brighter.

Sara got up and walked downstairs to sit on the stools near the windows. Stannum followed, floating in the air beside her.

"I've been thinking," Sara said, "that Mirmina is broken again."

"Are you tired of fixing it?"

"I'm just tired."

Sara looked out the window where the dark sky met the sea.

"I've been broken many times," Stannum said. "When I needed to be fixed the first time, Shift became frustrated and trashed me, but every time since, Thatch has fixed me without complaint. He understands I'm not perfect and I will endlessly need fixing. Shift believes my programming doesn't allow me to understand such things, but it is because I'm imperfect that I understand."

"I don't like turning my back on anyone," Sara said, "but it's hard when you win and lose at the same time."

Sara held her mother's teardrop gem between her fingers. She sighed and let it fall back onto her chest.

"Can you tell me about Morica's Councilors?" Sara asked.

Stannum's eye glowed. "The hierarchal ladder of Morica is based on both seniority and inheritance. When Morica was first formed, status was based on age, but in the event of any individual member's death, their position, even that of a High Councilor, is reassigned to the oldest living relative of that member, regardless of how young such member might be.

"The lowest status is that of a guard. Guards are young and not paid very well for their services."

Stannum's glowing eye projected the image of a Morica guard. The guard wore a blue and silver uniform and carried a black baton.

"After the guard, the next status level is that of the Councilor. The Councilors are close relatives of the High Council apart from a few non-blood members. These fictive kin are carefully chosen by the High Councilors. The Councilors' duties include giving orders to the guards and standing at ready in the event that a High Councilor's position becomes unoccupied."

The hologram image showed a Councilor dressed in a deep blue uniform. His hair was gray, but a darker gray than Veil's had been. He looked like one of the men who attended Veil in Caleena.

"The members of the highest rank are the High Councilors. Morica has six High Councilors represented by the six spokes on the wheel of never-ending change."

Stannum projected a hologram of Morica's flag depicting the wheel of never-ending change.

"Surnom is the oldest of the High Councilors. He is a scholar who survived the second Dustpath storm and recorded it for historical purposes."

The image of Surnom showed his long robes and light gray hair, the signature of the High Council.

"The second seat on the High Council is filled by Romulus. He was part of the Resistance. He and his twin brother founded Jetty Verte, but his brother died when he fell into one of the rifts created by an earthquake.

"High Councilor Caduceus was a Tosian alchemist. Aldo of Tosia was his apprentice. Caduceus is famed for finding a way to extract water from the waterfall at the Cliff of Broken Promise, allowing those brave enough to peer into the future."

"Of the High Councilors, the most hated is Mordecai. Mordecai murdered three Elementals in their sleep. He was condemned to serve a life sentence in the dungeons of Jetty Verte, but he escaped when an earthquake collapsed the wall of his cell. He was later caught and thrown into the dungeons of the deserted Vella City. No one knows how he got out."

The hologram showed an old man. Wrinkles made his eyes droop. His dark brows framed his narrow eyes. The nose stood like a pillar above his thin lips. His mouth was twisted into a frown.

"Jove is the fifth High Councilor. He mapped Mirmina years ago. Some of his maps reside in the library of Lumina City.

"The sixth High Councilor is Veil. Of the High Councilors, he is the most revered by the people for the good he does."

Veil smiled, but the smile did not seem to visit his narrow eyes. He stood tall and waved.

The image disappeared. Stannum's eye dulled.

"Can you tell me more about Veil?" Sara leaned forward in her seat.

Stannum blinked his eye.

"He is the youngest member of the High Council and has the most exposure to the public. He speaks at events, attends social gatherings, and shakes hands with the people. He inherited his seat on the High Council when Cronus, his father, died. A point of much social controversy is the fact that Veil does not have an heir nor is he married. It is rumored that his father did not properly groom him for his seat on the High Council. If he does not produce an heir before his death, his seat will be taken by a non-relative chosen by the High Council."

"What are you doing up?" Farah stretched as she walked up to the seat next to Sara.

"We didn't wake you, did we?" Sara asked.

"No, I just came down to get something to drink, but Rai snores like a beast. So, what are you both doing?"

"Stannum was telling me more about Morica Council."

"Oh, those puffed pigeons," Farah said.

"Morica seems to be gaining a lot of influence," Sara said. "Maybe they can help us find out who's taking the spheres?"

"Morica hates Elementals," Farah said. "Those superficial buzzards want nothing to do with us. The cowards hid when Hephaestus was running the show, and once he was gone, they came out of the shadows to take back power, power they didn't earn."

Stannum blinked his eye and floated away.

Farah yawned. "I'll see you in the morning." She got up from the stool and climbed the stairs to the loft.

Sara closed her eyes. The grain of the wood burnt into the paper as the charcoal swept across it. The dark waves loomed in front of her. The warmth radiated off his skin as he stood beside her.

5

PLAYING WITH LIGHTNING

IT was called the Healing Room where Dawn took care of the sick and dying. She took in strangers in need of help, and the people of Tosia didn't appreciate that. Even though she could only see light and shadows, Dawn could feel the disdain in their hearts as they glared at her in the streets.

She pulled the thick, dandelion-colored shawl up to the chin of the bandaged man as he muttered in his indefinite slumber. Thin, bony hands took the mortar and pestle and grinded herbs into a fine powder. She mixed the powder in water and tried to get the man to drink.

The man swallowed some of the medicine, but coughed up the rest. Dawn wiped the dribble from his chin.

A knock came to the door.

Dawn rose and answered it. "Fulgur?"

The man entered the Healing Room. His skin was papery and yellow. Beneath his bald head was a prominent brow with eyes peeking below. His long nose drew down to his lips surrounded by a gray beard and moustache. His cheeks were sunken and cheekbones high. His body was bony and aged, but he walked with the gait and stature of a much younger, stronger man.

"You've faked that raspy voice for so long, you've forgotten your real one. You have made quite a life for yourself," Fulgur said.

"As much of a life as we can have," Dawn said.

Fulgur could not sense her anger as he looked up at the branches that held up the ceiling of the Healing Room. Moss covered the floors like thick carpet, and roots and vines grew up the walls. It was a *living* room, the best hope for the suffering man lying on the bed.

"What have you come for?" Dawn sensed his straight-lined lips and cold, neutral eyes.

Fulgur held up his hand, his fingers wide apart. Sparks of lightning danced between his fingers.

Dawn could see the light that played between his fingers, and she could hear the static.

"I thought you used to like this. Gathering us together for meetings."

"I didn't call a meeting," Dawn said, "and I'm quite busy."

"As the people of this town say you are. It amazes me that you stayed with the people who shunned us."

"They feared us."

"They had reason." Fulgur's blank expression never changed.

"I'd appreciate it if you saw yourself out," Dawn said.

Fulgur grabbed Dawn's spotted arm in his hand. The lightning swept through her body faster than a rushing stream. She didn't flinch or react to Fulgur's assault.

He released her arm.

"Death does not come naturally to us." Dawn's arm did not feel the heat of the lightning.

"Nor does it come unnaturally." Fulgur's static fingers fell unhindered at his side. He neither looked surprised nor disappointed.

"You have no purpose," Dawn said. "Your soul is gone because you held the sphere for too long. You need a project to busy yourself in your endless years tied to this earth."

"I have found one. The world is picking up pace again," Fulgur said. "They've forgotten who their gods are. It is our duty to remind them."

6

STRIKES IN THE SAME PLACE TWICE

DARKNESS fell on Vella City and made the Council Palace look sapphire in the blackness. One thin, wispy cloud cut the crescent moon in half. In the uppermost room of the palace, Mordecai opened a letter with his pen knife.

He poured over the contents, having to look closer with his aged eyes. The letter was from the leader of Lumina. He had accepted the request to become a Councilor of Morica and to accept the large sum of money offered.

Mordecai beamed at the idea. The High Council was building power again. He liked that. Scurrying like a rat through the Vella City tunnels reminded him of his days in the dungeons.

A life sentence for killing Elementals, that's what the Resistance dealt down.

The condemned served their sentences in Jetty Verte. There were few guards. The prisoners were tucked away and forgotten beneath the green plain.

For nineteen years, his once youthful body became thin and pale in the dungeons. But a storm came and shook the ground above and beneath his feet. Lightning accompanied that storm and swept the plain. The bolts were as plentiful as falling rain.

The guards ran, leaving the prisoners in their cages. One guard was crushed beneath the falling clay. His dagger fell, the blade standing on its point.

A man entered the dungeon, walking past the prisoners yelling for help in their cages.

He was old and his skin was yellowed with age spots dotting the flesh like a speckled snake. Yet, his walk was firm and strong like the gait of a younger man. His head was bald, the forehead high, cheekbones pronounced.

He disappeared around the corner. Lightning crackled. He was thrown against the back wall. He stood, unharmed, and made his way back down the hall, empty handed.

The clay ceiling came down inside Mordecai's cell. He climbed the bars up to the ceiling and escaped through the hole.

The lightning quickened, and the earth shook.

DEEP in thought, Mordecai swept his elbow across the desk, and the pen knife fell to the floor, the point embedding into the ground.

A knock sounded at the door.

Mordecai's bones cracked beneath his robes as he rose to answer it. His feeble hand and knobby fingers wrapped around the handle. As the door parted from its frame, Mordecai once again met the face of the man who had entered the dungeon the night of the storm.

He was still old, but he hadn't aged a day since he last saw him. If he counted the years, the man before him should have been long dead.

The man stepped into the room.

"What's the meaning of this?" With effort, Mordecai lifted one aged eyebrow from its natural droop.

"I am Fulgur. I heard that this establishment does some dangerous work."

7

A New Order

JUST before dawn, Shift landed the Chariot in a clearing near Dustpath Road. Thermal kept his mouth and eyes closed as the dust swirled around him.

In the morning, they exited the Chariot. This time, Thatch and Shift followed. As they entered Lumina, Farah shouted, "We're just in time for the Games!"

The banners for the Element Games hung on every lamp post and inside shop windows.

"I thought we were here to ask questions," Rai said.

"Exactly," Farah said. "The Element Games draws everyone to Lumina. This is the perfect time to find out more about the element spheres."

Farah led the way to the ticket booth. In the port past the ticket booth, a large ship had docked. The ship had blue-violet and silver sails with the image of a wheel with six spokes.

"Hey, look," Farah said. "The Blue Jays have migrated."

Blue and silver uniformed guards lowered a ramp on the side of the large ship. Down the ramp glided four people dressed in blue-violet robes.

Sara recognized them from the hologram images Stannum had shown her. They were the High Councilors Jove, Romulus, and Mordecai. Veil was among them.

Veil walked behind the other High Councilors. He did not look pleased.

"I wonder what they're up to," Rai said.

"You don't think they're going to make a public statement about Veil's actions in Caleena?" Sara asked.

"They wouldn't do that. It would make them look bad. The people love Veil. Outing him would turn the people against the rest of the Council."

"Whatever they're up to, it can't be good for us," Shift said. "Their focus is preaching against Elementals, telling the people how dangerous we are and insisting we not use our powers."

"Farah, you get my ticket," Thatch said. "I'm going to go to the market and get food for Thermal."

Sara watched as the Council and their guards headed for Fletzi Manor. There lived the lord of the Manor, Jei Fletzi, surrounded by his advisors. The Fletzi family had long controlled the city's trade routes.

The Council and their guards disappeared within the stone walls of the Manor. Sara's eyes lingered on the building as if she could see through the thick stone.

INSIDE, Jei Fletzi sat at a half-moon shaped table. His advisors discussed matters related to trade. The room quieted as the servant announced that the High Council waited beyond the door.

Jei Fletzi rolled his eyes and beckoned for the young man to invite them in.

The silver-haired High Councilors walked through the doors escorted by their guards, bordering their persons on all sides.

As Jei Fletzi drummed his fingers on the arm of his chair, the golden bracelets on his arm jingled. This sound echoed through the high-ceilinged room.

"You don't trust me, High Councilors?" Jei Fletzi asked.

Councilor Mordecai stepped forward to set himself apart from the rest of the Council. "Lord Fletzi, we mean no offense. The High Council has become quite cautious due to prior experiences."

"What do you want High Councilor?" Jei Fletzi gazed at the vaulted ceiling.

"Morica requests a place on the Lumina City Council," Mordecai said.

Jei Fletzi spread his arms out to his advisors who filled every seat at the table. "But I already have a full council."

"We see that, my lord, but it never hurts to lend an ear to persons outside Lumina," Mordecai said. "We were honored when you accepted our request to become allies. We have much to offer as fellow leaders, and we share strong ties in trade. Most of the stone purchased to build this fine manor came from Vella City."

"Now, you want to be my advisors." Jei Fletzi waved his hand. "Well, advise away."

"Lord Fletzi, the High Council recommends you postpone the Element Games," Mordecai said.

The advisors whispered among themselves. One leaned in and spoke into Jei Fletzi's ear.

"High Councilor," Jei Fletzi said, "from my limited knowledge of your character, I take you to be a person of above average intelligence."

"As I do you, my lord." Mordecai cringed at his own words.

"Then you'll understand, why this proposal makes absolutely no sense to me," Jei Fletzi said. "After all, Lumina is not only a city of trade, but of tourism. To do such a thing as postpone this long-awaited event would lead to many disgruntled citizens and even more unhappy travelers, people who traveled hundreds of miles to see the Games. So, can you clear up this discrepancy?"

Veil's robes swept the floor until he stood in line with Mordecai. "High Councilor Mordecai, if I may?"

Mordecai nodded. "You have the floor, High Councilor Veil."

Mordecai leaned in to whisper to the young High Councilor. "Tell him I'd like to gut him like a hog and let those golden bangles of his decorate the dinner platter."

Veil frowned.

"Lord Fletzi, the people will miss the Games to be sure," Veil said. "And it seems wrong on its face to punish the people. But this isn't about punishment. Elements unfettered have caused significant hardships to the people. To encourage such an open display of power may only work to craft a new tyrant. Although it is not in my heart to control the innocent, sometimes it is in their best interest."

"The Games didn't create Hephaestus," Jei Fletzi said. "And fortunately, the Games for me have been nothing but positive since they fill my coffers."

"My lord," Mordecai said, "Vella City has more gold than you could earn in a lifetime hosting the Games."

Jei Fletzi settled back in his chair as his advisors whispered around him.

"I doubt that, High Councilor."

"We have vaults and vaults of gold," Mordecai said. "Enough to fill your coffers to the brim and keep them full year-round. People have reasons to come to Lumina other than the Games. The High Council is promising revenues of three times as much as you earn hosting the Element Games.

Think about it carefully, my lord. The Games are losing favor because of recent events."

"You mean the attack three years ago?"

Mordecai nodded.

"Are you threatening me, High Councilor?" Jei Fletzi asked.

"No, my lord," Mordecai said. "I'm simply directing your attention to the facts. The Games are losing popularity, less and less ticket sales, more and more empty seats."

The golden bracelets jingled as they hit the table.

"Three times as much?"

Mordecai nodded. "Not only that, my lord, but if you allow the High Council a seat on your committee, we will provide guards to patrol the city and guard the dungeons. You will have so many men, small battles like the one three years ago will never plague the city again. We can make sure of that."

Jei Fletzi nodded. "I'll sign the decree, but you are delivering the message to the people. Why do the dirty business yourself when you can have a blackguard handle it for you?"

The High Councilors descended the steps of Fletzi Manor.

"He disrespects us," Romulus said.

"He's an annoying creature," Mordecai scoffed. "But he gave us a bit of power, and power only grows."

AFTER they purchased their tickets, Sara went to the market. She found a merchant selling charcoal and paper and purchased both. She placed the charcoal and paper into the satchel slung across her body from shoulder to hip.

The crowd moved toward the center of the market where a Lightning Elemental practiced before the Element Games. Lightning zoomed through the air above his head.

Sara stared at the show. The Lightning Elemental moved with grace and commanded the Lightning with skill and passion.

"We meet again."

Sara turned, startled.

Veil stood beside her. "It is a crime to force someone to ignore his own nature."

"You don't agree that Elementals need to be . . . contained?"

Veil watched as the Lightning danced through the sky. "It's what my father believed."

"But you believe something different," Sara said.

Veil smiled.

Blue and silver uniformed guards pushed through the crowd and approached the Lightning Elemental. "Hey, you can't do that here!"

Veil shook his head.

After the Lightning Elemental was warned, he stepped down, and the crowd dissipated.

"I don't understand," Sara said. "The people of Mirmina owe so much to Elementals. We stopped Hephaestus. Why would Morica want to shun us?"

"Fear," Veil said. "They don't want another person to become that powerful again. That I understand."

"But at what cost?" Sara asked.

"And that's what I struggle with," Veil said.

"Hey, Sara!" Farah yelled from the balcony above the market. "The Games are about to start!"

"I have to go."

"I'm sorry you've wasted your money," Veil said.

"What?"

"High Councilor Mordecai will not let the Games go on this year."

"He can't stop them," Sara said.

"I didn't want you to be surprised," Veil said.

Sara met Farah on the balcony. "Come on. Rai, Thatch, and Shift are saving our seats. Was that that Veil guy?"

"Yes," Sara said.

Veil watched Sara from the market.

"Why does he keep bothering you?" Farah asked.

"He wanted to tell me that the Games will be cancelled this year."

"Cancelled?"

"He said High Councilor Mordecai would not allow them to go on."

"We'll see about that!" Farah said.

*   *   *

SARA and Farah took their seats beside Rai, Thatch and Shift. The field was renewed after having been blasted by Wind, scorched by Lightning, upheaved by Earth, and burnt by Fire. The seats were filled, and the audience talked and laughed as they waited for the Games to begin. The contestants stood on the sidelines waiting for the first round.

The announcer began: "Welcome to the annual Element Games!" A handheld device projected his voice across the field.

The crowd cheered, and Orka chirped as the noise grew.

"It is my pleasure to announce this year's new competitors—"

Blue-and-silver guards invaded the announcer's balcony.

"It looks like we have company . . ."

A guard ripped the device from the announcer's hands. The guard cleared his throat: "People of Lumina, please direct your full attention to this message from Morica High Council."

Mordecai, Romulus, and Veil stepped forward followed by a group of guards and other members of the Council. Mordecai took the device from the guard. His long fingers wrapped around the device, and he put it to his lips. "The Element Games have been cancelled." His voice came out like fine sandpaper, abrasive and stiff, unrelenting.

A hush swept the audience as they internalized what was said.

Wasting no time, Farah stood from her seat and expressed her disfavor. "Boo . . ."

Disdain and confusion erupted from the crowd.

"What?"

"You can't do that!" someone shouted.

"What does High Councilor Veil have to say about this?"

"High Councilor Veil agrees with our decision," Mordecai said, although the look on Veil's face said otherwise. As Veil looked upon Mordecai, unease lurked in his eyes.

Sara had not seen such a look on Veil's face, but even from a distance she could see darkness in it.

"You all remember what happened at the Games three years ago," Mordecai said. "This is a new age. The Games are dangerous, and a ban has been placed upon them for the safety of the citizens of Lumina. In excess, there is sin. Lumina shall no longer be a city of excess, but an example of hope for the rest of Mirmina. There will be a curfew, a limit on the alcohol served at bars, and Elementals are no longer permitted to perform publicly in the streets."

"That's not fair!" Farah shouted. The crowd joined her. Orka chirped in agreement.

"Any Elemental found using his elements publicly in any town or city of Mirmina will be arrested and charged as a danger to public safety."

The crowd's disdain rose to a roar.

Mordecai whispered something to Veil, and Veil took the voice device.

The crowd hushed as Veil spoke. "I know you all believe that the order raised by High Councilor Mordecai is unreasonable."

The crowd cheered their assent.

"But we only stand for the safety and benefit of the people. Years ago, we were plagued by a tyrant. An evil man who wanted to do harm to you all. Without order, that evil rose to power. We must put measures in place to prevent such an evil from rising again. I ask that you all help us to do that. Rules are never enjoyable, but they keep us safe. I fully support Mordecai's decision."

The crowd echoed some of its previous words of contempt, but Veil had quelled some of the resisters.

"Your strings are showing!" Farah shouted. "This is ridiculous. They can't do this." Farah slumped into her seat.

"They can do whatever they want," Rai said.

"Well, we can't just let them," Shift said.

Farah beamed. Her rebellious attitude was rubbing off on her older brother.

"What?" Shift asked.

"Nothing." Farah smirked.

Veil gave Mordecai the floor. "There have been reports from Caleena as well as other regions home to the sphere sanctums. The Protectors have gone rogue. It is of yet unclear why this has occurred, but the High Council is focusing all our efforts on discovering the cause for this disturbance. This is not the time for games. We must all be vigilant and stay together."

"We should find out more about the spheres," Thatch said. "Shift and I will ask around the market and get more supplies. You three go to the docks"

SARA, Rai and Farah walked to the docks, crossing paths with the High Councilors as they headed back to their ship. As Mordecai and Romulus walked on, Veil stayed behind. The guards escorting him stayed behind as well.

"Where will you be going after you leave Lumina?" Veil asked Sara.

Farah looked at Sara and shook her head.

Seeing this gesture, Veil said to the guards, "Follow Mordecai and Romulus back to the ship. I will be there shortly."

The guards nodded and left.

"Sending your guards away doesn't make us any more comfortable letting you in on where we're headed," Rai said.

"I understand," Veil said. "I live in Tosia. If you pass that way, please let me know when you arrive so that I may see you."

He walked back to the ship.

"What is he up to?" Farah asked.

"He likes her," Rai said.

"Me?" Sara asked.

"You're a missionary for the people of Mirmina, so I guess it's fitting," Rai said.

"He's a fraud," Farah said. "I don't believe for one second that he cares about the people. He's Morica's peacock, that's all."

"I don't know," Sara said. "He seems genuine."

They split up to ask questions and met back in the town square.

"Find out anything?" Rai asked as Farah and Sara approached her.

"Nothing. How about you?' Sara asked.

"Nope," Farah said. "Nobody knows anything about the spheres or has seen anything strange going on around the sphere sanctums."

"We should keep searching," Sara said. "After that speech from Morica, the people here might be too afraid to talk about what they know. Maybe we should go to Wyvek. We can travel by foot and ask travelers along the way."

"Good idea." Farah touched her earpiece. "Thatch, we'll walk from here. We're thinking about going to Wyvek."

"Okay," Thatch buzzed. "Shift and I are making our way back to the Chariot. We'll follow you from above."

"So, I guess it's on to Dustpath," Farah said. "I really hope—"

"Listen." Rai held her hand out to quiet her.

"And this thing attacked me . . ." Not far away a young man was trying to tell his story to a diminishing crowd. When the last visages of human interest faded, and the people walked away, Sara, Farah, and Rai approached him.

"What do you know?" Rai asked.

The man jumped. "Oh, you startled me." He scratched his blond head. "You won't believe me. You'll only laugh and walk away." The man turned to leave.

"Please, tell us," Sara said. "We won't laugh, and we won't walk away. I promise."

"Okay." The man sighed and faced them. "My name is Tacitum the Quiet. I came to Dustpath to work at my brother's inn—"

"Hey," Farah said, "does your brother work at Dustpath Inn?"

Tacitum nodded. "Yes, my brother is Solace the Calm. My brothers shamed me into working at the inn to carry on my father's legacy, but I'm an artist. All I sell are my own paintings, I wouldn't know the first thing about running an inn. I was standing outside the inn, contemplating whether I should knock on the door when I decided to run. I heard there were jobs at Wyvek Temple so I went there."

"What kind of jobs?" Farah asked.

"They wanted people who could build things," Tacitum said. "I'm no builder, but being an artist, I thought I could learn."

"Build things? Like houses?" Sara asked.

"No, machines," Tacitum said.

"Who runs the place?" Farah asked.

"I don't know his name. Everyone calls him *Boss*."

"So, what happened?" Rai asked.

"Boss was not impressed with my building skills," Tacitum said, "so he sent me to get scrap metal from the storeroom by the big boulder. Something was there with me."

Tacitum's eyes darkened and became distant. "I could feel it in the darkness. It sounded like teeth grinding against bone, trying to get all the flesh off. The cave . . . it went on for miles . . ."

"The cave?" Sara said.

Tacitum shook his head. "No, I mean what I saw by the big boulder. It was so bright. It looked like a horse with a spear coming out of its head."

"The Sphere Protector," Rai said.

"What would the Protector be doing outside the sphere sanctum?" Farah asked.

"That was a Sphere Protector?" Tacitum wiped his brow with a handkerchief. "I'm lucky I lived."

"Now it's even more important we get to Wyvek," Farah said. "The Sphere Protector has gone rogue there too."

8

Puppet Master

Throngs of people filled the market square of Elementa as the High Councilors Veil and Mordecai stood upon the platform to make their announcement. The other High Councilors would make the same announcement in Caleena and Lumina.

Guards stood around the pavilion and lined the streets of the town. More guards hung Morica banners from the roofs of buildings and across the tops of sales stands.

The crowd was loud as people questioned the High Council's presence in Elementa. After the news about their disruption of the Element Games in Lumina, many thought they had come to shut down Element.

At the pinnacle of the crowd's canticle, Mordecai raised one hand, and an eerie hush went through the multitude.

"Friends," Mordecai said, "there is no need to question our arrival. We are here for your protection. Although Elementa fortunately has no sphere sanctum, the danger for you all is still very real. I say this because you live in the town that houses the school of the Elementals, whose powers can shake cities and bring storms of destruction.

"For those of you such gifted, I apologize if my words are harsh, but, in my experience, I have seen such destruction. When backed against a wall, it is only human nature to use our every advantage, and those with such power do. We all should be aware of it and steel ourselves against it.

"Now that the spheres have been taken from their houses and the Protectors have gone rogue, who knows who else will go rogue.

"We can protect you against such a threat. I have decided to leave some of my most trusted guards here to protect you all, but if we are to be sister cities, it will require devotion on your part.

"A town tax will be instated immediately.

"Guards you may collect from the worthy citizens."

The guards jostled the crowd.

Some were willing to pay the tax. Others were more resistant.

A young woman with two children clinging to her skirt, fought with a guard in the crowd over a coin purse. The woman's fingers bit into the coin purse as the guard tried to wrench it from her grasp. She stomped on the guard's foot, and when he released his grip, the woman and children ran with the coin purse through the crowd, but guards blocked her escape.

She ran to the stage. Tears cascaded down her face. Her desperate hands clung to Veil's robes. "Please, please, High Councilor, this is all we have."

Veil looked down at the woman, and the pain in her eyes was reflected in his.

"Guards," Mordecai said, as Veil reached out to the woman.

A guard grabbed the woman by the shoulders and threw her into the crowd. Her two children fell, scrambled back to the stage, and clung to the wooden ledge. Their tears mingled with the dirt on their faces as their high-pitched wails echoed their mother's screams.

Veil clenched his fist, and between thin lips, he said, "This can't go on."

"Stop," Mordecai said as the guards circled the trapped woman. The guards backed away from her.

Her tensed fingers clenched the coin purse as Mordecai approached.

"Your tax, my dear." Mordecai held his hand out.

The desperate woman looked to her children, crying by the stage. With shaking hands, she gave Mordecai the coin purse. Mordecai pocketed it and walked back to the stage. The children ran into their mother's arms and took shelter there.

AS night fell, Veil and Mordecai retired to the inn outside the market square. It was the largest inn in town, and the only one befitting of the High Councilors' tastes.

Veil sat across the long table from Mordecai. Food filled the large expanse between them: two large bowls of salad with fresh mint and salted cheese, soft-boiled eggs in pine-nut sauce, lentils with coriander, a platter of roast boar, fried veal with raisins, and a dish of almond tart.

Mordecai cleared his plate with an appetite uncommon for a man of his age.

Veil moved his food around in his plate as if he was searching for something.

"That woman . . ."

"What woman?" Mordecai asked.

"The one in the market. She had children."

Mordecai wiped his mouth with a napkin. "We collect from the people to give back to the people. Sacrifices must be made for the greater good. You understand that."

Veil stared across the table at Mordecai and back down at his plate before his expression betrayed his feelings.

"We have to talk about other matters," Mordecai said from across the table.

"I'm listening." Veil put down his fork.

"How are you getting along with the Lady Sara?"

Veil hesitated before speaking. "She's intelligent. She's wise beyond her years. Why do you ask?"

"I want you to marry her."

Uncomfortable, Veil took an undesired sip from his cup. He held the wine in his mouth before letting it slide down his throat. "I don't understand."

"It's no secret you have a soft-spot for Elementals."

"I have a soft-spot for equality, for fairness, for humanity."

"And we will never have equality as long as their powers hold us prisoner, ever holding our breath until one of them decides that what we have to offer is not enough.

"If you marry Lady Sara, it would unite us. We would have a stronger hold on the Elementals. She could help us lead."

"I've only known her for a short time." Veil picked up his fork and knife to cut his meat, but the knife slipped from his inattentive fingers and fell to the floor. The blade stood upright as the point jammed itself into the floorboards.

Veil reached down to pick up the knife.

"No," Mordecai hissed. "Don't pick it up."

The door opened. It was Fulgur. He took a seat at the table.

Mordecai's hands trembled as he placed his fork and knife back down upon the white table cloth. "I didn't expect you."

"I was visiting an old friend in Tosia." Fulgur said, his face expressionless. "I thought to see you there."

"I'll have a place set for our guest," Veil said.

"No need." Fulgur stopped him. "I don't eat much."

Silence hung in the room.

Mordecai and Veil stopped eating. The room was so quiet, their breathing could be heard. Fulgur sat and respected the silence for a while.

"What brings you here?" Mordecai asked.

"I need to be occupied." Fulgur, twined his fingers together.

Mordecai stood from his seat. His hands still trembled as he pressed his fingers onto the table to help himself up, but his eyes glared at Fulgur.

Mordecai escorted Fulgur out of the dining hall and left Veil alone.

Veil stared at the knife still lodged in the oaken floor. He reached down to retrieve it but thought better of it. He retracted his hand, his fingers only a fraction of an inch away from the metal.

He gazed up and imagined his mother's portrait on the wall. It used to hang on the stone and earthen walls in the tunnels of Vella City. His father had placed it there, long after her death.

As a child, he had wanted the painting for his own. His father had slapped him for taking it down. That was the most contact he ever had with his father.

When his mother died, his father would spend hours locked in his room. Even before then, he had barely noticed his son. The boy was more like a piece of polished china to him than flesh and blood. His son served a purpose somewhat distant because Cronus believed he would never die.

Veil looked down at the knife and thought of his father.

THAT night, Veil took some money from his personal trove and wandered the streets of the city. He dropped money into the sleeping hands of beggars camped out in the alleyways.

As he turned a corner, he saw the sleeping mother and her children, keeping each other warm under a canvas blanket. The mother slept propped up against the brick wall of the building, and her children slept, one at each side, their heads leaning against her arms.

Veil dropped the rest of the money into her lap.

The heaviness of the coins woke the woman. Her eyes blinked open in surprise. She stared at the glittering coins resting in her lap and up at Veil.

"Thank you." A wide-eyed expression lingered on her face.

Veil knelt. "Take care of your children, and hide this when they come to collect."

The woman nodded.

Veil stood and walked back to the market square.

"High Councilor."

He turned.

Mordecai stood not far from the empty poultry stand. "Doing a bit of charity work?"

"She has children," Veil said.

"Your heart is soft. That's why the people like you," Mordecai said. "But remember: your loyalties lie with the High Council."

9

THE SEARCH FOR ANSWERS

SARA walked along Dustpath Road. Farah and Rai journeyed beside her. They hoped to make it to the inn by nightfall. When they reached the sign that read *Welcome to Dustpath Inn*, the sun hung low in the sky.

Solace ran from around the bend in the road.

"Solace!" Farah said. "What are you running from?"

Solace stopped.

Rai turned her face away from the innkeeper.

"Nice to see you again," Sara said.

Solace put his hands on his knees and leaned over, struggling to catch his breath.

"It's destroying my inn," Solace said between gasps.

"What's destroying the inn?" Farah asked.

"It's some kind of buzzing machine," Solace said. "It's pulling down everything from the shelves and tearing up the feather pillows. It's from Wyvek. I know it. I don't know what they're trying to do up there, but they're making monsters."

They walked to the inn, and Solace followed behind them. Behind the door, glass crashed and heavy objects thumped against the wooden floor.

Rai swung open the door and stepped back.

Inside the inn was a sputtering, jiggering little contraption that reminded Sara a lot of Stannum. The little machine crashed into Solace's merchandise and knocked down jars and packages which fell to the floor in a heap of glass and wrappings.

The machine buzzed toward them. They ducked, and it went over their heads, floated, and crashed into a nearby ruin by the cliff.

Farah ran to the little machine and picked it up. She turned it in her hands. It was smaller than Stannum, but had the same glowing eye and wiry arms that were signatures of Thatch's upgraded design.

"Looks pretty well put together despite the malfunction," she said.

Solace stooped and inspected the machine with Farah.

"You know a lot about machines," Rai said.

"My father saw to that," Farah said.

"Your father?" Solace asked.

"Tag, the leader of Breeze." Farah stood.

"We're traveling with royalty." Rai smirked.

When Solace looked at her, Rai turned her eyes to the road.

"Reluctant royalty," Farah said. "As far as I'm concerned, being my father's daughter has been more of a pain than an advantage. When I was little, I was kidnapped by *Lacwanx* for ransom because my father tried to cheat them."

"*Lacwanx*, where have I heard that name?" Solace asked.

"They're *Jabec Kunvanx*," Farah said. "Metal Workers. People say they look different from us because of the explosion years ago. It released lots of radiation, and they were exposed to it. The radiation stunted their growth and led to a bunch of deformities. They've created a home for themselves in the ruined sector of Breeze. It's been that way since the Great Raid, but the radiation doesn't seem to affect them anymore. The people of Breeze often trade with them. I learned to speak *Lacwanx* before I could walk."

"I remember now. The *Lacwanx* are working for Boss in Wyvek," Solace said. "Mean little creatures."

"That's strange," Farah said. "*Lacwanx* are very stubborn. What could have gotten them to leave Breeze?"

"The people of Wyvek cleared out months ago," Solace said. "The land became barren. No way to make a living. Now Boss moved into the temple and is having the *Lacwanx* build all kinds of new machines for him. I heard he was selling them."

"That's what your brother, Tacitum, told us," Sara said.

"Tac!" Solace said. "I've been waiting for him to get here for days. Where is he?"

"We ran into him in Lumina," Farah said. "He saw a Sphere Protector. He's really scared."

"He'll be really scared when *I* get to him. That's for sure," Solace said.

"Where did the people of Wyvek go?" Sara asked.

"From what I heard, they spread out and settled all over Mirmina. A lot of people are doing that now-a-days. A few people from Breeze left, and there were even some runaways from Tosia all headed to Lumina and, from there, who knows where." Solace looked at the darkening sky. "I would offer you a room, but my inn is in no shape for guests."

"We could help you clean up," Sara said.

"No," Solace said. "Even with your help, I doubt I could have it up and ready by nightfall. You should hurry to Wyvek. Boss is running the place. I'm sure he has an inn for travelers."

They left Dustpath Inn and continued their journey to Wyvek.

"Who is this *Boss* anyway?" Farah asked as they traveled up the road to Wyvek. "I bet he's some ignorant, tough guy who's full of himself."

The dust kicked up as a machine zoomed ahead and stopped in front of them. It looked like an IMT, only a little more like the model Thatch designed than the one Solace had crafted.

A helmet covered the driver's face. "You ladies need a lift?"

"We shouldn't go with him." Rai eyed him and kept her hand ready on her sword.

"Are you headed to Wyvek?" Farah asked.

"Yeah. I live there actually. I came from Lumina to get some supplies."

"We'd never all fit on that thing," Farah said.

"No problem." The driver pressed a button, and the back of the vehicle extended to provide additional seating.

"I don't trust him," Rai said.

"Look, sweetheart, you can ride behind me with that sword to my neck all the way to Wyvek if you don't trust me."

"Tempting."

Farah and Sara got on the back of the vehicle. With reluctance, Rai followed.

The driver took them to Wyvek. He stopped near the bridge, and they got off the vehicle.

The water under the bridge was murky, and the chemical scent rose in the air. "My father was from Wyvek. I've never been." "Where are you from?" "The Insula Somnia Perpetua, didn't you hear?"

"Well, here we are." The driver removed his helmet. Under the helmet, he had been hiding his thin angular face and a mess of black hair.

"Atrus!" Farah said.

"Oh," Atrus said, "if it isn't Tag's daughter."

Farah rolled her eyes. "I have a name."

Orka squeaked.

"That bird never liked me." Atrus smoothed his hair and circled Farah with one hand behind his back and the other to his chin. "But you. You've grown up, haven't you? Last time I saw you, you were a head and a temper shorter."

Atrus noticed Rai standing far off with her arms folded. He looked at her like he recognized her.

He stopped circling Farah and approached Rai.

"What are you do—"

"Name's Rai." She extended her hand.

Atrus shook it. His o-shaped mouth eased into a smile. "I see."

He turned away from Rai. "Well, who do we have here?" he asked.

"My name's Sara."

"Sara, where have I heard that name before?" Atrus teased.

"She's only the Water Elemental who saved all of Mirmina!" Farah said.

"Not exactly," Sara said. "And I'm not a Water Elemental anymore."

"Well, you could still work for me," Atrus said.

"I don't think that's possible right now."

"Work for you?" Farah said. "So, you're Boss."

A person the size of a small child ran up to Atrus. A gas mask covered his face. Tiny gloves encased his hands, and he wore a jumper that went all the way up his neck.

Atrus knelt to speak with him. They spoke in a language Sara was not familiar with.

Atrus nodded.

The *Lacwanx* ran back to the temple.

"I should go deal with this," Atrus said. "But you're welcome to stay a while even if you won't work for me. Once I'm done, I'll explain to you what we do here."

He winked and hurried off toward the temple.

"Well, I was right," Farah said. "Boss *is* full of himself."

Orka bobbed her head and chirped.

"How do you know him?" Sara asked as they approached the temple.

"Atrus used to live in Breeze," Farah said. "We grew up together. We got kind of close one summer, and then he was gone. His parents took him to live in Lumina. That was almost five years ago."

"Is he a Wind Elemental?" Sara asked.

"One of the best," Farah said.

"No wonder he's full of himself," Rai said. "He has you to boost his ego."

Near the temple, hordes of people carried metal scraps and machines. The *Lacwanx* all wore gas masks.

"Why do they wear masks?" Sara asked.

"They don't like the air up here," Farah said. "They live underground. No one knows where the entrance to their home is. I'm surprised Atrus got them to work for him like this. I wonder what he's giving them."

Atrus walked back to them after having a short discussion with a group of *Lacwanx*.

"Sorry about that," Atrus said. "The *Lacwanx* are complaining about the shortage of supplies. That's why we're constantly needing new people: supply collectors."

"What exactly are you building?" Farah asked.

"We've been commissioned," Atrus said.

"Commissioned by who?"

"I don't give out my clients' personal information."

"At least tell us what you're building," Farah said.

"I'm sorry," Atrus said. "I can't."

"You're serious?" Farah asked.

"How can you expect your workers to trust you?" Rai asked.

"Well, the sparklings are good, so no one complains."

"We got a complaint," Sara said.

"What's that?"

"Tacitum said he saw something at a boulder," Farah said. "We think it might have been the Sphere Protector."

"Tacitum?"

"He used to work for you," Rai said.

"Really? A Sphere Protector?"

"You probably ran it off by taking over the sanctum like this," Rai said.

"Well, I didn't mean to upset the locals," Atrus said.

"Can you tell us where he saw it?" Farah asked. "Tacitum said something about a big boulder."

"Ah." Atrus lowered his voice to a whisper. "He must have meant the entrance to Resistance Headquarters. They're allowing us to store scrap metal there as a cover up."

"Why would they need a cover up?" Sara asked. "I thought the Resistance works in the open."

"They're calling themselves the Rebel Resistance," Atrus said. "They're the ones against Morica. While their buddies, well, they're on Morica's side. Morica doesn't trust Elementals who are members of the Resistance, so it is rumored they actually have them imprisoned."

"That's terrible." Sara thought of Rodan. She hadn't heard from him in several months.

"Where's the boulder?" Rai asked.

"You know I can't tell you that."

"Why not?" Farah asked.

"You'd be lucky if they don't kill you when you get there," Atrus said. "They're being highly secretive. What's more, if they found out that I betrayed their trust, we wouldn't be friends anymore. That would be bad for me."

Rai removed her blade and pressed it against Atrus's neck. The workers around them stopped moving, and stared at their boss and his assailant.

"Rai!" Sara said.

Farah pulled on Rai's arm to get her away from Atrus. "Let him go!"

"Where's the boulder?" Rai asked.

Atrus laughed. "You won't hurt me. We're all friends here."

"There's one thing I've learned about friends," Rai said. "They can betray each other."

She pressed the blade closer to his neck. Blood dripped down and nestled in the hollow of his collar bone.

"Okay! Up the road to the left, there's a boulder cut out of the mountain. A gatekeeper will ask for a password."

"What's the password?" Rai asked.

"I don't know it. The boulder's kind of hard to see. It's around a bend."

Rai backed away from him.

"That was a dirty trick." Atrus picked up a soiled towel to wipe up the blood. It stained the front of his shirt.

Farah glared at Rai.

They turned to leave.

"Oh, and Rai," Atrus yelled as they walked toward the road, "be prepared to run into an old friend."

10

CONTROL OF THE CITY

JEI Fletzi paced his chamber. He had received news that the High Council was back in the city as he had requested.

The jingling of his golden bracelets bounced off the stone ceiling and met his ears. He was as used to the sound as a huntsman is used to the way the wind makes the leaves on the trees sing to life.

As the doors opened, his pacing stopped. The look of rage on his face deepened.

Romulus and Mordecai entered with two blue-and-silver guards.

"Get them out of my chamber." Jei Fletzi pointed to the guards.

"Have we offended you, my lord?" Mordecai asked.

"I want them out." Jei Fletzi's voice escaped through his teeth.

Mordecai nodded to the guards, and they left the room.

"You said you'd announce the postponement of the Games, not put a ban on them all together."

"My lord, I think there's some confusion," Mordecai said.

"Damn right there's some confusion. On your end," Jei Fletzi said. "I've been trying to get a hold of you for almost a month. Did you not get my messages?"

"My lord, travels these days are hard."

"By boat, you should have been at my doorstep within the week."

"Hardly within the week," Mordecai said.

"Because of you," Jei Fletzi said, "the people hate me. As soon as you gave your little announcement, I had open rebellion outside my Manor. You left me with none of the guards you promised while you escaped on your lavish boat to who knows where."

"I don't know what you mean, my lord. The guards promised to you now decorate your city streets."

"It is true your guards are here now, but where were they when the people stormed the steps of my Manor and tore down my banners?"

"On a ship from Vella City."

Jei Fletzi scoffed. "I posted new announcements for the Games at my own costs. Where is the gold you promised me?"

"A ship laden with gold is headed to Lumina Port as we speak."

"It better be."

"You were saying you rescheduled the Games, my lord?"

"Yes, you're in luck, High Councilor. You're late, but you've arrived just in time for the Games. They begin at high-noon."

"This decision is unwise, my lord," Mordecai said. "The Games are dangerous, and they encourage Elementals to display their power publicly."

"Publicly yes, and the public pays for it!" Jei Fletzi said. "The decision has already been made, High Councilor. If you happen to fall back into my good graces, next time I trust that you will keep your promises."

CROWDS of people gathered in Lumina Stadium and awaited the start of the Element Games. When Jei Fletzi stepped upon the balcony overlooking the Stadium, the crowd cheered.

"Ladies and gentlemen, it is my pleasure to announce the commencement of the Element Games!"

Cheers sounded, and the contestants took the field.

Jei Fletzi smiled. Each cheer sounded like the high-pitched chiming of silver coins hitting his coffers.

The contestants lined up. Dema, a Lightning Elemental, and Taryn, a Wind Elemental, were among them. They were both eager to get another chance at winning the crystal orb, the prized trophy of the Games.

The other contestants were eager as well. One of them wore a hooded cloak. This cloak shielded his face from the crowd.

The announcer began introducing the judges and the contestants. His voice excited the crowd, and cheering ensued. The hooded man was the last contestant waiting to be introduced.

"Sir? Sir? How did you get on the field?"

The hooded man raised his head.

"You're not on the list," the announcer said.

The crowd hushed as the man lifted the hood from his head.

It was Fulgur. His glowing eyes scanned the crowd. "Your games don't interest me."

Fulgur looked up to the sky. The clouds darkened and moved apart. From the center of the clouds, Lightning struck down on the field, scorching the grass, creating a large circular pattern on the ground.

The people in the stands ran.

Fulgur directed the Lightning toward the stands and struck one man trying to leave. The man's back arched to such a degree that the bones in his spine crackled. As the energy surged through his body, he collapsed between the stands.

Taryn tried to rush Fulgur, but he sent Lightning from the sky to shelter him like an energy cage. As she sped against him, her body hit the lightning bolts that stunned her to the ground.

Dema tried to counter his power and ease the bolts, but to no avail. Fulgur's strength was unmatched.

The stands were on fire, and the people ran in a sea and trampled the bodies.

Jei Fletzi peered over the edge of the balcony at Fulgur. Jei Fletzi's whole body shook in terror.

The Lightning caged the field and struck the bodies of the contestants and members of the audience. Hundreds of others still scrambled to safety.

Fulgur's face was expressionless. The immense power he expended did not make him weary. He continued to impale his victims with bolts. He didn't mind the pain. He sent them all to a place where he could never go.

The Stadium emptied of those who were able enough to escape. Fulgur replaced his hood, and left the Stadium, his charged feet, searing the grass where he stepped.

MORICA guards cleared the Stadium of the dead and wounded. No one in the city wanted to go near it because of the smell of roasting bodies. Some of the bodies had caught fire, and the guards had to peel their melted flesh from the stands.

Citizens and travelers mourned their loved ones by placing flowers near the Stadium. The guards detained people and trampled the flowers as they made their arrests. Wind swept the crushed flowers away.

Jei Fletzi, sheltered in his sedan chair, rode through the streets of Lumina. The sedan chair was box-like with cushions inside to seat Jei Fletzi comfortably. The sedan chair was carried on four posts by Jei Fletzi's personal guards. Curtains shielded him from the sun's harsh light. He pulled back the curtains to gaze upon his city.

Travelers congested the city. Jei Fletzi was pleased by this new influx of visitors who would require shelter and food from his markets. He could see the sparklings falling from their hands. From each head, he counted at least ten sparklings a day to fill his coffers.

Now that the Stadium was clear, and the weeks had passed since the attack, Jei Fletzi felt the anxiety leave him.

His sedan chair shook. A force acted on it from the outside followed by shouts.

"Come out, *Lord* Fletzi, and order us around yourself!"

The sedan chair tilted and fell to the ground.

Jei Fletzi was tossed about in the sedan chair. He climbed out from the other side to meet a crowd of angry citizens. Someone in the crowd threw mud. The thick sludge plastered onto Jei Fletzi's face and dripped down to his tunic.

The complaints of the crowd mixed and mingled in his ears.

"I was at the Games. No one's safe in this city."

"How could you let this happen to us?"

"Sell those gold bangles and hire more guards to protect us!"

The crowd moved in on Jei Fletzi. His men had fled. He turned to the guards in the silver-and-blue.

"Protect me!" Jei Fletzi shouted.

The guards did not respond to Jei Fletzi's request. Jei Fletzi screamed for help, but they ignored his pleas. They watched as the crowd swallowed him. They watched as they trampled on his silk-robed body.

11

THE REBEL RESISTANCE

"What's wrong with you?" Farah asked. "Why'd you attack Atrus like that?"

"It was the only way he was going to tell us how to find the Rebel Resistance," Rai said.

"You went too far," Farah said, "and what was that all about back there? Do you know someone in the Resistance?"

"The past is the past," Rai said. "No need to dig it up."

Rai's words made Sara sad. After all, she was digging, searching for something lost.

After rounding the bend, before them was the big boulder. The smallest fraction of light issued from tiny cracks outlining the edges of the boulder against the mountain.

A man stood guard. He wore a brown Resistance fighter uniform. At his side was a long-curved sword. The silver band around his arm had a thick black line painted through it.

"Password."

"Umm . . ." Farah cooed, tapping her cheek.

"Who are you?"

"We're friends," Sara said. "We want to help. We were hoping we could speak to your leader."

"You're the Water Elemental."

"That's right," Sara said.

"I can't let you through."

"Rai, I think now's a really good time to do your thing," Farah whispered. "You know, your rude sword-against-the-neck thing."

Rai glared at her.

"You see," Farah said to the guard, "Atrus sent us to talk to your leader about *the cover up operation*," she whispered. "We just came to discuss some things."

"Why did you come with weapons?"

"Oh, that." Farah removed her dagger from the side of her waist and put it on the ground.

"What are you doing?" Rai hissed.

Sara followed suit and removed her wrist gun and dagger and set them on the ground.

"Sorry," Farah said. "That was just for the trip here. For protection. We'll drop our weapons at the entrance. Farah turned to Rai. "Rai, put your weapon down."

"You must be out of your mind," Rai said.

"This guy is not even going to consider letting us in unless you put your weapon down," Farah said.

Rai shook her head, and laid her sword on the ground.

"You're Elementals. You carry your weapons with you," the guard said.

"I'm not an Elemental," Sara said. "I'm completely de-fenseless without my weapon."

"Not an Elemental. But you used to be?"

"Yes." Sara thought he might want an explanation, but he didn't ask for one.

The soldier contemplated. "If you're the Water Elemental, I assume you are friends with Rodan."

Sara nodded. "Is he here?"

"May we see him?" Farah asked.

"Rodan isn't here anymore."

"What happened to him?" Farah asked.

"He's out on a mission, which he insisted on taking despite my warnings."

"Your warnings? Where is he?" Sara asked.

"In enemy territory in Vella City."

Sara thought of Rodan, alone among the Councilors. She didn't want to think of what would happen to him if they found out who he was. "Please, let us through. We're friends," Sara said.

"The Commander is not going to like it," the soldier said. "Come on." He pulled a chain next to the boulder, and the large boulder sank into the ground.

"I'm Jin. You can pick up your weapons."

They walked into a large rocky courtyard filled with scrap metal. There were steps carved into the rock and rising into the mountain.

Jin led them up the rocky steps.

"If you're not an Elemental why are you part of the Rebel Resistance?" Sara asked.

"You assume I'm not an Elemental because I carry a sword?" Jin asked.

"I'm not used to Elementals carrying weapons."

"Well, like your friends," Jin said. "I too am an Elemental and carry my own weapon. I'm an Earth Elemental, but a weak one. My son is far stronger than I. Not that we don't have non-Elementals here who sympathize with us. But all the members of the Rebel Resistance carry weapons of steel. Besides the extra security, Morica has recently released an order that Elementals are not allowed to use their elements in the public eye. Members of the Resistance cannot risk imprisonment. Our numbers are dwindling as it is. If we were seen walking around in our uniforms without a weapon, Morica would detain us."

"I'm sure the High Councilors would much rather you fight them with swords and daggers," Rai said.

"Believe me," Jin said, "it may sound ridiculous, but they are more concerned with getting rid of non-violent Elementals than non-Elemental rebel attackers."

"What's their problem with us anyway?" Farah asked.

"We're powerful," Jin said. "Like Hephaestus, we all have the potential to overtake them. And what Hephaestus gave Morica was a reason to stop us. They're playing on the fear in people's hearts. Soon, we'll be shunned by everyone, and Morica will flock us like sheep into a pen, or worse, exterminate us all.

"The truth is, Lady Sara," Jin said, "what you and your friends did three years ago is keeping the people's trust. It's the only thing that stands between Elementals and certain death. Morica can't massacre us because the people would be against them, and what kind of power can they have without people to follow them? The people love and respect you as much as they do High Councilor Veil."

Jin led them to a tall rocky wall. He pulled the hidden chain that blended in with the rocks. The wall split in half, and the halves slid apart.

"This is where I leave you and return to my post," Jin said. "Good luck."

Sara nodded.

Through the crevasse were rows of tents and supplies, and in the center, was a larger building that rose above the tents. A balcony extended from the building.

"It's like a secret town," Farah said.

"That's the idea," Rai said.

People in tattered uniforms marched. They trained and saluted higher ranked officers. They all wore silver bands with black paint running through them.

Sara approached the tall building with Farah and Rai behind her.

Soldiers stopped them at the entrance.

"Why are you here?" a soldier asked.

"We're here to see your leader," Sara said.

"The Commander is very tired now and will speak to no one."

The soldiers stopped marching and stood at attention as someone appeared on the balcony. His black hair, streaked with gray, was cut short, coming down his forehead to a widow's peak. Lines gathered around his eyes and forehead. His beard was gray and so short that no hair hung below his chin and jawline. The hairs above his lip were still dark. His uniform was stitched in places. His right arm hung stiff at his side as he limped onto the balcony.

"Friends," he said, "comrades, soldiers. Some words. Morica thinks it can stand against us because it thinks it can stand against anything, but it can't stand against something it cannot see. I know preparation is slow going. Remember we are not hiding. We are building strength, and one day, we will open forces against Morica. For Mirmina!"

"For Mirmina!" The soldiers shouted in unison and saluted their leader.

Then Vassal turned around and walked stiffly back inside.

"I thought you said he would see no one," Rai said to the soldiers at the door.

"We have our orders, miss."

"Tell him the Water Elemental is here," Rai said.

Sara, Rai, and Farah waited outside the tall building. The soldier returned to announce that the Commander would see them. He led them to the upper floor of the building where the Commander sat at the head of a long, wooden table.

A young woman set a water basin in front of Vassal. She had long black hair like Rai's, and her face was equally slender.

Her features matched as did the confidence in the way she walked.

"My name is Vassal. Please, sit." Vassal's right arm rested on the table. As Sara sat next to him, she could see that the hand was made of wood.

"Nice to meet you," Sara said.

"Likewise," Vassal said. "I've always wanted to meet the young woman who saved Mirmina."

"It wasn't through my efforts alone," Sara said.

Vassal's eyes darted to Rai, and his gaze softened. He seemed to recognize her and was confused that she had not acknowledged him. Perhaps he marveled at how much Rai looked like his servant girl.

Sara broke the brief but biting silence. "We were wondering if you might know something about the element spheres."

The young woman walked over to Vassal and massaged his shoulders.

Rai tried to maintain her composure, but her discomfort showed on her face.

"Marissa," Vassal said, "please go into the outer chamber."

Marissa left the room. The silence hung like a dark cloud until she left.

Vassal diverted his eyes.

"I believe Morica is hiding the element spheres," he said. "Don't you?" He looked into Rai's eyes.

"Why would Morica have the spheres?" Farah asked.

Rai turned her head to break his gaze.

"Isn't it obvious?" Vassal asked. "Morica wishes to frame the Elementals. They want Elementals to seem responsible for all the mishaps that have been occurring—the missing spheres, the rogue Protectors. All to keep them out of the public's favor."

So, he knows about the Protectors. "Where do you think Morica is hiding the spheres?" Sara asked.

"I'm not quite sure. My best guess would be in Vella City where they have set up their Council."

"Then why don't you burst in and take back the spheres?" Farah asked.

"It's not that easy," he said. "There would be guards surrounding the entire area. Besides, you can never be sure, they may have them elsewhere. Maybe they assume Vella City would be too obvious, and they could have us walking into a trap. The ring of questioning will never end until someone finds the spheres. Unfortunately, none of my soldiers have gotten close enough to investigate the area. One was sent who never returned, but I doubt he knows anything. It was unwise for an Elemental to volunteer anyway. I warned him. They probably found him out and have him imprisoned already."

"Rodan?" Sara asked.

Vassal nodded. "You know him. He's a good soldier."

"But you're not sure about any of that? What you're saying about the spheres?" Farah asked.

"I'm sorry, all I can offer is my theories. And I would hope that you wouldn't try to take on Morica alone," he said with a quick glance in Rai's direction.

"Thank you for your time." Sara nodded and stood from the table. Farah and Rai rose to leave.

Vassal stood to see his guests out. His steps were labored and slow. As they turned to leave, Sara thought she saw Vassal reach out to touch Rai's hand, but the gesture was gone in the blink of an eye.

12

REFLECTION

SARA left the Resistance Headquarters followed by Farah and Rai. She stood by the rocky ledge overlooking the sea, and stared at the dark water below.

"Are you okay?" Farah asked.

She nodded. "I'm fine. Really." Sara forced a smile.

"You know what you need?" Farah asked.

"What?"

"A break. We could go back to Caleena, replenish our supplies, and visit with Spire."

"We just got a lead," Rai said. "It's not the time to be taking breaks. We break when we sleep."

"It's not like the world will collapse if we take a few hours to ourselves." Farah touched her earpiece. "Thatch, we're ready to go."

"Okay," Thatch buzzed. "Meet us at the entrance to the old road. There should be enough space to land there."

The Chariot landed at the junction between the old road and the new. They climbed the ramp and reported to the control room.

Stannum buzzed at his screens and buttons, and Thatch stared at the locator.

"They've been like that for hours," Shift said.

Thatch looked up from his screen. "So, what happened? What's wrong?"

"We got a lead on the spheres," Farah said.

"We heard the whole conspiracy theory," Shift said. "So, the leader of the Resistance thinks Morica has something to do with all this?"

"The Rebel Resistance," Rai corrected.

"Yep, that's what he thinks," Farah said. "We can look into it, but I doubt the High Council has the man-power or the skills to get out of a sphere sanctum alive."

"Perhaps he knows something we don't," Sara said.

"Then why didn't he just tell us?" Farah asked. "It certainly would have been more convincing if he had."

"So, where to now?" Thatch asked.

"We should go to Caleena and check on Spire and Decca," Farah said. "They have a rogue Sphere Protector to worry about."

Sara stared out the window as the Chariot flew over Lumina.

"You know what's funny?" Thatch asked. "We've been all over Mirmina in the past couple of months since I built the Chariot and no sign of Uncle Tag."

"Wait," Rai said. "The leader of Breeze is missing in action? Why isn't his son watching over his city instead of gallivanting all over Mirmina with the likes of you three?"

Silence swept the room.

"Did I say something wrong?" Rai asked.

Shift got up from his seat.

"What are you doing?" Thatch asked. "The Chariot can't fly itself."

"*You* fly it!" Shift marched out of the room and into the elevator.

Farah turned to follow him.

"Wait!" Thatch said. "Farah, I need you here to drive the Chariot."

"I don't know how to drive this thing," Farah said.

"You know better than anyone else," Thatch said.

"But he's my brother."

"I'll go talk to him." Sara turned to the elevator.

Farah jumped into the driver's seat and took the wheel.

Sara went up to the sleeping quarters. Shift sat at the bar. His head was in his hands.

"Are you alright?" she asked.

He looked up as Sara sat on the stool beside him. "I thought I was."

"I understand what you're going through," Sara said. "When I lost my element, it was devastating, and every day since, it feels like something is missing. Like I'm incomplete."

"My father says if I can't man up and use my element, how can I be in charge of his city?" he said.

"He doesn't know what it's like," Sara said, "and he's probably scared. Maybe he thinks it could happen to him. He doesn't want to face it."

"Then he doesn't want to face me," Shift said.

"Being without your element doesn't make you useless," Sara said. "We need you right now."

The Chariot jolted and jerked downward. Thermal dove in the direction of the reins. Shift leapt from his seat and rushed to the elevator. Sara followed.

Farah struggled at the wheel.

"We're not landing," Thatch said. "Pull up!"

"This thing's touchy," Farah said. "I don't know how Shift flies it."

Shift burst through the doors followed by Sara. "What are you doing?" He approached the driver's seat.

"Trying to fly this thing." Farah fought to pull the steering yoke back.

"I thought you said the steering wheel was touchy. You make it look stiff," Shift said. "Move aside."

Farah scrambled out of the seat, and Shift took his place at the steering wheel. He pulled up and righted the Chariot.

IN Caleena, Morica guards patrolled the wharfs. Guards were stationed at the gates to Cal Hill, and the silver-and-blue flags remained, waving in the soft breeze.

"What's with all the guards?" Farah asked. "It's even worse than it was last time."

"Looks like Morica is taking over," Rai said.

They walked to Spire's hut. Sara knocked on the wood paneling lining the doorway.

"Come in." Spire's voice echoed through the opening.

Spire sat on her cushioned sofa. "I didn't expect to see you again so soon."

"Rai's part of the team now," Farah said.

Spire nodded. "My invitation was less than warm last we met. You helped us cross the Lake de Somnia. Unkindness is not deserved for such a task. How has life been to you since then?"

"Not thoroughly unkind. I've been traveling."

"Traveling is good for the soul, but it makes the heart long for something more."

"What's wrong?" Sara asked. "You seem sad."

"It's Decca," Spire said. "Morica's working him too hard. They've instated this new head guard. He's brutal. I barely get to see Decca, and when I do, he's so worn out, he falls right to sleep. It's hard to tire him, and I believe the head guard is being particularly cruel to him. With the baby on the way, I need him here."

"Where can we find this guy?" Farah asked.

"I'm afraid there isn't much you can do."

"We'll see about that," Sara said.

Spire shook her head. "You should find him near the supply crates. Decca loads the ships bringing supplies to Vella City."

After leaving Spire, they walked to the wharf ends. Decca sat on two crates stacked together. His face was bright red, and thick beads of sweat wept from his brow.

"Decca?"

Decca shook off his stone gaze and looked up at them.

"Back already?" he asked.

Farah sat next to Decca on another stack of crates. "We heard an arrogant Blue Jay is giving you a hard time."

"It's not that bad, really," Decca said. "He's tough, but I can handle it. I'm just worried."

"About what?" Sara asked.

"I want to be there when the baby is born," he said. "I wish I had someone to talk to about being a dad. It's scary. When my big brother left, my mom kept saying I was the man of the house. I knew that meant protecting my family, but I never really knew if I was doing it right. I always felt unsure, and I'm afraid I'll have that same feeling when the baby is born."

"You'll be great at it." Sara patted his shoulder.

Decca nodded. "I've been thinking a lot about it."

"Thinking?" a cruel voice spat. "What about the work you're supposed to be doing?"

The voice came from a man wearing a silver and blue uniform. His dark crimson hair swept above his thick brows. His auburn beard was trimmed. His brow furrowed. "Did you hear me? You're supposed to be loading those crates, not sitting on them."

Sara stood. "It was my fault. I begged him to take a break. He looked exhausted. Perhaps your workers should get more breaks."

"Are you one of my workers?"

Sara shook her head.

"I suggest you mind your own business."

"Hey," Farah said. "You arrogant—"

Rai took her arm and squeezed.

"Ouch!"

"Get back to work," the guard said. "I want this wharf clear before sundown."

The guard turned and left.

"Hey, what was that for?" Farah faced Rai.

"You were going to get him fired. That wouldn't have been good with a baby on the way."

Decca got up and lifted one of the crates.

"Why are you listening to him?" Farah asked.

"She's right," Decca said. "I need this job. When you have a family, you make sacrifices.

"That guard is head guard now. His name is Sev. He's been working everyone in the village hard. Keep us working, stop us from gossiping. Wants to stop people from planning against Morica. Can't ever really stop the gossiping though. It would be like trying to stop the sun from rising."

SARA and her friends left Decca to his work. They returned to Spire and visited with her before boarding the Chariot.

"I'm starting to see a pattern," Farah said. "First, Morica puts a bunch of restrictions on people. Then, the Councilors send their guards to run the people ragged."

"They're taking Mirmina while it's still weak after battle," Thatch said. "Three years ago, there was disorder and chaos. People were looking for security and stability, and Morica offered it."

"They're trying to sugar-coat it," Rai said, "but they're tyrants. That's all they are."

"I don't like the way they're treating people," Sara said. "At first, I thought we could turn their influence into something good, but now I don't know. I think some of them have good intentions."

"You don't mean Veil?" Farah asked.

Sara nodded. "But we must stop them."

"It's not going to be easy," Shift said. "It's not just one man in charge. It's six. And they haven't hurt anyone."

"Taking away their freedom isn't enough?" Sara asked.

"I don't know if everyone will see it that way," Shift said. "Morica has convinced them that these precautions are for their own safety."

"I thought we agreed to take the day off." Farah folded her arms.

"Break's over," Rai said.

"I heard some news about Uncle Tag in Lumina," Thatch said. "Travelers say they saw Tag heading from Omega Ray."

"What would he be doing there?" Farah asked.

"Rumors are going around that he's trying to capitalize on the place by building a factory there where he can mass produce his machines," Thatch said.

"What?" Farah said. "I say we crash his party."

"Why?" Shift asked. "He doesn't know what we're doing. If we show up, he'll just order us back to Breeze."

"I guess I didn't fully emancipate you," Farah said. "So what if he orders us back? What can he do? We'll board the Chariot and fly away again."

"I don't want to see him," Shift said.

"You don't have too."

SARA sat on her bed and watched the sky through the windows above. Orka slept on her perch beside Farah's bed.

Orange light flooded the room.

Sara turned to see Stannum floating at eye level.

"They're beautiful. The stars," the machine buzzed.

"You think so?" Sara stared at them.

"I wouldn't know," Stannum buzzed. "I cannot see the stars, but I am told that they are very beautiful. It is a fact among humans, like the beauty of a sunset."

Orka rustled in her sleep.

"Can you tell me more about Morica?"

Stannum's eye glowed burnt-orange. "Two hundred years ago, a man named Thomas Morica, using the wheel of never-ending change, started what is now known as the Council."

A holograph image of the wheel of never-ending change with its six spokes was projected from Stannum's glowing eye.

"He created the Council in response to the Great Flood of Vella City. This flood spawned a fear of Elementals and the mysterious Keepers.

"The Elementals who once lived in the city were forced out by the Resistance, a group of military fighters who the Council had recruited. The Resistance guarded the borders of Vella City, keeping all Elementals out.

"As the years went on, Morica's influence grew stronger and spread to the outlying cities, including the great trade city, Lumina.

"Morica launched a campaign to rid Mirmina of Elementals so the people would not have to live in fear. He ordered the Resistance to hunt down and kill the Elementals.

"However, many members of the Resistance were displeased with this new initiative, so the group broke away from the Council.

"Meanwhile, certain members of the Council felt the plan to execute the Elementals was too cruel. They too broke away from the guidance of Morica and formed their own group, the Irradiatio.

"The Irradiatio wanted to study the Elementals and find the source of their power. For many years, they studied Elementals and Elemental writings. They compiled volumes of texts on Elementals and their abilities.

"Seeing the Irradiatio as traitors, Morica ordered they be found and disassembled. He used his remaining fighters and like assassins, they tracked down the Irradiatio and killed many. Those who were not killed found themselves kneeling before Morica and asking to be invited back to the fold."

"What's going on here?" Rai climbed the stairs to the loft.

Stannum's glowing eye turned dull orange.

"I was just . . ."

"Learning about the enemy," Rai said. "That's smart."

Sara folded her hands in her lap.

Orka awoke to the sound of Rai's voice and chirped with contempt for being awoken. Farah slept.

Sara looked up at Rai. "About Farah. I know she can seem overbearing at times, but she feels strongly about things. She gets feelings about people, but sometimes they surprise her."

"I don't think she and I will ever get along," Rai said. "She's stubborn, and she senses something about me she doesn't like. I can't blame her."

"*She* might surprise *you*," Sara said.

Orka lifted one foot into the feathers of her belly and went back to sleep.

13

COMMANDER

JIN issued the orders to the fighters. He separated them into groups to run circuits.

Rain fell, but training did not end.

Vassal hobbled from his tent to where Jin stood. Vassal stood up straight, unashamed of his disability, and clasped his arms behind his back.

"I miss Water Elementals," Jin said, rain dripping down his face. "Training days were always dry. They could shift the rain to some other town for the day."

"We have to teach the men to train without their elements," Vassal said. "Elements can become too easily exhausted."

"So can human bodies, Sir."

Vassal stared at the soldiers. "If I disappear, promise me you'll lead the men to Vella City and finish this war."

"But Sir, why would you disappear?"

Vassal turned to Jin, and his expression was unwavering.

"It would be an honor, Sir," Jin said.

Gallus approached Vassal, followed by a small group of people.

"Commander Vassal, these people want to join our cause," Gallus said.

"Who are they?" Vassal asked.

Dema stepped forward. Her short, dark hair swept across her forehead meeting at her narrow, determined eyes. "I didn't know the Rebel Resistance was so picky."

Taryn took Dema's arm and pulled her back in among the group. Dema shrugged away from Taryn with a look of disdain.

Taryn had tied her long hair back and dressed in her black training attire, which she purchased with the sparklings she won in various contests.

"Please," she said. "We are Elementals who have trained for years to participate in the Element Games. Now that the Games have been cancelled, we would like to focus our energy on bringing Morica down."

Vassal looked at her. "This is not a game, and it's not an outlet for revenge against Morica for taking away your playthings."

"We understand that," Taryn said. "But we don't want our talents to go to waste."

"People die in battles," Vassal said. "Being a skilled Elemental doesn't mean you're ready for war."

Dema glared at Vassal. "With no disrespect, Sir, but what do you know about training an Elemental?"

"Plenty," Vassal said. "I've worked with two of the finest."

Taryn stood her ground. "But we can be trained, Sir. Isn't that what you do here?"

"Jin, take these young Elementals and teach them to use a blade," Vassal said.

Taryn beamed. "We won't let you down, Sir."

Vassal hobbled back to his tent. His wooden hand had become saturated with water despite his attempt to shelter it.

With effort, he sat at the small wooden table and watched the water slush in under the hem of the tent as the door flaps fretted in the wind.

Marissa, her long, dark hair free, walked over to Vassal and rolled up the sleeve of his shirt to the shoulder. A leather padding encased his shoulder connected to leather straps that linked to the wooden hand. It stopped below the elbow.

Marissa unbuckled the straps and removed the wooden arm. It was hollowed out at the base to be fitted over what was left of Vassal's flesh and blood limb.

All that remained was a sock to prevent chafing. Marissa rolled the sock down Vassal's arm and off the stump. Vassal's arm ended above the wrist, leaving only a stump surrounded by pink flesh.

Before Marissa stood, Vassal ran his only true hand through her hair. "I told you to keep this tied back."

Marissa, thin-lipped, tied her hair into a quick and messy braid.

"Better?" she asked with contempt as she busied herself by putting Vassal's wooden hand and sock away in a box.

She set a plate and utensil out for him and scooped the boiled millet out of a pot and onto his plate.

Vassal rolled up his pant leg, unbuckled the straps and removed his wooden leg. He rested the wooden limb against the leg of the table and rubbed the pain out of the stump.

"You are good to me," Vassal said. "Will you go now?"

Marissa tossed the ladle back into the pot and marched out of the tent into the rain.

Vassal stirred the millet around with his wooden spoon and reflected.

14

OMEGA RAY

OMEGA Ray was shrouded by a dark cloud covering the summit of Regret Mountain. Wispy ash drifted through the deserted city. No longer were the streets lit up to swallow the darkness that hung like a thick black curtain, both dim and suffocating.

The roof of Hephaestus's stone palace lay on the ground, unrecognizable due to the debris and ash. The columns which once supported the roof were eroding. A thick sheet of ash and broken stone covered the abandoned bed.

Shift landed the Chariot where the road to Omega Ray was widest. The road wrapped around Regret Mountain and became narrower as it approached the peak.

Thermal dug his clawed feet into the snow and let out a loud caw.

"The cold reminds him of his home in Demlama," Thatch said. "Is everyone ready?"

"I'll stay," Shift said.

Thatch nodded. He and the others exited the Chariot and walked up Regret Mountain.

Sara stared up at the mountain's ashy peak. Her fingers pinched her mother's gem stone necklace.

"Are you okay with this?" Farah asked.

Sara nodded. "I'll be fine."

Sara tried to block the memories from her mind. There was a time for memories, but she didn't want to be swallowed up by them. Still, though she tried to put a dam against the memories, some leaked through, creating growing holes in her defense.

She journeyed back to a time when she gave the order to march onto Omega Ray. She wished she had chosen not to fight. No, we'll sneak in and save him. Then, we'll leave, build a better army and come back stronger. But in the meantime, we'll live. We'll have more time together.

Despite her efforts, a tear froze on Sara's cheek.

As they approached the narrow opening that led to the city, they stopped. Sheet metal rested in a nook in the mountain's rocky surface, and deep, labored footprints led into the city.

"Yep, he's here alright," Farah said.

Only a few vestiges of the city walls remained. The stones had resisted the flood that swept the city during the battle. A thick and heavy darkness hung over the city. Though it was dim, people could be seen moving through the darkness, their arms heavy with supplies and machines, sheet metal, gears, and glass.

Farah ran down past where the wall used to be, and stopped one of the workers.

"Where's my dad?"

The woman looked startled. "Miss, why are you not in Breeze?"

"I came here to look for my dad," Farah said. "Where is he?"

"Somewhere in the city. I'm not sure where. When he gave us our instructions this morning, we met at the cliff on the south side."

The others caught up with Farah, and she led them toward the cliff.

As they passed Hephaestus's stone palace, Sara recalled the clear sound of the sword cutting through Talon's body and the black bile that engulfed Eli and dragged him down with the shadow of his son.

The electricity ran up her skin as Bolton grabbed her hand.

Farah spotted Tag among the workers. He was barking orders, his face getting red.

"Dad!" Farah approached him.

Tag stopped shouting at the workers. "What are you doing out here? You're supposed to be at home in Breeze."

"What are *you* doing here?" Farah asked. "This isn't a playground. We fought here."

"There's no reason not to re-purpose the land. What we're doing here is for the good of Mirmina."

"It's for *your* good," Farah said.

"You." Tag pointed to Thatch. "You brought my little girl here?"

"I asked him to," Farah said.

As Farah and her father argued, Sara meandered to the cliff. Her chest burned when Fero used his element to destroy the Water Sphere. A part of her fell with Bolton that day and was still lying at the bottom of the gorge.

She looked down into the mist and tried to see what lie beneath it. A fresh tear joined the frozen one. She clenched the gem around her neck.

Rai walked to the cliff and stood beside her. "I'm sorry for your loss."

Sara dropped the gem. She feared she would break the golden string that held it around her neck. She kept her eyes down, searching the chasm.

"It's hard." Rai looked down at the black band around her arm. "There are so many things that remind us of our regrets and the people we have lost."

Sara stared into the chasm. *Mist. It's just water vapor. If I still had my element, I could clear it and see what lies beneath.* "Maybe it would bring me peace," Sara said, "but I don't want to forget."

Sara walked back to where Farah and Tag argued.

"Tag is right," Sara said. "This place shouldn't fall to ruins. People should remember what happened here. This reminds them. If the place lives on, so does the memory."

Tag nodded. "Come on. I have something to show you."

They followed Tag into a building. Sheet metal lined the sides of the building, and inside, a network of stairs rose to twenty feet, much like Tag's steel castle.

They climbed the steel steps to the second floor where Tag opened the door to a large room where workers were building various machines and contraptions.

Workers were lined up along long tables. Each doing a specific task before moving the contraption along to the next worker.

"They're working on machines to replace them," Tag said. "Isn't that ironic?"

At the back of the room was a machine that looked like Stannum, but did not have low hanging arms.

"What is it?" Farah asked.

Tag placed the contraption on the floor and pushed the button on its back.

The machine buzzed to life and rolled around them as it sensed objects in its way. Its eyes blinked as it moved.

"But what does it do?" Farah asked.

Tag grabbed the scurrying machine, and pushed the button to turn it off. He snapped off the panel from its back and pulled out a small cube encased in metal.

"Follow me."

Tag led them up another flight of stairs into a small, dark room. Another device sat upon a single table in the middle of the room. A bare wall of weathered steel panels was across from the table.

The device was a steel box, the size of an orange crate. On the front of the device was a large glass eye and, below that, a space large enough to hold the small metal cube which Tag had extracted from the rolling machine.

Tag placed the cube inside the box-like structure and pressed the small green button on the side of the device.

Light emitted from the large glass eye onto the sheets of metal in front of it. Then came a whirling sound, and the device projected an image onto the metal sheet.

The image was in gray tones and was distorted, but a careful eye could discern the outlines of the factory room from the perspective of the tiny rolling machine. It created a moving picture.

"We have one down there right now," Tag said.

"Where?" Farah asked.

"At the bottom of the gorge." Sara gripped the table.

"Once we retrieve the machine, we can project the image through this larger device. After we see what's down there," Tag said, "we'll find a way to retrieve his body and the Water Sphere."

Tag led them out of the steel building and back into the dimly lit streets.

"It was nice to see you again, Uncle," Thatch said.

"Listen to me, young man," Tag said. "I know you were the one responsible for all this. You've been corrupting my daughter since you were children. If your mother were alive, she would have set you in line long ago.

Where's Shift?"

"Shift is . . ." Farah started.

"Don't lie to me," Tag said. "I know Shift is not in Breeze. I do have eyes and ears there."

"Shift doesn't want to see you." Farah folded her arms.

"Why?" Tag asked.

"Really?" Farah asked. "How would you feel if your own father didn't trust you to take care of Breeze? The loss of his element is not his fault, and he can order people around like you do just fine without it."

"I know that," Tag said. "I just thought getting him all riled up would help him get his element back. I did it to challenge him a little, make him want it."

"He wants an apology," Farah said. "You should give him one."

"Me? I'm his father. He should respect my decisions."

"He doesn't understand why you did it," Farah said.

"Children were born to obey their parents' orders, not to understand them."

"You're both too proud for either one of you to give the other a chance," Farah said.

A growl sounded in the distance.

"We'll stop by again later," Farah said, "to make sure that thing in the mountains hasn't eaten you."

"I'm too busy," Tag said. "You should be going back to Breeze where I ordered you to stay."

15

BENEATH THE LAKE OF DREAMS

AS they boarded the Chariot, Farah ranted about Tag's behavior.

When the doors to the elevator slid open, a loud beeping met their ears.

"What's going on?" Thatch rushed to his seat.

"It won't stop," Shift shouted. "That weak signal that you were getting from the Lake is getting stronger."

"I can see that," Thatch said.

"What do you mean?" Sara asked. "What signal?"

The beeping continued.

"Turn it off!"

"There's been a weak signal over the Lake de Somnia," Thatch said. "I didn't think much of it. Sometimes energy settles in a place, but from this reading, it seems like there's a lot of energy stirring at the Lake. We should go."

Thatch typed a command, and the beeping stopped.

"Thank the Creator." Shift sighed. "That sound was really getting to me. It didn't seem to bother that buzz-can in the least."

Stannum's eye blinked. "Machines have their moments. Less so than humans."

Shift rolled his eyes, and pressed a button on the control panel.

Thermal cawed as the Chariot lifted into the air and zoomed toward the Lake de Somnia.

Sara went to the loft and sat on the stool near the window. She pulled paper and charcoal from her bag and sketched the clouds.

Starting on a fresh piece of paper, Sara let her hand wander. The charcoal outlined the curve of his jaw, and gentle strokes weaved the strands of his light hair. She let her hand work until the drawing was complete, and the face of Bolton stared back at her. His eyes were bright as if the luster had never gone out.

Tears dropped onto the paper. The tears mixed with the charcoal, which ran down the paper in watery black drips. Bolton cried with her in that moment as her tears dripped down his face. She let the paper fall to the floor.

SHIFT landed the Chariot, and Sara, Rai, and Farah exited. The Lake sparkled in the setting sun. The sun always seemed to be setting over the lake, but the darkness only existed below the depths of the water.

Sara gazed out into the water.

"Don't let it fool you," Rai said. "Remember what happened last time you crossed the Lake de Somnia."

"The next best landing place is in D'arkadia," Thatch buzzed. "Once you cross the Lake, go through Tosia, and meet us there."

They boarded the boat at the lake's edge. Rai untied the ropes securing the boat to the dock. Farah gave Orka orders to fly above the lake, but the little green bird refused, giving a defiant chirp.

Rai took the two oars at the back of the boat, and Sara and Farah each took an oar at the front. They rowed.

"What are we supposed to see?" Farah asked.

"No idea," Rai said.

"Keep your eyes open," Sara said. "I'm sure we'll know when we see it."

"I hope it's that easy," Farah said.

Orka chirped.

"You trust your little friend to come along?" Rai asked.

"No," Farah said. "Orka does what she wants most of the time. Once, she flew out of my window back home, and she didn't come back for days. I was so worried. She hasn't done anything like that since."

"I like having Orka along," Sara said. "She has good intuition."

They rowed in silence for a while.

"Hey." Farah looked back at Rai. "What did you do when you left the Lake?"

"I told you," Rai said. "I traveled."

"Yeah, but where?" Farah asked.

"Around," Rai said.

Farah turned her head back to the coast and sighed.

"Why do you want to know about it?" Rai asked. "It was childish."

"Just trying to get to know you better," Farah said.

"I can tell you something about me," Rai said.

"Fine," Farah said.

"I've never been in love," Rai said. "I thought I was once, but I was wrong. I thought he loved me more than I loved him. Wisdom only comes to us after we've made mistakes."

"What happened?" Sara asked.

"He turned out to be a very different person than I thought," Rai said.

Orka squawked.

"Drop your oars into the boat, and brace yourselves," Rai shouted.

The boat rocked.

"Orka, leave now!" Farah yelled, but the little bird refused to leave her side.

The boat jerked again. Sara felt the cool water touch her hand as she gripped the edge of the boat.

The boat lurched, and Farah reached up to Orka. As she did, her body was thrown. She would have fallen into the dark water if not for Sara who reached over to steady her.

"Hands on the boat!" Rai shouted.

But it was too late, the boat gave one final toss, and Sara fell into the water.

Farah and Rai reached out to grab Sara and pull her back into the boat, but she was jerked down beneath the surface of the water, deep into the dark depths.

SARA fell head first, her arms at her sides, but she blacked out before she hit the bottom.

Her eyelids fluttered open. She awoke on a grassy plain. Standing, she realized she was uninjured. There was no pain, though, as the wind had swept past her, it felt like she had fell from a great height.

A waterfall flowed in the distance, and humid mist surrounded her. Stars glowed in the dark blue sky. Above her was a rocky cliff.

Something glimmered among the grasses. Sara walked to it and stooped to pick it up. It was a medallion with a crack through the center.

She turned around.

From the depths of the mist, someone approached. Surrounded by the translucent haze was a man with light blond hair and familiar blue eyes. A new scar had formed below his jawline where the flesh had been burned away.

"It's you," Sara whispered. The words escaped her with difficulty. "But you're . . ."

He shook his head.

"They're searching for you down there," Sara said.

"I'm not down there anymore," he said.

Sara let tears fall. "I know, but your body is. They'll find you, so we can—"

"I don't think you understand." He hugged her. Sara could not hug him back.

"You have to go back now." His arms tightened around her.

Sara shook her head.

The waterfall had dried up, the grass and flowers in the field were dying, and a dark cloud covered the stars.

He pulled away from her, and his face and body burst into flames. "Go! Wake up now!"

SARA opened her eyes. The dull light of the sun wavered in the ripples. Darkness closed in. But among the darkness, something glowed in the mud. Sara scooped it up. It was cold and glassy.

She swam toward the dull light, clutching the newly discovered object to her chest. She did not look back to see the Nightmare approaching. She had a feeling it was held back by something.

As Sara broke the surface of the water, Farah and Rai grabbed the oars and rowed toward her. They reached over the edge of the boat and grabbed her hands.

Sara gripped the edge of the worn wood as Farah and Rai helped her into the boat. Sara's clothes were heavy with water, and she gasped for air as she held the object to her chest.

Farah knelt beside Sara in the bed of the boat.

Sara shook and clung to the object. Her fingers explored it. On one side, the surface was glassy, but on the other, it was ridged and uneven. Sara cut her finger as she ran it along a jagged edge.

The blood ran down the smooth surface, but some was absorbed into the porous, ridged side.

Sara held up the object.

"What is it?" Farah took it from her and examined it.

"Careful, one side is jagged," Sara said.

"It looks like half of an element sphere," Rai said.

"Half?" Farah asked.

"A broken sphere," Sara said. "Like the one the Beast guards in D'arkadia.

"But where's the other half?" Farah asked.

16

THE BANQUET

SARA looked back toward the Lake, treacherously beautiful under the setting sun.

"I don't know how you were able to wake up," Rai said, "but you're lucky that you did."

Farah shifted the half-sphere from one hand to the other. "We're lucky you found this too."

They walked down the path through the trees toward Tosia.

"I wonder if the Tosians have changed," Farah said. "People have been moving around a lot. Maybe it's influenced them."

"They're too stubborn," Rai said. "They think their elements are the most divine gifts of the Creator. Maybe one day, they'll be attacked and recognize how narrow-minded they have become."

They arrived at the ivy-covered door to Tosia. Roots and vines covered the walkway. Tosia was built into the trunk of a living tree.

"Maybe we'll see Lucerne," Farah said.

Hooded people passed with their heads diverted to the ground.

Sara, Rai, and Farah walked down the sloping trees that made up the walkway.

In the center of Tosia near the Domum Fidei, stood a hoodless man, wearing a blue and silver uniform. Sara recognized him as a Councilor because, although he wore the uniform of a guard, his short hair was light gray.

"Look," Sara said.

"Another arrogant Blue Jay," Farah said.

"No, he's different. His hair . . ."

"So, he's a higher rank," Rai said. "They're all the same. Come on. We should move on."

"I'd like to talk to him first."

"Why?" Farah asked, but Sara was making her way down to where the young Councilor stood.

"Sir," Sara approached the young man. "If I may ask, why are you guarding the Domum Fidei?"

"Domum Fidei? No, this is no longer a chapel. It is the home of High Councilor Veil."

Sara looked up at the high arches on the doorway to the Domum Fidei. She wondered why Veil chose to live in Tosia among Elementals.

"He needs guards to watch his house?" Farah asked. "I thought the people liked Veil. Not that I do."

"I'm not a guard. I'm the High Councilor's successor. My name is Pentagon. I am on watch for Lady Sara, the Water Elemental. High Councilor Veil asked me to keep an eye out for her."

"Do you know what Sara looks like?" Farah asked.

"Yes," Pentagon said. "She's standing right in front of me."

"Sorry for the pretense."

"No need to apologize. Your friend was doing the pretending for you. I can't see how that would ever work now. Everyone recognizes you as the woman who saved Mirmina."

"Why aren't you running to your master?" Rai stepped up to them.

"He's not my——" Pentagon stopped.

Rai shook her head, but realization didn't register before her name escaped his lips: "Rai . . . ahh. I mean . . . the reason why I'm not taking you to Veil right away is because I have a bad feeling about all this."

"All this?" Sara asked.

"There are things about the High Councilor I can't say," Pentagon whispered.

"You better talk," Rai said. "I don't like surprises."

"You know I can't do that."

"No, I don't know. Talk."

"Be on your guard." Pentagon walked to the door.

"Creepy," Farah whispered. "I never thought I would hear anything bad about Veil from a member of the Council."

"They would know best," Rai said. "They're probably hiding lots of dirty secrets. I'm not surprised."

"I think I should take his invitation," Sara said.

"What?" Farah said in half whisper, half shout.

"I still think he could help us," Sara said.

"We can't trust him," Farah said. "He's on Morica's side."

"Not completely," Sara said.

"He does what they tell him to," Rai said. "You saw what happened at the Games. He's a puppet, trying to hide its strings."

"I want to hear what he has to say," Sara said. "We don't have to ally with him, but let's at least see if he's willing to give us any information that could be useful. It can't hurt."

"From what that guy said, it sounds like it could hurt," Farah said.

"I'll be careful."

Farah folded her arms. With great reluctance, she and Rai followed Sara into the Domum Fidei. Pentagon opened the doors to them.

The ceiling was vaulted. Ivy grew on the walls, and tree roots covered the marble floors. A spiral staircase led to a room with tables full of food. Tree roots grew up the legs of the tables and fixed them into place.

"Wait here," Pentagon said. "I'll let the High Councilor know you have arrived." Pentagon walked through a door in the back of the room.

"Look at all this food." Farah picked a grape from one of the bowls and popped it into her mouth. She offered one to Orka.

"Wait! Don't let her eat that," Rai said.

"Why not?" Farah said. "It was left for someone to eat." She lifted the grape up to Orka.

"Poison," Rai hissed.

Farah threw the grape back into the bowl, and spit out the one she had been chewing.

Orka bobbed her head and chirped, amused.

"Orka!" Farah scolded. "How could you let me eat that?"

"It's not the bird's fault her master doesn't think before she eats," Rai said. "You should be more careful in the homes of your enemies."

The door at the back of the room opened, and Pentagon stepped out followed by Veil, who approached Sara.

"It's a pleasure to see you again," Veil said.

Sara's smile did not escape Farah who frowned. Still, Sara's grin only faded slightly. "Pentagon said you've been waiting for me."

"I didn't mean to be so forward. I was hoping that you would arrive soon. I'm having a banquet tonight, and it would give me great pleasure if you would attend."

Her face grew warm. "I'm sorry, but I . . . I don't have anything to wear."

"I'll send Pentagon to accompany you all to find the appropriate attire. It will be paid for, of course. It's not a problem."

"That is too kind."

"Lady Sara, if you don't mind, I would like to give you something." Veil walked into the back room. He came back moments later with a dress draped over his arm. He held it up for her to see.

The dress was intricately embroidered with pearl-white thread, and the fabric was of the lightest of blues.

"It was my mother's," Veil said.

"Oh, I couldn't . . ."

"Please," he said. "It is the very least I can do for the woman who saved us all."

With a weak smile, Sara awkwardly took the dress.

"Thank you," the High Councilor said. "I will see you at the banquet then?"

Sara nodded.

Veil returned to the back room.

Farah shook her head. "You're not going, are you?"

"We all are, apparently," Rai said.

Farah folded her arms. "I don't like that guy."

FARAH and Rai sat at a small table in the inn. Their long dress hems pooled around them on the floor. Sara was dressing in the next room.

"This is ridiculous," Farah said.

"It's an opportunity," Rai said.

"To what? Play dress up with the High Councilors?"

"Think. Veil is completely taken by Sara. He won't notice if we sneak into a few rooms and perhaps find dirt on the Council."

"We can't leave her alone with him," Farah hissed.

"I don't think we'll have a choice. Sara's strong, but she can be naïve. She'll go with him."

"You don't know her like I do."

"Just wait."

Sara came out dressed in the blue gown Veil had given her. "What do you think?"

"I think it's creepy," Farah said.

"The dress?"

"No, that Veil asked you to wear it."

"Let's go." Rai stood.

The entrance into Tosia overflowed with people from across Mirmina. They were all dressed for the banquet and flocking toward the Domum Fidei.

The Tosians locked themselves away in their houses as the intruders entered their home.

The new-comers' boots left imprints on the branch walk-ways of Tosia. Their voices were like a roar, disquieting the atmosphere of the ever-tranquil city. Their hot, humid breath mildewed the flowers.

Pentagon bowed to the guests as they entered the Domum Fidei.

Sara, Rai, and Farah stood among the masses, but when Pentagon spotted them, he ushered them inside.

They wandered in a sea of people. Voices clambered and feet tapped with an orchestra of soft music that lulled through the air. The smell of food being crushed by lazy mouths and coats flapping accosted their senses. The disease of decadence inflicted its poison on each person who entered.

As the crowd moved like a stream, Sara was swept away from Rai and Farah, who were forced to drift apart from each other.

"Farah?" Rai weaved through the dancers. Her eyes searched the congested room. She felt someone's gaze on her back. When she turned around, she locked eyes with the leader of the Rebel Resistance. "You!"

Before she could say another word, Vassal put his wooden arm around her waist and grabbed her hand into his living one. He swayed with her. "A dress. I'm surprised."

"I don't have time for this," Rai said.

"Then why are you here?" Vassal said.

"Why are *you* here?"

"If I remain invisible," he said, "how will I ever learn about my enemies? How will I ever gain allies?"

"In the home of a High Councilor?"

"It's not surprising that people stay so close to their enemies. This is the perfect place to find allies."

Rai looked away from him.

"Why are you playing this game?" he asked.

"It's not a game," Rai said. "I put that life behind me."

"There will always be things that remind us of our past." He pulled her closer and pressed the wooden arm into her back.

"You deserved that reminder." She pushed away from him and moved through the crowd.

Farah had found a seat against the wall. Even while standing, she was too short to see over the heads of the other dancers, so she had given up on finding her friends. Orka chirped at the passing guests, but riotous laughter drowned out her voice.

"Not enjoying the party?"

Farah looked up.

Atrus grinned. His hands tugged at his fitted coat. "Want to dance?"

Farah nodded and stood. She reached out to take Atrus's hand when someone else swooped in to steal hers.

"We have to get moving," Rai said.

"Hey," Farah said. "I was asked to dance."

Sara looked around her as the dancers pushed her toward the center of the room.

"The dress suits you."

Sara turned around.

Veil smiled.

He traded his blue-violet robes for a white suit with dark blue detailing. The jacket was buttoned and had a short, stiff collar that stood against his neck.

"I'm glad you decided to come," he said.

"This is quite a gathering," Sara said.

"I'm by far the youngest High Councilor," Veil said. "They should expect this of me."

"Well, I didn't," she said. "What is this all for?"

"You. You're my honorary guest. Shall we dance?"

From the balcony, Farah and Rai could see Sara and Veil like a beacon among the sea of people.

"We can't just leave her with him," Farah said.

"Come on. This is our chance." Rai opened the door to one of the rooms on the second floor, and Farah followed her inside.

A single chair faced the wall. In the back of the room was a fireplace, and above the fireplace was a painting of a woman. The smile on her face did not reach her eyes. She had a pale, long, angular face like Veil's, and her eyes, like his, were gray-blue.

The painting was not centered over the fireplace. It had been partner to another painting that had been removed. The nail that held the second painting was still hammered into the wall.

"Is that the dress he gave Sara?" Farah stared at the blue dress of the woman in the painting.

Rai pointed to the door leading to the adjoining room.

In the room was a four-poster bed and a small table with two chairs. As Rai stepped into the room, something crinkled beneath her slipper. It was a piece of paper, and torn bits of paper covered the floor.

Rai picked it up.

"Dear Father . . ." It began, but the rest had been ripped away.

"Father?" Farah asked.

"His father is dead," Rai said. "That's why he was ordained as the new High Councilor."

"It could be an old letter," Farah said. "If it's not, I'm severely uneasy about all this."

Rai looked around the room. She knelt and poked her head under the bed. "There."

Something rested between the wall and the headboard. Rai pulled it out. It was a painting of a man. His face was twisted into a frown, and he wore the robe of a High Councilor.

"I can see why he took that one down." Farah stared at the man's knitted brow and pursed lips.

"I think this is the man Veil was writing to," Rai said.

"This was his father?"

Rai nodded. "Let's go. I know more about Veil than I wanted to, and there are still rooms downstairs."

SARA'S hand rested on Veil's shoulder, and his was at her waist as they swayed in the center of the room. They clasped each other's hands although their fingers were not intertwined.

"How does it feel to move Water with your mind?" Veil asked.

Sara was taken aback by his sudden question. "I haven't moved Water in a long time, but it feels . . . I can't find the words. I felt empowered. I felt closer to my parents who died a long time ago."

"We share that in common," Veil said. "My parents are gone. My mother died when I was a boy. My father didn't know how to raise a child."

Veil became silent. He looked up past Sara.

Rai and Farah left the room on the second floor. "He sees us," Rai said. She and Farah hurried down the stairs.

"Veil?"

He looked back down at Sara. A smile spread across his face. "It's been a pleasure," he said. "I think I'll turn in now. I haven't been feeling well."

He hurried away to the back room.

Farah and Rai met with Sara in the center of the room.

Rai looked to where Veil had gone. *So much for checking the back rooms*. They couldn't explore with him stalking about. Councilors stared at them from across the dance floor. "We should leave," she said.

17

A PROPOSAL

THE next day, Sara and Rai sat on a tree branch that sloped to the ground.

Farah ran down the living walkway to meet them. Without having to catch her breath, she said, "I wonder where Lucerne is. I went to Madame Dawn's to find her, but some hooded guy stopped me and said Madame Dawn is nursing someone. I hope it isn't Lucerne."

Sara stared at the ivy-covered ground.

"What's wrong?" Farah sat beside her on the low-hanging branch.

"I don't understand what I'm feeling."

"If this is about Veil," Farah said. "I don't think you should pursue it. You probably don't understand your feelings because something's telling you it's not right between you two."

"Veil's a tormented soul," Rai said.

"But he's not a bad person," Sara said.

"From what we've seen," Rai said. "But who knows what he's hiding?"

"He'll show his true colors soon," Farah said. "Then you won't be confused anymore."

Rai spotted Pentagon watching them from the spring. Pretending she was only getting a drink of water, she walked over to him.

The water pooled into her cupped hands as she dipped them under the running spring.

"Why are you following us?" Rai whispered without turning to look at him.

"Did you have a nice time at the banquet?" Pentagon asked. "I saw you got a dance."

"It was nothing," Rai said.

"You don't have to explain yourself to me," he said. "I've learned a lot being part of Morica."

"You're a traitor like he was."

"I'm not at all like that." Pentagon's voice was calm and even.

"Stop following us," she hissed.

Rai walked back to where Sara and Farah sat.

Instead of heeding her words, Pentagon approached them. "Hello again."

"What do you want?" Rai asked.

"About before," Pentagon said. "There's a beggar in Lumina who can tell you things about the High Councilor that I can't. I think you should go to him and find out who you're really dealing with."

With that, Pentagon returned to the Domum Fidei.

"A beggar?" Farah asked. "Does he realize how many beggars there are in Lumina?"

"He's playing with us," Rai said.

Sara stood.

"Where are you going?" Farah asked.

"Aldo's shop," Sara said. "If things get bad, we might need his healing ointment."

Farah and Rai followed Sara to Aldo's shop and tried the door, but it was locked.

Farah knocked. There was no answer. She sighed and stooped to the ground with her back against the door.

"Let's use the Heiress's of Breeze sparklings to get supplies, and then let's get out of here," Rai said.

"You two go ahead," Sara said. "I'll meet up with you."

THE music grew louder as Sara wandered down the glittering path. She clenched the paper and charcoal in her hands. Charcoal dust fell onto the shimmering pathway.

The cliff was flat and brown. There was no grassy plain.

Sara stared out across the cliff to the waterfall under the dark blue sky.

"I was here. I know I was."

Sara knelt and used the rocky cliff as a surface for her drawing. She sketched the waterfall, the sky, and the plain. Pressing down onto the paper, she darkened the sky and picked up the texture of the rocky ground beneath the paper.

The smell of freshly turned dirt rose to her nose as her frantic movements loosened the earth under her drawing.

The paper tore, and the charcoal broke in half.

Black ash covered Sara's hands.

"I was here," she cried. Her voice faded into the expanse and journeyed to a place beyond her hearing.

On her hands and knees, she scrambled to the edge of the cliff. Below, all she could see was mist, and like the mist that filled the gorge in Omega Ray, no one could know what lie beneath unless they fell.

But Sara knew.

What lie below was a grassy plain, and on that plain, lay a broken man and a broken sphere.

Sara leaned over the edge.

"Don't!" a voice echoed.

Sara looked behind her, tears streaming down her face.

"Let me help you up." Veil took her arm and helped her to her feet. Without warning, he pulled her close to him and hugged her.

Sara kept her arms nestled between herself and Veil. The black soot on her hands stained his violet robes.

Sensing her discomfort, Veil released her. "I'm sorry. I was worried."

Sara wiped the tears from her eyes. "What are you doing here?"

"I come here sometimes. To think. There was something really important I needed to think about, but I don't believe I need to think about it any longer."

"What was it?" she asked.

"I wanted to give you this." Veil held up a silver ring with small diamonds embedded around the band.

Realization came upon Sara.

"I came here to think about this," he said. "At first, I wanted our union for the people of Mirmina. I knew that together, we could help them. I admire you, but until now I wasn't sure if I truly cared for you. But seeing you at the cliff . . . I felt a hole inside, thinking you would be gone."

"I don't understand how our union would benefit the people of Mirmina."

"I am the youngest High Councilor. The others will be gone long before me. I will gain seniority at a very young age. I want to gain the trust of the Elementals. They respect you. I want to give them back what they once had: freedom."

"I want that for the people," she said, "but I don't think marriage is the answer."

"Is there anything I can do to convince you otherwise?"

Sara shook her head.

Veil curled the ring into his hand and sighed. He turned and walked toward the gleaming path.

"Thank you for your kindness," Sara said. "I hope that we can still be allies."

Veil looked back and nodded. His smile was forced.

SARA met Farah and Rai near D'arkadia.

"Where were you?" Farah asked.

"I needed some time to myself."

"Farah wants to find the beggar in Lumina," Rai said. "Pentagon knows hundreds of beggars line the streets of the city. He's trying to slow us down."

"Well, right now we don't even have much of a lead," Sara said. "So, going back to Lumina wouldn't be a waste of our time. If we don't find the beggar, we might find someone who knows something."

Shift landed the Chariot in D'arkadia outside Tosia.

"You three don't check in, do you?" Thatch said as they entered the control room.

"Can't you hear everything that goes on through our earpieces?" Farah asked.

"Tosia is a dead zone. I get no readings from there, and I can't see your trackers on the map."

SARA stared out into the endless darkness. The light on her back streamed in from Tosia, but the illumination dimmed further out until it was swallowed by the overwhelming shadows.

Rai joined her on the roof and sat beside her.

"Shift says we take off in the morning," Rai said. "Who knows when night falls in this place?"

"You'll get tired." Sara continued to stare into the darkness.

They sat in silence before Sara spoke: "Veil wants to marry me."

"Did you say 'yes'?" Rai asked.

"Should I have?"

"Not unless that's what you want."

"I wasn't thinking about what I want," Sara said.

"Saying 'no' to a High Councilor," Rai said. "I wonder what happens now."

18

THE RUNAWAY

SARA, Farah, and Rai arrived in Lumina in search of the beggar Pentagon told them about. Thinking Pentagon was only trying to lead them astray, Rai felt that the trip would be a waste of time.

The city was crowded with people, many with sacks on their backs and children in tow. The city had become a beacon. Morica had control, but darker deeds went on outside the city walls. Morica guards were more carefree and power-hungry in the small towns. They worked the people ragged. Morica had bought out many of the small businesses and inns around Mirmina. This was why many people sought jobs in Lumina where treatment was less harsh. People attributed this to Veil's presence, because he frequented Lumina most often.

Banners were raised in honor of Veil around the city. On the banners, was a painting of Veil with the words: "Compassion in Action." His cloudy blue eyes watched Sara everywhere she went. Sara tried not to look at the banners.

Farah sighed. "Look at all these people. We'll never find him."

"Maybe we should split up," Sara said. "That way we'll cover more ground in less time."

"No," Rai said. "That's a bad idea."

"I don't understand," Sara said.

They moved through the city and weaved through the sea of people.

"When a High Councilor wants something," Rai said, "he will do anything to get it. We should stay together."

"What are you talking about?" Farah asked.

Rai looked at Sara. "Veil proposed marriage to Sara."

Farah stopped. "When did this happen?"

"Back in Tosia," Sara said, "before we left."

"And you told her?"

"Farah, I . . ."

"Doesn't matter. It's not like you're going to marry the guy." Farah craned her neck and tried to see over the heads of the people in front of her. Not watching where she was going, she bumped into someone, and Orka chirped.

"Sorry," Farah said.

The young woman Farah ran into was about her height with long black hair and eyes so dark, it was like looking down into the depths of a well.

"Lucerne!"

But she wasn't the reedy, young girl of three years ago. She was fifteen years old. She wore a long, traveling cloak and a satchel on her shoulder.

"Farah the Wind Elemental." She hugged Farah. "I changed it to Lucerna. Lucerne is a child's name."

"We looked for you in Tosia."

"If you two want to talk, let's go someplace less crowded," Rai said as a man brushed past her without an apology.

Lucerna led them to a temple. The temple was deserted apart from the priests that kept watch over the sanctuary.

"No one dares come worship the Creator for fear Morica is watching those who enter the temple," Lucerna said.

The floors were made of marble. Columns supported the ceiling. In the center of the room was an altar and above that hung a slab mounted against the wall. The element symbols were etched into the stone.

"Why have you left Tosia?" Sara asked.

"Madame Dawn told me it was time for me to seek my destiny," Lucerna said.

"She made you leave?" Farah asked.

"It wasn't like that," Lucerna said. "She let me go. My destiny always did lie beyond the reach of the branches of the Great Tree. Madame Dawn knew that.

"Everyone in the city is talking about you and High Councilor Veil. People saw you dancing with him at a banquet. They keep saying it is good he found someone since he needs an heir, but they're even more excited that that someone might be you. He reminds me of you. You're both so kind."

"He's nothing like Sara," Farah said. "He pretends."

Sara shook her head. "I don't think he's pretending."

Farah folded her arms.

"So," Sara said. "What adventures have you had?"

Lucerna's face spread into a grin. "I crossed the Lake de Somnia, and I worked in Wyvek for a year. I explored every inch of Dustpath. I found some old books and brought them to Lumina to see if they were worth something. The priests have been letting me stay in the temple."

"How long ago did you leave Tosia?" Sara asked.

"Three years ago," Lucerna said. "Someone was brought to Madame Dawn. Bandages covered his face, and he wouldn't wake up. Madame Dawn said she had to devote all her energies to the man. That's when she told me to seek my destiny. She gave me sparklings, and I left."

"What were the books you found in Dustpath about?" Sara asked.

"I can't read. I found them in an old chest. The pages are very thin. I could show them to you."

Sara nodded.

Lucerna led them to the back room of the temple. A small mattress rested against the front wall, and the room had no windows. In the corner was a dusty chest. The leather straps that served to close the chest were worn to the point of tearing.

Lucerna knelt, opened the chest, and retrieved one of the three books. The book was thick and heavy. She placed it on the floor, and sat. Sara and Farah sat cross-legged around the book. Rai stood over them with her arms folded.

Sara reached out to touch the book. "May I?"

Lucerna nodded.

Sara turned the book so its title faced her: "The Keepers: Volume 1." She turned to the first page:

They numbered seven: Seven Keepers, Seven Tragedies. They came to the doors of the Inn, each carrying a glass orb. When a guest asked to touch one of the orbs, its Keeper screamed and sheltered the orb close to his chest. They had fed their souls to those orbs.

All the Keepers were elders. Their skin a web of wrinkles. Their eyes dulled. But they walked with strong strides and un-labored steps. One had a scar in the shape of a teardrop. He held a Blue Orb clenched between his fingers.

They sat around one of the tables as we stared.

At the head of the table sat the One with diseased flesh. He had a Black Orb, and All there seemed to fear him. He demanded to see the town builder. The builder was sent for.

You must build a sanctuary for me. A part of me will be housed there and exist for all time.

The builder set to work designing and building the temple. The people helped him, and so it was built.

The One with the Dark Orb looked upon it and was satisfied. The Orb with the blooming flower, the Green Orb, was placed upon the pedestal in the inner room.

That day, an energy swept through the land and empowered the people while they slept. The People awoke moving mountains.

When asked, the Dark One said he was the Creator of such power, and that it had been bestowed on them for their kindness in building the sanctuary.

But he needed more.

That is how we became the Builders.

And so, we built more temples all over Mirmina, and in each sanctum, an orb was placed.

The Creator thanked us.

People across Mirmina had new-found powers. They summoned fire, water, wind, frost, lightning, and moved the earth, all without lifting a single finger. But there was also the darkness. It spread like a disease.

That's when the Builders were asked to build walls to keep it out.

The Keepers watched as the world moved around them. This was their curse. As we grew old, they stayed frozen in time. Not even the One with the Blue Orb aged.

The Creator had us build him a palace with no windows. Once a week he asked that someone of our village enter the Dark Palace for the chance to be enlightened. The Ones who Entered never returned.

The Creator explained that this was because they had reached Enlightenment.

The air around the Dark Palace began to smell.

Black birds would sit on the roof and Wait.

The Keepers would meet and stand in a Circle for long hours with their hands Held. They never Ate or Drank or Slept. At Night, their Bodies became ethereal and airy. They seemed to float instead of walk.

They were our gods.

One day, long after the temple was built, a youth entered it and went into the Forbidden Room that housed the Green Orb. What he found inside frightened him to his Bones. He described What he saw to the Elders.

It was then we Knew we had Bred Monsters.

The village Elders sent in our Finest Warriors to fight the Monster, but to no avail. The Monster would return to fight again. The Elders determined that it was the Orb that controls the Monster. So, it had to be removed.

The Pedestal that supported the Orb was taken from its Foundations. We never saw the Orb or the People who had chosen to remove it again.

This angered the Creator.

That Day a terrible Storm without end racked the village. The Rain flooded the crops, and the people had to wait in their houses with buckets to shovel out the invading waters.

Once the Rain had stopped, the Lightning came and caused Great Fires that Raged for Days. The Land became so dry that the crops Died, and the Wells dried up. The Winds were Wild and picked up the Sand so that We were breathing more Sand than Air.

The People got on their Knees and prayed.

The Creator said that in order to stop the Storm, We needed to sacrifice Seven of our Own. Their Bodies were to be boiled in a communal stew and Eaten by Everyone in the village.

This idea was Grotesque to Us.

For Months, We did not entertain the notion, but the Storm only became Worse. Because Our Crops were Lost, People became Weak from Hunger and eventually Died.

We lost more People than the Seven to be Sacrificed.

People Volunteered because they did not want to be in Pain anymore.

And so, we Sacrificed Our Own.

People lined up to Eat from the Communal Stew. Mothers lined up their Children. Just a spoonful of Flesh would do.

Once the Last in Our Village ate, the Creator was Satisfied. He asked that the rest of the Communal Stew be taken to the Dark Palace.

We had shown Our Obedience, and the Skies Cleared, the Winds Stopped, and the Crops grew once again sped by the power of Earth.

We will Never again anger the Creator.

Sara looked up from the book.

The room was so quiet, one could hear the flickering of the candle flame.

"I don't think you should try to sell these books," Sara said.

Lucerna shook her head. "You should take them. You could get more out of them than I could. I'm not sure I want to hear more."

SHIFT landed the Chariot a few miles from Dustpath Road. He didn't want Thermal scaring any travelers. Ruins and piles of sand obscured the road.

As they approached the Chariot, Sara and Farah held the handle on one end of the worn chest, and Rai held the other. They carried the chest to the Chariot and met Shift and Thatch in the control room.

"A friend found these old books," Farah said. "They're about the Keepers and the Sphere Sanctums."

"How many?" Shift asked.

"Three volumes," Rai said.

"Let Stannum have them," Thatch said. "He can read faster than any human."

Stannum floated over to the chest they placed in the center of the room and opened it with his long fingers. "I love a good read." He wrapped his fingers around volume one and floated back to his desk.

"Any sign of the beggar?" Thatch asked.

"No," Sara said. "The city is congested. It feels hopeless, but I think we should try again tomorrow. We came back because all the inns in the city are booked for the night."

"We'll stay here until morning," Rai said. "Then we'll find this beggar." She walked out of the control room.

"What's up with her?" Shift asked.

"She thinks we're wasting time," Farah said.

19

THE BEGGAR

SARA was worn out from the exertions of the previous day. It had not been an easy walk through the crowded city while handling a large, heavy chest filled with three over-sized, bound books, each five inches thick. This day promised no easier task. She had to find the beggar Pentagon spoke of. He would know more.

The city thoroughfares were calm in the morning. The guards had chased people off the streets due to the curfew. Many visitors could not find room and board. The inns were booked with no promise of a vacancy anytime soon.

Those who could afford it left by boat. Others, determined to stay near the city, slept on Dustpath Road and kept their noses and mouths covered by thick scarfs to stop the dust from invading their lungs. Some went still further to Dustpath Inn, where Solace had rooms for the night.

As daylight crept over the horizon, the people migrated back into the city in hopes that this time, they would be able to secure a room at one of the inns and stay the night.

Farah was becoming frustrated as the day inched on. She, Sara, and Rai had covered every inch of the city with their footsteps, passing banners bearing Veil's face everywhere they walked, which only served to fuel Farah's growing dissatisfaction.

Farah sighed. "If I have to see his face one more time, I'm going to start tearing each one of these banners down and rip them all to shreds."

Rai folded her arms. "Well, it was you who wanted to come here and find this beggar. You both failed to consider that Pentagon is the enemy, like the rest of Morica. Trusting him is like trusting the rattlesnake that slithers into your bed at night."

The sun was getting low in the sky, and people hastened to their sleeping quarters.

"Look over there," Sara said.

Near the market square sat a hooded man with a wooden bowl in his hand. The bowl was one meant for crushing herbs and spices, but it had another purpose now. The man had his head down and the bowl raised into the air. The skin on the hand that held the bowl was stretched, straining over the spidery bones.

"Yet another beggar," Rai said. "Pentagon would be laughing if he saw us now, approaching every beggar on the street."

Sara approached the hooded man and dropped a few sparklings into his bowl.

The man looked up at the sound of the coins hitting the wooden bowl. His face was shrunken from hunger, his cheekbones prominent. He lifted his hood. His clear, green eyes looked up at them. An inverted triangle with a line through the center was etched upon his forehead.

"Aldo!"

Aldo put his finger to his lips.

They knelt to hear him as he whispered. "They're looking for me."

"Why?" Sara whispered back.

"Because of what I saw."

"What did you see?"

"If you want information stay close and listen."

Sara nodded.

"Veil and his father High Councilor Cronus came to Tosia more than two years ago. I'd never seen a father and son colder to each other.

"High Councilor Cronus wanted to live in the Domum Fidei which was something of great contempt to the people of Tosia, but Cronus got what he wanted as he sent more and more guards into Tosia.

"It wasn't long before Veil asked me to gather water from the Cliff so he could see the future. Flask in hand, I walked to the Domum Fidei to deliver it.

"Inside, I heard screams coming from the room upstairs. I walked up to the door and listened. It sounded like a struggle. I was about to walk away when Veil came out. His hands and uniform were bloodied. I tried to ignore that and stay calm. He asked if the flask contained what he needed. I nodded, and he grabbed the flask in his bloody hands.

"I believed my expression of fear betrayed me at that point, but he didn't seem to note it.

"He threw his head back and drank the water in a few gulps. His eyes glassed over and his body became stiff.

"While he was in that state, I hurried away.

"The following day, news of High Councilor Cronus's death spread. The Council blamed the effects of old age. But I know that body was too bloodied for them to really believe that.

"After that, I got word that the Council was looking for me. I couldn't return to my shop for fear they would be waiting for me there. I left Tosia with what I had on me and came here."

"I knew it," Farah whispered. "I knew something was off about him."

Sara shook her head. That was not the man she had come to know. Veil had been kind to her and to the people.

Three guards approached.

Aldo put his hood over his head.

"It's past curfew!" barked one of the guards. He looked at Aldo. "Get up, beggar!"

Aldo rose to his feet, and the guard tore off his hood.

The guard retrieved a rolled-up piece of paper from his pocket, scrutinized it, and looked back at Aldo. "Come with me."

The guard grabbed Aldo's arm and tossed him into the hands of the other guards.

"Wait!" Sara pleaded.

A man approached. He was dressed in a long cloak. His eyes shone in the darkness. Rai focused on the man as he advanced.

"This man is under arrest," the guard said.

"I don't think so," Farah said.

"Don't," Rai said, but it was too late. Farah knocked the guard to the ground with a powerful gust of Wind.

The guard rose to his feet and pulled the crossbow from his back. "Stand down!"

A burst of flames flew toward the guard's face, and he ducked to avoid them.

"Run!" Rai yelled.

One of the two guards who had been arresting Aldo pursued them. The guard with the crossbow followed him.

"We have to go back and save Aldo," Sara said as they ran past the dried-up fountain filled with flowers. Their feet tapped upon the marble floor.

"You want to get caught too?" Rai said. "Look, there!"

The ticket booth window had been left open. Rai slid inside followed by Sara and Farah. The guards stampeded past them.

"We could have helped," Farah said.

"Or we could have stayed low," Rai said. "If Morica wasn't after us before, they're after us now. If we would have stayed to fight, we would have only given them more time to see our faces. That paper the guard was looking at was a sketch of your friend. If they got a good look at us, our faces will be posted all over Mirmina. We won't be able to walk into any city."

"He's a friend," Sara said. "We're going back." She tried to stand, but Rai pulled her back down.

"That man who was approaching in the distance," Rai said, "his name is Fulgur, and he is skilled with Lightning. He'll fry our brains if he gets the chance."

"He's an Elemental?" Sara asked.

"I don't know what he is," Rai said, "but he's not one of us."

"What's that supposed to mean?" Farah asked.

Rai was silent. She shook her head.

"I'm not leaving Aldo out there alone after he helped us," Sara said.

"Listen!" Rai hissed. "They'll bring him to Lumina dungeons to hold him until they receive orders from the Council on what to do with him. We'll break in."

"Into the dungeons?" Farah asked.

Rai nodded. "How close of a friend was he?"

"Okay," Sara said.

THE sun blistered the sky. Farah rested against Sara's shoulder as they slumped in a deep sleep. Rai shook them awake. They left the ticket booth, and went to the temple where they spoke with Lucerna.

"Are you all okay?" Thatch buzzed in.

"Yeah," Farah said. "We have a plan to save Aldo."

Lucerna came out from the small room the priests of the temple provided to her.

"Glad you're still in the city," Lucerna said.

"We need your help," Rai said.

Lucerna was taken aback by her sudden request. "Sure, anything."

"We're planning to break into the dungeons," Sara said, "and we need a lookout."

"The guards are looking for us, so neither one of us can do it," Rai said. "We need you to stand at the back entrance to the dungeons and signal to us when it's clear."

Lucerna nodded. "I can do that."

"If anyone asks you why you are there, say that you're lost, and bail."

Lucerna followed them as they allowed themselves to get swallowed into the crowd. They came to what was once the Manor of the Imperator and was now the Council Chamber. Below that was the dungeons.

Lucerna stood near the back entrance while Sara, Rai, and Farah hid around the corner and waited for her signal.

There were no guards in sight.

Lucerna was ready to wave them in when a young guard came out from the dungeon entrance.

"Can I help you?" the guard asked.

"Actually, I'm a little lost." Lucerna smiled. "I'm looking for the entrance to the Council Chamber. It's my first time in the city."

"Why would you need to visit the Council Chamber?"

"My father is a representative for the Morica Guards Union. He hasn't been feeling well so he asked me to issue the list of complaints such as low pay, long hours, well, you know."

"I've never heard of the Union."

"How long have you been a guard for Morica?"

"A few months," he said.

"Of course," she said, "they won't want you to know about the Union. You should join. Right now, we're just a whisper, but, with more members, we could be a roar."

Lucerna's speech mesmerized the young guard.

"So, can you help me?" she asked.

"Sure." The guard followed Lucerna like a moth attracted to the light of a lantern.

"She's a better talker than *you*," Rai whispered to Farah.

"Maybe just as good, but not better," Farah hissed.

"Now's our chance." Sara ran to the door and caught the gate before it slammed shut.

They rushed in. The light streamed into the dark hallway. In between the stones that made up the walls was thick mortar laced with dirt. At the bottom of the stairs leading down into the dungeons was a guard. Through the archway was a small room with a table in the center filled with food and tankards.

Farah sent Wind to knock over the table and distract the guard.

He rushed over to the table and looked around. He knelt and picked up the fallen food and utensils.

Sara, Rai, and Farah slinked down the stairs. They went into the room and through the doorway without being seen. Inside this room were cots where the guards slept and chests where they kept belongings taken from the prisoners.

Through the door in the back of the room were the prisoners' cells. A guard was making his rounds. Above him was a loft where a second guard was circling.

Rai pointed to the stairs leading to the cells on the second floor. She, Sara, and Farah crept up the stairs.

The guard on the second floor was coming around to the stairs.

Rai put her hand out, warning them to stay back. She drew her sword and gripped the hilt in both hands.

As the guard passed them, Rai hit him on the back of his head with the hilt of her sword. Before his body made its thunderous fall to the ground, Rai grabbed him in her arms and lowered him to the floor. She peeked over the banister.

The second guard was still making his rounds, unaware of what was happening above him.

Rai waved Sara and Farah on, and they followed her.

"Aldo," Farah whispered. She went up to one of the cells.

"You came." Aldo wrapped his hands around the bars of his cell.

Farah fished the lock pick from her pocket. "I learned how to do this after Fortress Tower. I never want to get locked up like that again."

The lock released, and Farah opened the cell door. The door shrieked.

Rai grabbed one of the bars to stop Farah from opening the door any further.

Aldo squeezed out.

Rai looked down at the guard below. He was rounding the corner to the opposite cells and would be able to see them if he looked up.

Rai pointed to the cell above the guard, and the others followed her.

As they passed one of the cells, a hand reached out to Sara.

"Come closer." It was a man. The skin on his face and neck was rotting and peeling off in layers, exposing the pink flesh beneath. His fingernails were dirty, and the skin on his hand was in the same state as the skin on his face.

In his cell was a table full of bread and cheese that had been untouched. Yet his body was wasting away under the heavy folds of his tattered clothing.

"I'm hungry!" His voice came out in a howl.

The guard rushed to the stairs.

Rai met him and cut him through with her sword aflame.

As they descended the stairs, more guards filled the room.

"Sara, go back up, and get ready!" Rai shouted. "We'll distract them."

Farah and Rai ran to the center of the room while Sara went up to the loft and stood facing the guards below. Aldo crouched behind the banister.

Rai held her sword ablaze, and Farah held out her dagger.

The guards were armed with black batons, swords, and crossbows.

Sara pointed her wrist gun as the guards backed Farah and Rai up against the wall. She focused her energy, and the Aether glowed, but the force of the Wind that issued forth knocked her back. The forceful rush hit the ceiling and sent a crack through it.

Sara thought the ceiling would collapse, but the heavy stone stayed intact.

Bracing herself, she tried again. The Aether glowed. The next shot sent out vines. The vines wrapped around some of the guards and pinned their arms to their sides. They fell to the floor and struggled as their fellow guards tried to cut the vines.

"Again!" Rai shouted from below.

Sara focused. The force of the Wind knocked the guards to the ground.

"Now!"

Sara and Aldo scrambled down the stairs and leapt over the guards as they tried to pick themselves up. Farah and Rai joined them. Followed by the guards, they ran through the sleeping quarters.

As they went through the archway, a guard approached them from the side.

Rai raised her sword and sliced through his shoulder. She removed her blade and kicked the injured guard to the ground.

The exit was up the stairs. They reached the gates, but they were locked. Farah got out her lock pick and proceeded to unlock the gates. Her hand fumbled with the pick, and it snapped in half.

Rai sent flames to the foot of the stairs to delay the guards. Farah retrieved another pick from her pocket and began to work on the lock again. The guards tore down the heavy tapestries from the walls and throw them down onto the fire.

The lock released with a click and Farah swung the gates open. They rushed out into the sunlight and took sanctuary among the crowds of people.

The guards were in close pursuit.

Sara weaved through the crowd, barely taking the time to look around. Someone grabbed her arm. At first, she thought Farah or Rai must have rushed ahead of her. But the hand that pulled her wrenched her through the crowd as she bumped into people. She cried out, but she could scarcely hear herself among the roar of the voices.

Orka flew overhead.

20

THE GUARDS OF MORICA

THE hand that grabbed her arm had bruised her flesh as it pulled her through the crowd.

Sara looked behind her, trying to catch a glimpse of Farah or Rai, but the crowd was packed with too many faces. *Who is this?* Sara wondered. *A friend?* Was she right to trust the unknown wave that was sweeping her through the sea of people?

A flash of blue, and then nothing but heads and elbows and the pummeling of sacks upon the backs of faceless bodies.

Her body was beaten by the crowd.

Orka flew above the sea, her green and blue feathers bright against the sky.

As the crowd thinned, Sara saw her captor. He wore a uniform of blue and silver. Around his waist was a holster with a dagger and black baton.

Sara twisted her arm, trying to loosen his grip, but without success. She was weak from the pummeling, and her feet were tired from the endless days of walking and lack of sleep.

At the entrance to Dustpath Road, several guards waited. A guard took her free arm. One of them took the tracker from her holster and smashed it beneath his boot. They confiscated her weapons and her earpiece.

"What is this?" Sara asked.

"You are under arrest," said Grayson, the head guard. His low hanging brow sat right above his wide set eyes. His skin was a fusion of pink and ivory, and his hair was kept short. His thin, pressed lips looked permanently sealed so it was a surprise when he spoke.

"Why didn't you take me to Lumina dungeon?"

The guard was silent.

"What are the charges?" Sara asked.

"You don't ask the questions," he said.

Behind the guards were several IMTs. The head guard forced Sara onto one and got behind her, his hands reached out to grip the handle bars. His arms barred her escape.

The other guards saddled onto their IMTs, and they zoomed down Dustpath Road. The guards pulled up to Dustpath Inn to get supplies.

"Be quick boys," Grayson said.

The guards walked into the inn.

Sara could hear Solace's booming voice greeting them. She hoped he could see her as the door swung open. As Solace grinned, Sara thought she had caught his eye. But as he said good-bye to the guards and "come back next time," Sara's hopes were dashed.

The engines on the IMTs roared to life.

"Just a minute!" Solace yelled from inside.

The door to the inn burst open, and there stood Solace, his feet wide apart and hands supporting a huge gun with a wide muzzle.

"Release Lady Sara, you Morica bastards!"

The head guard stared at Solace from his seat behind Sara on the IMT. "Put the gun down, old man."

Sara threw herself from the IMT.

Solace released fire on the guards. Two of the guards were hit. The others were quicker and took cover behind their vehicles. The bullets embedded into their IMTs. But Solace, unfamiliar with weapons and taking poor aim, had completely unloaded the clip.

A desperate click sounded, but the bullets were exhausted.

Black batons accosted Solace as the guards beat him to the ground.

"Stop!" Sara screamed.

The head guard walked over to Solace, and the other guards backed off. The head guard removed the crossbow from his back and shot Solace in the leg right above the knee.

Solace screamed in pain, and Sara ran to him, but Grayson caught her and dragged her back to the vehicle.

Solace lay on the ground and gripped his leg in his hands, his fingers wide and pressing into the flesh. The arrow had not gone all the way through.

The guards sped away.

Sara tried to look over Grayson's shoulder as they left Solace writhing on the ground.

SARA dried her eyes.

The sky darkened, and she wondered where the guards would decide to sleep for the night. She hoped it would be near Wyvek so she could alert Atrus and get help for Solace.

But as night loomed, the guards continued to drive with no talk of stopping to rest.

As they neared Wyvek, Sara hoped they would stop, but in vain.

She needed a way out. She shoved against Grayson's arm, and his grip slipped. Sara flung herself from the IMT and

scrambled to her feet. She ran for the gates of Wyvek, screaming Atrus's name.

The guards stopped their IMTs.

"Someone knows her here too?"

"Everyone knows her," Grayson said. "She's the Water Elemental." He ran after Sara.

Halfway to the gates, he caught her by the arm and turned
her around. Sara tried to pull back, and she kept screaming.

Grayson slapped her across the face.

The sting stopped her screams.

"You will not ruin this for me." Grayson grabbed her hand
and dragged her back to the IMT.

Sara tried to get away from him, but her attempts were
futile.

Grayson's grip was tight enough to make her skin red.

The gates of Wyvek disappeared in the distance.

As the road narrowed the guards had no choice but to
leave the IMTs behind and squeeze through the narrow fissure
in the rock to get to the Lake de Somnia.

Grayson pushed Sara toward the dock and threw her into
the boat. The boat tipped as Sara's sudden weight unsettled it.

The guards, taking little care, jumped into the boat.

Five guards remained, including Grayson. They took the
oars while Grayson watched Sara.

He must think I'm crazy to believe I would try to escape
by swimming across the Lake de Somnia, Sara thought.

As they rowed, Sara stared at the reflection of the moon
wavering across the Lake's surface.

"You said don't ruin this for me," Sara said. "What's *this*?
The mission to kidnap me?"

Grayson stared at her.

"By the time we cross the Lake, the sun will have risen.
That's a long time to sit in silence."

"Prisoners don't talk."

"Is that what I am? A prisoner? What have I done?"

Grayson looked out across the Lake and tried to judge the distance from the other side where the trees were black and blurred. "You are my prisoner until I release you to the High Councilor."

"To Mordecai?"

Grayson's pressed lips moved like he was trying to talk with his head buried in thick, wet mud. "High Councilor Veil."

Sara gulped. "High Councilor Veil would have sent for me. He wouldn't have had guards kidnap me and throw me into a boat." But she remembered Aldo's story. Was there a Veil she didn't know?

"I get orders, not reasons."

"Why do you follow those orders?"

He looked away from her for the first time since he took her from Lumina.

The boat rocked, and two oars were ripped from the hands of the guards.

"Row faster," Grayson ordered.

The two guards who still possessed oars, propelled the oars through the water, which splashed around them as the oars cut through it.

The dark water swam beneath them and lurked near the bottom of the boat.

The left side of the boat dipped into the water, and Grayson jumped to the opposite side to level it.

The boat kept rocking upon the unsteady waters, but Grayson had managed to use his weight to keep the boat stable.

A loud crash sounded as something broke the surface of the water. An immense shadow hung over the small boat. But it was more solid than the average shadow.

Sara thought she saw eyes within that shadow and mouths laughing.

The shadow swept down and grabbed one of the guards. He screamed, and his legs kicked as he was thrown into the water.

The shadow that lived deep beneath the waters, the Night-mare, wrapped around him and pulled him down into the Lake's depths.

Those still in the boat waited, frozen.

"Your oars!" Grayson shouted.

Two of the remaining guards each took an oar and rowed, but one had picked up the oar sooner than the other, and the boat turned in a circle. They tried to right the boat, but nerves were on edge, and they couldn't get it back on course.

Grayson shook his head and took one of the oars, pushing the guard aside.

He rowed until the boat pointed toward the opposite shore. "With me!" he shouted, and the other guard rowed.

Another crash.

The Nightmare loomed above them.

A guard shot it with a crossbow, but to no avail.

The Nightmare crashed down onto the edge of the boat and sent it rocking.

The sack containing Sara's belongings was nestled be-tween the knees of one of the guards.

"Give me my weapon," Sara demanded.

The guard looked over to Grayson, and Grayson nodded. He reached into the bag and retrieved the wrist gun. He tossed it to Sara. She strapped it to her arm.

As the Nightmare rose out of the water, Sara focused and pointed the wrist gun at it.

Lightning coiled around its body, and the Nightmare yielded back into the depths of the Lake with a resounding crash.

The guards breathed sighs of relief.

Grayson relinquished his seat at the oar to another guard.

He held out his open hand, and Sara unstrapped the wrist gun and placed it into his palm.

21

THE DARK MAN

VEIL sat alone and gazed at the images of his mother surrounding him. Ink spilled onto the floor and stained the carpet. He picked up the ink well and set it on the desk.

His father had transported a shrine to his mother when they first moved to Tosia. He built the shrine the day after she died.

The flowers that surrounded the painting had dried up, their petals curling at the edges. One touch, and they would crush beneath the pressure of the most careful fingers.

Jewelry Cronus had bought her rested in the tomb-like engraved box that had not been opened in years. Dust lived in the box, sticking to the velvet lining and sucking the color out.

Veil's fingers rounded the edge of his mother's journal.

His mother begged for her life, so she could take care of him.

Veil's hands, small then, gripped the earthen archway, the wooden door open wide enough for his small eyes to peer in and see the panic in his mother's face.

A blade invaded her body, and Veil could feel the coldness of the metal in his heart as it plunged into hers. His mind split in two, the duality cracking his personality until he could clearly identify what characteristics in him mirrored his mother and which bled into his father's side.

He had blocked the memory until one day, Mordecai, his protector, whispered it in his ear, like venom.

His father was crying in this room surrounded by his mother's portraits. It wasn't time, but he had to do it while he wasn't his better self. He plunged the dagger into the vulnerable flesh. But this time, he did not feel the coldness of the blade in his heart. He feared there was nothing left to cool.

Blood dripped from his hands.

Veil jumped back. He blinked and looked at his hands again. He turned them over. They were clean.

"What's the matter?" Mordecai approached him. His eyes held a look of concern.

"It's nothing."

"The Lady Sara is on her way. Have the arrangements been made to her new room?"

Veil nodded. "I don't like this."

"I don't either," Mordecai said. "I wish you could have convinced her that your union is what is best for Mirmina, but sometimes people need a push in the right direction. In time, she will learn that this was the right decision."

Veil took a deep breath. "She doesn't trust you."

"Oh."

Veil shook his head.

"That's understandable," Mordecai said. "My past hasn't been . . . clean. She will come to trust me as you have, but in the meanwhile, tell her that I am old, I will die, and my ideals will die with me."

"I don't think—"

Mordecai stopped him. "I understand you have your ways. But messes are hard to clean up. I will guide you as I did with your father, but you must trust me and do as I say and not before. It was messy what happened to Cronus. Follow me, and this can be a happy union."

Veil nodded, but his mind pulled away from Mordecai's words.

22

PRISONER

AFTER they docked the boat, a guard took Sara's arm.

"Stop," Grayson demanded. "Get out of the boat and wait for my orders."

Grayson offered his hand to Sara.

Sara looked at him quizzically, but took his hand.

He helped her onto the dock. "We were more than lucky back there. Thanks to you."

"You're welcome," Sara said.

They journeyed through the woods toward Tosia. A guard took Sara's wrist gun out of the bag and strapped it to his arm. He pointed at the trees. He swung his arm into the open air, but nothing happened.

"Are you an Elemental?" Sara asked.

"No," he said.

They approached Tosia. Inside, it was littered with guards. Pentagon waited outside the door to the Domum Fidei.

Grayson handed Pentagon the bag with Sara's belongings inside.

"Thank you for your services," he said to Grayson.

"Am I to report to Vella City?" Grayson asked.

Pentagon nodded.

The guards left.

Sara stood in front of Pentagon alone.

"Come this way," he said.

He led Sara through the door to the dining room.

"Please, wait here," Pentagon instructed.

"You wanted me in Lumina, didn't you?" Sara asked. "It was a trap. You needed to make sure I was separated from my friends."

As Pentagon was about to speak, Veil came into the room from the back chamber.

"Welcome."

"I don't understand what is going on here," Sara said.

"This is in preparation for the wedding," Veil said.

"But I said no to your proposal."

Veil nodded, and Pentagon returned to his post outside the Domum Fidei.

"I know." Veil took her hands in his. "But High Councilor Mordecai has convinced me that this is what will be best for the people of Mirmina. You above all others would know that sacrifices have to be made for the greater good."

Sara shook her head. "But Mordecai hates Elementals. Why would he want us to be together?"

"He wants the Elementals to trust us."

Sara was silent until reality hit. "He wants to control them through me."

Veil shook his head.

"Why would you allow this?" Sara asked.

"It won't happen. Mordecai is old, and he will die, but we will live. Think of the future: Elementals, strong again."

"We can be allies, but it doesn't have to be like this."

"This is your home now." Veil turned and walked to the back room.

Once he was gone, Sara rushed to the front door and pulled the handle, but the door would not open. Sobbing, she leaned her back against the door and slid to the floor.

Veil watched from the hallway as Sara cried, but he couldn't look for long. He disappeared into the room.

ONCE Veil returned, Sara's crying had stopped. She was slumped, sleeping against the door.

Veil lifted her into his arms and carried her up the stairs and into one of the bedrooms.

The room had been cleaned and redecorated. A carpet was placed in the center of the room and new tapestries hung on the wall. A canopy bed was positioned near the fireplace. The only thing that remained constant was the painting of the woman above the mantle, but the painting had been centered so there was no evidence of the second painting that had hung beside it.

Veil placed Sara on the bed, and she turned in her sleep. Veil brought the thick blanket gathered at the end of the bed up to her chin.

He stirred the fire with the poker and looked up at the painting of the woman. He stared at the painting until his eyes burned.

Veil walked back over to the bed where Sara slept. His hand touched the air around her face. She turned and smiled, her cheek touching his hand. He stared at her for a long moment. He stepped out of the room and watched her as he eased the door shut.

SARA awoke late the next morning and stretched. Her stretch was interrupted as she pulled her arms back to her chest. She lay in a bed without knowing how she got there.

Veil knocked on the door before entering. In his hands was a silver tray. On the tray was an ivory plate of barley cake, two hard boiled eggs, grapes, and three figs. Beside the plate was a bowl of barley porridge, and a silver spoon and knife.

Sara sat up. "You brought me here?"

"I'm sorry. I couldn't let you sleep on the floor." He walked around to her side of the bed and set the silver tray down at the bedside table.

Sara moved away from him to the center of the bed.

Veil sighed. "I'm sorry things turned out this way."

"Am I confined to this room?"

"You have the run of the house, and I hope you make yourself at home. Only I don't want you to go into the chamber on the first floor. I had the tub filled in the bathroom downstairs, and there are fresh clothes in the chest at the foot of your bed."

"How do you expect me to be a good ally if you're forcing me into this union?" Sara asked.

"The very idea of our marriage will inspire loyalty in the people, and I hope you will come to see this as something good. I know the only reason why you denied me is that you still hold onto unrealistic hopes."

"How dare you say that?"

"I'm sorry," he said. "I've said too much."

Sara stared at the painting on the wall. "Who is she?"

"My mother."

"This was her room?" she asked.

"No, she died before I moved to Tosia."

"Where did you live before?"

Veil pulled the chair by the fireplace closer to her bedside. "May I?"

"It's your house."

Veil took a seat in the chair. "I was born in Lumina. It was me and my mother for a long time. The Council was still operating in the tunnels under Vella City, and they were just a memory.

"When I was four years of age, my father entered the Morica High Council. It was never more important that he have a son. He tried to produce an heir but to no avail, so he came looking for his bastard.

"When he found us, my mother seemed happy. I didn't understand. At the time, I thought children only had mothers.

"But he told me who he was. He told me who *I* was.

"And we left to join the rest of the Council.

"Long after my mother died, my father decided to move us here."

"What happened to your father?" Sara dared to ask.

Veil rose from his chair. "He died in this house, cursing my mother's memory."

He walked to the door. "Come down when you feel comfortable. In the afternoon, we will sit for a painting."

"For what?" she asked.

"For our wedding announcements." He left the room and closed the door behind him.

SARA and Veil sat on a bench. Sara had one hand placed on top of the other, and Veil's hands were on her shoulders.

The painter told them to keep very still.

As time lulled by, Sara became more acutely aware of Veil's touch, and her growing discomfort was making her fidget.

"I want things to be amiable between us," Sara said.

"So do I." Veil tried not to move his lips too much.

"If there is to be a wedding, I want Rai and Farah there."

"They can be there. These announcements are to be hung all around Mirmina in the morning. We're inviting everyone."

Good, Sara thought, they can plan my rescue.

After the painting was complete, Veil reviewed the results. He stared for a long time and smiled. "This is good. Have your men start making the announcements and get them out by morning."

He took Sara's hands in his. "We'll have dinner together tonight. I'm so glad you're warming up to the idea of this union. It is good for the people." He retired to the bath.

Pentagon saw the painter out.

Sara watched as the door to the Domum Fidei opened, and the painter made his escape.

She raced for the door.

Pentagon grabbed her about the waist and stopped her from flying out.

"Not now," he whispered. "You run out there now and there are hundreds of guards waiting to stop you."

"What does that matter when I have the one guard here ready to stop me?" Sara asked.

The comment didn't seem to bother Pentagon, though his position on the Council was higher than that of a guard. "I will help you, but you have to wait."

"Until when?"

"Tomorrow night. Here." He handed her a small silver key. "Tomorrow, okay? I'll get your weapons. I've been watching the guards. By tonight I think I'll have figured out a pattern in their movements."

Pentagon opened the door and walked out.

Sara hid the key in the pocket of her dress. She turned around to go upstairs, but stopped. The back room was now vacant, and Veil didn't want her back there. Why?

She put her ear to the door of the bathroom. From inside the room came the sounds of water gently falling.

This was her chance.

She went to the room under the loft. The door was locked. Sara reached for the key in her pocket and placed the key into the lock. It worked.

Was it a skeleton key? Or did Pentagon want her in this room?

Sara placed the key back into her pocket and opened the door.

In the center of the room was a large rug. On the back wall was a bookshelf and a vanity. Upon the vanity was a journal and a small portrait of the woman whose painting hung above the fireplace in the upstairs bedroom.

Sara picked up the journal and turned to the first page.

No money today. A neighbor was kind enough to offer us some potatoes and old bread.

Sara leafed through the pages.

We should move to Caleena. Things are cheaper there, but I can't afford the boat fare. Veil was crying this morning. He's sick. The food he's been eating . . .

Sara turned a few more pages.

Cron came for us. After five years. Should I be happy?

Veil seems confused.

Cron says he will take us to Vella City to live. Do I have a choice? I can no longer feed my son.

Sara flipped through the pages and scanned them.

A wedding. I feel that this decision is not my own, but good things have come out of decisions that weren't mine. Like Veil.

I'll do this for him.

Sara sighed and flipped the pages.

Two years of marriage. Two years that I have been careful. They hate people like me, and Cron abhors us. He knows now, that I am one of them. I should have fought the urge. But it was too great. I felt the pull as vines crawled up the wall. I willed them. That was enough for me. I saw his fierce eyes staring back at me. I had committed a terrible sin.

No, I was the sin.

He will kill me now . . .

Sara turned the pages. All blank, but the last few.

Thick lines of ink bled through the pages and formed one word over and over:

Murderer.

The ink was smeared in places where tears had trailed down the pages.

Sara shut the journal. She stepped back.

A light breeze hit her face, but the room was windowless.

She looked around.

A small crack ran down the wall just at the edge of the bookshelf.

Sara pushed the shelf to the side, and the crack grew into a gaping hole. The hole was large enough for her to walk through. Inside, it was dark.

Sara grabbed the lit candle from the vanity and shined it inside the hole.

It was a tunnel.

Sara stepped inside and went down, guided by the light. She felt along the walls as she walked. The tunnel smelled like wet dirt. It was rich and intoxicating.

Something glowed up ahead.

Sara journeyed further down.

In a silver bowl resting atop a pedestal were the four remaining element spheres.

Someone grabbed Sara by the shoulder and turned her around.

Veil pinned her arms to her sides. "I told you not to go in here."

"I'm sorry." Sara could not control her breathing. It was becoming erratic as her brain boiled, and she tried to think of a way out. *This is it.*

But Veil let go of one arm and pulled her along as he marched to the entrance of the tunnel. Veil let go of Sara and pushed the shelf back into place. He leaned against it with his head in his hands. "You read my mother's journal?"

Sara nodded, realizing Veil could not see her. Still, she couldn't speak.

"He killed her in front of me. Stabbed her in her bedroom. I was six years old. And I didn't have a mother anymore.

"I could hear the rattle when she died. It was so final. But I don't think I really understood what happened until I found her journal."

Veil sighed. "That spot beneath the rug is where he died. I couldn't look at him anymore. He said we moved here to remember my mother. The Council covered it up like they covered up my mother's murder.

"It was so strange. I didn't remember it. Just like I didn't remember when he killed my mother until much later. She was just gone one day."

Veil sobbed.

Sara knelt beside him. "You don't want to do this, do you?"

Veil shook his head.

"It's Mordecai?" Sara asked.

"It's always been Mordecai," Veil said. "He gave me the journal."

"You don't have to listen to him anymore. I can help you." Sara took one hand away from his face and held it.

A knock came to the door.

"High Councilor Veil?" Pentagon said. "High Councilor Mordecai is here to see you."

23

FIRE REKINDLED

JACOPO sat among the rocks and ruins with his followers. His fire-red cloak tossed across his shoulder was reminiscent of his late leader, who also gave power to the flames.

Thirty-four men were within his company, all possessors of the Fire Element.

The sand of Dustpath Road covered the roof under which they sat. The sand spilled into the ruined fortress like an hourglass.

Jacopo held out his hand to catch the sand that fell at his side. It spilled over his fingers and onto the floor.

An old friend, Gerwald, sat beside him on the next stone. He had fought with him at the Element Games, three years ago, at his leader's request. "When will we take back Omega Ray?"

Jacopo dumped the remaining sand from his palm. "It never made much sense for Fire Elementals to rule in the snow. I like it here in this dust palace, and the heat of the sun matches my body temperature. This is where we'll build our army, and soon every inch of Mirmina will be ours just like Hephaestus would have wanted."

Jacopo stood and breathed in the sunbaked air. His lips spread into a smile. "Did you bring the wine?"

"Took three kegs from Lumina," Gerwald said.

"Well, pour it then," Jacopo demanded.

Gerwald dumped his canvas bag. Four cups tumbled out. He uncorked the bottle and poured the deep red wine into a wooden cup and passed it to Jacopo.

Jacopo lifted the cup and drank it down in one gulp. He passed the cup back to Gerwald, who refilled it.

"You know why those old men in robes hate us?" Jacopo didn't wait for an answer. "They're afraid of us. They think their rules and fancy clothes scare us. I'll burn them to the ground. And steal their wine and their gold and their power. And then I'll make the rules."

The rest of the men sat among the ruins. They talked and laughed as they enjoyed the stolen wine. Without Hephaestus, they had wandered Mirmina, and the people scorned them for their power. They walked around with so much anger and no-where to focus it, until Jacopo made his decision.

He gathered the wanderers from the far reaches of Mirmina and asked that they gather in Dustpath where he would build his army to march upon Vella City.

He would gather more followers, take the city, and set up an outpost.

Hephaestus had been foolish, he had let his passions get the better of him, but Jacopo only had passion for one thing: power.

A cat settled in the sand by his feet, her long front legs stretched out in the sand. Her eyes were orange like the flames.

Jacopo reached down to pet the creature. Her head arched up to his hand.

He downed another cup of wine.

24

THATCH'S RESCUE

MORICA guards grabbed Rai.

"Rai!" Farah turned back.

"Get out of here!"

A baton hit Rai on the back of the head and knocked her out.

THE cold stone chilled her body. Her eyes blinked open. The blurred image of Farah was kneeling over her.

"Are you okay?" Farah's voice echoed in her head.

Rai waited as her vision focused. She sat up on the stone floor. "I'm starving."

They were in a cell in Lumina dungeons. A cot rested in the corner of the room, and a wooden tray of bread and cheese was on the floor. Rai picked the bread up and pulled at the hard crust with her teeth. The smell of sewage issued from a hole in the ground. Their cell faced the loft, and a guard waited outside.

"They took our stuff," Farah whispered. "I hid a lock pick, but I can't use it with that guy there."

Rai, still a little dazed, looked around.

"Aldo got away," Farah whispered. "Orka too."

"Where's Sara?" Rai asked.

Farah shook her head.

"Dead?" Rai asked in alarm.

"No. I saw someone grab her. A guard maybe, but I'm not sure. Anyway, they were headed away from the dungeons. I didn't see where they went because the guards grabbed you. I tried to help but—"

"You should have run," Rai said.

"And leave you like that?"

"What you did is exactly what could get you killed one day."

"Like you wouldn't do the same," Farah said.

Rai stood. "I wouldn't."

Farah frowned. "So, what do we do now?"

"Let's hope Aldo or your little bird friend can get to Thatch and tell him where we are."

Farah slumped onto the cot. "So, we wait. Do you have any stories?"

"You're not a child."

"Tell me more about you and the leader of the Rebel Resistance," Farah said. "I could tell you knew each other."

"Let's keep our pasts to ourselves."

"So, you did know him?" Farah asked.

"Nonsense."

Farah put her face in her hands and sighed. "Who knows how long we'll be down here." She sat for two minutes in silence, and then declared, "I'm bored."

"Get a hobby." Rai leaned against the wall.

Farah stood. "I can't take this anymore. You were out for two days. I can't stand it in here." She approached the cell door.

Rai grabbed her arm. "I know what you're thinking."

"Let me go."

A loud crash sounded from above. The fissure in the ceiling grew. The stone ceiling rained down like heavy hail.

A loud caw rang through the dungeon.

"What in Mirmina?" The guard staggered from his seat on the wooden chair outside Rai and Farah's cell. As he stood, a hooked beak grabbed him by the shoulder and threw him from the loft. Thermal's claws wrapped around the bars of Rai and Farah's cage and ripped them from the wall. They settled with a crash on the floor.

On the back of Thermal was Thatch. "Come on."

"Just a minute," Farah said. "Our weapons."

She rushed to the chest outside their cell and picked the lock. After tossing Rai her sword, she grabbed her weapons and their trackers and earpieces.

"Hey," said a guard below them on the first floor. He drew his crossbow and aimed at Thermal.

The arrow hit Thermal under his wing and embedded.

Thermal cried out in a high-pitched screech.

"Let's go," Thatch shouted as guards flooded into the room.

Farah and Rai climbed onto the edge of the banister encircling the loft and hopped onto Thermal's back.

Thermal rose through the fissure in the ceiling. As he peeked back into the Council Chamber, people screamed and ran to get away from the monster.

Thermal staggered across the floor and made his way down the stairs outside the building's entrance. At the foot of the stairs, Thermal swayed and slumped to the ground.

Farah, Thatch, and Rai slid off his back.

The people outside continued to run in panic.

Thatch stroked Thermal's feathers.

"Look," Farah said.

Banners lined the walls of the buildings surrounding them. Next to an image of Veil and Sara was an announcement: "Lady Sara and High Councilor Veil are to be united in Marriage in a Public Ceremony in Vella City on the Thirteenth of April at the tenth hour."

"We don't know where she is now," Rai said, "but we know where she is going to be."

"That'll be too late," Farah said.

Guards rushed down the steps of the Council Chamber and around the corner of the building.

"It's going to be okay," Thatch said to Thermal. "I need you to hold on for me a little longer, and I'll get you patched up."

Thermal cawed and rose to his feet.

"Come on," Thatch shouted. "But be careful."

He, Farah, and Rai ascended onto Thermal's back.

Thermal flapped his wings, building momentum and lifting himself into the air as arrows flew around him. He caught the wind and soared away.

THERMAL landed near the Chariot, and his passengers dismounted.

Thatch grabbed Thermal's reins and guided him toward the shelter of a ruined building. "Come on. Just a little further.

"Could you go get the med kit?" Thatch asked.

Farah and Rai ran to the Chariot and retrieved the med kit from the control room. Orka perched on the back of the chair next to Stannum. She chirped when she saw Farah.

"I've read through the three volumes," Stannum started, but he was cut off.

"Hey," Shift said. "Is someone hurt?"

"Thermal," Farah said as she and Rai ran to the elevator.

Their feet sank into the sand as they made their way to the ruined building where Thatch had taken Thermal.

Thatch stood on a broken column so he could reach Thermal's injury. He broke the shaft of the arrow, and Thermal cawed in pain. The arrow had gone all the way through. Thatch pulled out the other end. "He'll be fine. I'm going to get him patched up, and he should be ready to fly again in a couple weeks."

"Weeks?" Farah said.

"It will still be healing, but he should be able to fly with little discomfort."

"We only have nine days before the wedding. We have to get to Sara before then."

"We'll never make it if we travel by foot," Rai said.

"I have motor vehicles in the back of the engine room. Grab them. They should get you there in time."

Farah and Rai ran back to the Chariot. Farah grabbed the cubes from the engine room.

"What are those?" Rai asked.

"Motorbikes like the one Atrus has." Farah threw the cubes outside the engine room, and they expanded. The cubes unfolded into two fully functioning motorbikes.

"Okay." Rai grabbed the bike and revved the engine.

Farah picked up the bike beside Rai and got on. They sped down Dustpath Road.

Night fell on Dustpath as Farah and Rai neared Wyvek.

Rai stopped her engine. "Atrus might have a place for us to hold up for the night."

Farah pulled up beside her. "Should we stop?"

"We have to sleep and eat. We'll be no good to Sara if we drag ourselves into Vella City half dead."

Farah got off her bike and pressed the button between the handle bars. She backed up as the bike folded into a cube. Farah put the cube into her canvas bag. "Let's go."

The *Lacwanx* worked well into the night, shuffling sheets of metal into the temple. The area around the temple stayed lit by the flames atop tall poles, encircling the temple on all sides.

Atrus poured over his blueprints in his office.

"Boss, you've got company," said one of the human workers.

Three *Lacwanx* trailed in, carrying tin buckets full of gears and bolts. Atrus moved past them to the elevator. As the elevator descended, Farah and Rai waited at the door.

"Ladies," Atrus said, "I was wondering when you'd come back around."

"We need a place to stay," Rai said.

"Well, ask me nice, and maybe I'll hook you up."

"We're not kidding." Farah folded her arms.

"Whoa. She's rubbing off on you." He pointed to Rai.

"Always joking. Never helping," Rai said.

"You can't stay in the temple," Atrus said. "And the inns in town are all abandoned, but I'm sure I can set one up for you. Are you hungry?"

"Starved," Farah said.

"Okay. There's an inn around the corner from here. You can't miss it. I'll send *Lacwanx* to bring you food and blankets."

"Thanks," Farah said. She and Rai turned to leave.

"I'll see you in the morning?" Atrus asked.

"No," Rai said. "We're leaving early."

"What happened?" Atrus asked. "Where's the Water Elemental?"

"Haven't you seen the announcements?" Farah asked.

"I've been working. This is the first time I've left my office in two weeks."

"We have to save Sara before Veil forces her to marry him," Farah said.

"You want to help?" Rai asked.

"I would, but I try not to get involved in Morica business. I'm sure you both will do fine without me."

"Thanks for that," Farah said. She and Rai left the temple and made their way to the inn.

"I thought you liked that guy," Rai said.

"I thought I did too," Farah said.

The streets of Wyvek were deserted. Lanterns whose flames had long gone out hung on posts. The doors to the homes had been boarded up.

The inn towered over the surrounding buildings. Rusty nails poked out of the boards that crisscrossed the door.

Rai put her foot high onto the frame of the door for leverage and used both her hands to pull at the boards until they loosened. With effort, she removed the boards and threw them to the ground. "Looks like they might not have wanted to come back."

"Or maybe they wanted to keep others out," Farah said. "This was their home."

"Then why leave it?" Rai opened the door and walked inside.

Thick dust decorated the shelves and corners. It crept along the bell on the innkeeper's desk and clung to the unlit lanterns. Their footsteps disturbed the dust. In the back of the room was a fireplace. Dust settled on the mantel.

"Why would you need a fireplace in this kind of heat?" Farah asked. "It never gets cold in Wyvek, not even cool."

"The fireplace is probably for cooking," Rai said, "which you've never had to do a day in your life."

"Hey. Quit with the royalty jokes. If we have to travel together, we might as well be nice to each other until we find Sara."

Rai sighed. She lit the lantern without a match and moved into the dark hallway. "There are more than enough rooms. We don't have to share."

"That's a relief."

Later that night, a group of *Lacwanx* brought food and blankets.

Farah and Rai settled down to a dinner of cheese, rye bread, and barley cakes. After the meal, they retired for the night into separate rooms.

Farah tore off the sheets from the bed, and the room was filled with a cloud of dust. She coughed and waved the dust away from her face.

Orka kept her beak against Farah's hair as the dust wafted through the room.

"Sorry, Orka." Farah petted the green bird.

Once the dust had settled, Orka perched on the window sill. She raised one foot into the feathers of her belly and closed her eyes.

Farah spread the blankets the *Lacwanx* had given her across the mattress and laid down.

She sighed with relief as she blew out the light from her lantern on the table beside the bed. She closed her eyes and sank into sleep.

THE sound of static awoke Farah. She kept her eyes closed and listened. The noise became louder and more pronounced.

Farah sat up in bed, and Orka opened her eyes.

Something darted across the floor. It was like a thin snake. A jet of light sparked when it moved, creating a sound that was distinct and loud.

More lights appeared sweeping across the floor. The tiny strings of energy darted under Farah's bed.

She jumped up from the bed and ran to Rai's room. She could hear the static roar following her as she moved down the hall in the dark and struggled to find the doorknob.

She burst into Rai's room.

"Rai!"

Rai got up from bed. "What is it?"

The tiny strings of energy moved up Farah's legs and traveled over her body to her mouth. They forced their way inside. Farah's head leaned back, and a loud popping sound came from her neck as the energy invaded her body.

Rai approached her. "Farah?"

Farah's head snapped forward with a crack. Her eyes glowed white in the dark. "We are your gods!" A voice echoed from Farah's lips.

The energy escaped Farah's throat, and spread out in all directions across the floor.

Rai backed up as Farah leaned over and coughed. When she stood up straight, her eyes had returned to normal.

"What was that?" Rai asked.

"They look like those things we found in Caleena, in the sphere room," Farah said between breaths.

"Come on," Rai said. "Grab your things. Now I know why they left and boarded up the doors. Let's get out of here."

Orka flew to Farah's shoulder as she grabbed her bag and rushed to meet Rai outside the inn.

As soon as Farah made her exit, Rai put the boards back against the door and hammered the nails in with a rock. "I'm going to kill him."

"You don't think Atrus knew?" Farah asked.

"I don't trust him."

"You don't trust anybody," Farah said.

Rai stopped hammering in the nails and turned to Farah. "You all right?"

Farah hesitated. "Yeah. I'm fine. Why are you worried all of a sudden?"

"I've seen those things before," Rai said.

"Yeah. I know," Farah said. "Back in Caleena. We all did."

Rai walked down the street toward the entrance to Wyvek. "No. Before that."

"What are you talking about? Where?" Farah ran to catch up with her.

Rai stopped. "I don't think the spheres were meant to be off their pedestals for this long." She continued down the street.

"We have to tell Atrus what happened."

"There's no time," Rai said. "Let's forget about this and get to Sara."

"Stop." Farah rushed up and grabbed Rai's arm.

Rai pulled away from her. "There's no time."

"What do you mean?" Farah asked.

"It's almost morning," Rai said. "We have to get to the Lake."

"I'm not going anywhere until you tell me what you know." Farah planted her feet in the ground.

"Do you want to get to Sara before she says yes to Veil?" Rai asked.

"Morica kidnapped her," Farah said. "She won't say yes to him."

"She might not be given a choice."

Farah slumped her shoulders and followed Rai. They walked to the Lake de Somnia. When they arrived at the Lake, the sun peeked over the horizon.

They approached the dock.

"Oh no." Rai walked to the edge of the water.

"What?"

"A large group must have crossed. All the boats are on the other side." Rai sat on the ground. "Looks like Sara's wedding won't be interrupted."

A forceful gust of wind caused the pilings on the dock to split.

"What are you doing?" Rai asked, shouting over the thunderous sound. She was surprised Farah had the strength to summon such a powerful force of energy.

"We can make a raft." Farah focused on the dock as the Wind pushed down on it.

"Are you crazy?" Rai asked. "We can't cross the Lake on a raft."

The pilings cracked and gave way. The surface of the dock lay floating on the water. Farah pulled up the two pilings closest to the water's edge. "Oars." She handed one to Rai.

"You're crazy," Rai said.

"I'm not about to let my friend marry a monster."

Rai took the oar.

Farah jumped onto the raft. Rai sighed and followed her. They rowed in silence. Even Orka was quiet as they rowed to the middle of the Lake.

"What do you think my dad will find down there?" Farah asked.

"What?"

"In the gorge. Do you think he'll find Bolton's body? And if he does, it's been over three years."

"Why are you thinking about that right now?" Rai asked.

"Every time I've crossed this Lake I remember when he fell in."

"He fell in because he was being a fool," Rai said, "and you're a fool too if you think we can cross this Lake on a raft."

"So, what? You think we're going to die out here?"

"That would be my guess." Rai watched the dark shadow approach the raft.

"What is it?" Farah asked.

"It's here."

The raft rocked.

Farah tried to steady herself by wrapping her fingers around the boards.

The Nightmare rose from the water.

Rai stood on the raft and drew her sword.

"What are you doing?" Farah shouted.

"Expediting my prediction." Rai swung her sword and sliced through the Nightmare, but it was in vain. The dark cloud still loomed over them.

Rai set her feet wide to steady herself as the raft rocked on the water. The raft jolted, and a jar fell from Rai's side and rolled across the raft. Rai scrambled to pick it up. The jar contained her Aether. She unscrewed the cap and released the Aether.

The Aether floated into the air above her head. It glowed, sparked, and flamed. Every element within seconds fumed from its transparent body until light flashed.

Farah and Rai shielded their eyes from the brightness.

When the light was gone, so was the Nightmare.

"What was that?" Farah asked.

"I don't know." Rai stared into the air where the Nightmare had risen. She did not blink.

Farah hurried to the edge of the raft and looked down into the dark waters. The Nightmare wasn't lurking below. "It's gone."

Rai coaxed the Aether back into the jar. "Whatever that was, it saved us."

25

PLANS FOR A WEDDING

HIGH Councilor Mordecai waited in the entrance hall. He wore his councilor's robes, and he had an air about him, like he had won.

Sara leaned against the wall, hidden in the hallway. She listened to their conversation.

"High Councilor Mordecai," Veil said, "what brings you here?"

"I want to move you and Lady Sara to Vella City."

"But the wedding's not for several days," Veil said.

"I know you want to have time with your young bride, and you'll have plenty of time in Vella City."

"And very little privacy."

"What would you do with privacy?" The High Councilor laughed. "You're not married yet. Besides you're a High Councilor marrying the woman who saved Mirmina. There will be little privacy in your future."

"That's why I'm grateful for it now."

Mordecai clapped Veil on the shoulder. His wrinkled face crinkled into a smile. "You'll come to Vella City. I've provided guards to escort you. You'll leave this evening."

Sara swallowed. Tonight, Pentagon had planned to help her escape. But if Mordecai wanted them to journey to Vella City, the plans must change. She would have to tell Pentagon.

The door closed behind High Councilor Mordecai.

Veil approached. "I'm sure you heard everything. I'll have your dresses packed."

"Those are not *my* dresses," Sara said.

"They are now." Veil touched the doorknob.

"What are you doing with the element spheres?" she asked.

"You shouldn't have seen that." Veil opened the door, walked inside, and closed it behind him. The lock clicked.

Sara rushed to her feet and ran to the door in the entrance hall. Pentagon waited beyond it. But she couldn't signal him for fear Veil would hear. She tapped on the door and whispered his name, but Pentagon could not hear her through the heavy oaken door.

She sighed in desperation. She would leave for Vella City that evening. It would be surrounded by Morica councilors and guards. How would she escape?

TWO guards carried the chest containing the dresses of Veil's deceased mother. Guards bordered Sara on all sides as they journeyed through D'arkadia. The lanterns at their sides made Sara nervous because the Beast would be irritated by the light.

Veil was several paces ahead of her with his own group of guards. Pentagon travelled with him, but Sara couldn't speak with him without being heard by the others.

As they moved across the plain, the lantern light hit upon where the ground was marked. Talon had said this meant they were halfway across.

The lightning flashed, and the Beast roared as he slashed Bolton's chest.

Sara tried to shake the memory, but it was too vivid. A distant roar and the hammering of heavy feet sounded, but this time it wasn't only Sara who heard it.

The guards drew their swords, and the procession stopped.

The roar became closer and louder. A guard in Veil's company screamed, followed by the sounds of ripping and tearing. The air smelled like copper.

Another guard was taken. His lantern light snuffed out.

The guards in Sara's troop looked around. The hands that clenched their swords shook, causing the steel to waver.

One by one the guards in Veil's troop were swept into the blackness. The remaining guards scanned the darkness with their lanterns.

Veil's left side was exposed. No guards protected him.

Snarling and growling, the Beast emerged from the darkness. Its claws high, it rushed Veil. But it stopped mere inches from him. Its massive feet plummeted to the ground, and its lips dropped down over its sharp teeth.

Veil was so tall, he matched the height of the Beast on all fours.

But the Beast cowered until its back was hunched. It sank back into the darkness.

Why didn't the Beast attack Veil? Sara wondered. What did it see in him that caused it to shrink back into its black solitude?

Shaken, but not deterred, they continued their journey to the city. They arrived in Vella City when the sun was high. The city sat on a cliff overlooking the vast sea. Years ago, a flood destroyed the city. The citizens died in the flood only to be swept off the cliff with the water that splashed onto the rocks below.

When Hephaestus rose to power, the Council used the tunnels under the city as their hiding place. Once he was defeated, they planted their roots, but they had failed to make the city any less cold and ghostly with their presence.

"A wedding would warm the city," Mordecai had suggested to Veil.

The guards escorted Sara past Fortress Tower to the Council Palace. The Palace was pale blue marble with a silver balcony high up over a marble platform meant for spectators.

On the first floor, no windows lined the walls. On the second, windows no larger than a hand whispered the secrets of the world outside. The windows grew larger with every floor. Inside, the walls and floors of the building were made entirely of marble. It was a marble prison.

Veil stayed downstairs to meet with High Councilor Mordecai while the councilors escorted Sara up the stairs. They released her into a room on the top floor of the Palace.

The room was large with a four-poster bed in the center, a chair and reading desk, a full-sized mirror, and a small rug to warm the marble floor. The only window faced the sea. The window had no glass or curtains. The edge of the building met the edge of the cliff. A drop from that window would mean a drop to one's death.

Sara looked out the window. The building had no ledges or cracks, but was smooth pale blue marble all around.

Sara sighed. She felt for the key in her pocket and walked to the door. She tried the key. It wouldn't unlock the door. She threw the key to the floor with an exasperated gasp.

A click sounded, and the knob turned.

Sara backed up and dried her eyes.

Veil walked inside and closed the door behind him. "I'm sorry. It wasn't supposed to be like this."

"I don't think you should be in my room," Sara said.

"You're right. I wanted to see that you made the journey comfortably." Veil spotted the key on the floor near the door. His tall form stooped to pick it up. "What's this?"

Sara remained silent, and Veil placed the key on the table beside the bed.

"What stake does Mordecai have in this?" Sara asked.

"High Councilor Mordecai wants the same thing that I do. He wants the Elementals on our side."

"Mordecai hates Elementals," Sara said. "He's like your father."

Veil's face changed. His usually calm and gentle demeanor turned fierce. "He's not like my father," Veil yelled, raising his hand into the air.

Sara backed away from him.

"I'm sorry." He put his hand down, shocked by his own anger, and rushed to the door. He left, shutting the door behind him and locking it.

Sara moved the chair to the window and stared at the sea wavering in the breeze. The same breeze hit her face and brought the smell of the sea to her.

A Councilor came to escort Sara to dinner.

He brought her to a large dining hall with a long table.

The Councilor pulled out a chair for Sara at the head of the table. The Councilor took his place against the wall, awaiting further instructions.

Veil sat at the opposite end of the table.

The table was set for two with a dinner of mountain herbs, baklava, grilled leeks, seared pigeon, onion soup, pomegranates, pears, chick peas, beans, and boiled lentils. Beside the dinner plate was a glass of fermented nectar.

"I shouldn't have yelled at you," Veil said. "High Councilor Mordecai raised me after my mother's death. My father couldn't even look at me."

Sara nodded. "Do you want to marry me, or are you just following orders?"

"What I said to you on the Cliff was true," Veil said. "I was told to get to know you after I met you in Caleena, but then I wanted to. You are like me in many ways. I wish you could see that we want the same things."

"Do you know about Mordecai's past? Why he was put in the dungeons in Jetty Verte?" Sara asked.

"He has turned his back on that. He loved my mother like my father never could."

"Did he tell you that? Did he tell you why your father killed your mother?"

Veil stood and slammed his hands down on the table. "Because she was an Elemental!"

His wine glass fell onto the floor, shattering it and spilling the nectar.

The Councilor rushed from his place behind Sara and knelt to pick up the shards of glass.

"I'm sorry." Veil eased into his chair. "Please, let's not talk about High Councilor Mordecai."

Sara nodded. *He's on edge*, she thought. "How do you know I won't run as soon as we are married?"

Veil sighed. "It is my hope that you will not flee your obligation. That you will one day understand why this needs to be done."

"It's my understanding that we were friends, and now this. I would have joined you in defending Mirmina and the Elementals. It would have been clear I was on your side."

Veil looked down at his plate.

"I'd like to go to bed now," Sara said.

Veil looked up. "But you haven't eaten."

"I'm not hungry."

"Councilor, escort Lady Sara back to her room, and bring her food up to her."

The Councilor bowed and led Sara back up the stairs to her bedroom prison.

*   *   *

SARA looked out the window and down to the sea crashing against the rocks. The morning light made its way over the horizon, and seagulls like roosters brought the dawn with their calls.

Sara moved the table to the window and sat with her paper and charcoal to sketch the sea.

The Councilor brought up her breakfast which she left untouched.

The door opened, and Veil walked in carrying a cream-colored dress. He held the dress up for Sara to see. Lace covered the top. The sleeves were short and fanned out below the shoulder. The sleeves and waist were trimmed with embroidery. The silken skirt flowed to the ground like a gentle waterfall into a stream.

"Your mother's?" Sara asked.

Veil nodded. "I want you to wear it for the wedding." Veil laid the dress out on the bed. He glanced at Sara's breakfast of barley cakes and porridge. "You're not eating."

"No," Sara said.

"You'll starve." Veil gazed at the open window that led to the treacherous rocks below.

Sara followed his gaze. "I would never do that."

"When I found you at the Cliff, it worried me."

"That's because you didn't understand. I was looking for someone."

"I stood at the edge of the Cliff many times," Veil said, "wondering why I wasn't blessed with the Creator's gifts like my mother. I wanted to be like her because, if I wasn't like her, I was like him."

"Your mother was brave," Sara said. "She left everything for you. She married a man she didn't love. You don't have to have her element to be like her. The way you treat the people with kindness, that's what she would want. Your father, he's the one who took things by force."

26

PENTAGON'S PROMISE

SARA'S fingers grazed the embroidery on the dress. She had never dreamed of a wedding. Before the battle with Hephaestus, she thought her life would be short. And after that battle, she never thought about love or family, just duty. Although Spire had warned her against this, it was easier this way.

What would have happened if she had gone with Bolton like he had asked her so many times? After all, she hadn't saved Mirmina. It had been the efforts of many. Maybe they would have fought despite her absence.

Sara shook the thoughts from her head. She had promised herself she wouldn't dwell on them.

Night fell. She moved the dress from the bed onto the back of the chair, and crawled in between the firm mattress and the heavy blankets. She closed her eyes and drifted.

The knob turned.

Sara opened her eyes. She wasn't sure how long sleep had claimed her. The door opened.

It was Pentagon. He came in. On his back was a small satchel. "I've come to get you out of here," he whispered.

Sara climbed out of bed. She wore only the nightgown which she had found among the clothes in the chest.

"You're going to freeze to death," he said. "Grab a coat."

Sara shook her head. The chest only contained heavy dresses that would burden her. "I'll be fine. Let's just go."

Pentagon opened the door and slinked into the hallway.

Sara followed.

The Councilor who guarded Sara's door lay unconscious on the floor outside her room.

Turning the corner, Pentagon pointed to a window down the hall. It was wide and open, but on the top floor of the building.

Cutting through was the main hallway.

"Wait here," Pentagon whispered. He looked around the corner and crossed. He waved for Sara to come over.

Sara started to cross the hallway when Veil came from around the corner.

Their eyes met.

Sadness settled in Veil's eyes, but he made no move to stop her.

Sara crossed over to Pentagon.

"Veil saw me," she whispered.

"Come on. He might warn the guards."

"I don't think so."

"You can't take that chance."

They hurried to the window.

Sara looked down. She could make out the figure of a man wearing the tawny uniform of a Resistance fighter. He waved to her.

Pentagon threw the sack down, and the man below caught it.

The man sent a vine up to the window sill. The vine was met by more vines that wrapped around it, adding to its thickness.

"Go ahead," Pentagon said.

"Aren't you coming?" Sara asked.

Pentagon shook his head.

Sara nodded, gripped the vine, and climbed out the window. Her hand slipped and she slid halfway down. She tightened her grip on the vine and braced her feet against the wall of the building. Hand over fist, Sara lowered herself to the ground.

The man touched the small of her back and helped her down. "You act like this is your first climb." He smiled, his white teeth shone in contrast to his tan skin. His sandy brown hair wafted in the breeze.

"Rodan!" Sara wrapped her arms around his neck and hugged him.

Rodan pulled her away. He saluted Pentagon and took Sara's hand.

27
THE RESISTANCE FIGHTER

RODAN led Sara through the city to the waterfall at the edge of the forest.

Sara's thin nightgown did nothing to shield her from the chilly night air.

"What are you wearing?" Rodan took off his cloak and wrapped it around her shoulders.

"Thanks."

Rodan and Sara wandered through the Crystal Forest and made it to Jetty Verte before dawn. They sat on the grass of the plain. The cool night breeze wavered through the air.

Rodan sighed and leaned his head back. "I thought I told you to call me if you ever needed help."

"Well, that wouldn't have been easy. I haven't seen you in over two years."

"Sorry about that," Rodan said. "I wanted to come, but things weren't going well."

"Are you helping Morica now?" Sara asked.

"Why would you ask me that?"

"I was told you were here, and I believed that. But, how would Pentagon know to call you? I thought, maybe, you switched sides after coming here to spy on them. They told me that you had been gone for so long. I thought you were found out and captured, but seeing you here like this . . ."

"Captured? Give me more credit. I'm part of the Rebel Resistance," Rodan said. "Commander Vassal did not like the idea of an Elemental going in. I think he respects me because of my part in the battle at Omega Ray."

"So, you're not—"

"Helping Morica?" Rodan asked. "I'm not him, Sara."

"I know you're not." Sara's eyes trailed toward Regret Mountain.

"Here." Rodan handed her the bag. "I think these are yours."

Sara searched the bag, and found her earpiece and what remained of her tracker. She snapped the earpiece into her ear. "Hello."

"Sara?" Thatch's voice came through. He sounded relieved. "Where are you?"

"Jetty Verte."

"Farah and Rai should be on their way," Thatch said. "They're headed for Vella City. I need to tell them you're safe."

"They're not on the Chariot?" Sara asked.

"Something happened to Thermal. He was hurt, but I bandaged him up. He should be fine in a week or two. Farah and Rai went off looking for you. There are banners up saying that you're marrying Veil."

"Morica guards took me from Lumina and smashed my tracker," Sara said.

"I'll let Farah know before they reach Vella City." A loud click sounded, and Thatch was gone.

"One of Thatch's devices?" Rodan asked.

Sara nodded and took her drawings from the bag. She set the drawings on the grass in front of her.

"At it again?" Rodan picked up the drawings and looked through them. "These are really beautiful." He turned to the drawing of Bolton, tears bleeding the charcoal down the paper. He put the drawings back down.

"How are you holding up?" Rodan asked.

"I thought it would get easier, but I still have the nightmares."

"And your element?"

Sara shook her head. "It's gone. I can feel it. I've tried, but I know it's for nothing."

"A part of you died back there. Strength visits us for many reasons, but it turns its back on us when we no longer need it. It will come back to you."

"How's the Rebel Resistance treating you?" Sara asked.

"It was interesting in the beginning. They taught me how to fight using this." Rodan patted the sword in the sheath at his side. "I got to spend a lot of time with my father, which was a nice change. I can't say he was happy with my decision to leave. At first, he thought it was Commander Vassal's idea, and he hated him for it. Now, I guess he hates me."

"I'm sure that's not true."

"You always did see the best in people." Rodan stared at the trees bordering the plain.

She felt the shadow of shame creep in. Was he referring to how she had so foolishly trusted Bolton? But hadn't he trusted him too?

"Can you show me how to use a sword?" she asked.

"Really?"

Sara nodded.

Rodan stood and unsheathed his sword. Sara stood next to him and let the cloak drop to the ground.

"Okay, grab right below the guard with your right hand and grip the pommel in your left." Rodan demonstrated the correct hand position and offered Sara the sword.

Sara took the weapon and placed her hands in the correct position. She was surprised by the weight of the sword.

"When striking, use your right hand to guide the blade and your left to control the force." Rodan stood behind Sara and helped her to adjust the sword so the pommel was waist high.

"Now place your left foot behind your right. When you're ready to strike, push with your left and pivot with the right. Keep your arms out, but not locked. Give it a try."

Sara struck out into the air. The weight of the sword made her balance waver, and she leaned back against Rodan.

"Not bad," he whispered into her ear.

She looked up at him. "I need practice."

"Lots of practice," Rai said as she and Farah approached them.

Sara stepped away from Rodan. The sword pointed to the ground.

"We thought we would be too late. We were making our way through the forest to Vella City," Farah said. "Rodan? Where have you been? The Resistance doesn't let you send letters?"

"It would have blown my cover," he said. "I'm stationed in the city."

"You're one of Vassal's men," Rai said.

Rodan nodded. "That's right. You know him?"

"We met him when we visited Wyvek," Sara said.

"Sorry to cut this short," Rodan said, "but I'd better get back to the city before morning or things will look suspicious."

"Be careful," Sara said. "And thank you for rescuing me from yet another prison." She handed him back his sword.

Rodan sheathed it and hugged Sara good-bye. "When this is over, I'll visit. Stay out of trouble you three." He walked back to the Crystal Forest.

28

OLD SCARS REOPENED

SARA watched Rodan disappear among the trees. When would she see him again?

"Come on," Rai said.

"We've been walking all night," Farah said. "Can't we rest?"

"Would you like to rest in the abandoned inn up ahead?" Rai said.

"No way." Farah's voice squeaked. "I'd rather walk."

Orka chirped and flew off into the distance.

"Let's go," Rai said, "before Morica catches up."

"I'm sorry," Sara said. "I was wrong about Veil."

"Yes, you were," Rai said. "But I'm not one to dwell on the past." She turned around and led the way. Sara and Farah followed.

At mid-morning, they were half-way across the plain, headed for Regret Mountain.

"Rest now?" Farah asked. "I'm hungry." Farah stopped. As her shoulders slumped, Orka moved up to stay perched atop the descending appendage.

Rai did not turn back.

Sara stopped beside Farah. "You okay? You look exhausted."

Farah raised one tired hand into the air and swept it down. "I'll be fine." But her feet were slow to respond.

Rai stopped and folded her arms. The ground was soft where she stood. The earth moved downward until, under the pressure of Rai's weight, the surface gave in, and Rai fell with the raining dirt.

She fell into the earth among the dirt and stony pebbles until she hit harder ground. Rai scrambled to her feet and pulled out her sword. Her weapon raised in front of her, she scanned the darkness from the light of the blazing steel.

It was a tunnel, either side disappearing into darkness.

Sweat grew on Rai's brow. Strands of hair escaped her long braid. She dug her boots into the earth, her arms heavy with her sword.

"Rai? Are you down there?" Farah called from above.

The light streamed down from the hole like a spot light. Rai stepped into it. "Down here!"

"We're going to look for rope at the inn. We should be back in a few hours."

The sweat rolled down Rai's cheeks and off her chin. "No, don't leave me here."

"We'll be right back. We promise," came Sara's voice from the light above.

Rai listened. "Hello?"

Their voices were gone.

"Hello?"

A loud static zip came from one end of the tunnel.

Rai turned in the direction of the sound.

The zip became a roar, and that side of the tunnel exploded with light. Tiny strings of energy darted across the walls of the tunnel and along the floor and ceiling.

Rai ran in the opposite direction and held her sword out in front of her. Her feet pounded upon the hard earth. Her braid whipped her back as she ran down the tunnel, the opening becoming narrower and narrower until the glowing light of the sun streamed in.

Rai ran toward the light, and stopped, her feet about an inch from the edge. The tunnel ended at the cliff and opened far above the sea. The buzzing grew louder.

With nowhere left to go, Rai jumped.

The wind rushed past her.

She let go of her sword. The force of the wind put out the flames. Her hand gripped a branch and gravity yanked her arms.

Reaching out her hand, she grabbed the pommel of her sword before it descended into the water.

She hung there, one hand gripped around the branch, jetting out from the side of the earth, the other hung at her side as she held onto her sword.

Another tunnel was carved into the earth near the branch where she hung.

Her arms were becoming fatigued. She threw her sword into the tunnel, and it disappeared into the darkness.

Gripping the branch in both hands, she leaned forward and back until she got the right momentum. She jumped into the tunnel in the side of the cliff.

Rai rolled once onto her feet and felt in the darkness for her sword. Her hand touched upon the warm steel. Finding the pommel, she lifted the sword ablaze into the air and searched the darkness.

She stepped further into the tunnel and quickened her pace until she was running in a feverish panic.

She scanned the darkness. Ahead of her was a stone wall. Rai dropped her sword. The wall was solid and unyielding. She beat the wall and screamed. The force of the scream caused tears to issue from her eyes.

She leaned against the wall and slid down to a slumped position beside her sword. Putting her head in her hands, she cried fresh tears until her body forced her into a long-denied sleep.

SHE awoke. The air had grown cool and less humid. She stood and leaned against the wall. Her breathing was ragged and desperate. Though the air had become cool, she still felt the walls closing in and growing tighter.

She picked up her sword and set it ablaze. The earthy walls of the tunnel lit up as did the stony wall behind her.

Taking a deep breath, Rai turned around and kicked the wall with forceful, practiced kicks. She pulled her leg back to a bent knee and extended her leg straight out until it made contact with the stone wall.

Her heavy boot pounded into the wall with each kick until the sound of stone rubbing against stone met her ears.

Rai kicked harder, sending one stone brick loose from its mortar. As four more stones were released, Rai rushed to the wall and pulled loose the surrounding stone.

The gritty stones rubbed against the skin of her hands and caused the flesh to become raw and bloodied.

Her breathing got faster and more frantic. She ignored the empty pain in her stomach, the ache of her arms and legs, and the tearing of the flesh on her fingers.

She pulled the last stone free as the stony dust blocked her lungs. Coughing, she climbed through the hole she created, carrying her sword and satchel.

In front of her were the bars of an open cell. She grabbed the bars and collapsed into a hallway lined with dungeon cells.

Rai looked around, panicked and exhausted.

"Not here!" she screamed. She put her face in her hands. Dust dirtied her cheeks and forehead.

Rai stumbled along the hallway. "Somebody help me!" She rattled the bars of the cells with her blade.

She entered the sphere room. She breathed heavily and dragged her sword at her side, her arms too tired to hold it out in front of her.

The Sphere Protector stood before her, its rows of thorny teeth bared. Vines sprouted from its budding head, speckled with leaves and thorns.

Strings of energy issued forth from its mouth and beneath its body.

"We are your gods." A deep voice rumbled from the depths of its body.

Rai put her arms out at her sides and leaned her head back, but as the strings of energy zipped toward her, she swung her sword into their static bodies.

The Sphere Protector screamed, a high-pitched inhuman screech.

Blood issued from Rai's ears as she raised her sword against the monster.

The blade cut through the ethereal mass in vain. Sweat rolled down Rai's neck and matted the hair in strands at her brow. She swung again.

The Sphere Protector let out another screech as the blade tore through its wraithlike body and lighted upon the strings of energy.

The blood rolled from Rai's ears down her neck and onto her shirt. The blood was warm on her heated skin.

A vine whipped across her face as the monster screamed and left a long, angry cut across Rai's cheek. The blood joined the blood pooling in the hollow of her neck and dripped down her chest. It bloodied her shirt.

Her arms grew heavy and her legs sore. She was light-headed.

A chirp echoed through the dungeon.

"Rai?" Farah's voice rang in her head.

Gentle arms grabbed her shoulders and led her away. Disoriented, Rai allowed herself to be guided away from the monster.

LIGHT bathed her vision, as Rai's eyelids blinked in the sun.

"Is she awake?" Farah asked.

"I think so," Sara said. "Let's get her back to the inn."

Sara tried to take Rai's sword, but Rai's grip was like iron. "It's okay. It's me, Sara."

Rai loosened her grip on the sword, and Sara eased it out of her hand. They lifted Rai from the ground. Sara put one of Rai's arms around her shoulders and Farah took the other. They helped Rai to the inn.

Sara bathed Rai's wounds with water from her canteen and wrapped her hands in cloth ripped from her long nightgown.

Sara put a blanket from one of the bedrooms around Rai's shoulders as she sat beside the fire. Rai had not said a word since they found her in the dungeons.

Farah sat away from the fire, and Sara joined her.

"That screaming," Farah said. "I never heard anything like it. To be able to hear it all the way across the plain."

"I never saw Rai so scared before," Sara said.

Farah sighed.

"What's wrong?" Sara asked.

"She freaked out at the inn in Wyvek. I mean, don't get me wrong," Farah said, "she had reason. But it was so sudden. It was weird."

"What happened?"

"These things, like the ones in Caleena. Long, glowing worms took over my body. It was so strange and scary. Rai didn't want to talk about it. But it was like she had seen it before."

Sara looked back at Rai, who stared blankly into the fire. "How long do you think she'll be like this?"

Farah shrugged.

"I don't like this," Sara said, "that fear in her eyes. I've never seen someone so scared."

SARA walked to the edge of the lake surrounded by blue crystals.

A tapping sounded behind her.

Veil held an abacus. The wooden beads tapped against each other as he slid them down. The frame that held the abacus together fractured and the beads rolled into the water and disturbed its smooth surface.

Panic rang on Veil's face as he scrambled to the ground to catch the beads, but with no success. They were lost to the waters which they had disturbed.

Across the lake, Bolton waved for Sara to come.

She held her foot out over the water.

"No, Sara, you can't." He pointed to a raft wavering in the water. The raft was made of uneven branches, some short, others longer, and woven together with dried reeds.

Sara stepped onto the raft. The raft rocked in the water, and Sara stooped to keep her balance.

The raft moved toward Bolton. The bright light of the rising sun peeked through the trees behind him.

The raft was tossed into the water, and Sara went under. She tried to break the surface, but all she could see was the light reflecting off the water.

She swam in the direction of the light.

Bolton knelt and watched his reflection waver.

Sara burst through the water. Bolton tried to help her up, but in vain. She grabbed his shoulders, and they were both pulled under.

Sara shot up, gasping for air. The campfire lighted beside her. The cool night was dark and quiet as Rai, Farah, and

Orka were still asleep. The green plain stretched out before her, and the lake was far away hidden in the trees and crystals of the forest.

29

FINDINGS

AS the first vestiges of light made their way over the horizon, Rai prepared to leave. She had her sword at her side, and her satchel was heavy with supplies from the abandoned inn.

"Are you alright?" Sara asked.

Farah yawned, and Orka flew from the gate to her shoulder.

"Farah was right," Rai said. "We needed rest. We should get going now. There's death in the sedentary life." She didn't want to talk about what had happened the day before.

Sara looked in her bag. Her weapons and earpiece were there. She wore the nightgown from the night of her rescue. "I'll be right back." She made her way to the inn.

The door screeched open, upsetting the dust that had settled there.

Sara walked down the hallway to the bedrooms. She walked into one room and opened the wardrobe. It was empty of all but dust and spiders.

She tried the next room. On one of the shelves was an old, beige dress. Sara shook out the dust and pulled the dress on over her nightgown. She tied a piece of hemp around her waist.

Back in the hallway, a door hung open. Sara peered inside, and swung the door open the rest of the way.

The bed in the corner of the room was soaked in blood. It wasn't fresh. It had settled into a red-brown stain against the white sheets.

She walked in and looked around the room. "Is anybody here?"

Lifting the bed skirt, Sara searched under the bed. She walked back into the hallway. "Hello?"

She checked each room, but found no one.

The morning light hit her eyes as she exited the inn.

"Ready." Sara picked up her bag.

Orka perched upon Farah's shoulder and ate a small piece of bread which she held in one clawed foot.

"Here." Farah tossed Sara a piece of bread torn from her loaf. "It's getting a little stale, but it's all we have for now."

"It's not from the inn?"

"You kidding? It would be well past stale."

Sara bit into the loaf. Bits of crust flaked down onto the grass. The bread was dry and tasteless.

"Let's go," Rai said. "Hopefully your father feels like having hungry guests."

Farah sighed. "All the way up Regret Mountain without food."

TAG'S tower had only grown taller as Breeze's citizens added floor upon floor of sheet metal bolted together. Torches lit up the area around the tower and the cliff.

"You're back," Tag said.

Sara nodded.

Farah ran up to hug her father. "I'm starving."

"You wouldn't be hungry if you were back in Breeze where you belong," Tag said. "We have food. Come in."

Tag led them to a large mess hall where the workers ate. "Go through there. The workers haven't eaten yet so there's plenty of food."

Inside were tables full of mountain herbs, baklava, grilled leeks, roasted hares, onion soup, pomegranates, pickled pears, chick peas, fried beans, lentils, and salads of lovage leaves, celery, and olives. Pitchers of boiled nectar were at the ends of each table.

Farah rushed to the nearest table and helped herself to a plate full of food. She piled everything she could fit high on the plate and took a seat at the empty table. It wasn't long before she cleared her plate and was up for seconds.

Sara and Rai took a seat beside her and ate.

While they sipped their nectar, Tag settled down across from them on the wooden bench facing the table. He leaned his arms down on the worn wood.

"How has the traveler's life been treating you?" Tag asked.

"Fine," Farah said. She took a gulp of her nectar.

"You sure you wouldn't want to be home," Tag asked, "eating like this every day?"

Farah nodded her head as she leaned her cup back, trying to get the last drop of nectar.

"Was there any luck with your device?" Sara asked.

Tag got up from the table. "Come on. There's something I have to show you."

They followed Tag to the room with the projector. Tag snapped the switch, and the projector lit up. An image appeared on the wall in front of them.

The image was distorted in tones of gray. It showed the body of a man face-down in the gorge. The image went black.

"That's all we got." Tag walked to the back of the room and reached into the supply closet. "When we pulled the machine back up, this is what happened." Tag turned around. He was handling what was left of the device that recorded the image. It was mangled, its glass eye cracked. "I don't know what's down there, but it didn't seem to like my invention."

"You only found one body?" Farah asked.

"That's right," Tag said, "and no sign of the sphere. The image isn't good, and it's been so long, the body's been exposed to the elements. It could be anyone. I'm sending a man down in the morning."

"Is that a good idea?" Sara asked. "Whatever's down there destroyed your machine. What would it do to one of the workers?"

"No scavenger's going to scare *my* men off." Tag sighed.

"Dad, what's wrong?" Farah asked.

"It's nothing. It's nonsense."

"Tell us."

Tag pressed his lips together and let out a whistle of air. "There's this awful howling at night. Like no animal I've ever heard. Not even the Beast. And the men say they see this strange man walking the streets at night . . . like he's looking for something. They say they can see right through his body. I never saw anything, but the men are getting spooked. I'm afraid they're going to cut out on me."

"They're your people," Farah said. "They'll always stand behind you."

Tag scratched his head. "If you're looking for a place to stay for a while, I've got some extra beds. Interested?"

Farah nodded. "Looking forward to breakfast."

*   *   *

SARA, Rai, Farah and Orka shared a room with two bunks. A wide window opened to face the cliff where the torches shined in the darkness.

Farah wrapped the blankets around her to trap in the warmth. "I've slept in the sand, in the bed of a ship, on wooden floorboards, in the dirt, and in the trees. Finally, I get to sleep in a soft bed in a warm room again."

"You don't have a traveler's spirit." Rai sat on the empty bunk.

"Because I know what comfort is?"

"Count on a palace princess for that."

Farah rolled over and faced the wall.

Sara settled down in the bunk below Farah's. "I'm just happy to be free, moving from place to place."

Orka perched on the ladder beside Farah's bed.

"You haven't found a place to call home yet," Farah said. "I feel the same way."

"How about you, Rai?" Sara asked.

Rai looked up at the steel ceiling. "No, I guess I haven't either."

"Maybe we're all travelers at heart," Sara said.

Farah rolled over, head turned to the ceiling.

A loud howl sounded through the air. It echoed. The volume rose like the roar of a couple thousand wild dogs.

They jolted up from bed.

"What could that have been?" Sara asked.

"It couldn't have been one animal," Rai said.

"How do you know it's an animal?" Farah asked.

"Humans don't make that sound," Rai said.

"Animals don't make that sound," Farah said.

Sara hurried to the window and peered into the misty skies. "I can't see anything."

The roar came again.

Orka flew to the windowsill to join Sara.

"What if it hurts someone?"

"We can't fight something if we don't know where it is, much less *what* it is," Rai said. "Choose your battles, and get some sleep."

Rai settled into a deep slumber. Farah managed to eventually drift to sleep. Sara stared, unsettled, into the thick mist.

*   *   *

IN the morning, Tag walked through the city streets. His workers hauled a pulley system three times his size.

The pulley system had a wooden tripod as its base with a pulley at the apex. Through the pulley was a thick rope that pooled at the base of the tripod. Tied to the rope was a harness large enough for a man.

The men carried the pulley system to the edge of the cliff.

A man stepped forward, and the others helped him into the harness. They lowered him down into the gorge. His body disappeared beneath the mist.

Tag watched as the seconds ticked by.

Then came the screams. "Pull me up!" The man screamed at the top of his lungs. His voice was shrill and panicked. "Pull me up!"

The unearthly roar echoed from the gorge along with the sound of heavy feet.

Without waiting for Tag's orders, the workers wheeled the crank, pulling up the rope until the man was lifted from the mist and over the edge of the cliff.

The man was shaking as the workers removed the harness.

Tag placed a hand on the man's shoulder to steady him. "What did you see down there?"

The man's lips trembled. He didn't speak.

"I am ordering you to tell me what you saw!"

The man looked at his leader and said, "A monster."

30

WANDERINGS

RAI looked down into the gorge. "What exactly did he see?"

"I don't know," Tag said. "I'm moving the men out."

"Really?" Farah choked out in surprise.

"That howling . . ." Tag's eyes were distant. He shook off the stare. "I don't want anything to happen to my men."

"And you say they're seeing a man at night?" Sara said.

"It's not your friend," Tag said.

"You've seen him?" Farah asked.

Tag nodded. "He wanders the streets like he's looking for something. I yelled at him from the window, and he didn't even look up. When I went down to the street, he was gone."

"Like he disappeared?"

"Like he walked away." Tag sighed. "Look, I don't believe in that kind of stuff, but the men are scared, and the howling, whatever my man saw down in that gorge, that was real. It's time for us to move back to Breeze. I'm sorry we couldn't find your friend's body. He deserves a proper burial.

"I'm telling the workers the journey home starts in the morning. They'll sleep better knowing that." Tag turned and walked back to his tower.

"Nothing scares my dad like that," Farah said.

"Maybe we should stay and find out what's going on," Sara said.

"It's not your friend Bolton," Rai said. "We need to keep moving. These people are leaving in the morning. We should join them."

"I'm not taking the first ship to Breeze," Farah said.

Sara shook her head. "We can't do that. Morica has the spheres."

"How do you know that?" Farah asked.

"Where are they?" Rai asked.

"In the Domum Fidei. I saw them. Veil's got them tucked away in a tunnel under the temple."

"Did anyone see you find them?" Rai asked.

"Yes, Veil did."

"Then we'll be lucky if they haven't moved them by now," Rai said.

"I don't think Veil would have thought of that," Sara said. "He listens to whatever Mordecai says. We left for Vella City after I found them. And now, he's probably distraught, knowing I ran away." Sara felt pain for Veil. "He won't think to hide them or to tell Mordecai."

"I hope you're right," Rai said.

"I'm not saying we have all the time in the world," Sara said. "But we need a plan. At least Morica has lost our tracks. Now, we have to go back."

"Think again," Rai said. "Tosia, Lumina, even Wyvek will be crawling with Morica guards."

"So, what do we do?" Farah asked. "We have to get the spheres. The Protectors are out of control."

Their earpieces buzzed.

"Shift?" Farah asked.

"It's Thatch."

"How's Thermal?"

"He seems to be feeling better," Thatch said, "but not top notch. I don't think he should be flying yet."

"We know where the spheres are," Farah said. "Tosia. We're planning on heading back."

"I don't think that's a good idea," Thatch said. "Once Thermal heals, he can fly you out of the village. Do you still have the object Sara found at the bottom of the Lake?"

Farah pulled the jagged glass out of her bag. "Yeah, why?"

"Stannum finished analyzing it from the scan he took of it on the Chariot. From the size and shape, he thinks it's an element sphere. Half of one anyway."

"What element is it?" Farah asked.

"We don't' know. When Thermal's better, you can bring it back to the Chariot, and we'll go from there."

"We can't wait for Thermal," Farah said. "They might move the spheres, if they haven't already."

By the time Sara, Rai, and Farah journeyed down to the base of the mountain, the cold had long invaded their boots and chilled their feet to numbness. Sara wore only the night slippers she had on when she escaped from Vella City. Their faces were red from the blasts of wind that escaped Farah's control.

As they approached Jetty Verte, the air became warmer until the sun washed away the frigid cold.

They camped near an abandoned inn.

Rai drew a map in the dirt with the point of Farah's dagger, and they all sat around the diagram. "This is Tosia, and here is the Domum Fidei. Okay, so we need to cause a distraction. Sara, you still have the key, right?"

Sara nodded.

"Okay, so once the guards are out of the way, Sara, you will unlock the door and sneak inside." Rai drew a line to the door of the Domum Fidei.

"Right through the front door?" Farah asked.

"Is there a back door?" Rai asked.

"Not that I know of," Farah said.

"Then, yes," Rai said, "right through the front door."

"But what about Veil?" Sara asked.

"I'll handle Veil," Rai said.

"Farah, you will be waiting here." Rai pointed the dagger toward the spring. "Sara will come out and hand off the spheres to you. Then we leave quickly and quietly. Okay?"

They nodded. Orka chirped.

"You'll have to leave the bird," Rai said.

"Orka knows how to stay quiet," Farah said.

"If anything happens to us, we need someone to get back to Thatch," Rai said. "If Orka can do that, Thatch will know we've been captured."

31

THE OTHER HALF

AS they stepped upon the hard ground of D'arkadia, the Beast could sense their presence. The hairs on the back of its neck prickled. Its large eyes glowed within the mass of black fur. Saliva dripped from the points of its teeth, down its coarse chin.

It waited in the darkness.

Farah cowered in the gloom as Rai led the way. Floating above the palm of Rai's hand was a flame that did not burn her, but she could still feel its heat, even when it was not blazing.

Half-way across the plain, Rai paused. "Stop here."

As she was about to sit, Farah pulled her up by her arm. "I'm not resting here."

"Do you want to exhaust your energy before we arrive in Tosia?" Rai asked.

"Rai's right," Sara said.

"No way," Farah said. "I don't want to see its face ever again."

"Rai, your bag," Sara said.

A glowing light emitted from the satchel secured around Rai's waist.

Rai pulled out the jar containing her Aether. The tiny, semi-transparent mass of energy shone so brightly they could see more than five feet in front of them.

Rai extinguished the flame in her hand. She stepped forward, and the light dimmed. She stepped back, and the glow was strong again. "It's trying to lead us somewhere."

Rai stepped to the right, and the Aether glowed brighter. As she continued, the Aether's glow became stronger. Farah and Sara followed her.

The closer they got, the more the Aether attached to Sara's wrist gun glowed as well.

"I see something over there," Sara said.

It was a cave, jetting out of the rocky ground. Darkness flooded the opening of the cave.

As they moved closer, the Aether's light lit up the mouth of the cave, and dark shadows played on the walls within.

Sara touched the wall of the cave. It was rough, jagged, and bare. Sara entered. Rai and Farah followed close behind her. The Aether lit the way. Orka stayed quiet upon Farah's shoulder.

A sharp curve in the wall led them west. The air became damp and warm the farther they walked into the cave. It was a contrast to the cool, dry air of the rocky plain.

Stalactites hung like stone teeth, some reaching down to the floor of the cave. The ground was difficult to maneuver because of the bumpy, rocky surface. Beneath the rocks was the tiled floor of what was once a temple, lost to the rocky earth.

A glass pedestal rose from the ground, and upon the pedestal was the jagged edge of a broken sphere, its smooth glassy surface hugged by the pedestal.

The Beast emerged from the darkness. Its body crept around the pedestal. It curled its lip up to bare its yellow, dripping teeth.

Rai put the Aether back into her satchel and drew her sword, but its blaze was a poor substitute for the Aether's glow.

Sara pointed her wrist gun toward the Beast. The Beast leapt at her with a roar, and flames emitted from Sara's wrist gun. The flames hit the Beast's face.

The Beast rolled upon the rocky ground, extinguishing the flames with the fur on its legs.

"Grab the sphere," Sara shouted as the Beast lunged for her.

Sara ran towards the entrance of the cave, the Beast biting at her heels. She tripped on the rocky ground and turned over onto her back. The Beast leaped, his body hung in the air above her as she lifted her wrist gun, and lightning flooded the area. A bolt hit the belly of the Beast.

Its feet hit the rocky ground, and its body covered Sara. The Beast rose upon its beefy legs and hovered over her. She could see into its eyes, not like a mirror but like a dark well. She felt lost in its depths and saw despair, the overwhelming need not to be fooled. The more she looked, the more she became immersed in its eyes until she was no longer herself, no longer in her own body.

A man entered the cave. He wore a long cloak to hide his aged body. Beneath his cloak, a strange, red light glowed. His face was like fall leaves, yellowed and wrinkled. Among the age spots that marked his face, a scar stood prominent. It looked like a permanent tear.

Sara tried to speak to him, but this place lent her words no power. They fell like rain too far off to be noticed. She had no bodily presence. It was as if she only sensed the man approaching the sphere. She knew he had come for the sphere.

It was a cave no more. The floors were marble with statues decorating the altar and candles lining the walls.

Sara followed the old man as he entered the sphere sanctum. As he entered, she felt an overwhelming need to protect the sphere. She was looking through eyes enmeshed in a sea of black fur. The Beast had appeared as was a Protector's duty when the sphere is threatened, but the man was prepared. He had a weapon. A gun. He shot, and the Beast staggered, the steel bullet embedded in its leg. The pain was hot, like its leg had touched the surface of the sun. Sara could feel it as she inhabited its body and felt its need and its fear. Still, it lunged, and the man shot it between the eyes. The Beast, bleeding, tried to stand. Unable to be killed, it crawled upon the ground in circles in its own blood.

As the man lifted the sphere from the pedestal and held it up to the glowing light of the candles, the Beast turned to dust and disappeared, but its aura was still strong. Through its bodiless presence, Sara could see what would unfold.

The man turned the sphere in his hands. "It's beautiful," he whispered, "and wrong." His voice was youthful despite his aged appearance.

He clasped the sphere in both hands and sent Water into it until the pressure sent a fissure down the center of the sphere. It cracked in two.

The man placed one half of the sphere onto the pedestal and clenched the other to his chest.

The Beast reappeared upon the return of the half sphere. Once again, Sara's eyes and the Beast's eyes were the same.

The man ran, the Beast quickening at his heels, following the man to the mouth of the cave.

There, an aged woman stood in a brown cloak.

Sara could not see her face through the Beast's colorless vision.

The woman gasped when she saw the man.

With a flick of her wrist, the woman sent the earth down and around the temple. Boulders rolled down, shutting the Beast inside the cave. Darkness spread over its eyes.

*   *   *

SARA blinked as her eyes adjusted to the darkness. The Beast was upon her. "Never again!" a scream echoed through the cave as the Beast lifted one clawed foot, ready to bring it down when it turned to dust.

The Beast disappeared, but its smell lingered, and Sara knew it wasn't truly gone. The Beast's presence hung in the air, like a spirit, stuck and undying.

Sara stood and rushed back to the sphere room where Farah was holding the half sphere.

"You okay?" Rai asked.

Sara nodded. "Let's get out of here."

32

MENDING THE BROKEN

SARA took the jagged glass from Farah's hand. "Where's the other half?"

Farah reached into her canvas bag and retrieved the object Sara found at the bottom of the Lake. She handed it to her.

Sara held both halves in each hand and brought them together. The jagged parts joined like two pieces long separated.

"Stan was right," Farah said.

"So, we have a broken sphere," Rai said.

"Yes," Sara said.

The sphere was devoid of life, no essence swirled inside.

A deep, defeated roar resonated, and a thunderous crash echoed through the cave.

They rushed to the cave's entrance. Boulders fell at the mouth of the cave and blocked their escape. Rai's fingers gripped a stone, but it would not budge. She kicked the boulders and tried to loosen them. Rai's breathing spiked. Sweat poured down her forehead, and her face flushed.

Sara put a hand on her shoulder. "It's alright. We'll find another way out."

"I'm fine." Rai wiped her brow with the back of her hand. "It's just stuffy in here."

Orka's chirp echoed through the cave.

"Come on," Farah said.

They walked past the glass pedestal. Sara felt the pull of the sphere's connection to the pedestal, like a soul to a body.

The further they walked, the smoother the ground became until water touched the tips of their boots.

Sara nodded, and they continued.

As they walked deeper into the cavern, the stagnant water rose to their chests. Rai held her sword ablaze high in the air as she walked. Orka flew from Farah's shoulder as the water touched her clawed feet. The water rose to their chins.

The heaviness of the steel made the muscles in Rai's shoulder and arm burn the longer she held it up above her head. As the depth of the water increased, Rai sheathed her sword. When the blazing sword hit the water, steam hissed.

But they were not plunged into darkness. Light glowed in the distance, and they swam to it.

Light streamed from an opening in the cave wall where the water pooled. The oculus bathed the cave in light. Flowers grew along the cave wall.

Sara touched the ledge and lifted herself up through the opening. The light emitted from the glow of crystals nestled at the base of the trees.

Farah and Rai joined her. Orka flew back to Farah's shoulder.

Sara looked at Farah, but neither said a word.

They walked to the clearing where they had rested three years ago among friends. They sat on the ground where fire had scorched the earth.

Sara's eyes were distant. Farah knew she was reconstructing the past from memory. Farah turned to Rai and broke the silence. "You know Pentagon, the Councilor from Tosia, don't you?"

Rai had thought the name slip had gone unnoticed. "Yeah," Rai admitted with a sigh, "once, a long time ago."

"How do you know a Morica Councilor?" Farah narrowed her eyes.

"We crossed paths in my travels. He wasn't a Councilor then."

"What about Atrus and the leader of the Rebel Resistance?"

"Why are you asking me this?"

"Because," Farah said, "we're going to break into the Domum Fidei and take back the spheres. You're keeping something from us. Don't think I didn't notice all those familiar glances."

"We met in my travels," Rai said. "You think I'm a traitor?"

"You stole a sphere."

"You stole them all."

"Stop," Sara said. "It's no good fighting amongst ourselves."

Farah leaned her chin in her hands.

Night fell, and Rai and Farah slept around the long-extinguished campfire. Sara left the clearing and journeyed to the lake nestled among the crystals.

She knelt and placed her hands on the surface of the water. The gently wavering water felt cool upon her palms. Closing her eyes, she let the silky waves drift between her fingers.

Bolton's promise echoed in her mind. *I'll never leave your side.* Someone took her hands and lifted her. The water drifted across the bottoms of her feet. She looked up.

"I'm here," Bolton said.

"I wish you were," Sara said, "but this is a dream."

"No." He took her hand and placed her palm against his face. "It isn't."

Sara awoke at the edge of the lake. She hadn't remembered falling asleep or taking her slippers off. Her feet were wet. She spotted her slippers at the water's edge. She looked around, daring herself to shout out his name. She sat back down and traced the golden string around her neck.

"It's okay to miss what you once had."

Sara stood. A mouse with a flute and a bloated lizard emerged from among the trees. Sara had met such creatures before—Milbill and Omar.

"Sara?" Farah's voice carried through the trees.

Founten floated above the water, his face surrounded in silver feathers, his owl-eyes calm and alert. "I have come to reveal something to you."

Sara turned around at Founten's voice and faced him. "I'm ready."

"No human has known this. I and my friends have lived for many years. We were here when the world was barren, a blank canvas ready for painting. Energy never dies. It drifts. It becomes something new. But when a light goes out, the energy remains."

"Like when someone dies?" Sara asked.

The feathers on Founten's head wavered as he nodded. "You have a broken sphere."

Sara removed the two halves from her dress pocket and held them in each palm. An Aether appeared, forming in droplets until it was the size of a shield. The Aether glowed, and the two halves of the sphere shined.

Founten nodded, and Sara gave the broken sphere to the Aether. The Aether absorbed the halves into its body until the two pieces floated inside its translucent essence.

Sara watched and waited.

The Aether brought the two halves together inside itself. A brighter, blinding light emitted from the Aether.

Sara turned away and hid her face from the light. When the light was gone, something rolled and knocked against her heel. She picked it up. It was the sphere. The surface was smooth as if no fissure had ever been made. Inside, it swirled dark energy like the dark depths of a well.

Sara turned the sphere in her hand. "The element has been restored?"

Founten backed into the trees. "This is my world as much as it is yours. The spheres must be replaced and the balance maintained. The Protectors have become wandering souls. And you can put a stop to it."

33

OF WAR AND ITS WEAPONS

MORDECAI glided through the streets of Vella City. In the center of the city was Fortress Tower, and the streets branched out from it like the spokes of a wagon wheel. The tunnels beneath the city matched this pattern. The winding dirt trails flowed to every corner of the city like veins beneath the marble surface.

Mordecai's violet robes dusted the cobbled floors as the sun bared his shadow over the stones.

A chariot the size of a shipping vessel waited behind the Resistance barracks. Councilors and Resistance fighters lined up, their hands behind their backs. A man with black hair leaned against one of the large wheels of the chariot.

When the High Councilor approached, the young man extended his gloved hand.

"You must be Boss." Mordecai shook the man's hand.

"That's right."

"Do you go by any other name?"

"Now, High Councilor, are we here for business or to re-hash our life stories?"

Mordecai looked at the chariot. "Does it fly?"

Boss nodded. He patted the cannons affixed to the side of the chariot. "Missile-ready, just like you asked."

"Pay the man," Mordecai instructed one of the councilors, "and see that he is treated to a good supper."

Boss waved his hands in front of him. "No to the supper, but I'll take the money."

"Of course, you will. How many more of these can you have ready for me?"

"I had a feeling you'd like it," Boss said, "so I took the liberty of getting my workers started on two more. They should be ready in a month's time. I have the other one you ordered waiting to be delivered. It should be here by nightfall. For now, you have this one."

"And the weapons that shoot steel?" Mordecai asked.

"Just delivered them along with the chariot. You'll find crates and crates of them in the control room. I could have more for you easy. For the right price, of course." Boss rubbed his fingers together.

"No doubt," Mordecai said.

A blade clamored to the floor. A Resistance fighter stooped to retrieve it.

Mordecai cringed and hurried away.

MORDECAI retired to his room at the height of the marble palace where he kept the ledger of all the tithes that had been collected.

The sky became dark since he left the barracks. Lightning flashed outside the small window of Mordecai's room. But it was a cloudless night. The stars and the moon shone in the dark sky.

A shiver went through Mordecai as he sat on his bed.

A knock like thunder clamored at his door and shook the wooden panels.

Mordecai became quiet and waited.

But the visitor persisted, knocking thunderously once again.

Mordecai got up from his bed. He opened the door only a crack. Fulgur stood outside, his face expressionless and unbothered by the slow response.

"What do you want?" Mordecai asked.

"Entertainment," Fulgur said.

"You won't find it here."

"I always find it here." He pressed his hand against the door.

Mordecai, knowing Fulgur could get in if he wanted to, stepped back and allowed the door to swing open.

Fulgur stepped into the room and sat on the chair in the corner, like a spectator. Mordecai felt like a caged monkey meant to perform tricks for a watchful yet unrewarding audience.

Fulgur, thin-lipped, watched Mordecai's chagrined expression. He needed inspiration. "You're picking off the weak Elementals."

"Does that bother you?" Mordecai asked.

"I'm curious. Where's the threat?"

"In my experience," Mordecai said, "even the weakest Elemental can still breed the strongest foe. I'm eliminating that possibility."

"And your plan is to wipe them out."

"Everything is eventuality."

"Your method is curious," Fulgur said.

"Take out the weak, lower their numbers. Influence the strong to find a reason to side with us, and then control them," Mordecai said.

"How?" There was no look of interest. Mordecai wondered if the man had just come to annoy him.

"A union. An Elemental, a once-Elemental," he corrected, "and a High Councilor. It'll be big news and the gossip of ages. But most of all, it will leave a lasting impression. I can convince Elementals that their powers are a sin against nature."

"You act as if you're going to live forever," Fulgur said.

"I don't have to," Mordecai said. "I have my protégé."

"You know that's not true. Veil is broken, but he doesn't harbor the same personal hate that you do. Elementals didn't murder his parents in the streets for stealing their wares to survive. They didn't leave him an orphan beggar and, later, murderer."

Mordecai cringed at such knowledge, but he was no longer surprised by Fulgur's familiarity with his past.

"My only regret is that I didn't find the Elemental-scum who killed my parents and deal down to him what he deserved," Mordecai said.

"Death?"

"I tried to smash the spheres when they were in my hands, but no human hand can destroy them, isn't that right?" Mordecai asked.

Fulgur cocked his head to the side, his big eyes staring up at Mordecai. The sudden crack of his bones rang through the room. "There is only one Elemental that you didn't kill in her sleep."

"Because she never slept," Mordecai said.

Fulgur's eyes glowed in the dark.

"Are we done?" Mordecai asked.

"There are as many people who love without expression as there are those who express without love," he said.

"What is that supposed to mean?" Mordecai asked.

"How should I know?" Fulgur said. "I am told I am an empty vessel."

34

TAKING BACK THE STOLEN

SARA, Rai, and Farah faced the entrance to Tosia.

"Are you ready?" Rai asked.

Sara nodded and pulled the hood over her head.

They each wore a long, beige cloak to blend in with the townspeople. Farah branched away from Rai and Sara. She positioned herself near the spring where she could be on the look-out.

"Alright, keep your head down," Rai instructed Sara.

Rai and Sara approached Pentagon at the door. Rai lifted her head. Sara stood behind her. Sara's eyes were to the floor, and the hood hid her face.

"What are you doing here?" he whispered.

"I need to see Veil," Rai said.

"Who's with you?" he asked.

"Not your concern," Rai said. "I said I need to speak with Veil. I have a deal to strike with him."

"I don't understand."

"You don't have to," Rai said.

"You know where Sara is," Pentagon said.

"And?"

"Are you going to . . . No, you wouldn't do what Vassal did. You're not a traitor."

"I don't need the moral lesson," Rai said. "I need to get inside. This is what's best for all of us."

"You know the guards are watching," Pentagon said.

"Then they're seeing your suspicious behavior. We used to be a team. What happened to that?"

"We lost our leader," he said.

Rai's eyes deepened. "You can put on that pretend suit and make believe the Morica Councilors aren't a bunch of unjust, lying thieves, but you know better. All those years of fighting by your side must have counted for something."

Pentagon sighed and nodded. He unlocked the door to the Domum Fidei, and Rai stepped inside. Sara followed.

He shut the door behind him. "This way."

Rai followed Pentagon while Sara stayed behind. Pentagon led Rai up the stairs.

Sara darted to the back room. She used the key and tore open the door. She moved the bookcase to reveal the tunnel. Climbing through the hole in the wall, she raced down the tunnel to where she had seen the spheres. The glowing orbs sent a dull gleam through the dark tunnel. Sara withdrew a canvas sack from beneath her cloak, and placed the spheres within the bag.

RAI entered Veil's meeting room. Veil sat at the head of a small table. His eyes were hard and sad at the same time.

"Sit."

Rai sat at the opposite end of the table. She lifted her hood.

"You're Sara's friend," Veil said.

"You could say that."

"Why are you here?" Veil asked.

"She wants to make a deal with you."

"She does?" Veil said in disbelief.

"Her hand in marriage for the spheres," Rai said.

Veil chuckled. "I can't make that deal."

"Because Mordecai won't let you?" Rai asked.

"I don't want to marry her."

"Then I'm talking to the wrong man." Rai stood.

"Wait!" Veil put out his hand.

Rai settled back down.

"May I speak with her?" he asked.

"When an agreement is reached."

FARAH waited at the spring. Orka perched atop her shoulder.

Guards crowded into Tosia. They focused in on the Domum Fidei and carried black batons and crossbows.

"A trap," Farah whispered. She spoke into her communicator. Her voice buzzed to Rai from her earpiece. "We're surrounded."

Rai leapt from her seat, rushed over to Veil, and grabbed him by the collar of his robe. She pulled him from his seat. With her free hand, she drew her sword from beneath her cloak.

"Pentagon didn't check you for weapons," Veil said.

"Is there another way out of here?" Rai hissed.

Veil shook his head. "You shouldn't have brought her here."

Guards burst through the doors of the Domum Fidei, and marched up the stairs.

Pentagon stood at the balcony. Guards grabbed him and secured his hands behind his back. "You are under arrest for crimes against Morica and the High Council."

Rai came through the door, her blade close to Veil's neck. The flames licked the underside of his chin.

"It was a trap for you too," Veil said to Pentagon. "To prove you've been unfaithful."

Pentagon struggled in the hands of the guards.

"Check the tunnel in the bedroom downstairs." Veil's voice was flat. "You'll find her there."

The guards made a move for the stairs.

"Don't move!" Rai pressed the blade against Veil's neck and blistered the skin. "Drop your weapons."

A clatter of batons and steel crossbows hit the floor.

Footsteps sounded on the marble staircase. Fulgur emerged, dressed in his burnt orange robes. He sent an electric current through Rai. She dropped her sword and staggered back as energy invaded her body.

The energy passed from Rai's body to Veil. He knelt as the pain became white-hot.

The guards rushed to detain Rai.

"I'm sorry, High Councilor," Fulgur said.

SARA clenched the bag of element spheres to her chest as she opened the door to the entrance hall. Emerging from the Domum Fidei, she was met by a sea of guards.

Farah was in the distance, her hands secured behind her back by a guard. Several others stood around her.

Sara pulled the clasp at the neck of her cloak, and the cloak pooled to the ground. She raised her wrist gun and shot, sending Wind to knock down the first line of guards.

As her energy became one with the Aether, she sent lightning through the body of a guard, and he knelt before collapsing to the ground.

The guards moved in, backing her against the door to the Domum Fidei. A guard grabbed her arm as she concentrated on fighting off the guards on her right flank.

Flames flew into the faces of the guards, but they overcame her and clasped her hands behind her back. They removed her wrist gun from her arm. As they pulled it away, Sara felt the pull of the Aether holding on, binding to her. But in the end, the guards won. They tore away her wrist gun along with the Aether bound inside.

The guards brought Farah to join Sara outside the Domum Fidei. They pushed Farah to the ground. Orka flew into the face of a guard. His hands buffeted the air in front of him to get her away from his face. Orka screeched as his hand came down on her, and she flew away to a nearby tree where she was lost in the leaves.

"Orka!" Farah screamed.

The guard tried to lift her from the ground.

"No!"

A gust of wind pushed the guards away and knocked them to their backs. Farah put her head down and focused, summoning the energy for her next assault.

Fulgur came through the doors of the Domum Fidei followed by the guards carrying Rai, who had been tortured to exhaustion by Fulgur's biting energy.

Fulgur reached out his hands, and a jolt of energy ran up Farah's spine. Her head shot back in pain. Fulgur stopped, and Farah's head slumped onto her chest.

The guards took her arms and dragged her to her feet.

THE guards dragged them through the streets of Vella City to the marble palace.

The large balcony casted its shadow over them as they approached the palace. Only Sara had energy enough to struggle in the arms of her capturers. She didn't stop, even when Fulgur eyed her.

As they entered the great hall, Mordecai stood in his long robes with two other members of the Council, waiting for them to arrive.

The guards took Farah, Rai, and Pentagon to the dungeons.

"High Councilor Veil," Mordecai said, "You should get ready for the ceremony."

The two councilors escorted Veil to the stairs and down the hall. He looked back at Sara. Guards held her arms. Her hands were bound.

Mordecai noticed Veil's pained expression. "Release her," Mordecai demanded.

A guard untied the rope binding Sara's hands.

Sara rubbed her sore wrists. The ropes left the skin pink and raw like a sunburn. She was grateful that the ropes no longer rubbed against the tortured flesh.

"You've given us quite the adventure," Mordecai said.

"I wasn't trying to entertain," Sara said.

"Well, now there'll be no more adventures," Mordecai said. "You've made it just in time for the ceremony. At dawn, ships will come in from all over Mirmina to watch the marriage of High Councilor Veil and Lady Sara. Take her upstairs to get dressed. We don't have much longer."

35

NUPTIALS

GUARDS escorted Sara to the balcony. She wore the embroidered, cream-colored wedding dress Veil's mother wore when Cronus forced her to marry him.

The balcony was of blue marble, and the marble railing was a silvery gray. Water flowed over the top of the balcony down to the moat surrounding the palace.

A crowd gathered on the floor below the balcony to watch the ceremony. More ships were arriving, and the people flooded in.

Sara's marriage to Veil was to be a public spectacle.

FARAH, Rai, and Pentagon shared a cell in the dungeon of Fortress Tower. The dungeon was cold and damp. Farah sat slumped in a corner. Rai was semi-conscious while Pentagon held her head up from the ground.

Rai turned her head, her eyes fluttering. "Vassal?" Rai blinked twice and opened her eyes. She sat up and looked around.

Pentagon pressed her shoulders back, urging her to lie down, but Rai fought him.

"No," she said. "I'm fine. Farah? Are you okay?"

Farah didn't speak nor did she look up from her slumped position.

"She's been like that since we got here," Pentagon said.

"She's focusing," Rai said. "Gathering strength."

Farah gritted her teeth, and a powerful gust ripped the cell door from its hinges. The barred door clambered against the stone wall.

Farah lifted her head. She stood, staggering until she found firm footing.

The noise alerted the guards, and their voices carried through the dungeon as they descended the stairs. Holding their batons, crossbows, and swords they scrambled through the entrance to the dungeon. As they met Farah, Rai, and Pentagon, a strong blast knocked them off their feet. Heads hit the stone floor.

Farah hurried around the stunned guards followed by Rai and Pentagon.

The guards scrambled for the entrance. Rai sent Fire to block their pursuit. The flames rose to the ceiling, licking the stones above.

Farah knelt by the chest outside the entrance to the dungeon. She used her last lock pick to open the chest where the guards had stored their belongings. Inside was Rai's sword and Aether, Farah's daggers, Sara's wrist gun, and their communicators and earpieces.

Farah put in her earpiece and spoke through her communicator. "Thatch?"

"Are you alright?" Thatch buzzed.

"Who's that?" Shift's voice was distant.

"Farah."

A heavy sigh came from across the room.

"I can barely hear you," Thatch said. "We're following the location on your tracker. We've been flying all night. We're close, but I'm sure we'll make it in time."

"Is Thermal alright?" Farah asked.

"He's not tip-top," Thatch said, "but he's managing."

The connection was lost. "Thatch?" "Thatch?"

"We have to find the spheres," Rai said.

"Sara first. Then the spheres." Farah ran for the exit.

Emerging from Fortress Tower, Rai cut through one of the guards standing watch outside. Pentagon elbowed the other in the face and took his sword.

"You're armed," Rai said. "That means you'll help us."

"That was my plan," Pentagon said.

On the balcony, A councilor escorted Sara to Veil's side. Veil wore his white suit with the short, stiff collar.

Rai, Farah, and Pentagon pushed through the crowd of onlookers. They headed for the palace. In the sea of people, they were unnoticed by the guards.

A burst of wind forced the palace doors open, and the guards standing vigil looked on in shock. Farah swept the guards to the side, knocking them from their posts.

They drew their weapons, and hurried up the stairs. Half-way down the hall to the balcony, Rai's Aether glowed. "The spheres."

"We have to help Sara," Farah said.

"They're distracted," Rai said. "This could be our last chance." She raced down the enjoining hall as the Aether glowed brighter.

SARA took Veil's hand as the councilor led her to the center of the balcony to stand beside him.

The crowd was growing, and the noise was thunderous, but a hush went through them as Sara took Veil's hand.

Veil's gray eyes were regretful, but hopeful at the same time. He grasped Sara's hand tightly so that the quiver in her hand was barely visible.

Four councilor escorted Mordecai onto the balcony. The other High Councilors were seated at the forefront. Mordecai stood in front of Sara and Veil and began the ceremony. They exchanged rings. Veil pulled Sara in for the kiss, but she resisted. Mordecai warned her with his eyes.

Veil neither pulled nor loosened his hold as he waited for Sara. She leaned in. Veil's lips pressed against hers. Once they touched, Veil pressed his lips hard against hers with bruising pressure.

The crowd cheered, unable to comprehend that this was a forced union.

"Stop!" Farah and Pentagon rushed onto the balcony. They detained the guards outside and had their weapons drawn.

"Step away from her, both of you." Farah raised her daggers.

"You've exhausted your energy, Elemental," Mordecai said.

RAI rushed down the hall. The Aether's light glowed several feet in front of her until she came upon a door, guarded by two men.

She approached the men with her weapon drawn. The men withdrew their swords and readied themselves for her attack.

Rai's sword clashed with the sword of a guard, but she had to block the other who swung at her. Fire flew into the face of the second man as her sword remained locked with the first.

The man held his face in his hands as the flames seared his skin. Rai kicked the man down, her sword scraping against the sword of the first guard.

She pushed against the first man until the space was wide enough for her to lift her leg between them. She kicked him in the stomach, and he staggered back.

She raised her sword and cut through the body of the second guard who held his face in his hands as he rolled on the ground.

The first guard cut through the air, his sword once again meeting hers as she drew her blade out of the body of the dead man.

Rai sent flames to surround her blade. The flames licked against the blade of the guard and melted the edge until it was blunt.

She ran her blade up the guard's sword to the tip, forcing him to raise his arms high into the air. Her blade skirted off the tip of his, and Rai turned around, knelt with the guard behind her, arms in the air, body exposed. She pointed her sword behind her, between her arm and the side of her body, and sank her blade into his stomach.

She kicked the guard's body off her sword, and approached the door. It was locked. With no time to search the guards for the key, Rai kicked the door open.

Inside, the spheres rested in a glass bowl on a pedestal. Rai placed each one within her satchel and raced to the balcony.

Guards met her at the end of the hall.

Rai's sword blazed, but only with a dull glow.

The guards in the front of the group matched blades with her. She sliced through the first two guards.

Rai tried to keep the adrenaline up, but she was losing momentum. Cringing, she forced her blade against the blade of a guard. But the remaining guards had their swords and crossbows drawn.

An arrow flew towards Rai. But inches before it hit her, the wood of the arrow cracked in half in mid-air.

Living branches emerged from the walls of the marble palace and wrapped around the arms of the guards and pinned them to the wall.

Rodan focused on the branches. Strong vines wrapped around the sword of the man fighting Rai and ripped the blade from his hand.

"Go!" Rodan shouted.

Rai hesitated.

"Now!"

She ran down the hall, embers falling from her blade.

A guard pinned against the wall withdrew a pistol from his holster. He aimed at Rodan and pulled the trigger. The bullet buried itself in Rodan's shoulder.

Rodan had never seen such a weapon. The wound broke his focus, and the branches disappeared. The guards moved in on Rodan.

THE councilors gathered around Farah and Pentagon. Farah summoned the energy to send a gust of wind, but it wasn't even powerful enough to stagger the many councilors in their steps. Only one lost his balance and fell over the balcony railing.

But the councilors made a wider circle when Rai emerged, her sword blazing. Guards filled the balcony and drew their swords and crossbows.

"Detain the Elementals!" Mordecai shouted.

The roar of the Chariot's engines filled the sky. Shift butted the Chariot up against the balcony, cracking the marble railing.

Rai and Farah pushed through the guards. Rai threatened Mordecai with her sword. The old man raised his hands. "My little thief. At it again."

Farah grabbed Sara's hand, but Veil's grip on her was strong. He clasped her hand in his.

"Let her go," Farah shouted.

Sara pleaded to him with her eyes. Veil looked down at the marble floor and loosened his grip. Sara's hand was torn from his.

Sara and Farah ran to the Chariot. Rai cut down the guards at their heels and cleared the way. Sara and Farah leaped onto the back of Thermal. The engines roared as Shift accelerated.

"Wait! Rai!"

Rai raced to the Chariot, leaped, and caught the railing before Shift took off.

Pentagon was left behind. He was still dressed as a Councilor, and the guards did not recognize him as the enemy. In the chaos, he pushed through the guards. He grabbed the streamers that hung over the balcony connecting the roof of the palace to the ground.

His hands slid against the streamers as he descended. He hit the ground, rolled and landed on his feet. Running for the forest, he looked back. Two chariots, identical to Thatch's apart from their smaller size, raced through the sky. Large cannons were attached to the sides of the chariots, and guards stood on the roofs with guns.

Rai pulled herself up over the railing and onto the roof of the Chariot. Against the wind, she made her way to Thermal. Sara and Farah clung to the back of Thermal as the Chariot tore through the sky, and the wind roared in their ears.

Sara struggled to see Farah, but the wind was so loud and burdensome, she couldn't lift her head from Thermal's back.

Rai lost her footing as the Chariot shook. A missile grazed the side of the Chariot and caused it to shudder. Two smaller, faster chariots flew behind them. Unlike Thatch's Chariot, these vehicles flew without the aid of a large bird like Thermal.

"Morica," Rai hissed.

Thermal screeched as the heat of a missile touched his body.

Rai ran to the railing. "You have to get aboard the ship!" she shouted to Sara and Farah.

Farah climbed along Thermal's back and reached for Rai's hand. Their fingers were less than an inch away.

Shift flew the Chariot lower. "There's nowhere to land." He searched the sea below them.

Lights flashed on the machines lining the control room wall. "The Chariot won't hold up," Thatch said. "We have to release Thermal."

"No way," Shift shouted. "My sister's up there."

"She'll have a better chance with Thermal than we have in here," Thatch said. "Stannum, release the harness."

"No!" Shift shouted.

Farah's fingers grazed Rai's as she balanced on the back of Thermal. The latches securing Thermal's harness released. Farah lost her footing and was torn away in the wind.

"Farah!" Rai screamed.

Sara, still clinging to Thermal, watched helplessly as Farah was swept away. Thermal bolted through the sky. Sara buried her face in his feathers.

36

THERMAL'S PASSENGER

NIGHT fell, but Sara refused to sleep for fear of falling. Thermal, frightened, flew without aim, not stopping. He flew over the endless sea. The ointment Thatch put on his wound was caking and needed to be cleaned and reapplied. The clay ointment became itchy, and in his discomfort and panic, Thermal's wings dipped into the sea.

Sara clung to his body. Her stomach was taunt and empty. Her wedding veil had been lost to the wind, and the roar of the gust bit at her ears.

Thermal's flying became less erratic. He reached his head back to scratch his wound with his beak. His rough beak flaked away the clay salve. Blood dripped into the blue water below him. As it fell and hit the water, it was bright red, but soon dissipated into the blue, dulling to brown and getting lost in the sea of cerulean.

The clouds raced across the sky. Sara had seen night come and go and the sun peek back over the horizon twice.

Sara's eyes begged her to shut them. Her mind drifted. When she awoke, she was belly down in the sand, her face turned to the side. Water came up to the shore to caress her feet. The smell of salt stung her nose.

She lifted her head from the sand. A blurred figure with blond hair approached her.

37

THE DARK ELEMENT

RODAN sat stiffly in the marble chair. Rope bound his feet and arms. His bullet wound weakened him. The steel bullet was lodged inside his shoulder.

He was in a dim lit, round windowless room in Fortress Tower. The heavy oaken door opened, and a man walked in.

This man was bald with yellowed skin. He was old, but his stature made him appear much younger. He turned his pale face to the light and soaked in the silence, tainted with Rodan's ragged breathing.

"My name is Fulgur." He pointed to Rodan's wound, and Rodan felt sharp, excruciating pain ride down his arm to his fingers and back up his nervous system.

His jaw clenched as his body seized.

"Any idea where your friends might be taking the spheres?"

Rodan's body was still shuddering when the question was asked.

Fulgur walked behind his chair and put his fingers on Rodan's temples. The shock that ran through Rodan's body did not affect Fulgur.

As the pain dulled, a second shock ran through Rodan's head. He blinked, seeing only white.

THE High Council gathered in Lumina to make their announcement. They came in a ship with blue and silver sails.

The city of Lumina was crowded. The guards had trouble keeping people off the streets at night, and the jail was at full capacity.

Lucerna walked from the temple to Lumina Stadium.

The stands were full. Many had slept in the rows the night before, not in anticipation of the High Council's announcement, but because the inns were overflowing, and it was easier to hide from the guards between the rows of seating.

Mordecai stepped forward onto the balcony overlooking the stadium. His leathered skin had been assaulted by the sun. His blue and silver robes streamed in the breeze.

Mordecai's voice boomed. "It is with great regret that I inform you all of this. A group of Elementals have kidnapped High Councilor Veil's young wife, the Lady Sara. She did not go willingly, but was ripped from the arms of her husband shortly after her wedding ceremony. The High Councilor is in severe distress and cannot make any public appearances at this time. I ask that with faith and loyalty, you hold out your hearts to High Councilor Veil in his time of need."

VEIL brought his hand down hard upon his mother's desk and knocked down her perfume bottle, which cracked, filling the room with her fragrance.

Tears fell. She had left him. Again.

Anger took him. He stood from his chair and thrashed the desk against the wall. Darkness crept into the room. Not any darkness, pitch black, nothingness.

Veil blinked, and the darkness receded back into his mind.

Something dripped from his hand and landed on the floor. He lifted his hand, blackness covered it, dripped to the ground, and created a gaping chasm of darkness. At first, he thought ink had spilled, but it was something more. He knew that blackness was not flat. It extended down like the depths of a well.

He knelt and reached into the hole. As his hands searched, the hole grew wider. He grasped something and pulled it out. It was heavy and difficult to move, like he was pulling it through thick tar.

He pulled the figure out from the darkness. It was a body, covered in sticky, black mucus. The figure opened her gray eyes, the eyeballs shining white in the blackness.

Veil's blackened hands shook, and the tears in his eyes dried. "Mother?"

38

THE KEEPERS

THE old man walked upright from the cave as the boulders blocked the Beast's escape.

Dawn, an old woman with papery yellow skin and silver hair, waited outside. Her pale blue eyes could see only shades of dark and light.

"Destan," Dawn said. "You are unwise. Erebus will be angry."

"What I did," Destan said. "That was power, and it was wrong. These are my efforts in setting it right."

"Vella City flooded because you were sad. We Keepers have stronger emotions. We have to be strong and forget."

Destan walked away from the cave.

"You must stop this."

"That's what I'm doing."

Dawn reached out as he passed and grabbed him by the shoulder. She looked at him with her sightless, pale blue eyes. "We are their gods."

39

PAIN AND DISCOVERY

SARA'S eyes blinked open. In the blurry haze, she saw a figure standing on the beach. His blond hair was bright under the sun. Before her vision cleared, the figure disappeared beyond the sand.

Sara turned her cheek to the side, and the grains of sand stuck to her warm skin. Her whole body ached from the fall. Her wet hair revealed that she had hit the water first and washed up upon the shore, but her mind could not remember those near fatal moments.

The tide touched her legs as it came in. Seagulls sounded overhead, and the smell of sea-salt sobered her.

Her vision returned, becoming clear for the first time. She blinked against the sun and lifted her arm to shield her face with her hand. Her shoulder ached.

Someone turned her over onto her back. She looked up at the strange faces of men and women. They blocked the sun with their bodies as they looked down at her. Among them was

the blond figure, a young boy who had run for help when he
saw her.

The strangers lifted her from the ground and brought her
to their village.

Sara tried to turn her head to get an idea of her surround-
ings, but it hurt to try. She felt the flaps of a tent sweep past her
body and the softness of the cushions the strangers placed her
upon.

Sara tried to thank them, but her throat was so dry all that
came out was a raspy whisper. She pressed her lips together.
They felt flaky and blistered.

A woman brought a cup to her lips and lifted her head.
Sara ignored the pain as she drank the water from the wooden
cup, her lips pressing hard against the edge.

When the cup was empty, the woman pulled it back. She
wore a beaded veil atop her head, and her clothing was bright
and covered in beads as well. Her face showed her age with its
many lines running through the tan skin, but her hair was black
without a hint of gray.

"Thank you," Sara managed to say.

"You must have come a long way. We saw a massive
shadow over the island. We thought it was a bad omen. And
here you are."

"Island? Where am I?" Sara asked.

"You are on the Insula."

Sara tried to sit up, but she cringed.

The woman shook her head and pressed Sara down into
the cushions. "You should rest."

"I've been looking for this place," Sara said.

"So have many others. It was luck that you washed up
here. It would have cost you to come, and the ferryman is hard
to find."

The tent was large with beads decorating the inside and
pottery small and large at each corner.

"Who is the lord of this place?" Sara asked.

"Lord? We don't have one."

"I'm looking for someone," Sara said.

"Someone who lives here?"

Sara tried nodding her head, but sharp pains ran up her neck. "A man who used to live here when he was a boy. Maybe he returned?"

"I'm sorry," the woman said, "You are our first visitor in over ten years."

"Are you sure?"

"The island is small. I know everyone who lives here. I'll get you some food."

The woman drew away from Sara's bedside, but Sara clasped the woman's hands and pulled her back.

"Do you know everyone who has ever lived here?" Sara askcd.

"You must rest." The woman pressed Sara back against the cushions and stood. "My name is Abby. I will be your nurse until you are better, which should be by tomorrow morning. What's your name?"

"It's Sara."

"Well, Sara, I hope you feel comfortable here. The ferry-man doesn't come to the island unless someone pays him. If you're lucky, he'll come in the next ten years, and you can go home."

The woman left the tent.

THAT night, Sara managed to sit up despite the pain. She felt stronger now that her thirst was quenched and she had eaten. Her legs wobbled as she stood.

She took one labored step at a time until she reached the entrance of the tent. She pulled back the tent flaps. Fifty tents filled the area surrounded by a bamboo gate.

The night was dark, but as Sara turned her gaze back inside the tent in the hopes of finding a lantern, she realized that the inside of the tent was even darker.

She decided to let the stars be her guide. Under the light of the moon and the stars, her legs, gaining strength, brought her to the entrance of the gates, which were unbarred.

She moved through them undeterred. The land was raised so she could see the beach in the distance beyond the balmy trees.

The path down to the beach was bordered by high, rocky plateaus. She followed the path until it split in two. In one direction, the sand and dirt gave way to grass, and in the other, the path sloped up and became long and narrow.

She followed the long, narrow path to a wooden bridge above a gorge. Trees with large smooth leaves grew on either side of the bridge.

The bridge gave way to a natural path with a stream, which led to a ledge with a small waterfall spilling into a lagoon.

Three years before, Bolton told Sara that when he was a boy, he hid a box under a waterfall. Sara dared to think that this could be the one.

She looked down into the lagoon. A gentle slope allowed for clear passage further down without touching the water.

Sara descended upon the slope. A small nook hid behind the waterfall. She reached inside and felt a wooden object, which she pulled out.

It was a box about the size of a brick.

Sara lifted the latch on the wooden box and opened it to reveal its contents. The box contained coins and pretty stones.

Sara lifted a metal plate from the box. It was the size of a handheld mirror and had holes at the top and bottom. A ribbon ran through each hole, looped around, and was tied tight.

There were symbols on the plate. On one side was a triangle, the symbol for Fire and on the other was a bolt, the symbol for Lightning.

Sara's foot slipped upon the wet slope. She landed in the lagoon with a splash. The box slipped from her hand, but she still grasped the metal trinket between her fingers.

She peered into the green waters and hoped that the little, wooden box would float up, but the coins and stones weighed it down. Sara ducked her head under but could not see the box within the dark waters.

Swimming back to the ledge, she clutched the metal trinket, afraid to lose it. She tried to pull herself up from the wet slope, but her fingers slipped from the rocks and wild grasses.

Seeing nowhere else to go, she swam further out, and the sky darkened. The lagoon led her into the mouth of a cave. On the ceiling and walls of the cave were tiny specks of light like stars.

She swam until she saw a ledge leading out of the cave. She pulled herself up with some effort. Her body was still sore. Her hair and clothing dripping, she walked to the village, the metal trinket clenched in her hand.

40

THE OLD SCHOLAR

SARA sat outside her tent. She studied the metal trinket. As she held the ribbons taunt, the metal plate twirled. The images on the plate tricked her eye as they spun, and the symbols intertwined.

Two villagers passed her tent.

"The Old Scholar will help us. He is wise. He will tell us what the shadow means."

The Shadow? He must mean Thermal. When he flew over the island, Thermal casted his great shadow over their village and eclipsed the sun.

"Hey, what's that?" The blond-haired, young boy who found Sara on the beach stared at the metal trinket.

"I think it belonged to a friend of mine," Sara said.

"What is it?" the boy asked. The beads on his shirt clinked together as he sat crossed-legged beside her.

"Maybe a toy," Sara said.

"Where did you get that, girl?" Abby put down the basket of yellow fruits she was carrying and knelt next to Sara. Abby took the metal trinket from her hands.

"Please, give it back," Sara said.

"Where did you find this?" Abby asked again, this time looking Sara right in the eye. The intensity of her gaze frightened Sara.

"Why?" Sara asked.

"You shouldn't be playing around the island. These things aren't yours." Abby stood, trinket in hand, and turned her back on Sara. "Come, Balin." The boy joined Abby.

Sara stood. "I know the man who owns that."

Abby turned back to Sara. "A man never owned this. He was a boy. He never grew to be a man."

Abby again turned to walk away.

But Sara persisted. "His name was Bolton. He was my friend."

"How do you know that name?" Abby asked. "You are a cruel-hearted girl who washed up onto this island and started taking things."

"I know him," Sara said.

Abby struggled to keep her voice firm, but it shook as she said, "He died. He burned to death with his mother. And the bodies, the ashes washed away with the sea."

"Did you know him?" Sara asked.

"Who are you to ask questions of the people of this island, to bring out memories of our past that hurt us?"

"Who is the lord here?" Sara asked.

"I told you. We have no lords."

"Who is the Old Scholar?" Sara asked.

"He is not our lord," Abby said. "He's been a father to Balin. His true father left him to travel the world. The Old Scholar is wise, but he is no lord."

"I want to speak with him," Sara said.

"Why? So, you can pry more into our lives."

"What is the meaning of this?" One of the islanders stopped to intervene. He was a tall, broad man. His skin was browned from the sun. "Oh, Abby, are you trying to stop our guest from seeing the Old Scholar?"

"She's here to pry and disrespect us," Abby said.

"She came from another world and is here to learn about ours. Show her kindness."

"You are not my keeper, Cirtus," Abby said.

"And you are not hers," Cirtus said.

Abby turned and left with Balin following behind her.

"Thank you," Sara said.

"So, you want to see the Old Scholar," Cirtus said.

"If it wouldn't cause trouble."

Cirtus looked to Abby who glared at him from her tent. "You don't have to worry about that now. The bridge is already burned as they say. Come on, I'll lead the way."

"Who is the Old Scholar?" Sara asked. "What's his name?"

They passed the rows of tents. Though Abby had given Sara a beaded dress to wear, the people still stared at her like an outsider. She could feel their stares as one feels the heat of the flames while sitting around a campfire.

"His name?" Cirtus said. "We call him the Old Scholar. That's his only name. He claims to have lived here all his life, but he's well-traveled. He tells the children stories of his journeys, especially the one about the great orb."

Sara grabbed his arm, and they stopped outside a large tent covered in wooden beads. "What are you talking about? The great orb?"

"The one that took his youth," Cirtus said. "Here's his tent."

Cirtus pulled back the flap, and Sara stepped inside.

A beaded mat adorned the floor of the tent and led to a pile of cushions. A man of eighty or ninety years of age rested upon the cushions. He faced the back of the tent and muttered a prayer. He was dressed in blue pants that fanned out and a beaded shirt. His white-blond hair was long and full and braided down his back.

Sara felt uncomfortable, like she intruded on something sacred. She turned to leave when the old man lifted his head and said, "It's alright. Please, sit."

His voice surprised Sara. Though the man looked ancient, his voice was clear and youthful, strong and firm.

Sara sat on the beaded mat.

The old man turned where he sat until he faced her. His beard covered his neck, it was thick, blond, and curly with streaks of white running through it. His mustache was the same: thick with streaks of white. His mouth disappeared in the mess of curls. His forehead was high and broad. Heavy, dark brows hung above his eyes, which were crystal blue beneath the dark clouds.

He held a look of calm seriousness cloaked with a touch of sadness that he carried with him through the ages. "Have you come for my stories, Traveler?"

"Perhaps," Sara said. "I hoped you could tell me the story of a boy. His name was Bolton."

The look of sadness that hung over him deepened, and the clouds above the crystal blue eyes darkened. "I'm afraid I can tell you only a few short years of his story. After that, I wish I knew. Where did you hear his name?"

"Can you tell me what you know about him?" Sara asked.

"I know he was an adventurous child, curious and daring. And loyal to his mother . . . and his father. Innocent. What happened to him was a crime, and no one paid for it."

"That isn't true," Sara said. "The man who took him, Hephaestus, he paid in the end. I suppose he's in the dark now . . . forever."

"What do you mean, Traveler?"

"My name is Sara," she said. "Bolton was by my side when we fought Hephaestus. He died in that fight."

The old man's eyes were distant, and his mouth hung open.

"Did you know him well?" Sara asked.

"Yes, I knew him well. How did he die?"

"He fell . . . from a cliff, to save me."

"He must have loved you." His eyes were distant and his voice ominous.

41

BETWEEN THE SEA AND THE SKY

SARA pulled back the flaps of the tent and stepped outside. Cirtus was waiting for her.

"Was this helpful?" he asked.

Sara shook her head. "The Old Scholar knows him, but he can't tell me what I need to hear."

"That he lives?" Cirtus asked.

Sara took a deep breath. "I know that's not possible."

Balin ran up to them. In his hand was the metal trinket. "I took this back for you. You seemed to like it very much."

"Thank you," Sara said. "I don't think your mother would like that you gave it back to me."

"I don't care what she thinks," Balin said. "She shouldn't have taken it from you." He turned and ran off toward the entrance gates.

"Where's the boy's father?" Sara asked.

Cirtus looked in the direction the boy had gone. "No one knows. He never married Abby. She was his comfort when his wife and child died in a fire."

"What fire?" Sara asked.

"They lived on a boat at sea," Cirtus said. "His name was Benn. He built that boat for his family at the coast because they were always afraid. Of what, no one knew, but they were ready to leave at a moment's notice. They were a good family. They raised their child here. Everyone on the island loved them."

"Benn, the Lightning Elemental?" Sara asked.

"That's right," Cirtus said. "Did the Old Scholar tell you?"

Sara shook her head. "Benn was Bolton's father. I knew Bolton."

"The boy died in the fire."

"I wish people would stop saying that. He didn't die." Sara failed to stop the words. He had died, but not the way the islanders thought.

"Someone who came from the island must have lied to you. The boy died with his mother. For years, Benn mourned them. Abby comforted him, and he fathered a child with her.

"But he never stayed to see his child grow. He left the island, driven mad by memories of his wife and son, and never returned. No one has seen him in over ten years.

"That's when the Old Scholar came. The boy was only five when the Old Scholar descended in a lightning storm. He favored the boy and raised him as his own.

"Abby was relieved because she had no way of helping the boy control the Lightning that issued from his very being. He still struggles, but the Old Scholar has helped him to calm and control his powers."

"They're brothers," Sara said under her breath.

"Say again?" Cirtus asked.

"Balin and Bolton. They're brothers."

"Had Bolton lived, yes."

"Why are you so convinced Bolton died that day?"

"Because we all heard the screams."

Sara closed her eyes and tried to think of something other than the screams of a mother and her child. Her eyes popped open. "You said Balin struggled with his element. When was the last time he had trouble? Was it three months ago?"

"How did you know?"

"My friends. They can track energy. They can see it on a map. To send a message to them, I need Balin to use his element. He must bring another lightning storm."

42

AIR ASSAULT

BLASTS shook the Chariot. While Rai tried to keep her footing on the roof, Shift and Thatch attempted to avoid the missiles from the control room.

"Tell me this thing has something we can shoot back at them," Shift yelled over the squealing of the missiles.

"I didn't build this ship for battle," Thatch shouted.

The Chariot rocked, throwing Stannum against the wall. The little machine shook himself until something rattled inside his head.

"Then there's only one way out." Shift aimed the Chariot toward the sea.

"Rai, get off the roof!" Thatch said into his communicator.

"Farah fell!" Rai shouted.

She could sense Thatch's teeth clenching from across the air waves.

"I'm turning around," Shift said.

The Chariot jerked and rattled.

"We can't," Thatch said. "Shift, we won't make it."

Shift punched the steering wheel.

"We'll go back for her," Thatch said.

"Do you know where Thermal's going?" Rai asked. "Where he could be taking Sara?"

"The chariot is going down. I need you inside now!" Thatch's voice boomed through Rai's earpiece. The door to the roof opened for her, and she escaped into the Chariot before it hit the waves.

The Chariot broke the surface of the water with a crash, and the sea swallowed it.

AS the Chariot washed up upon the shore, the occupants emerged from the ship, tired and hungry, having exhausted their rations. From the shore, out into the distance, were miles of sand.

"Where are we?" Rai asked.

"The shores of the Windy Desert," Shift said. "Beyond is the City of Breeze, my people."

"How far?" Rai asked.

"Too far," Thatch said. "More than two weeks without food or water. There's an oasis halfway between, but the chances of us reaching it before nightfall are slim. And when night comes, so do the coyotes and the cold."

"So, what then?" Rai asked. "We stay here to die? We have no food, no water."

"The Chariot can move across land," Thatch said. "But if I can get it back up and running for long enough to get us to Breeze, it would be a miracle. At most, it can get us to the oasis. From there, I'm not sure."

"If there's no other choice," Rai said, "let's get back into that contraption and try to make it move."

They climbed back into the Chariot from the roof.

Thatch turned to Rai. "There's a generator in the engine room. Can you get down there and pull the starter switch?"

Rai nodded. She descended to the engine room through the ladder in the elevator shaft.

Shift sat in the driver's seat.

"Are you there?" Thatch spoke into his communicator.

"Here," Rai said, "I can see the switch."

"Alright, give it a go." Thatch's voice buzzed over Rai's earpiece.

Rai flipped the ignition, pulled the starter, and the engine roared to life.

"Ready," Rai said.

Shift increased the throttle and brought the wheels out. The wheels lifted the Chariot from the sand. Shift pulled back on the steering wheel, and the Chariot launched across the desert.

By nightfall, they made it to the gates of Breeze. The Chariot's engine gave out a few feet from the entrance.

"We were lucky," Thatch said. "I'll need to inspect further and find the parts I need. I have to get the Chariot up and running again."

"This time put missiles on it," Shift said.

At the gate, the guards let them in, recognizing Thatch and Shift. All three passed through the gates. Stannum floated at their side.

"It's getting dark," Thatch said. "I'll have to start work in the morning."

"Where's the nearest inn?" Rai asked.

"We're not staying in an inn," Shift said. "My father is the leader of this place. We'll stay in his palace."

"That would require you to face the man your father asked to rule in his stead," Thatch said.

"I'm not going to let a man keep me from my home. My father didn't."

Shift marched up to the door of the steel palace and pressed the buzzer.

"Yes?" a woman's voice sounded.

"It's Shift. I've come home."

"Welcome back, sir."

The door to the steel palace slid open.

Shift ascended the many steps leading up to the higher levels of the building. Thatch, Rai, and Stannum followed him. He stopped at a heavy metal door and opened it. "This is my room, you two can share the room across from mine."

"Share?" Rai said.

"What about me?" Stannum asked.

"The machine too." Shift opened the heavy metal door in one swift gesture, stepped inside and shut it behind him.

"That man hasn't said a word about his sister," Rai said.

"He's worried about her," Thatch said. "He's just not the type to say it."

RAI fell asleep in the armchair by the window. A knock sounded at the door. The sun set on the desert, and a cool breeze issued from the glassless window.

Thatch went to the door and opened it as Rai blinked away her sleep.

A woman dressed in silver handed Thatch a note. She nodded to him and descended the stairs.

"What is it?" Rai asked.

Thatch unfolded the note and read. "General Riee wants to have dinner with us tonight."

"Who's General Riee?" Rai asked.

"The man Uncle Tag asked to rule while he's away."

Loud banging came to the door.

Thatch opened it.

"Did you get this?" Shift crinkled the letter in his fist.

Thatch held up his note. "I think we should go. Out of respect."

"Respect?" Shift said. "This is my home, not his."

"I could use a hot meal," Rai said. "And if this general has offered, I will certainly take."

"It's dinner. Perhaps an act of good will," Thatch said. "Riee did not ask Uncle Tag to offer him the city."

"He's a dog for accepting it," Shift said.

"Really?" Thatch said. "You don't know your own father. Tag doesn't ask. He demands."

"If the old man wishes to serve me," Shift said, "I can't say I won't let him, but he has no right to offer me to dine in my own house."

A couple hours later, women dressed in silvered escorted Shift, Rai, and Thatch into the dining room. Three candles rested on the long metal table covered with silver plates filled with wild seeds and pinon-nuts, a large bowl of soup made with rice, beans and mustard, a platter of dried raspberries, elder-berries, and rose-berries. The main course was dried fish.

At the head of the table sat General Riee. His gray suit came up to his neck. His sharp pointed chin covered the only flesh that escaped the collar. His dark skin was thin and weath-ered. His nose was large and hooked over thin lips. The eye-brows had gone white as had his hair which floated atop his head like wispy white clouds. His eyes were big and intense, light-gray steel.

Shift took a seat at the opposite end of the table.

Rai and Thatch sat opposite each other on either side.

The room was quiet as the women prepared their plates and poured the wine.

Once everyone was served, General Riee interrupted the silence. "It's nice to have you all here. Thatch, I'm glad you have returned. You're the only one who knows a thing about energy in this city, and we're in desperate need of someone to help the workers and to teach the little ones.

"And who are you, young lady?"

"A friend," Rai said.

Riee turned to Shift. "You haven't commented on the fish. Fish is a delicacy in the desert, or have you forgotten that in your travels?"

Shift looked up from his plate, knife and fork in each hand. His lips were pressed hard together. "This is *my* food and *my* home," Shift said. "You are *my* guest. I am not yours."

"You're right, son, but your father has put me in a certain position of power."

"That position belonged to me as his son," Shift said. "A stranger does not belong as leader of Breeze."

"Am I a foreigner to you, then?" Riee asked. "I am not a stranger to your father. I fought beside him in many wars."

"As have I," Shift said.

"Correct me if I'm wrong, but you have fought beside him in one battle. You are hardly fit to run a city or to defend one, especially now, that you are significantly . . . disempowered."

Shift stood and would have lunged at him from across the table had Thatch not rose from his seat and took him by the shoulders.

"Not wise," Thatch whispered.

"We've had a long trip, General," Thatch said. "You'll understand if we're all very exhausted and frustrated from the journey."

"Of course. We can try again tomorrow evening."

Shift was still fuming, but Thatch managed to turn him around by the shoulders.

Rai ate the fish.

"Rai?"

She downed her cup of wine and grabbed a handful of dried berries before joining Thatch and Shift.

When they were outside the door, Shift shook Thatch from him. "You should have let me punch him square in his leathery face." He marched back toward his room. Thatch and Rai followed.

"And then what?" Thatch asked. "You need to rest. You know he's not your only concern. Don't let that affect your judgment."

Shift stepped into his room and slammed the door.

*　　*　　*

A commotion from the street below woke Rai and Thatch.

Rai's fingers clenched the windowsill as she leaned out to look.

Men dressed in rubber suits from head to toe were holding onto thick silver ropes. Tied to the ropes was a horse, its body made entirely of Lightning. It reared up, causing one of the men to lose his grip on his end of the rope. He scrambled on the ground to find it, his sight hindered by the rubber mask.

The street was clear except for the Protector and those men. The citizens watched from their houses as Lightning glowed in the still dim morning.

Thatch joined her at the window. "A Protector?"

"Why do you seem so surprised? Your people have taken a Sphere Protector before." Rai rushed to the heavy metal door, sword in hand.

"Where are you going?" Thatch shouted, his eyes still glued to the scene outside the window.

Rai skipped steps as she launched down each stairwell. She burst through the door of the steel palace and marched into the square.

The Protector was still rearing up, trying to free itself of its captors. It saw Rai. Its glowing yellow eyes met her black ones.

Rai lifted her sword and brought it down on the silver ropes that bound the Protector. The ends of the ropes snapped into the faces of the rubber-suited men.

"What are you doing, girl?" General Riee tore off his rubber mask. He was at the forefront of the square.

The Protector reared up as the final rope was cut, and a burst of Lightning flew into the face of the General. The bolt stunned him to the ground as the sensation like white hot fire seared his temple.

The Protector turned and galloped through the open gates of the city and into the desert.

The men rushed to the general's side. Someone proclaimed him dead.

Shift joined Thatch at the window.

Thatch's eyes anchored to the scene outside. "You're the leader of Breeze now, cousin. Just like you wanted."

"I didn't want the man to die," Shift said.

Thatch shook his head. "I'm going to inspect the Chariot. I hope you're with us when we decide to leave. Farah would want you to be there when we find her."

Thatch clapped his cousin on the back and exited through the north gate to service the Chariot.

Rai approached Shift, her fiery sword still drawn.

"Why?" Shift asked.

"A Sphere Protector has no place among the people. Your general found that out first-hand."

That evening, Rai and Shift sat at the large metal dining table. Eating the cold dish that was to be General Riee's dinner.

"How do you like no longer being a guest in your own home?" Rai asked.

"I was never a guest," Shift said. "Riee was mistaken if he thought so."

"What will you do if Thatch gets the Chariot running?"

"Dare I say he might never get it flying again? Morica somehow got theirs to fly. Thatch will take it as a challenge. If he does, I'll have to stay here with my people."

"Who will fly the Chariot?" Rai asked.

"I'll teach you."

"Me? My feet have served me just fine."

"Your feet have served you on your travels before?" Shift asked.

"Yes."

"I'd like to hear of these travels," Shift said.

Rai sighed. "There's nothing to hear. I got bored, so I journeyed to see what lie beyond the Lake de Somnia."

"And you saw?"

"Nothing you haven't seen on your travels with Thatch and Farah."

Shift frowned at the mention of his sister, an expression so slight Rai missed it.

THATCH sighed.

"What is wrong?" Stannum asked in his metallic voice.

"I can replace the metal siding that was damaged from the bursts, but the engine is shot. I'd need a jolt to get her started again. It would power down the whole city."

"What about the windmills?"

"I don't think there's enough energy stored. I guess I'll get the scraps. If the Chariot is dead, I'm not going to let her die bruised."

Thatch's arms were heavy with scrap metal. He piled the sheets of metal in front of the Chariot, open to the engine room. When Thatch turned around, he froze.

Not far from where he stood, was the Sphere Protector. Its static head was pointed toward the Chariot's engine room. Lightning buzzed around its body, which was made of the same.

Thatch felt numb. He wanted to run, to duck into the engine room and hide among the machines. He saw what this creature had done to the General.

But he stood, wide-eyed, staring at the Protector as it reared its head, and Lightning zoomed toward him.

Thatch ducked, but the Lightning wasn't headed for him. It struck the engine of the Chariot inside the gaping engine room. The engine whirled to life, and the pistons shuttered.

Thatch looked up at the sound, and the Protector was gone. He looked back at the engine room and its many machines working away.

"I'll be damned," he whispered under his breath.

"SHIFT!" Thatch rushed up the metal steps and burst into the dining room.

"Decided to join us?" Shift asked from the table.

"I need you, now!"

Shift rose from his seat and put his napkin down. He and Rai followed Thatch out through the gate and to the Chariot.

"I need you in the driver's seat," Thatch said.

Ascending to the control room, Shift took the steering wheel while Rai and Thatch looked on. Shift increased the throttle.

The hatch to the engine room shut, and the wheels extended from the Chariot to the ground. The Chariot picked up speed, racing through the desert.

Shift pulled the steering wheel back, and the forefront of the Chariot lifted into the air. The wheels retracted into the body as the Chariot sailed into the sky.

"Whoa!" Shift said. "Thatch you're a damn genius. You did it!"

"The Protector gave us the jolt we needed," Thatch said.

"What?"

"Yeah, it was weird. I could have sworn the thing was going to hit me, but it aimed for the engine as if it knew," Thatch said. "Let's go back to the city and get some supplies. Then we can all get out of here."

"Don't get too excited just yet," Rai sobered him. "Our driver wants out."

"I have a duty to the people of Breeze," Shift said. "I would be leaving them leaderless."

"Install a new leader," Thatch said.

"I need to take my rightful place," Shift said.

Thatch put a hand to his temple and shook his head. "This is about your pride? You promised me you wouldn't think about that mess when you left. This isn't about your role in the city. It's about proving yourself to your father. To him, you'll never be good enough for the city. When Tag returns, you'll get a heap of criticism with zero acceptance or gratitude."

"I'm teaching Rai to fly," Shift said.

"Wait a minute," Rai said, "I told you . . ."

"I know. Your feet have served you well. And how much better will flying serve you?" Shift said. "We've covered miles in hours. It's time you learn to travel efficiently."

"We don't have time for flying lessons," Thatch said. "Sara and your sister are out there somewhere. We have to find them before Morica does."

Shift landed the Chariot, diving it into the sand. He was breathing heavy.

Rai thought he might be sobbing.

Without turning around, he said, "I must be here for my people."

43

SO GOES THE CAPTAIN

RAI grasped the steering wheel of the Chariot as it sailed through the skies. Never had she handled something with more masterfulness than she did her sword.

She took to flying with ease. So much so that after instructing her for less than an hour, Shift had called her a liar. She kept many things in her past cloaked, but flying wasn't one of them.

Thatch sat at his seat and stared at the blue screen above his head. He was angry at Shift for his arrogance and inability to see his father's impenetrable opinion of him.

Farah, his own sister, was out there somewhere, and Shift had chosen to stay behind. Farah was strong. Thatch didn't want to believe she was gone.

Thatch worried for the great bird, Thermal. Never, after he had been taken from Demlama, had Thermal stayed this long out of Thatch's presence. Thatch didn't doubt the bird could find food, but he didn't want the great creature coming against Morica only to be slaughtered by their metal bullets.

He pondered how Morica could have obtained those chariots so like his design.

"It's a long way to the coast of Vella City without talking," Rai said.

"What do you want to talk about?" Thatch asked.

"Do you think we'll find them?" she asked.

"We can hope," Thatch said. "You said Farah was lost over the sea. She may have washed up on shore. Knowing Farah though, she'd make it to the city on her own. Her communicator may have been water-logged. With no way to reach us, she would have moved on.

"Sara could still be with Thermal. But it's unlikely she would find us."

"What will we do if we don't find them?" Rai asked.

Thatch shook his head.

Rai rubbed her eyes. "How did Shift fly through the night like this?"

"He slept when he could, but you haven't quite built up the resistance. We should land and find a place to sleep."

"No . . . I mean, I'll be fine."

Thatch looked outside the window. "There! There's the coast. Can you land?"

Rai nodded. She pushed the steering wheel in, tilting the forefront of the Chariot downwards. She landed the Chariot along the coast.

"Let's get out and search." Thatch stood.

He and Rai exited from the engine room. From the coast, they could see the cliff where Vella City was perched. The blue marble palace gleamed in the sun. The wedding banners were still streaming.

"Do you think they spotted our Chariot?" Rai asked.

"No," Thatch said. "We flew above the clouds."

They searched the coast for hours shouting Farah's name until their stomachs growled for food and their lips ached for water.

"This is hopeless," Rai said as Thatch met her in the cabin room. She downed a bottle of water and opened the trunk to take what she could of the bread and cheese.

"You're right. We could spend a year on this coast and never find her. The tide has washed away any tracks that might have been. And I'd hate to think of the alternative." He shook his head. "We need to go. I guess Lumina would be the best place. That's where Farah would go to find us."

After a night's rest, they went up to the control room, and Rai took her seat at the steering wheel.

The Chariot lifted into the air toward its new destination.

As the day faded to night, they were out over the sky and still many miles from Lumina.

"Look," Rai said. "I don't want to talk. Looks like you don't either, but if I'm to stay awake over the water, we'll have to make conversation."

Thatch shuffled in his seat. Sleep had assaulted him, and Rai had pushed back the intruder.

"I think once we reach Lumina," Thatch said, "we should speak with Jei Fletzi. Tell him what Morica has been up to."

"After what happened at the Games," Rai said. "Jei Fletzi doesn't have the people behind him anymore."

"But maybe he still has enough clout to get them to hear us out. The people will be with Sara."

"Wait, a public announcement? Morica will have us jailed. Someone will recognize us, and we'll be tortured until we reveal Sara's location, which can never happen. So, we'd be dooming ourselves to indefinite pain. They might decide to take limbs."

"We have to—" Thatch stopped. His eyes were glued to the blue screen above his seat.

"What?" Rai asked.

"It's taking over the map."

"What? What's taking over the map?" she asked.

"Energy."

Rai flew toward the pulse. It was morning before they reached the spot where the energy flared. Rai shook her head. "I can't see anything above these clouds." She angled the Chariot downwards.

Below, a thick, black cloud, emitting glowing bolts of lightning, surrounded an island. The lightning entangled the landmass like an intricate web.

"We're landing." Rai pointed the Chariot toward the cloud and dived into the darkness.

44

LIGHTNING

OUTSIDE their tents, the islanders sat beading clothes, cutting fish, gossiping, grinding vegetables into paste, and peeling fruits for their next meal.

Sara ran past the tents until she spotted him. "Balin!"

The boy turned around. His mother stepped in front of him. "What do you want with my son?"

"Lightning," Sara said as she panted for air.

Abby wore a confused look on her face, sobered by a tint of disgust.

"You want me off this island?" Sara asked. "Then I need your son to start a Lightning storm."

"Just because we don't have a lord, doesn't mean we take orders from anyone who washes up onto this island."

Balin pushed past his mother. "I'll do it."

Abby molded her mouth into a surprised 'O'. "You will not!"

"If it will help you get home," Balin said.

The islanders gathered around the highest mound on the island to the north. At its pinnacle stood Balin and the Old Scholar. The Old Scholar whispered something to the boy, and Balin closed his eyes.

With this, the Old Scholar backed up until he stood among the islanders.

Sara could see Abby standing across from her. The woman's lips were pinched together as if she had tasted something sour, and her eyes were so narrow, Sara could not make out the color of the irises.

Balin lifted his hands. Lightning sparked from his palms. The bolts flew through the sky where they grew and entangled, creating a growing mass of Lightning.

As the Lightning stormed above them, growing in force, the islanders backed away, some retreating to their tents. Many of the brave stayed.

Sara looked on in amazement. Never had she seen a Lightning Elemental possessing such power.

The static sound of the Lightning above them rose to a roar.

"Balin! Stop!" Abby screamed. "Look, look what you've done to him!" She glared at Sara.

Abby ran up to the mound and shook her son.

"Woman, get down from there!" the Old Scholar shouted.

Balin blinked and opened his eyes. The Lightning that lingered in the sky descended to the ground.

The on-lookers scattered, only to be struck by the bolts. Their bodies convulsed and dropped to the ground.

The boy panicked. His body shook.

The Old Scholar, with strength and swiftness beyond his years, scaled the mound and grabbed the boy's two hands in his.

"Meditate with me," he ordered.

Balin closed his eyes.

His mother had her hands on his shoulders.

The Lightning drew back into the sky, and the bolts faded.

Abby sighed. She turned Balin around, hugged him, and glared at Sara over her shoulder.

Sara ran to one of the islanders who was struck. She was still alive but convulsing. Several others had come to the aid of the fallen, seven total, one dead.

Sara stood aside to let the islanders take the woman back to the village.

Abby marched toward Sara. "See what you've done? An eighth of the village on the edge of death because of you."

Sara's eyes darted from Abby.

Something large and metal flew down from the sky and landed on the distant coast. They heard the sound first, a screeching whistle cutting through the wind.

Abby turned in the direction of the sound, and Sara ran toward the coast where the object landed. When her feet touched the shore, Sara saw the Chariot, the wheels digging into the sand.

The hatch door to the engine room opened. Rai and Thatch emerged.

Sara ran to them. "You found me."

"We thought you were dead." Rai reached out to hug Sara. Sara was surprised by the gesture, pausing for a moment before hugging her back.

"Farah?" Sara asked.

Rai shook her head.

Tears and exhaustion painted Sara's face. She turned to Thatch.

"We'll find her," he said.

Sara nodded and wiped the tears from her eyes, but she failed to stop the fresh ones. "I washed up here on the Insula."

"This is the Insula?" Thatch asked.

Sara nodded. "The people here, they knew Bolton."

Sara led Rai and Thatch into the village. The islanders nursed the fallen and wrapped the dead man in a beaded cloth. The family gathered around to watch the ceremony in tears.

Sara regretted asking Balin to use his element to help her find her friends.

Cirtus approached her. "I know what you're thinking, but you didn't cause that death, Abby did, with her carelessness. But the islanders are an ignorant people, they will blame you too. If your friends have provided a ship, you must leave before they start throwing sand in your faces. But first, the Old Scholar wants to ask a favor."

Sara entered the Old Scholar's tent. His head was bowed in prayer.

"Sit," he said.

"I'm sorry," Sara said, "about what happened with Balin."

"Sad business that," the Old Scholar said. "But it had to be done. I have something to ask of you."

"Anything."

"I need to go with you on your journey."

"But what about Balin and his mother?" Sara asked.

"The ferryman has not come for ten years. I have the glistenings to come back, but I can no longer wait for someone to come here so that I can make the trip to the mainland. There are some things I need to do there."

"You're welcomed to travel with us," Sara said.

Amid the angry islanders with their killing stares, Sara, Rai, and Thatch, followed by the Old Scholar, made their way to the Chariot on the coast.

Balin watched his surrogate father walk toward the Chariot before turning to wish him goodbye. He approached the boy, ready to give his speech about not being gone long and coming back soon. But before he could get out a single word, the boy ducked under his mother's arm and ran toward the lagoon.

"You can't blame him, old man," Abby said. "His father left the same way as you. I always thought I could see him in your eyes."

The Old Scholar nodded to the bitter woman and entered the Chariot's engine room. The hatch door closed, and Abby turned her back.

From a tall palm tree, Balin watched as the Chariot took off into the distance.

45

CAUGHT

FARAH was alone in a dungeon room. Shackles hanging from the moldy, stone wall bound her hands.

When she fell from Thermal's back into the Altasi Sea, she dove and called Wind to slow her descent. Her hands, in prayer, broke the surface of the sea. She jettisoned down until the water submerged her body. She swam for days and hoped she headed for the shore. She slept when she reached the warm shores outside the Crystal Forest.

Voices greeted her in the morning. "Take her back to Vella City. We'll question her there." She tried to blink the sleep from her eyes, but her vision was blurred as strong hands clasped her arms and lifted her body from the sands. Without food or water and inadequate rest, Farah was weak. They dragged her away.

Her legs and feet brushed the rough ground. The skin bruised and bled in places, especially her knees. She blacked out from pain and exhaustion. When she opened her eyes again, she found herself in this dismal dungeon.

The hanging shackles were not made for someone of her size. Her feet were a head above the floor, and the manacles bruised her wrists.

Footsteps sounded from outside. A key turned in the lock. Farah lifted her head as Mordecai entered the dungeon room.

"How are we today, young heretic?" he asked.

Two Blue Jays entered behind him. Farah pressed her lips shut. Without any continuing formalities, Mordecai went on, his expression growing grave as he spoke. "Where are your friends taking the Lady Sara?"

Farah looked away from him.

Mordecai grasped her chin and turned her head to face him. "Where is Lady Sara?"

Farah's body was tired, and she had lost all her strength, but her eyes burned with that spark and venom which she flung at the High Councilor. She moved her head and tried to bite his hand.

Mordecai pulled his hand away from her.

"Ask me what you *want* to ask me?" Farah asked.

Mordecai glared at her.

"Go on, or do you need some reminding," Farah said.

"Guards," Mordecai said, "wait outside the door."

The Blue Jays nodded and exited the small room.

"Where are your friends taking the spheres?" he hissed.

A devilish grin spread across Farah's face. "Wouldn't you like to know?"

Mordecai slapped her. "Tell me where they are, girl!"

"You puffed pigeon, why should I tell you where to find them? You're trying to destroy them, so I can be as defenseless as you are. I'm sure you've found that steel doesn't work."

"You'll regret not talking to me," Mordecai said. "There are worse ways to get information.

"Guards!"

The two guards came back into the dank room.

"Take her down from that wall and throw her into the main dungeon," Mordecai ordered.

They released Farah from the shackles bruising her flesh. The guards dragged her to the dungeon. She recognized this place. It was the dungeon of Fortress Tower, the lowest level of the tower, going deep into the sea.

The guards shoved her into one of the cells and strong arms caught her before she fell to the hard stone floor. The stranger helped her to her feet. The blue sleeves of his uniform filled Farah's vision.

She recoiled from the man and backed into the bars of the cell.

"It's alright. It's me."

"Rodan?"

A bloody bandage patched his shoulder, and his face was bruised, but it was Rodan.

"Are you alright?" he asked.

"Why are you here? I thought the Rebel Resistance sent you to feign an alliance with Morica?"

"Shh," Rodan cautioned. "Right now, all they know is I'm an Elemental and I'm a friend of yours. How did they get you?"

"I fell from Thermal's back. They have strange weapons of steel. They blasted the Chariot."

"The marriage . . . were the vows exchanged?" Rodan asked.

Farah nodded.

Rodan sighed. "I've been here for days waiting for a storm."

"Why?" Farah asked.

"If a good thunder storm comes, they won't hear us break through our cages. They've been dragging me out to beat me, trying to weaken me so I'll be too exhausted to use my element. But training with the Resistance has taught me to save my strength. They won't beat it out of me. They ask me about Sara and the spheres, hoping I'll break."

"How did Mordecai get the spheres anyway?" Farah asked. "We fought to get the spheres away from their sanctums. It's hard to believe a bunch of old men and some Blue Jays armed with batons could take on a Sphere Protector."

"They have an Elemental working on their side. Fulgur. He's strong. A Lightning Elemental. They have him torturing people."

"Did he do that to your face?" Farah asked.

"No, the guards did that. He uses his element, not his hands. He may look like a fragile, old man, but he moves and talks like a much younger one. He never gets exhausted. He never stops. Only when Mordecai needs him."

Rai had mentioned Fulgur. "Why would an Elemental want to be on Mordecai's side? Doesn't he know what he is up to?"

"I don't know. The man is strange. He tortures without passion, like he's sitting down to a meal."

Farah sat on the cot stuffed with coarse hay.

"The guards gossip like old women," Rodan said. "Morica is blaming us for the disappearance of the spheres."

"Stupid old men," Farah hissed. "Sara's with us. The people won't believe the Council. Sara wouldn't put them in danger after she fought so hard to save them."

"That doesn't bother Mordecai," Rodan said. "They announced that Sara has been kidnapped by the Elemental traitors. He has put a price on her head. And Veil has locked himself in a room and hasn't come out for days. The guards believe he's gone insane. They say that the guards in Tosia claim they hear hysterical laughter coming from Veil's room. And talking, but he's alone in there."

46

FROZEN ARMY

THATCH stared at the blue screen above his seat and searched for Farah's locator. A signal from Demlama appeared. He had kept quiet about it for days. The signal was too weak. It could be anything, and it was unlikely that Farah would go to such a remote place without food or water. But as his head ached from staring at the bright screen, he realized he had been foolish.

"I'm receiving a signal from Demlama," he said.

Sara and the Old Scholar gathered around the screen. Rai craned her neck to see.

"I'm not sure," Thatch said, "but Farah could have found another way to reach us as Sara did."

"Where can I land?" Rai asked.

"The temple floats above a chasm," Sara said. "You'll have to land in the snow."

Rai landed the ship on the ice outside the Crystal Forest. They crowded out of the ship except Stannum, who stayed with his machines. As they journeyed up the narrow, ice path, a shadow loomed over them. Within the shadow were tiny facets of light.

They met a wall of ice. The sun through the wall created the facets of light that danced upon the snow. Trapped within the wall were the skeletal bodies of the warriors that had fought for the city.

Rai approached the wall of ice. "What's this? How would Farah have made it through?"

Sara touched the ice wall. "We put this here."

"This must be the reason the Resistance gave the Wind Sphere a new sanctum."

"A new sanctum?" Thatch asked. "How do you know that?"

"I've traveled," Rai said. "So, how do we get through?"

"Melt the ice," the Old Scholar said.

Rai laughed. "With Fire, old man?"

"It is your element, isn't it?"

"If I melt this entire wall, if I can, I will be of no use to anyone for days. You might as well chuck me into a boat and let me fall asleep on the Lake de Somnia."

"Maybe we can crack it," Sara said.

"Say again?"

"Rai, if you could melt a weak spot in the ice, the whole wall would come crashing down."

"If this wall comes down, I hope you're all prepared to run." Rai focused on a section of ice near the snow. The ice melted. A crack developed, followed by a sound like crystal breaking.

As the sound grew louder, Rai said, "It's time to run."

They turned and sprinted through the snow. The Old Scholar led the troop. Heavy bulks of ice fell from the wall, crashing down upon the snow. A block of ice fell in front of Sara. She skirted around it and kept running as ice rained down like hail.

The bodies of the dead twitched within their icy tombs. But as the wall fell, their skeletons fractured, and the snow buried them.

Sara and the others stopped at the edge of the forest where the snow thinned. The remainder of the wall tumbled down until only fragments rose above the snow.

The assault over, they approached the temple across the narrow, icy bridge. Sara and Thatch chorused Farah's name.

Rai shook her head. "You all saw what it took to bring that wall down. What other way would Farah have had into this city?"

"We're here now," Sara said. "It might seem impossible. But a few days ago, we didn't believe the Insula existed." Sara entered the temple. The statue of Clara, the warrior who fought the Dark Elemental, rose at the end of the hall. Her sword hung at her side and her right hand drew forward, palm upwards.

A misty image emerged from the cold stone. The ghost of Clara beckoned for Sara to follow. Clara led her out of the temple and into the snow.

Rai watched as Sara followed the misty shadow, but she could not make out the semblance of the female figure. To her, it was formless, faceless like the warm air one breathes out into the cold.

At the snowy ledge, Clara pointed to the snow. Sara stared at the ground.

Rai watched until passion seized her, and Rai knelt in the snow and dug, pushing away the snow with her hands. Fingers numb from the cold, she lifted the object she found. She held up a sphere with a deep fissure running through its center.

Sara looked for the warrior ghost, but she was gone. She turned to Rai. "Watch out!"

Rai threw the sphere to Sara. Sara caught it and stumbled towards the ledge leading to the precarious depths. Rai drew her sword and turned to see an undead man carrying a war axe. The flesh hung from his face, frozen in time. Rai cut through him, her sword ablaze.

The dead man's bones rattled to the ground. Rai and Sara rushed to the door of the temple.

"Thatch," Sara screamed, "Scholar, it's time to go."

The undead now free of their icy prison approached. Rai kept her sword out and ready.

47

STORM

FARAH, her stomach half-full of clear soup and dry bread, slept on the hay-stuffed cot.

Rodan leaned his head against the wall and cringed from the pain in his shoulder. The steel bullet was still lodged inside, hugging against his sinews and stopping the wound from clotting or healing. The injury drained his energy.

Footsteps echoed through the small dungeon. Farah stirred in her sleep. Two Morica guards faced the cell.

"The girl." A guard pointed to Farah.

Rodan rose to his feet. He knew they would take her to Fulgur. The guards unlocked the cell. Rodan stood in front of Farah.

"Move aside, traitor!" the guard said.

Rodan swung back his uninjured arm and punched the guard in the jaw. The guard staggered back, and his partner rushed to his aid. Rodan grabbed the second guard's shoulders, forcing him toward the ground. He kneed him in the stomach as he descended.

The first guard recovered.

Rodan tried to elbow him as he approached, but the guard was quick and pinned Rodan's arms to his sides. Rodan attempted to send a branch to wrap around the man. The stone ground cracked as the branch emerged, but the festering wound in his shoulder weakened Rodan. The branch shrunk away.

Farah woke from her sleep. Seeing the commotion, she jumped on the back of the guard attacking Rodan. The guard, backing up into the bars, banged Farah's body against them. He maintained his hold on Rodan.

Farah was tired from exhaustion and dehydration. She could not summon the strength to call Wind.

The second guard stood and removed his baton from his side. He beat Rodan with it. The guard buffeted his shoulder, and Rodan screamed. Satisfied they had exhausted Rodan, the guards let his beaten body slump to the floor.

They took Farah from the cell. She struggled against them and shouted Rodan's name. They took Farah to a dark room at the top of Fortress Tower. They tied her to the chair in the center of the room. The guards left, locking the door behind them.

A small lantern swung above her head. Darkness skirted around her and deepened at the corners of the room.

Footsteps sounded, so faint, Farah doubted the sound existed. The sound was unnatural as if the darkness crept toward her.

The outline of a man emerged from the shadows. He walked into the light. He had a bald head and papery skin. Farah guessed he must be a hundred years old, but as he approached her, his straight back and strength showed no signs of age. His face was expressionless.

"Who are you?" Farah struggled in her binds. "Can I get some water?" She tried to appear unafraid.

Fulgur leaned in. Farah could not detect signs of breathing from the strange man. She waited. Air did not issue from his lungs, nor did his chest heave with evidence of in taking air.

"What are you?" Farah's voice rippled on the air and dragged her fear along with it.

"The reason the sky lights up in the storm."

Biting energy zoomed through Farah's body. Her teeth clinched.

Fulgur stopped.

"You want me to tell you where the spheres are?"

Fulgur's head lulled left to right and back.

He sent Lightning through Farah's body again. Farah jolted up in her seat, but the straps bound her hands and feet and pinned her to the chair.

The energy ceased, and Farah sat with her head down. "When will this stop? What do you want?"

"A release from the endless burden of existing."

RODAN sat up and dragged himself to one wall of his cell where he leaned back and gulped air. He reached out his hand and tried to upturn the stone, but it would not budge. He attempted to send vines, but in vain.

He was weak from the beating, but what stopped him was the bullet buried in his shoulder. It sapped his energy.

Rodan focused on the bullet. He knew it was made of metal from the earth, but he had not wanted to feel its coldness slide through his muscle once again. He could sense the bullet as the force pulled it, but it remained wedged between his sinews, buried deep beneath his flesh.

Rodan closed his eyes. He needed strength to move the bullet. He needed to concentrate. If he could summon enough force to remove it, he could heal.

He focused on the metal. It tunneled through the muscle. Rodan leaned his head back, his mouth open in a silent scream.

He clinched his teeth as the bullet popped from his flesh and dropped to the ground. It bounced, sending infinitesimal droplets of blood to stain the stone floor.

He passed out against the wall.

He awoke as the guards jostled Farah back into the cell. Her body hung lifeless in their arms. The guards tossed Farah on the straw cot.

Rodan scrambled across the floor to where Farah lay. He shook her arm. She remained unconscious.

The storm had come, but from his windowless cell, Rodan could not see the lightning flash. Still, he could hear the storm, thundering against the marble building. The rain beat down like hail, and every time the sky opened, thunder loud and foreboding, shook his eardrums.

Rodan put his hand out in front of him. With effort, he called vines. He let them shrink back, and hurried to where Farah lay. He shook her. She would not wake.

He stood. The pain in his shoulder lessened. Thick vines wrapped around the bars. He thrust the vines forward. The vines pulled the bars from the hinges, causing them to crash against the marble wall. The crash sounded like the crash of the thunder.

He lifted Farah over his shoulder. He cringed as the weight put pressure on his injury. He cursed. He placed Farah back onto the cot and lifted her over the other shoulder.

He carried Farah to the marble wall. Summoning the energy, he sent a crack through the marble. The fissure grew, giving way to smaller fractures until the wall crumbled in front of him.

Farah stirred. The rain misted against her skin. Her fingers pressed into Rodan's back.

"I've got you," he said, but Farah continued to lift herself from him. He put her down. When Farah's feet hit the floor, she staggered.

Rodan put his hand on her shoulder to steady her. "You okay?"

Farah nodded.

48

BENEATH THE SNOW

THE undead lifted themselves from the ice.

"What is this?" Rai asked.

"Energy animates them," Sara said. "They can't be stopped. We need to go. We have to find Thatch and the Old Scholar."

Rai and Sara backed up against the temple walls as the undead rose around them. Sara leaned through the doorway to the temple. "Thatch!" She pointed her wrist gun at the approaching attackers. Energy zoomed from the Aether and strong Wind knocked down the front line of undead. Their axes, swords, and shields clashed against the rotting skeletons behind them. But they stood from the ice and continued their approach.

Rai slashed a skeleton through with her flaming sword. Sara pointed her wrist gun at the fast approaching undead, but the Aether would not respond. She picked up a small statue resting at the entrance to the temple. The statue was heavy in her hands. She brought it down on a rotting corpse in front of her.

Footsteps echoed down the halls of the temple and sprinted toward them. Thatch and the Old Scholar emerged with their weapons drawn. Thatch held a dagger, while the Old Scholar removed a long sword from the folds of his cloak.

The Old Scholar took initiative and cut down the undead in front of them, clearing the way to the icy bridge. "Let's go!" His voice rang out clear and youthful. He ran to the bridge followed by Sara, Rai, and Thatch. The undead clambered toward them and raised their weapons against the cold wind.

Once they had crossed the bridge, Rai turned back.

"Rai, let's go!" Thatch shouted. He, Sara, and the Old Scholar rushed down the sloping ice path to the Chariot.

Rai closed her eyes. A mass of undead soldiers ran across the bridge. The others followed, pushing forward. The top layer of ice melted, and the warm water spilled over the bridge into the chasm below.

Heat invaded the cold air.

The melting increased as Rai focused, her brain burning with heat. The ice cracked from the warmth and the weight of the skeletal army fast approaching.

Rai's body temperature rose, and heat emitted around her until the bridge could no longer sustain itself. One final crack, and the bridge split and fell into the chasm. The undead who remained on the bridge fell with it. The others incapable of crossing, raised their weapons in disdain.

Rai collapsed in the snow.

"RAI!" "Rai!"

Rai woke up among the trees of the Crystal Forest.

"Drink this." The old Scholar held a canteen to her lips. "You exhausted your energy."

Thatch and Sara knelt by her side.

Rai sat up. "Why didn't you bring me back to the Chariot?"

"We have to mend the sphere," Sara said.

"You don't know what we created when the first one was mended," Rai said.

"We didn't create anything," Sara said. "We restored the balance."

"You believe that?" Rai asked.

"If we restore the spheres, we may be able to set things right," Thatch said.

"If we return the spheres to their sanctums," Rai said, "we would be able to set things right. That's what we should be focusing our energies on. By restoring the spheres, we could be breeding enemies."

"Or allies," Sara said. "Regardless, the balance must be restored. We cannot bandage one problem just to hide it away and let the other fester when we have the cure."

Rai stood. "I know what this is. You want to make sure it will work the second time, so you can test it on the Water Sphere when we find it."

Sara looked to the trees and stared in the direction of the lake. "You're right. My reasons for doing this are not wholly unselfish."

Rai sighed. "Give it to me." She held out her hand.

Sara looked at her.

"We'll mend it." Rai took out the jar, containing her Aether. The Aether floated into the space between them and grew. It gathered energy from the forest until it was the size of a large shield.

Sara handed Rai the sphere, and Rai fed the sphere to the Aether. The Aether absorbed the cracked sphere. A blinding light emitted from the Aether. Once the light dulled, the sphere, now solid, floated inside the Aether.

Rai reached inside her Aether. The substance of the Aether was warm and gel-like. Because Rai's body temperature matched the fire, the substance was not too hot for her, but had any of the others reached in, their hands would have been scorched. She pulled the sphere out, and the Aether contracted, allowing Rai to recapture it inside the jar.

The Old Scholar marveled at the sphere, but his eyes were gloomy and tainted by disdain.

49

THE BEATEN PATH

FARAH and Rodan raced to the side of the building opposite Fortress Tower. They avoided the guards patrolling the wet city streets.

Rodan peered around the corner of the building.

A guard passed. His sloppy footsteps made squashing sounds as he walked.

Rodan pinned his body against the building and held Farah back with one hand. They waited while the guard passed.

The guard turned.

Rodan could have sworn he felt the eyes of the man on him, but the guard whistled and walked away.

He and Farah let out sighs of relief. They rushed to the Crystal Forest, out of sight of the guards. The rain fell, leaving the ground muddy.

Farah and Rodan walked deep into the forest headed toward D'arkadia. Once the rain slowed, Farah stopped and let out a shrieking whistle, which surprised Rodan.

"What is it?" he asked.

She whistled again. Nothing. She slumped her shoulders and knelt to the ground, her face in her hands.

"What's wrong?" he asked.

"Orka. I thought she'd be waiting for me. I thought she might have followed me," she said.

"She'll be okay," Rodan said. "Orka can take care of herself. She takes after you."

Farah nodded, but didn't lift her head from her hands.

They needed to get far from Vella City before Morica realized they were gone. They would send guards and Resistance soldiers to find them and bring them back. Mordecai would see to that.

"I need to find Thatch," Farah said.

"How?"

"I need a transmitter," Farah said.

"A what?"

"Something to contact the Chariot. A transmitter."

"I don't know what that is or how we're going to get one," he said.

"Breeze."

"Are we going to swim there?" Rodan asked.

"No, wait. Atrus!" Farah said.

"I'm not following."

"He's an old friend. He's staying at Wyvek temple. We'll go there. And I can get the materials I need to build the transmitter. Then we can contact Thatch and find out where they are."

Farah and Rodan journeyed through the Crystal Forest and went on to D'arkadia. Farah was not sure how to build the transmitter, but she hoped Atrus knew. They walked through D'arkadia without stopping. The entire journey took two days, and when they arrived in Tosia, they were hungry and needed sleep.

"The guards said Veil locked himself up in the Domum Fidei," Rodan said.

"Guards are perched all over this place," Farah said. "We need to find a way to disguise ourselves."

Farah and Rodan ducked into a shop. Hooded robes hung behind the counter.

"We have a problem," Rodan whispered. "No sparklings."

A woman's shoulder brushed past Farah.

"Oh, sorry, dear," a young woman's voice issued from the mouth of an old woman with thin-yellowed skin.

"Madame Dawn?" Farah recognized the woman.

"Wind Tamer and Earth Mover. You need money."

Farah nodded. "Yes. We need to get robes."

Dawn took Farah's hand and forced her palm up. She took a satchel from her side and poured the four glittering coins into Farah's palm.

"Thank you." Farah tried pull her hand back, but the woman grasped it.

"A young man was taken to me," Dawn said. "He was badly ill, delirious, talking in his fevered dreams. He whispered Lady Sara's name."

"What?" Farah asked.

Rodan's eyes darted. He furrowed his brow.

Dawn's grip on Farah's hand tightened.

Farah wanted to pull her hand away, but she couldn't. "What did he look like?"

Dawn chuckled.

Farah looked into her milky, sightless eyes. "Right. Sorry."

"Where is this man now?" Rodan asked.

Dawn shook her head. "He left my care weeks ago. I'm afraid he still has a bad fever. He was fighting an infection that spread." She released Farah and left the shop.

50

Commissioned

FARAH and Rodan rented a room at the inn and purchased food and wine for the road. They slept through the day, and at night, they left Tosia.

The hooded cloaks disguised them as they passed the guards on patrol. Outside Tosia, Farah whistled for Orka with no response. They boarded the boat at the edge of the Lake de Somnia and rowed to the other side.

They disembarked.

Farah's steps, quick before, were now sluggish. At first, Rodan amounted this change to exhaustion, but now he worried Farah was losing hope.

As the sun rose, they stepped upon Wyvek's hard soil.

The temple was like a factory. Humans and *Lacwanx* entered from one door and exited the other.

A *Lacwanx* recognized Farah. He stopped and said something to her in a language Rodan did not understand.

"*Sa chrysta,*" Farah thanked him.

The *Lacwanx* walked away toward the temple.

"What did he say?" Rodan asked.

"He said Atrus is on the second floor."

Farah and Rodan walked into the temple. A stream of energy powered the elevator. Atrus sat at a table on the loft. He scanned a large unrolled sheet of paper. A hammering noise echoed from the sphere room, but the door was shut.

"*Ka qaaus juna aqanfo* . . ." Atrus stopped mid-sentence as the elevator rose and Farah and Rodan stepped off.

"Sorry to interrupt," Farah said, "but I need your help."

"What is it?" Atrus's hands shook as he rolled up the large sheet of paper.

"You alright?" Farah asked.

"Yeah." Atrus wiped his hands on his pants. "What do you need?"

"I lost the Chariot," Farah said. Do you know how to make a transmitter?"

"How could you lose that big old thing?" Atrus laughed.

"Do you know how to make a transmitter or what?" she asked.

"Are *you* okay?" Atrus asked.

"Can you make it for me?"

"Sure. Let me get a team together," Atrus said. "Do you have a place to sleep? It should be ready by tomorrow."

"Thanks." Farah forced a smile. "I'll get the sparklings for it when my friends arrive."

Farah and Rodan left the temple.

"Can we sleep outside?" Farah asked.

"Are the houses all boarded up?"

"Yes," Farah said.

"We could pop the boards off and—"

"I'd rather sleep outside," Farah said.

"Yeah." Rodan eyed her. "We can do that."

* * *

FARAH and Rodan returned to the temple in the morning. They waited on the first floor. Farah was silent. She remained anchored to the spot where she stood among the stone statues.

Rodan wanted to say a few words to her, but thought better of it.

The doors to the temple opened, and a Morica councilor followed by four guards stepped inside. Rodan and Farah hid deeper among the statues. The guards rounded the corner and disappeared from their view.

"I wonder what they're up to." Farah stepped forward.

"Don't wonder." Rodan grabbed her arm and held her back.

She wrenched her arm free of Rodan's grasp and rounded the corner.

Rodan followed her up the elevator to the loft.

On the loft, Atrus again gazed at the large sheet. But this time, the councilor stared at it with him as Atrus pointed to things on the blueprint and explained the design to the Morica councilor.

Atrus led the councilor to the Sphere Room. The councilor and the guards walked in. Atrus hesitated at the door. He spotted Farah on the elevator. He closed the door behind the councilor.

"I told you to wait downstairs." Atrus rushed to the table and rolled up the large paper, but before he could finish, Farah darted to the table and slammed her hand down on one end of the page. With her free hand, she unrolled the other side.

"Thatch's blueprints." She backed away from the table. "You stole his blueprints."

"He left copies in Breeze. I modified them."

"To be built with missiles. To attack us," Farah said. "You sold these chariots to Morica, and you're making more." Realization hit Farah. "And you have been using the Sphere Protector for energy. That's why you chose Wyvek."

Atrus shook his head. "I was commissioned. I didn't know what they'd be using the chariots for."

"You're a traitor and a thief!"

A *Lacwanx*, carrying a small metal device, came from the back room. "*Yiyer* transmitter, Boss."

Before the *Lacwanx* could present the device to Atrus, Farah snatched the transmitter and ran to the elevator. The elevator rose. Rodan stood upon it.

The councilor and the four guards exited the Sphere Room. A guard shouted, "Those are the escaped prisoners!"

The councilor nodded to the guards.

In place of their black batons, the guards carried snub-nosed guns, which they released from their holsters and aimed at Rodan and Farah.

"Jump!" Rodan took Farah's hand. He and Farah jumped from the elevator to the floor below. They hit the ground hard. Rodan scrambled to his feet. He helped Farah up, and they ran for the exit.

Once outside, Rodan looked both ways.

"Where to?" Farah asked.

"The village."

"No," Farah shouted. "The Rebel Resistance."

"We can't lead them to headquarters."

"We don't have a choice." Farah grabbed Rodan's arm and ran as the guards' footsteps thundered down the temple halls.

Bullets flew at their heels.

Rodan screamed. A bullet went through his leg and blood dripped onto the rocky ground as he stumbled.

They stopped outside Resistance Headquarters. Jin guarded the entrance.

"Rodan," Jin said.

"Dad, we need to get through. Guards are chasing us."

Jin triggered the hidden latch, and the large rock moved aside. Jin followed them through the opening as the rock shifted back into place.

51

ROGUE PROTECTOR

NOON approached. Decca sat with Fre, a fellow worker and villager, on the wharf.

"Those guards are still patrolling Cal Hill," Fre said. "I don't understand it."

Decca stared at his hands.

"My cousin in Lumina says the Council has taken over." Fre swatted a gnat against his neck. "The crowd stomped Jei Fletzi like a bug after the attack at the Element Games."

Decca looked back toward the village.

"Hey, man, you okay?"

Decca shook his head. "Yeah. Sorry. I care, you know, about what's going on in Mirmina, but now with the baby coming and everything. I just . . ."

Fre clapped him on the back. "I know. When my first little one was on her way, I couldn't think about anything else. Even today when I think of her, it crowds everything else out."

"What's going on here?" Sev, the head guard, approached them. "It's not your break yet."

Decca stood, and Fre busied himself with the crates. Fre carried a crate to the ship. As Decca passed, Sev took his arm. "You're a family man, right?"

Decca nodded.

"Do your job. Provide for them."

Decca shrugged free of Sev's grasp and grabbed a crate from the wharf.

That night, Decca, trying not to wake Spire, crept into bed.

Spire turned over as his body hit the cushions. "How was work?"

"Fine."

"Liar."

"It was boring," he said.

Spire placed a hand on his chest. "Well, I've been slaving away all day on the sofa so I feel your pain."

Decca rested his hand on her stomach.

"Movement?" she asked.

"She's sleeping."

"Or he," Spire said.

"No, this one's a girl. We'll have a boy next time."

"Next time?" Spire rested her head on his shoulder. "If there is a next time. I can't bear any more days sitting around at home."

Decca laughed.

The next morning, Decca piled crates onto a ship bound for Lumina. A vessel approached. It sailed alongside the dock, and a silver-and-blue guard stepped out to tie the ship to the pier.

A man dressed in a guard's uniform stepped out. His brow hung above his eyes, and his hair was trimmed. He looked to be about Decca's age. He approached him.

"You're one of the workers here? I'm looking for a man named Sev."

"He's my boss," Decca said.

"Right. Where is he?"

"He patrols the wharfs," Decca said, "makes sure we're working hard. He should be coming around."

The man smirked. "Do you like your job, worker?"

"Yes."

"Then you'll go find your boss right now and tell him that I am here waiting for him."

Decca put down the crate he was carrying and walked down to the pier.

The guards laughed.

"Caleena. They really are sheep people."

Decca turned around. "What did you say?"

"Go along, worker."

"I asked you a question," Decca said.

"You don't ask the questions. Now get along like a good dog."

Decca lunged at the man and pushed him to the ground.

The man scrambled to his feet and withdrew his sword. "Animal."

Decca swung, and the blade met his forearm. The edge dug into the flesh. Decca pushed the man away. He staggered back with the force of Decca's push, but he maintained his balance. He raised his sword against Decca. "You're going to pay for that, swine!"

"What's the meaning of this?" Sev approached the men.

"Your worker attacked us."

"What are you doing here, Parvel?" Sev asked.

"I've been given orders to take control of this village."

"Why?"

"I don't ask questions. I just obey orders."

"I'm not giving up this village," Sev said. "These are my people."

"Your people?" Parvel laughed.

Sev stared back at him.

"I want that man arrested." Parvel pointed to Decca.

"I won't arrest this man without hearing his side."

"His side?" Parvel said. "I'm a Morica guard."

A roar sounded in the distance.

"What was that?" Parvel asked.

"The Protector," Sev whispered.

"Spire!" Before Decca could run, a Morica guard grabbed him and pummeled him on the back of the head with a baton. Decca staggered, and his vision blurred.

Seeing Decca on the ground, Sev slammed Parvel in the face with his fist. The other Morica guards piled off the ship to defend their captain.

Sev grabbed one man by the back of the shirt and tossed him off the wharf.

Decca blinked. A guard blocked his path to the village. He tried to punch him, but the guard was quicker. He hit Decca in the ribs with his baton, and Decca keeled over. The guard smashed him on the back with the baton.

Through the blows, Decca rose and punched the man in the stomach. The man backed up, holding his gut. Decca's fist landed against the side of his head, and the man staggered to the ground.

SPIRE stood outside her hut and stared into the distance toward Cal Hill. Something rushed through the trees. The trunks swayed as if tossed by a tornado, making its way to the village, and as the thing passed, the trees went ablaze until the forest outside Cal Hill was red with black smoke pillowing out into the sky above.

The gates to Cal Hill burst from their hinges, and then came the screaming.

Spire climbed down the steps to the wharfs. People rushed past her.

"Water! We need water!"

Men rushed back carrying large buckets.

"Stop!" Spire said. "You'll get yourselves killed!" Holding her stomach, she raced along the wharf.

The Protector of the Fire Sphere loomed above her. The men threw buckets of water at the Protector, maddening it.

Spire looked up at the great monster. She turned her eyes to the forest. She darted for the trees, but the Protector slammed one flaming hoof down in front of her.

Spire turned to the Protector. "You remember me, don't you, beast?"

The Protector roared, revealing its thick bronze-coated tongue.

Spire put one hand on her stomach. She focused on the Protector. Feeling a strange surge of energy from deep within, she called a gust of Wind. The Wind knocked the villagers carrying the buckets back. Water spilled onto the ground. The gust forced the Protector past the opening in the gates. Its hooved feet dug into the earth, leaving behind deep grooves.

The wind raged around Spire, and she was surprised by how little control she had over it. She felt kicking beneath the taut skin of her belly as the folds of her dress flapped in the wind.

"Spire!" Decca grabbed her hand.

Sev, the Morica guard, followed him.

They cut through the wind and headed for the trees. They journeyed deep into the forest until the winds calmed, and they could no longer hear the roar of the Sphere Protector.

Spire held her stomach and gasped for air.

"What's wrong?" Decca held her arm.

"I think she's ready," she said.

"The baby?"

Spire nodded.

Decca found a patch of grass and helped her to lie down. "It's going to be okay."

"Do you know what you're doing?" Sev asked Decca.

Decca's grasp on Spire's hand tightened. He nodded, but his eyes were to the ground.

"I can handle it," Sev said. "Just stay there."

Sev knelt.

Spire pushed with all the strength she could muster until she felt she would push out her heart and all that surrounded it. She screamed from the pain and the sharp ache of pushing.

The wind picked up through the trees, causing the leaves to fall around her. They landed on her face and chest and fell off her rising stomach.

As she grinded her teeth, the wind tore through her hair, and its chill bit her face.

A cry sounded through the forest, and the tension left her. Her vision blurred as she saw Sev hand something to Decca. Decca cradled it in his arms. "She's bloodier than I am after a fight."

Spire turned her head up to see her. She was beet red, and her skin looked soft as tissue paper. Decca handed her to Spire. Spire looked into her eyes, light like Decca's. As her cries calmed, so did the wind.

52

BOLTON

PEOPLE crowded the city of Lumina, one of the few habitable places not within a sphere's throw of a sanctum and its Protector. People had grown to fear the new-found mobility of the Sphere Protectors and had taken to the city and adopted its isolation.

Morica added coal to the flame by announcing Protector attacks and blaming it on the missing spheres and the Elementals. The High Council concentrated in the city and carried promises and assurances that they would protect the people. The councilors, however, came with a caravan of pushy guards. Many of the guards were later deposited into the city to join their large number of residing brothers.

Bolton looked around him. What he needed was a ship.

He had traveled non-stop for days with one objective: to get to Elementa so he could find Sara.

He doubted she would recognize him. His face was scarred and not only by the flames. A long, jagged scar swept across from the cheekbone to the jaw where he had been clawed by a Maledixit. Fortunately, it wasn't a bite, and Dawn knew how to stop the infection before it spread. Now he was left with only a slight fever and a headache. He had been knocked out. For how long, he didn't know.

He remembered falling from the cliff with Fero. He stayed face-down at the bottom of the gorge for three days before he regained consciousness, and when he did, he barely had the strength to stand.

He reached out and found the broken Water Sphere. He journeyed at the bottom of the gorge for days and found pockets of water along the rocky ground to quench his thirst.

He encountered the Maledixit, the creature swallowed by the darkness. It clawed his face, but he managed to escape it by hiding in the mist. His brain boiled after the creature attacked him. He became dizzy and his vision unfocused.

He found a place where he could climb up from the gorge. He was blasted by the wind and the cold of the mountain. When he made it to Jetty Verte, having no food or water, he realized he could go no further.

The Water Sphere sanctum was far within the cave. He entered the cavern and collapsed. The Water Sphere rolled out of his hand and into the darkness.

When he awoke, he found himself bandaged and laying in a bed in Tosia. His caregiver was gone. He got up and stumbled out the door.

Bolton ran his fingers along the inside of the scar. It had healed, but left a narrow, shallow valley in its wake.

He went down to the decks of Lumina Port where a large ship docked, letting off about forty or so people. The captain of the ship stepped off.

"Excuse me," Bolton said. "Is this ship sailing for Caleena?"

"Just came from Caleena," the captain said. "What do you want there? Most everyone is leaving. You didn't hear about the attack, did you?"

"What attack?"

"That damn Protector. It attacked the whole village. People are still coming on boats outta there."

"What about Elementa?" Bolton asked.

"You want to go to Elementa? Fine, but it'll cost the full price plus some. I didn't plan on stopping. Let me tell you, though, it's a bad idea. With Caleena becoming a ghost town, Elementa's going to run outta the necessities, and everyone from there's gonna come here."

"I need to get to Elementa," Bolton said.

"Suit yourself. Twenty sparklings will get you there."

"Twenty!"

"That's the cost. You in or out?"

Bolton had only one sparkling to his name and fifty glistenings hanging from a small sack at his side. But glistenings were of no use in Lumina, nor any other city. They only had value to the ferryman who knows the way to the Insula. "Can I get it to you by sundown?"

"You have till morning. That's when I set sail with my crew. We were headed to Vella City, but if you're on board, and you have the sparklings, we'll stop in Elementa."

Bolton left the port and headed for the marketplace. The customers outnumbered the shopkeepers. Maybe he could help a shopkeeper in exchange for sparklings.

He approached a middle-aged man selling potatoes and carrots.

"Excuse me, do you need a hand running this shop?"

Beside the vegetable stand was a jewelry shop. The man declined Bolton's offer, but Bolton was distracted by the jewelry shop owner who batted away a green bird.

The bird swooped down and stood among his jewels. It grabbed a necklace of cream-colored pearls before flying off.

"Damn that feathered demon!" the man shouted. "Come back, you wicked creature."

Bolton left the vendor as he lamented his stolen jewels. He wandered out onto the pavilion and spotted the green bird hiding her stolen treasures atop the sloping roof of a nearby building.

"Farah!" He searched the area.

He felt something light land on his shoulder. Orka chirped in his ear.

"Where's Farah?" Bolton asked.

Orka squawked.

"Okay, okay. Calm down." Bolton tried to pet her, but she snapped at his fingers. "Hey." Bolton withdrew his hand. "Alright, maybe you can help me." He reached into his pocket and withdrew the only sparkling he had. "Can you get me more of these?"

Orka bobbed her head and flew off into the distance.

Bolton overheard the conversation of two blue-and-silver guards who walked by. "Yeah, they say Veil's gone loony, never comes out . . ."

Since the day Bolton left the room where he passed his feverish slumber, he had seen many of these guards in blue-and-silver uniforms. He wondered who they were. The only members of the guard he was used to were Resistance fighters.

As Bolton stared at the strange guards, Orka dropped a silver coin into his open palm.

53

CONTACT

"THATCH, come in. It's me, Farah."

Sara rose from her seat on the steel steps. She rushed over to Thatch.

"Farah," Thatch said. "Where are you?"

"Resistance Headquarters."

"Can we land there?" Thatch asked.

"I don't care," Rai said. "We're landing."

The Chariot passed over Wyvek and was on the way to Lumina, but Rai veered the ship around, causing Sara to have to cling to Thatch's seat so she wouldn't be tossed to the floor.

Rai landed the ship in a remote area of Resistance Headquarters, but the wind caused by the ship's landing knocked down a row of tents.

Sara ran to the elevator followed by Thatch and Rai. They raced through the engine room to the hatch door.

Resistance fighters grouped in front of Vassal's large tent. Farah stood among the fighters. Sara embraced her.

Farah took her hand. "Come on, there's someone who wants to see you."

She led Sara into Vassal's tent. Inside the tent was a bed, and on the bed, was Rodan. His leg was bandaged.

Sara knelt beside the bed. "You're hurt."

Jin sat in a corner close to Rodan's bedside.

"It's nothing," Rodan said. "They gave me something for the pain. It's making me feel a little drunk. But, it's not like I can't stand on it."

"It's the infection we're worried about," Jin said.

"Then give me meli and send me on my way," Rodan said.

"Do you want to lose the leg?" Jin asked.

Rodan turned to Sara. "You'll stay, won't you?"

She nodded, taking his hand.

"Where's Vassal?" Sara asked.

"No one's seen the Commander for days," Jin said. "He left with some of our fighters to escort new recruits from the Crystal Forest, but he hasn't returned."

A man burst through the flaps of the tent. "Forgive me, Captain, but there are *Lacwanx* banging at the rock entrance. They're trying to pry it open with metal tools."

Jin walked to the entrance of the tent. He turned his head, "Lady Sara, please stay with my son."

JIN climbed the battlements and stared down at the hundreds of *Lacwanx* hammering away at the rock entrance. More flooded in from Wyvek and gathered around the stone. Humans joined them.

"Let them in," Jin commanded. He descended the battlements.

"What's going on?" Farah asked.

Jin shook his head.

The rock moved aside, and the flood of *Lacwanx* streamed into Resistance Headquarters. Once the flood thinned, Jin, Farah, and Rai rushed to Wyvek.

Humans and *Lacwanx* alike ran out of the temple. As Jin, Rai, and Farah pushed past the hysterical stream, a group of humans and *Lacwanx* closed the doors. Screams came from inside.

"Let them out!" Farah demanded.

"No," a man said. "There's something in there. Something dark."

"Where's Atrus?" Rai asked.

"Na ta beigheid, Menslike, nos het dit ondor muqnuç," barked a Lacwanx.

"Oael cuuv cyva by," Rai challenged. "Quk juha. Bacc Boss klana ouin."

"You speak *Lacwanx*?" Farah asked.

The banging on the temple doors grew louder together with the screaming.

"You're looking for Boss," said a man, his back against the door. "He ran. He pulled a gun on those guards, and killed their leader, that guy in blue. They didn't like that very much. They chased him all the way to Dustpath, bullets flying."

"What's happening in there?" Farah asked.

The man shook his head. "After Boss left, these things invaded the temple. They were fast, like snakes. They went down the throats of human and *Lacwanx* alike. And they turned against us. Their eyes were solid white."

"You have to let these people out," Rai said.

"They're not people anymore." The man backed away from the door and ran. As did a few others. Without their help, those who remained could not keep the door shut. They scattered.

Rai, Farah, and Jin watched as the door swung open. Rai and Jin drew their swords.

Throngs of humans and *Lacwanx* flooded through the entrance.

Farah, Jin, and Rai stepped inside. Farah picked up a long, jagged piece of scrap metal that lay abandoned at the doorway.

The screams deafened, and the only sound was that of lips smacking.

They turned the corner, Rai at the forefront followed by Jin and Farah. As they rounded the corner, they saw six people, men and women, *Lacwanx* and human, standing along the hall, three on one side and three on the other, facing each other. Their eyes were closed and their heads bowed.

The smacking sound accompanied with the grinding of teeth against bone echoed from the loft. Blood dripped down onto the broken elevator and spilled over the floor.

A man stood on the loft, his eyes white with no pupil or irises. Blood dripped down his shirt, issuing from the dismembered arm he clenched in his fist. His mouth was bloody as he took another bite.

He pointed to the intruders, and a high-pitched inhuman scream issued from his red mouth.

The people who lined the hall turned their faces to the intruders, and their eyes popped open, solid white.

Rai looked up to the loft. Thousands of white worms crawled down, creeping along the walls and racing across the ground.

Rai cut at them with her sword. Farah and Jin followed suit, but the worms kept coming, more interested in the living than the dead.

Rai gathered the strength to summon Fire. She blasted the worms, searing their bodies, which curled up like burned papers.

The white worms circled Rai, and she backed up toward the loft.

"We remember." She heard a voice behind her. She raised her sword and thrust in the space between her hip and her arm. It sliced into the body of the man who approached her.

Rai withdrew her sword, turned around and backed away from the man who was now on his knees. From his mouth, the white worms issued until he was an empty vessel.

The people dropped to their knees, the worms coming out of them and disappearing from the room, retreating to the boarded village. The people gasped and crawled upon the ground. They looked at their hands and rubbed their faces.

Rai, Jin, and Farah helped them to their feet.

The man who stood upon the loft dropped the dismembered arm and stared. His hand touched his bloody mouth. Shaking, he stood, leaned over the loft and allowed himself to fall.

"No!" Farah shouted.

The man's body went over the loft, and his head took a fatal blow as it hit the railing of the elevator. His lifeless body pooled on the floor. His head leaned up against the rail, face turned to the side, staring into nothingness.

54

THE LOSS OF THREE LEAD-ERS

EVENING came to Lumina as Bolton wandered the streets alone. At intervals, Orka flew by to drop a glitter-ing coin into his hand.

Bolton sighed. He had four coins to his name. As he stared at the coins in his open palm, he knocked shoulders with one of the blue-and-silver guards.

"Hey, watch it!" the guard snapped.

Bolton was about to snap back, but seeing the guards lining every inch of the place, he thought better of it. He needed to get to Sara.

The people crowded in like a wave gathering force. Shouts came from near the Stadium. Bolton was swept up in the wave of people rushing and pushing.

The people formed a circle around three men. One wore a blue suit, his hair was white-blond. The second fighter was a tall, thin man with black hair and pale skin. The third wore his shoulder length hair tied back. His tattered and beaten uniform needed mending. His movements were stiff, his arm pinned to his side.

The crowd that surrounded this unlikely group had come to watch them brawl in the street. They were evenly matched. Bolton could tell they knew each other by the way they fought, predicting each other's moves and dodging their blows.

Amid the crowd, Orka flew down to Bolton's shoulder.

The fight was nothing more than a series of failed hitting attempts and swearing, coupled with very detailed and drawn out insults.

"I'm not the one who joined a band of power-hungry, old misers in silk dresses!" the mechanic shouted.

"No, you're only the one who stole energy from a Sphere Protector to help those 'power-hungry, old misers,'" the councilor hissed.

The mechanic lunged at him, and the councilor moved aside like a matador captivating the bull.

The mechanic shook off his shame. "You're one to talk. You joined them after you knew they were a bunch of rotten sphere-stealing . . ."

"That's enough!" The wooden soldier glanced at the growing crowd. "We're all a bunch of worn-out villains," he hissed. "But do we want those guards to know that?"

The mechanic and the councilor stopped shouting insults, but the guards were alerted, pushing past the crowd of people to the center.

"Hey, what's going on here?" asked a guard who made it to the inner circle. The guards had their batons ready.

"It's one of those rebels," a guard said, "and Councilor Pentagon, the traitor."

The tattered soldier stepped back and whispered something to the councilor and the mechanic.

As the guards stepped forward, the mechanic moved in front of the soldier and the councilor. He spread his arms, and a gust of Wind knocked the guards off their feet. A guard fell to the ground hard, sending an audible crack down his back while the other three tumbled over each other.

The trio of worn-out villains pushed through the crowd and ran.

Orka flew from Bolton's shoulder in the direction of the three. Bolton chased after her.

The guards scrambled back to their feet and pursued the trio. The crowd dispersed. The guards were about to cross the bridge to pursue the trio to the docks, but a Lightning bolt zipped from one end of the railing to the other, blocking entry to the bridge.

Bolton looked at the guards from the other side of the Lightning bolt. He had to find Orka.

The trio turned back to see this rogue Lightning Elemental helping them.

"Looks like he's having fun." The mechanic saluted him from a distance.

"Let's go. He's just going to get himself into trouble," the soldier said.

"But he's helping us." The councilor hesitated.

"A long time ago we were helping *each other*," the soldier said.

The councilor ran toward Bolton.

"Pentagon, what are you doing?" the mechanic shouted.

"Returning a favor."

"Come on, we have to leave him," the soldier said, but the mechanic refused to move.

"You can leave," he said.

The councilor reached Bolton. "You can't stand here all day."

"I thought I was helping you get away," Bolton said.

"But at what risk?" the councilor asked. "You don't know us."

"Well, it's a little late to consider that now," Bolton said.

The guards shouted and glared at them from across the lightning barrier.

"Come with us," the councilor said.

Bolton looked toward the docks. "I guess I don't have much of a choice."

Bolton and the councilor took off toward the docks. Once Bolton had taken his focus off the ban of Lightning, it disappeared, leaving the guards free to pursue them.

The councilor waved on the soldier and the mechanic. The group darted to the loading docks. The soldier and the mechanic were in the lead, and Bolton and the councilor were behind them as the guards pursued.

As they rounded the bend and took refuge among the crates on the dock. The guards' feet thundered down the marble walkway past the crates.

The group sighed as one.

"Pentagon, did they bleach out your brains when they bleached your hair?" the mechanic asked.

"I thought we were going to stay low," the soldier grunted and looked away.

The soldier's hand was stiff, most likely made of wood. Judging from his limp, Bolton assumed his leg was wooden too.

"Why were the guards after you?" Bolton asked.

The three looked from one to the other. None of them volunteered an answer.

"Who are you?" the mechanic asked.

Bolton returned the silence he was offered.

The soldier looked at Bolton. "Likes to walk in the dark."

"You know him?" the mechanic asked.

The soldier nodded. "Rescued him from a cave."

Bolton narrowed his eyes.

L. M. PERALTA

"I don't think you'll remember me," the soldier said. "You were bloody and blacked out. You were lucky the ship left without me. I was journeying home on foot when I found you."

"You go cave exploring for fun?" the mechanic asked.

"It's a hobby," Bolton said.

"Like helping criminals, I suppose," the soldier said.

"We're lucky he got Morica off our trail for now." The councilor offered Bolton his hand. "I'm Pentagon. My unruly companions are Vassal and Atrus. We're on the run from Morica. Each for his own reasons."

Bolton shook Pentagon's hand. "Who's Morica?"

"You've been out for a long time, haven't you?" Atrus laughed.

Bolton glared at the mechanic as Orka landed upon his shoulder.

"Hey, isn't that Farah's bird?" Atrus asked.

"How do you know Farah?"

"We grew up in Breeze," Atrus said. "We were good friends."

"She never mentioned you," Bolton said.

"Did she mention all her friends to you?" Atrus asked.

"Is Sara with her?"

"Who's asking?"

"I fought with her in the battle against Hephaestus," Bolton said. "I'm looking for her, and I'm starting in Elementa, but I need a ship."

"Well, going to Elementa won't help," Atrus said. "I doubt she's going back there. She's on the run from Morica."

"I don't understand," Bolton said.

"All you need to know is Morica Council wants the Elementals under control," Atrus said. "You and I, we're liabilities, possible Hephaestuses who will drive them all back underground. Prevention is key. Sara's a pawn in this game. They see her as a tool to get Elementals to bow.

"Now that we're on the same page."

"Hardly," Bolton said.

"Sort of," Atrus said. "Would you like to join our band of thieves and gamblers?"

Vassal's expression was bleak.

"First," Bolton said, "tell me why you're on the run."

Vassal warned Pentagon with his eyes.

"I can't speak for them," Pentagon said, "but Morica wants to lock me away for helping Lady Sara escape her forced wedding."

"Forced wedding?" Bolton asked. "To who?"

"High Councilor Veil," Pentagon said.

"Who's that?" Bolton asked.

"He's a member of Morica," Atrus said.

Bolton's head hurt. "Were you able to get her out of it?"

"Yes," Pentagon said, "but there was a second wedding. Morica claims the vows were exchanged before we came to her aid. The High Council is saying she was kidnapped."

55

SPHERES THIEVES

"WHO taught you *Lacwanx*?" Farah asked Rai.

"I can't see how that's relevant," Rai said as they neared Vassal's tent.

Farah ran ahead of her. Turning around, she stopped in front of Rai. "How do you know Atrus?"

"I've traveled," Rai said. "I know people. Satisfied." Rai took a step forward.

Farah held her ground. "No."

"Well, I'm not in the mood for telling stories." Rai pushed her aside and entered the tent. Farah followed.

Sara sat by Rodan's bedside. The medicine caused him to doze off. "Where have you two been? It's been hours since you left."

"Only that long?" Rai slumped in a chair at the wooden table.

"What's wrong," Sara asked.

"Something weird happened," Farah said. "Something attacked the sanctum. A man was ripped to pieces . . ." her voice trailed off.

"What attacked the sanctum?" Sara asked.

"Something not human," Rai said.

"Whatever it was, it possessed people," Farah said. "Their eyes . . . I think we should leave."

"I can't," Sara said. "Rodan asked me to stay."

"If he took meli, he'll be knocked out for a while," Rai said. "You need to eat. We all do. Then we must get back to work. Morica is after us. We need a plan."

THAT night, Sara waited by Rodan's bedside. He was still lost in the deep sleep that had command over him when she left. She took his hand and held it.

Rai pushed back the tent flaps and walked inside. She stood next to the bed.

Sara looked up. "Is something wrong?"

Rai shook her head. "I'm just tired. Tired of looking at that dagger on the wall and pretending like I don't know where it came from."

Sara looked at the dagger stained with blood. It was mounted against a board on the back wall of the tent. "Where did it come from?"

"It's mine," Rai said.

"How did Vassal get it?" Sara asked.

"I stuck it in his side."

"Why?"

"Did you ever wonder how Morica got the spheres?" Rai asked.

"Many times."

Rai folded her arms. "When my father died, he didn't leave me with anything except that lake. No one wants to cross it. I couldn't afford food. I was miles from any town. So, I left.

"Along the way, I met Atrus, Pentagon, Vassal . . ." Rai paused. "Somehow they had gotten wind of this job. They had a paper. No name. No job description. Just a location and the promise of more sparklings than I could spend in a year.

"So, we traveled together to the location in Dustpath. We shared stories and adventures.

"When we arrived, there were thirty or so other applicants. A man walked in wearing a long, violet robe. He asked anyone without a weapon to leave. No one did. After all, who doesn't carry a weapon these days?

"I thought for sure I wouldn't be selected. If they were looking for weapons, they were looking for warriors. I wasn't a warrior. I was a ferryman's daughter.

"But all the applicants were selected. The whole thing was run by High Councilor Mordecai. The orders were to rid the sanctums of their spheres. We went in groups. Vassal, Atrus, Pentagon, and I stuck together.

"We fought Protectors with elements and steel. We ripped the spheres from their pedestals. A councilor always waited outside to receive the spheres, which we gave him.

"We all came together in the end to take the Earth Sphere from its dungeon. But as soon as that sphere touched Mordecai's palm, he ordered the guards to lock us all down there. He told us to fight to the death. The last man would be allowed to breathe the air of freedom. If we didn't, we would all starve down there in the crypt."

Rai shuttered, but she continued, "The men down there did not want to die. It was a horrible desperation. People were cut down in the dark in front of me.

"But then, Vassal grabbed my arm. He led me to a tunnel near the back wall. Atrus and Pentagon went with us. It was narrow. I could smell the earth. It was suffocating. There was a fissure in the ground above. We each in turn climbed on Vassal's shoulders to pull ourselves out. We reached down and pulled him up.

"We ran until we collapsed outside Omega Ray. Then we took a ship out of there.

"I don't know what happened to Mordecai's victor, but I can't imagine he allowed anyone to live. He wanted to cover all of it up. He wanted to kill us, and we all knew it.

"For weeks, we jumped from place to place. We spent a lot of time together. We became friends in the fight, but we became even closer friends on the run.

"One night, we stayed in an inn after gathering supplies from a small town nearby. The inn was in the middle of nowhere. We thought we were safe. We played cards, drank, relaxed.

"But then, Vassal wandered off in the middle of the night. When he returned, he was followed by Morica guards."

Rai's eyes watered, and she grimaced. "I stabbed him. Pentagon pulled me away. But then, Vassal was kneeling. These . . . things were coming from his mouth.

"He stood, confused, I think.

"But the guards . . . they weren't. The worms had invaded their bodies. They hacked off Vassal's hand and his leg.

"We ran. All of us," Rai said. "We left him to die. Signed him off as a traitor. He was my friend the night before." She shook her head. "I've been trying to make it right."

Sara looked up at Rai. She had taken the spheres, and she had kept it from her. Another betrayal . . . like Bolton's. But oddly, this time, the betrayal endeared Rai to her. Sara marveled at this strange mix of feelings. "It will be right again."

56

DARKNESS

A knock came to Dawn's door. She rose to answer it. Three men stood outside.

Dawn greeted them and ushered them in.

"Why did you call us here?" Vjetar's voice rang out clearly though his skin was aged and beaten like tanned leather. His azure irises shown in the depths of his dark skin. Wrinkles gathered in the corners of his eyes. His once blond hair had turned white.

Glaciem stood next to him. His nose and lips were blackened and blue around the edges, fading out to pink. His ears were ridged with black from the frost, and the fingers on his hands were shriveled with a grayish pigment. The nails that remained were blue-violet. Some had fallen away.

The other man, too, remained silent. He gave himself the name Vuur because the fire had consumed him. The only place untouched by the flames was his face where his hands had been pressed to shield himself from the fire. Pink, waxy skin covered the rest of his body, and the hair on his head could no longer grow. Sometimes the fire still roared in his ears.

"Where is Destan?" Dawn asked.

"Did you really think he would leave his watch?"

"Fulgur is out of control," Dawn said. "He's messing in matters . . . entirely human."

"You mean what he did in Lumina?"

"I mean everything he's been doing with the High Councilors. I don't know what game he's playing, but—"

"We don't have games," Vuur said. "All we have is time. Fulgur has found something to do with his."

"Is that your answer?" Dawn asked. "He's destroying the balance, and we should stop him."

"There isn't a balance anymore," Vuur said. "The Protectors are a testament to that."

"You sound like Destan," Vjetar said.

"So, that's it then?" Dawn said. "We watch like gods from the clouds."

"That's what we have always done," Vuur said.

"No," Dawn hissed. "We let humans handle themselves, but let gods police gods."

Panicked screams came from outside the door and throughout Tosia.

"Should we police that?" Vuur asked.

"That is a human matter." Dawn's crystal blue eyes aimed for the sky. "Dark Elementals are surrounded by pain, engulfed by it. Let nature run its course."

"That is not nature," Vuur said.

57

THE THREE WORN-OUT VILLAINS

BOLTON tried to pet the green bird on his shoulder, but the creature snapped at his hand.

"Guess she doesn't like you very much," Atrus said.

"Farah would never leave Orka. Something must have happened to her."

"Not Farah," Atrus said. "The bird probably flew away on its own.

Vassal headed the group. "You're sure the sphere rolled into that cave?"

"Yes," Bolton said. "It was in my hand when I passed out. It must be there."

"Morica has no use for a broken sphere," Pentagon said. "We're wasting our time."

"Would you rather wait around in hiding?" Vassal said. "We were very good at that back in Lumina. Besides Mordecai has his head up his ass. He fears Elementals so much, he'll believe the sphere is still whole if we tell him so. We could use it to control him when we need to."

Bolton kicked up the sand on Dustpath Road. They neared the inn.

"Brings up old memories, doesn't it, Vassal?" Atrus taunted.

"Ancient," Vassal said without emotion.

Bolton approached the inn and knocked on the door.

"I don't think we're welcome," Vassal said.

"Whose fault is that?" Atrus asked.

Bolton heard labored steps coming from inside. The door swung open.

"Welcome to—" Solace stood in the doorway. He stared at Bolton. "You're alive?"

"Was I dead?"

A grin spread across Solace's face. "You're alive! This is incredible!"

"What happened to your leg?" Bolton asked.

Solace's leg was bandaged above his knee. Blood soaked through.

"Ran into some Morica guards," Solace said. "The cowards! They shot me while I was down. I was defending Lady Sara against those brutes."

"Defending her? What happened?" Bolton asked.

"They kidnapped her, it seems" Solace said. "She definitely didn't want to go with them. I wasn't able to help her." Solace looked down.

"They've taken her?" Bolton asked.

"Last I heard, she escaped from Vella City," Solace said. "She must have gotten away eventually. After that wedding. I won't believe her friends captured her. Morica is lying to us!"

"I'm looking for her, Solace," Bolton said.

"You must have traveled a long way. You'll need rest if you wish to find Lady Sara." He grabbed Bolton by the arm and ushered him inside. "Board's on me for the night. Please, please come in!"

Vassal loudly cleared his throat.

Solace looked up to see him, Pentagon, and Atrus standing near the gate. He glared at them.

"Get away from here!" Solace shouted. "You will not bring any more of those guards here. Get away from my inn."

"Sir," Pentagon started, "we have no need to stay at your inn. If you'll let our friend go, we'll be on our way."

Bolton stood with Solace in the doorway.

"Sorry we bothered you." Bolton stepped back outside.

"You're traveling with them?" Solace asked.

"They're going to help me find Sara."

"I wouldn't trust them," Solace said. "They're wanted men. They've probably had Morica at their heels since the night they stayed here. Where are you headed?"

"Jetty Verte," Bolton said.

"If I see Lady Sara, I'll tell her you came this way. I don't know how I will get her to believe me." Solace shut the door, and the lock clicked.

Bolton turned back to the three worn-out villains. "You must have done something terrible to make a man like Solace hate you."

"All we did was bring guests," Vassal said.

"They weren't *our* guests." Atrus shot a glance at Vassal.

"I don't understand," Bolton said. "Are you friends or enemies?"

"Who do you keep closer?" Vassal asked.

They walked down Dustpath onto the new road.

"Then why are you still together?" Bolton asked. "Why don't you go your separate ways if you hate each other so much?"

As they stepped upon the new road, Vassal said, "For one simple fact. We fight better as a team, whether we like each other or not."

"Once we get the sphere, what exactly is the plan?" Bolton asked.

"So many questions?" Vassal taunted.

"I have a lot of questions you still haven't answered," Bolton said.

"Being knocked out for three years will do that to you," Atrus said.

"Maybe we should knock him out for three more," Vassal suggested.

Bolton stopped and turned around.

"Where are you going?" Pentagon asked.

"Sorry. It's been nice and all," Bolton said, not turning back. "But I can't stick around to be bitter with you."

"That's probably not a good idea," Atrus said. "Morica's on your trail just like the rest of us. If they catch you, they'll kill you or throw you in a dungeon."

"Let him go," Vassal said.

"Wait!" Atrus said, a sense of urgency in his voice.

Bolton turned his head, but his body was half-turned to the road.

"Call me a saint," Atrus said, "but I can't let you walk away without paying you back for what you did for us in Lumina. Besides, Farah's mad at me, and if I let you go get yourself killed, she might be liable to kill me too. That girl's a tiger."

Bolton turned to face them.

"You want to ask another question, don't you?" Vassal asked.

Bolton shook his head and sighed. He rejoined the group, and they headed for Wyvek. Atrus promised that when they got to the temple, he would have his workers make a transmitter to reach the Chariot.

When they arrived, the place had been abandoned. The temple doors were open. Pieces of metal and bolts littered the floor.

Atrus ran into the temple. The others followed.

"What happened here?" Pentagon asked.

"I don't know," Atrus said. "I wasn't here."

As they rounded the bend and stepped into the elevator room, the gory sight met their eyes.

A man, his neck broken, was tossed like a ragdoll across the rails of the elevator. The dismembered arm of one of Atrus's workers rested on the floor in a pool of blood.

"You're kidding me," Pentagon muttered.

"We should leave," Vassal said. "This is not the work of Morica guards."

Atrus weaved between two columns to the back wall where he pulled out the wall panel.

"Can you still make the transmitter?" Bolton asked.

"Afraid not." Atrus continued his task. "I need the materials and the workers. Looks like most of the materials are destroyed, and the workers have fled."

"So, you're taking your aggression out on the wall?" Pentagon asked.

"Secret stash," Atrus explained. He successfully ripped the panel off the wall. Reaching into the edifice, he pulled out a shiny, metallic weapon and tossed it to Pentagon.

"What is this?" Pentagon asked.

"In the old days, they called it a gun," Atrus explained. "Morica has them. Now, we do too."

Pentagon turned the metal object in his hand and marveled at the weight of it.

Atrus took out two more pistols and offered one to Vassal.

"I prefer the old way," Vassal said, refusing the weapon.

"This *is* the old way," Atrus said. "I don't have anything more primitive."

"That's alright." Vassal's long sword zinged as he pulled it from its sheath. "I have my weapon."

Atrus offered the gun to Bolton.

"I wouldn't know how to use it," Bolton said.

"I'll teach you."

"I'm better with my element."

Atrus put the gun into the waistband of his pants and stuffed his pockets and satchel with steel bullets. "Suit yourselves."

From Wyvek, they traveled to the Lake, boarded a boat, and rowed to the opposite side, to Tosia.

Orka chirped the whole time, but Bolton could not understand her.

"At least that bird seems to like you more than it likes me," Atrus said.

"She puts up with me," Bolton said.

"She tried to bite me the first time I spoke to Farah."

Orka bobbed her head and squawked at Atrus.

"Angry, little, green monster."

Bolton tried to pet Orka to calm her, but she arched away from his touch and snapped at him.

They got out of the boat when they made it to the opposite shore and walked to Tosia. Outside the entrance to Tosia, the trees were dying. They were blackened and withering.

When Bolton and the three villains stepped upon the marble floor in front of the entrance, the roots covering the floor cracked and splintered under their feet.

They looked up at the great tree. It was black, and the leaves had fallen, coating the branches of the trees below with dried, dead foliage.

"What did this?" Atrus asked.

Vassal reached for the handle of the door, which used to be formed from a living branch, but it crumbled in his hand. Vassal shouldered the door and shoved. The door gave with a squeal.

Inside, the sloping walkways cracked. Pools of blackened ash crept along the floor, the walls, and the upper branches. The town looked like a starless night.

The hooded victims were scattered and crawling on the splintered floor.

Bolton stepped along the fragile wood to a hooded figure on the ground. Her face pointed down. Bolton knelt beside her.

"What happened here?" he asked.

The woman grabbed Bolton's arms and lifted herself up onto her knees. Her face was blackened on one side, and her eyes were like deep, dark wells. Bolton could not see his own reflection in them.

"The High Councilor . . . he has power . . . strange power. It moves in shadows. There was a woman with him. She dripped with black ooze. She told him to hurt us."

The woman let go of Bolton and resumed her aimless crawling.

Bolton stood and backed away from the woman.

"She's gone mad," Vassal said.

"She said a High Councilor did this," Bolton said.

"High Councilors don't have this kind of power." Pentagon eyed the dark walls.

Bolton looked at the black pools on the ground. He had seen this before, back in Omega Ray.

"We have to go," Vassal said.

"And leave all these people?" Pentagon hissed.

"You want to try to help these people, you go right on ahead," Vassal said. "But, it doesn't look like they can be helped."

Pentagon approached a man creeping along the ground and tried to help him up, but the men shook him off and stared at him with unreflective eyes.

"Let's go," Vassal said.

THE atmosphere of D'arkadia had changed. The sky was dim, but no longer as dark as before. Bolton wondered at this and half expected the Beast to jump out, open its great maw, and pour the darkness out again.

Vassal stopped and settled onto the ground. "We'll rest here." He took a swig of water from his canteen.

Bolton looked around.

"The Beast has been tamed," Vassal said.

"You didn't stop at your headquarters," Atrus said. "Why?"

"Don't you think it's a little late to ask that question?" Vassal said.

"We've been walking for days," Atrus said. "We walk and sleep and then walk some more. My mind has been on other things."

"Right," Vassal said. "You didn't have the courage to ask until now. But why?"

"You won't do anything when we're this close to Vella City," Atrus said. "Morica guards took your hand and your leg. What will they take next?"

"We didn't need to be side-tracked," Vassal said. "I'll return to my soldiers when we have the sphere."

"Why did you leave in the first place?" Pentagon asked.

"There were men who wanted to join us," Vassal said. "Well, supposedly. When we got the message, I and four of my soldiers journeyed to Dustpath to meet them and lead them to headquarters. It was a setup. I don't know how word leaked out about us, but Morica fighters met with us, and they knew who I was. They killed my men before I could put a blade in their hearts. I recognized one of the men. He used to fight alongside me. He was a Resistance fighter faithful to Morica. They walk around, thinking they're not puppets. They think that they fight for Mirmina, but they fight for the High Council."

THEY entered the Crystal Forest. Morica guards marched through on their way to Tosia. Vassal was the first to hear their marching.

"Hide in the trees," he hissed.

They followed his command and watched through the leaves as the guards passed. There were eight guards dressed in blue-and-silver. As the troop marched on, the guard at the end of the line stopped and stared into the trees where Bolton hid.

The sweat on Bolton's forehead dripped down his nose. The guard was still staring.

Bolton stepped back. A twig cracked beneath his feet.

"Halt!" the guard shouted. "I think I heard something."

"You don't say when to halt, boy." The head guard thundered toward him. "It was just a bird."

Orka chirped to affirm.

"See, be on alert, but don't let your imagination run away with you—"

"But, sir, birds don't break twigs."

"I've heard they can imitate all kinds of sounds," another guard said.

"Are we going to stop and talk about birds, or are we going to follow orders?" the head guard asked.

"Sir, I want to investigate."

The head guard laughed. "Go on, boy, and when you find nothing, I'll hit you with the flat of my sword."

The other guards gathered around as the lone guard made his way through the trees.

"Now!" Vassal shouted.

As the group moved through the trees, Vassal slashed the searching guard across the belly, and the guard watched his own blood spill upon the ground.

The remaining guards pulled out their weapons. Some carried swords, others carried guns.

Swords clashed and guns fired.

The head guard shouted, "Save your bullets men! We don't need to be wasting them on this lot."

Atrus showed off the store of bullets lining the inside of his vest. "Don't worry, you can always buy more."

The head guard dashed for Vassal, and their swords met.

Atrus managed to shoot a guard down in the fray, taking their number down to six.

Orka flew into the face of a guard marching towards Bolton. While the guard was distracted by the bird, Bolton stunned him, sending Lightning through his body until he shuttered on the ground.

Pentagon tried shooting at the guards, but he was not familiar with the weapon, and years of retirement left him with poor aim. As a guard approached, the gun locked.

Pentagon hit the weapon with his hand and tried jamming down on the trigger.

The guard grinned, getting closer and closer to the white-haired councilor.

Pentagon grasped the gun in his hand and hit the guard in the head with the butt of the weapon, knocking the man to the ground.

Atrus had to reload. As he loaded the gun, a guard made a mad dash at him with a dagger. Vassal stepped between them and slashed the guard with his sword. The guard fell to the ground.

"That's why I prefer a sword," Vassal said.

Atrus finished loading his gun. He pointed the gun over Vassal's shoulder and shot the guard who was running up behind him.

"It's not the weapon," Atrus said. "It's the wielder."

"Can't argue with that, my friend," Vassal said.

While Pentagon brutalized another guard with the butt of his pistol, an injured guard rose from the ground. Pentagon felt the cool blade of a dagger against his throat.

"Stand back and drop your weapons or I'll kill your friend."

"You think we care about him," Vassal said.

Pentagon stared wide-eyed at Vassal, not knowing whether the man was serious.

"Besides, do you really think you could take us all? Even without our weapons? Especially not with that injured leg." Vassal pointed to the huge gash in the man's calf. "And you're asking at least one of us to perform the impossible, Bolton's weapon can't be dropped."

Vassal looked at Bolton and nodded toward the guard.

"No," Bolton said, "I might hit Pentagon."

"We don't care about him, remember?" Atrus said.

"Thanks," Pentagon said through his teeth.

The guard's eyes glued to Bolton, and he awaited the attack.

"It's too dangerous," Bolton said.

As the grin spread across the guard's face, Atrus sent Wind, which knocked the guard and Pentagon to the ground. The guard's head hit the jagged edge of a crystal, knocking him unconscious. Pentagon stood, his hand clasped across his neck, but he was unharmed.

"You could have gotten me killed!" Pentagon said.

"But I didn't."

Something slipped from the guard's pocket. It lay on the ground beside him. It was a silver box with several little holes at the top.

"What's this?" Vassal scooped up the small device and tossed it to Atrus.

Atrus caught it and looked at it. "It's a communicator, a transmitter, whoever has this one can talk through it and send their voices to whoever has the one like it. It's only a one-way though. Thatch uses them. We make them in Wyvek. Well, we used to."

Bolton took the transmitter from Atrus.

"How does it work?" he asked.

"You can't reach Sara with it. It's on a different frequency," Atrus said.

"What?" Bolton asked.

"Use that," Atrus said, "and you'll probably contact a Morica guard or High Councilor, whoever is on the same frequency. That's not the frequency Thatch uses."

"Ah," Vassal said. "There's always a language barrier when talking to the people of Breeze."

"How many gadgets did you give them?" Pentagon asked.

"Not give. Sold," Atrus corrected.

"That's still helping the enemy," Vassal said.

"Guess you and I have switched places then," Atrus said.

Bolton felt something hit him in the back of the head. Then came a cold sensation. Orka, from the safety of the trees, chirped to warn them.

Before Bolton loss consciousness, he heard movement through the trees and Atrus say, "Damn it! He must have used it to call in reinforcements!"

"Things have a way of coming back to bite you," Vassal mused.

58

TRIAL BY COUNCIL

WHEN Bolton awoke, he was chained to a wall in a large room. As he blinked and tried to focus, he could see his three companions at the front of the room facing the High Council. The High Councilors sat high above them on a wooden platform. A long table served as a barrier between them and the three villains.

Bolton's new friends were chained in hand-cuffs and stood behind a low wooden barricade.

He began to get feeling back. He realized he was hanging, his feet dragged to the ground while his wrists suffered from his own weight against the shackles. He stood to relieve the pressure, but as soon as he did, two guards hit him in the ribs with their batons.

Bolton doubled over in pain.

"Is that really necessary?" Pentagon asked.

"To keep him weak so he cannot use his element against us," High Councilor Surnom said.

"I can knock you over by just looking at you, old man!" Atrus shouted.

"I know of your power, boy. Rather weak for an Elemental."

Atrus glared at his customers, five old men, dressed in long robes, praying the world would not turn against them as Hephaestus had.

Vassal was only interested in one of them. "Why taunt us with a trial, Mordecai? If these guards would have brought us to *you*, we wouldn't be standing on ceremony, would we? Is that why we're not dead yet?"

"All people have the right to a trial," Mordecai said, "even criminals."

Vassal smirked. "Who is the real criminal? The puppets or the puppet master?"

"Silence!" Councilor Romulus said. "This trial will proceed in an orderly fashion or we'll toss you all in the dungeons. State the charges."

Councilor Jove stood and read: "For the assault and injury of three Morica guards and the death of five, for the disruption of the peace in the City of Lumina, and the tragedy in Tosia—"

"Wait a minute!" Atrus said. "Whatever happened in Tosia, that wasn't us."

"Can you prove it?" Mordecai asked.

"So, that's the way it works."

"That's the way it works here," High Councilor Cadueus said.

"Who accuses us of the crime in Tosia?" Vassal asked.

The High Councilors were silent.

"Who?" Vassal demanded. "Oh, please, don't make me argue with shadows."

Mordecai shifted in his seat.

"Is something wrong, High Councilor?" Vassal asked. "I noticed one of you is missing from the bench. Any thoughts on that?"

"This is your trial," Mordecai said.

"Why did you attack the guards?" Surnom asked.

"They would have attacked us," Pentagon said.

"Do you have a grudge against Morica?"

"Everyone has a grudge against Morica," Atrus said. "Do the questions and answers get more obvious or is someone ready to really stump us?"

"Many now seek the protection of Morica," Romulus said. "Like the mechanics of Wyvek who were attacked after their leader left them."

"I'm sure you had no hand in helping them," Atrus said."

"How would you know?" Romulus said. "You weren't there."

Bolton lifted his head, and the guards battered his ribs again, making him cry out.

"Stop this!" Pentagon shouted. "We've done nothing that wasn't in self-defense . . . unless High Councilor Mordecai wants to charge us with *another* crime."

Mordecai shuffled in his seat.

"You need us, don't you," Vassal said. "That's why this trial. So, let's negotiate."

"Defeat Veil, in the name of Morica, and the charges will be dropped, and you will be free to go."

"Defeat a High Councilor. All that will take is my dagger in his gut."

"Now, when you say the charges against us will be dropped," Atrus asked, "is that including just the charges listed today or any charges prior to—"

"All of the charges," Mordecai said, "if you survive."

"First, let our friend go," Pentagon demanded.

"Release him," Surnom commanded the guards.

The guards unlocked the shackles around Bolton's wrists and he fell to the floor. The guards snickered.

When Bolton found the strength to stand, he punched a laughing guard in the throat, and the guard knelt and gasped for air.

His fellow guard lifted his baton in the air above Bolton.

"Enough!" Surnom shouted. "Find and kill Veil, and Morica Council will thank you."

"We don't need Morica's thanks," Vassal said as the guards ushered them out the room.

59

LUCERNA

"CAN you stand on it?" Sara helped Rodan out of the bed. She supported his back with one hand and placed a hand upon his chest so he wouldn't fall. His arm rested on her shoulders.

Rodan didn't dare tell her that he was fine for fear she would leave his side. He squeezed Sara's shoulder. He was delirious from the meli. "I never really got to be angry."

"What?" Sara asked.

"I mean . . . I was angry," he said, "but I had to be happy too. Bolton was my best friend. I couldn't just be angry."

"Sara?" Farah entered the tent. "Come quick!"

Sara attempted to help Rodan back into the bed, but he stopped her. "No, I can walk."

He and Sara followed Farah.

Lucerna arrived at Resistance Headquarters with a message for them. Rai and Thatch talked to her. Sara and Rodan joined them.

"Is there somewhere we can go that's more private?" Lucerna asked.

They walked to the entrance right outside the rocky wall.

"I have something to show you." Lucerna reached into the satchel around her waist and pulled out something wrapped in a cloth. She unfolded the cloth to reveal an orb devoid of light. A crack ran through its center.

Sara recognized it. "But how?"

"Madame Dawn sent me to retrieve this. She was nursing a traveler and she began to believe his unconscious ravings. He kept muttering in his sleep about the sphere and the cave. Madame Dawn said you need it, and I was to get it for you."

"She sent you in there alone?" Farah asked.

"It wasn't deep in the cave. It was right at the entrance. I shined a light, and I saw it."

Sara took the broken sphere. "We have to go to the Crystal Forest."

"I have an Aether," Rai said. "We can do it here."

"No," Sara said. "It won't work here. Your Aether needs to draw its energy from the Crystal Forest. We need to see Founten."

RAI flew the Chariot to Jetty Verte outside the Crystal Forest.

They walked into the forest and to the clearing.

"Founten?" Sara called. A large owl-like creature appeared. With him was an Aether.

"You found it," Founten said.

"Can it be repaired?" Sara asked.

The white feathered head nodded. "Nothing is lost."

Sara placed the sphere inside the Aether. This Aether's substance was cool to the touch. It did not burn like Rai's Aether. Removing her hand from the cool, gel-like substance, Sara stepped back.

Light shone, making them all look away. Floating inside the Aether, the surface of the sphere was smooth.

Sara reached in and took the sphere.

"Do you feel any different?" Farah asked.

Sara shook her head.

Lucerna looked on in amazement. "I didn't think it could be done." She reached into her bag mechanically. "Madame Dawn said if I gave you the sphere, and you were able to repair it that I am to give you this." She handed Sara a piece of paper.

"It's a map." Drawn on the paper, Sara recognized Omega Ray. In the center of the city was a symbol with seven circles going around a smaller circle in the center.

"She wants me to find this?"

Lucerna nodded.

THEY traveled the snowy mountain to Omega Ray. The city was abandoned. Tag and his workers packed up and left. The lights were out in the city, and the mist drifted through.

"Looks like my dad finally gave up on this place," Farah said.

Sara held up the map. "It looks like whatever the symbol is marking must be over there." Sara pointed toward the center of the city where Hephaestus's stone palace had fallen to ruins.

She led the way with Farah, Rai, Rodan, and Lucerna in pursuit.

An unearthly howl sounded in the distance.

Rodan and Rai drew their swords.

They continued toward the center of the city.

They approached the ruins to Hephaestus's palace. Sara looked at the map and down at the cold stone floor. "It should be here." She kneeled, touching the stones.

She put her fingers between the cracks and lifted the stones from their beds. With effort, she removed one of the stones and placed it on the floor beside her. Rodan sheathed his sword and knelt to help her.

Farah held the lantern over them.

After four stones were removed, they stood. Beneath the stones, were seven hollowed round edifices, and in the center, was an eighth.

Sara compared it to the map. It was the same. She knelt and touched the places where the stones were hollowed out. Above each was an element symbol.

"Give me the spheres," Sara said.

Farah reached for her bag and handed it to Sara.

"Sara, wait!" Rodan said. "We don't know what this does."

"Madame Dawn led us to it." Sara reached into the bag and planted each sphere into its place. Once the spheres were set, Sara stood. "There's one missing."

In the center, the eighth hollowed edifice had no symbol above it.

"So much for that." Rai knelt to remove the spheres. Her hand touched the Fire Sphere.

"Wait!" A loud voice echoed around them.

A figure approached from the mist.

Rodan unsheathed his sword with a zing and stepped in front of Sara.

"Dawn sent you?" The figure stepped into the light and removed the hood he wore.

He was an old man. The mark on his face looked familiar to Sara. It was shaped like a tear. Something else was familiar. A glowing, red light emitted from beneath the sleeve of his robe. Unlike Sara and her company, this man's breath was not visible in white mist against the cold.

"You'll need this." He reached into his cloak and pulled out a sphere. He offered it to them.

Sara stepped in front of Rodan and approached the man.

Rodan kept his sword ready.

Sara took the sphere. "Who are you?" she asked the man.

"I've been guarding that sphere and this place."

"Why?" she asked.

"This is my city. I've been searching for that very spot. Years ago, I built that mechanism."

"What does it do?" Sara asked.

"Set the spheres, and find out."

Sara looked down at the sphere. She walked to where the other spheres rested, knelt, and placed the remaining sphere in the center.

The circle of spheres turned, and each of the spheres shone from its place in the circle.

Sara backed away.

When the other spheres went dull, the one in the center brightened. The sky erupted with light, and Aethers burst into the air. The light from the center sphere dimmed, but did not go out. Sara knelt and removed it. It was warm.

"Lucerna, are you okay?" Farah asked.

Sara turned to Lucerna.

Lucerna's hair had turned as white as the snow on the ground, and her eyes were pale blue.

"What?" she asked.

"Your hair. Your eyes."

Lucerna picked up one end of her long hair and brought it up to her face. "Where is all that light coming from?"

"The light's gone," Farah said. "It's dark again."

"No," Lucerna said. "It's as bright as day out here."

60

THE ONCE OLD SCHOLAR

WHILE Thatch and Stannum waited in the control room, the Old Scholar sat on the roof of the Chariot. He was wrapped in a wool blanket to keep warm in the cold air.

He had been a traveler. He had seen all Mirmina, searching for someone he could not find.

In his travels, he went to Omega Ray where he met a man who promised to help him find the person he was looking for so desperately.

The man was old and had an odd shaped mark on his face, like a tear.

He had a sphere, and he told him to hold it, and to think of the people he had missed, and of all the pain and the happiness he had witnessed in his life.

The Old Scholar thought of those things, and his body began to age. Scared, he dropped the sphere.

But it was too late.

The man picked up the sphere and was not satisfied. Nothing happened. The sphere had life but no substance.

The Old Scholar asked about the man's promise, but he said he couldn't keep it.

And so, he left.

The Old Scholar curled his hand into a fist as he gazed into the night sky, not really seeing the stars.

A burst of light erupted into the sky. It was followed by a brighter light that shone for several minutes before fading.

The sky was suffused with glowing Aethers.

When the Old Scholar opened his eyes, he gazed upon the hand he had used to shield his face from the light. The skin was less wrinkled, and the veins were just barely visible beneath the flesh.

He felt his face. The skin was firmer. His hair fuller.

The curse was over.

61

DARK STORM

RAI took the jar from her satchel and released her Aether to join the others in the sky.

Farah bagged the spheres.

At dawn, they journeyed back to the Chariot where Thatch, Stannum, and the Old Scholar waited for them.

"So, when do we return the element spheres?" Farah asked.

"It's not safe yet," Rodan said. "Morica is on our heels, and they're probably guarding every sphere sanctum in Mirmina."

They entered the Chariot and took the elevator to the control room.

"What happened out there?" Thatch asked. "We saw a burst of light. It flooded the sky for several minutes."

Lucerna stepped into the light.

"Whoa!" Thatch's eyes grew wide.

After they explained what happened in the abandoned city, Stannum spoke up. "A Keeper."

"A what?" Farah asked.

"That man you met in the city," Stannum buzzed.

"From the book?" Sara asked.

Stannum's eye blinked. "The Keepers, the men who came to Dustpath. They told the Builders to create the sanctums."

"That's impossible," Farah said. "If he was a Keeper, he would be dead, long dead."

"He was guarding that sphere," Sara said. "But from who?"

"We don't have time for riddles." Rai took her seat at the steering wheel. "We have to return the spheres before the Protectors terrorize every city in Mirmina."

"It's too dangerous right now," Rodan said.

"Well, Resistance fighter, tell me, when is it going to be safe to enter a sphere sanctum?" Rai asked.

"Rai, you should rest," Thatch said. "You can't fly tired."

"Who said I was tired?" Rai asked.

"We're all tired." Thatch rose from his seat and took the elevator to the cabin room.

"Thatch is right." Sara placed her hand on Rai's shoulder. "I need some fresh air." Sara walked to the elevator. The hatch door opened to the roof.

The Old Scholar marveled at his hands. He stood on the roof and let the wool blanket fall from his shoulders.

"Scholar?" Sara stepped closer.

The Old Scholar turned around.

"Who are you?" Sara approached him. His face was visible in the dim light under the cloudy sky. Bolton's eyes looked back at her.

The Old Scholar didn't speak.

"Did you hear me?" Sara asked. "Why are you wearing the Old Scholar's clothes?"

"I . . . I *am* the Old Scholar."

"No." Sara shook her head.

The man nodded.

"Come with me," she said.

The man followed her to the control room.

"I don't know what we did back in that city," Rai said, "but I don't like it."

"What happened to Lucerna?" Farah asked. "Her hair . . ."

"It's the spheres." Rodan sat with his hands clasped in front of them. "We have to return them or—" He looked up.

Sara stood at the elevator with the man.

"Who . . .?" Rodan rose from his seat.

"He says he's the Old Scholar," Sara said.

The man smirked. "I was never that old. I just thought it was stolen from me."

"How did you get on the ship?" Rodan asked.

"You let me on. I'm the Old Scholar."

"Like hell you are," Rai said. "Do you think we lack eyes?"

"He looks like Bolton." Farah approached him. "Only older."

"I don't know what to say," the strange man muttered.

"The truth," Sara said.

"My name is Benn. I come from the Insula. I've been looking for my son, Bolton."

"Really?" Rai laughed.

Farah placed her hands on her hips. "Is this a joke?"

"He's lying to us." Rai put her hand on her head. "Maybe Thatch is right. I need sleep." She walked to the elevator.

Farah, Rodan, and Sara stood in silence and waited for the man to tell them something they could believe. When he offered nothing, Sara spoke, "You were another man when we brought you on this chariot. What happened to you?"

"I don't know," Benn said. "But I was never that old man you saw back on the Insula. I should have been younger. When that light in the sky, when it came, I changed back. Well, I got younger, not as young as when it all started, but probably as young as I would have been had it never happened."

"I don't understand anything you're saying," Farah said. "What do you mean *it*? When what happened?"

"The traveler asked me to hold a sphere," Benn said, "and it took my youth. It took my soul, and that wave of light released it."

"You're Bolton's father?" Sara asked.

Benn nodded.

"You're the coward then?" Sara glared at him for a long moment. No one spoke. Sara walked away, her footsteps loud across the metal floor. If she could have slammed the steel doors of the elevator, she would have.

THREE nights later, Rai flew the Chariot over Lumina.

"What's that?" Farah's eyes focused outside the large window in the control room.

"What?" Thatch asked.

"The sky looks darker. Over there. You see how the stars disappear just over that large patch of sky."

"I see," Rai said. "It might be a cloud."

"Smoke?"

As day dawned, the darkness remained. It hovered over Lumina. It was thicker than smoke and blocked the city lights. As Rai landed the Chariot on Dustpath Road, the cloud gathered size until it engulfed the entire city.

They met in the control room.

"We have to enter the cloud and see what is affecting the city," Sara said.

Thatch shook his head. "Not a good idea. We don't know what that thing is."

"But what we do know," Sara said, "is that the people of Mirmina are in that cloud. Thousands of people have flocked to Lumina on the belief that they would be safe. Now we must protect them."

"I'm coming," Lucerna said.

"Your skill with a weapon is untested," Rai said.

"But I can see in the dark," Lucerna said. "You may need me."

"She's right," Sara said. "Lucerna comes too, but stay close.

"Rodan, how's your leg?"

"It's fine," he said.

They approached the elevator, Sara in the lead. But before they got there, Benn stepped in front of Sara. "I have an element. I want to use it."

Sara swallowed what she wanted to say. *Why didn't you use your element to save your wife and son?* She wanted to jab at him, but she pressed her lips closed and nodded.

62

INSIDE THE STORM

BOLTON and the three pardoned villains were off to Lumina. The Council received distress signals from the city. Vassal, Atrus, Pentagon, and Bolton boarded a small chariot piloted by two Morica guards.

They saw the cloud miles before reaching the Port. It grew over a large portion of the city.

When they landed in the water by the dock, and the hatch opened, Vassal rushed out and vomited in the water.

"Air sick?" Atrus clapped him on the back.

"Just another reason to prefer the old way." Vassal coughed.

"This is 'the old way,'" Atrus said.

Vassal wiped his mouth with the back of his hand.

"We're not going into that thing, are we?" Pentagon stared up into the looming black cloud.

"Like Tosia," Bolton said.

Orka perched upon his shoulder. "Go, Orka. Farah would kill me if anything happens to you."

The green bird flew into the distance.

As they left the deck, a crowd pushed past them as the people tried to escape the cloud. Some dove into the water. Others ran toward Dustpath.

SARA exited the Chariot followed by Rodan, Farah, Rai, Lucerna, and Benn.

"The cloud is spreading from the pavilion," Farah said.

People rushed past them as they entered the city. A man ran up to Sara. His face and hands were blackened, and his eyes were darker than the night.

"Get them off me!" he screamed. "Please." He grabbed Sara's hands. "The rats. They're everywhere. They're eating me!" He let go of Sara and brushed his shoulders and his chest.

"Calm down." Sara placed her hands on his shoulders. "There's nothing there."

The man fell to his knees. Sara tried to help him up, but he refused. "I can feel them. Help me," he begged.

"He's delusional," Rai said.

"A nightmare," Sara said. "Like in the Lake."

"What are you saying?"

"The Dark Sphere. This is an Elemental."

"How do we stop this?" Rai asked.

Sara looked at Lucerna.

VASSAL, Pentagon, Atrus, and Bolton neared the pavilion. The cloud rose over the tall buildings of the city, over the Stadium.

"So, Veil's in that cloud?" Pentagon said.

Vassal nodded. "He let darkness consume him, and we have to clean up the mess."

"Wait," Atrus said, "Pentagon, give me your gun."

"Why?"

Atrus took it from him and loaded it with bullets. "You don't know how to load." He handed the gun back to Pentagon.

"Thanks," Pentagon said with a sneer.

The marble floor was blackened and splintered. People ran, hiding their faces, crying and crawling away from the cloud.

"How do we keep that thing back?" Pentagon asked.

"Kill what's controlling it," Vassal said.

"We should go in," Bolton said.

"Two of us will," Atrus said. "The other two should get these people out of here and onto Dustpath. I volunteer to enter."

Vassal stepped forward.

"No." Pentagon stopped him. "If anything happens, we don't want to lose our best swordsman. I'll go. You give the finishing blow."

"Generous of you," Vassal said.

Atrus and Pentagon entered the dark mist. Inside, darkness curled around them.

"This must be the base work for nightmares," Atrus said. "Think warm thoughts: the comfort of a woman's embrace and the savory taste of wild roast boar."

"Are you serious?" Pentagon asked.

"How should I know? Thanks by the way."

"You mean Vassal?"

"Yep."

"I know. I wouldn't have wanted to travel through a dark cloud with the guy. I barely trust him in the light of day."

Without end, the darkness stretched in front of them. Not like a dark room, but instead a dark, empty nothingness, all consuming.

"I'm starting to think it would have been better to be wrapped in chains in Fortress Tower," Pentagon said.

Two heavy chains came out of the darkness, wrapped around Pentagon, and pinned his arms to his sides.

"Get me out of this!"

"What? I can't see anything." Atrus reached inside his satchel and felt for his lantern and matchbox. Striking a match, he lit the lantern. He tried to remove the chains.

Atrus put the lantern down, and tried to loosen the chains. But the lantern fell as if no floor rested beneath it.

"What the . . ." Pentagon's voice trailed off.

"A woman's embrace," Atrus said.

"Shut up and get me out of this or I'm going to kill you."

"Seems like you would have a harder time killing me with these chains on." Atrus tried to unwrap the chains in the dark, but they wouldn't budge. "Looks like you're stuck, Pent."

The chains hit the floor and fell away from Pentagon's body.

The lantern jettisoned down from above, and Atrus caught it by the handle.

"Ah hah!" he cried.

"It's taunting us," Pentagon said.

"At least it gave this back to us." Atrus held up the lantern.

"Watch out!"

They dove to the floor as a winged shadow swept for them.

"What in the hell?" Atrus said under his breath.

Winged, shadow demons with fingernails that reached their knees surrounded Atrus and Pentagon. The demons flew low, clawing at the two men.

"Can they be killed?" Pentagon asked.

Atrus rolled on his back and shot at one of the shadows. The bullet hit the demon in the chest. The shadow fizzled out.

"That works," Atrus said. "Get up and shoot!"

Atrus and Pentagon shot at the dozens of shadows surrounding them.

Pentagon ducked as a jagged claw brushed his face.

A shadow swept low, and Atrus fell onto his back to avoid it. His gun was knocked out of his hand, and it skirted across the ground to where Pentagon fought. The bullets rolled across the floor.

In the dim light of the lantern, Pentagon gathered the gun and some of the bullets. He reloaded the weapon and threw it to Atrus.

Atrus raised the gun and shot the demon that dove for his face.

Atrus got to his feet. He and Pentagon moved closer to each other. They stood back-to-back and commenced shooting.

"So, you *can* load," Atrus said.

"Lucky for you."

"Now there's always that question," Atrus said as he continued to shoot at shadows. "Would you have acted so urgently to save me if you weren't trying to prove me wrong?"

"You'll never know."

SARA stood between the darkness and the light.

"We have to get Lucerna to the center of the cloud," Rai said. "Whatever this is, it's growing from the center."

As the cloud grew, darkness engulfed Sara. The others followed.

Within the blackness, tissue rustled in a stiff breeze. A gun shot echoed. The bullet landed, and the shadow, deeper than the darkness, fell behind them.

"You should watch your backs," Atrus said.

Pentagon held up his lantern. "Rai? What are you doing here?"

Rai stepped aside. Behind her was Lucerna. Her hair and eyes glowed so brightly, the darkness around her faded into light. But the light was more blinding than the darkness.

Atrus shielded his eyes. "What is that?"

"A weapon," Rai said.

Pentagon stepped forward. "Where did you come into the cloud?"

"The market," Rai said.

"That doesn't make sense," Atrus said. "We came in from the port, and we haven't moved."

"It's a directionless void," Pentagon murmured.

"Then how can we get to the center?" Farah asked.

"You mean to Veil?" Atrus reloaded his weapon.

"Veil's doing this?" Sara asked. "I don't understand."

"Veil's a Dark Elemental," Atrus said.

"Sara, there's something else we have to tell you." Pentagon stepped into Lucerna's glow.

Lightning struck within the void. Farah screamed and hid behind Rodan. It struck again. Heat rippled across her skin.

"That's happened before, Pentagon thought of chains, and they appeared," Atrus said. "Farah, you thought of lightning, didn't you?"

Farah nodded. "How did you know?"

"I've known you since we were children," Atrus said. "It's what you're most afraid of."

"Our worst nightmares come to us in this void," Pentagon said.

"Then," Rodan said, "we must make Veil our worst nightmare."

"That won't be too hard." Farah removed her dagger from its sheath.

"Close your eyes," Sara said. "Focus on Veil." Sara closed her eyes against the darkness.

Laughter echoed.

Veil stood among the blackness as it radiated from his body. A shadow laughed beside him. The shadow was the figure of a woman, her form covered in thick, black muck that dripped as she walked.

The darkness seemed darker, but not just because of Veil's presence.

"Orka!" Farah screamed. "Answer me!"

"Orka's not here." Sara placed a hand on her shoulder.

Rai looked behind her. "Where's Lucerna?"

They searched the darkness, Lucerna had disappeared. Her light was nowhere to be found.

Benn was also gone.

Rai turned to see Veil's body, and the darkness flooding from his soul. Her eyes glazed over, and she knelt.

"Rai?" she could hear Sara's voice in the distance.

Rai was on a ship. The sea stretched out in all directions with no land to be seen. The sky was dark and starless. A bright, white moon shone above, offering the only light.

Pentagon and Atrus stood on the deck, whispered to each other, and looked her way, not directly at her, but at someone behind her.

Rai turned around. Vassal.

He reached for her arm, and Rai flinched, but Vassal was insistent. He led her away to the stern of the ship.

I remember this, she thought. She knew what he was going to say, she knew the words, but he did not speak them. Instead, he removed a steel blade from his side, wrapped his arms around her, and stuck the knife through her back.

Rai fell to the floor and gasped. Her hands touched the knife in her back. The pain radiated up her spine.

Vassal stood above her and watched her suffer.

She climbed up his body, her bloody hands reddening his pants and shirt. She stared into his unfeeling eyes as she reached for the knife in her back. With a scream, she pulled out the knife. She grasped his collar as she raised the knife above her head. She stabbed him in the chest over and over again, screaming.

Her eyes were squeezed shut.

"Rai!"

Released from her nightmare, she opened her eyes. The shadow woman stood in front of her. Pentagon and Atrus had their weapons raised. Rodan clang to Farah and pinned her to his chest as she screamed Orka's name. Sara rushed to Rai and stood between her and the shadow. Veil was on his knees. He struggled to stand as the darkness consumed him.

The shadow woman reached out to Sara.

Smoke filled the burning cottage. Sara's eyes darted, searching for her father and mother. She ran to the back and tried to pry the window open, but it wouldn't budge. Banging on the window, she screamed for help.

The smoke made her eyes sting, and she coughed. Through her blurred vision, she could see the dining room. She ran and grabbed a chair as the smoke obscured her vision further. Weak from being unable to breathe, she stumbled to the back window. She hit the window with the chair, and the glass shattered.

She reached up to grab the sill, the remaining glass digging into her palms. But the window was too high and far too small.

Above the roar of the flames, footsteps sounded from inside the house.

"It hurts now," an echoing voice said, "but you should inhale the smoke. Let it kill you before the flames do."

Fire had filled the kitchen, and from those flames came a figure. Around his neck was a medallion. The skin on his face was scorched by the flames, but she knew him.

"Bolton."

Something urged her to join him in the fire, but a voice sounded all around her. "This isn't real!" Talon's voice bit through the roar of the flames in her ears. "Leave this place!"

Sara shut her eyes, and when she opened them, cavernous walls surrounded her.

"Hello?" her voice echoed.

The voices of two men resonated through the cave, and she followed their voices through a narrow space to a large, secluded section of the cavern. All along the walls, she saw strange markings, some she recognized as sphere symbols.

In the space stood the men, one with a strange birthmark on his face. The mark was shaped like a tear.

The other man had patches of skin eaten away from his face and hands.

Against one wall was a pile of bones, some with the flesh ripped from them, others still wrapped in the sinews. The smell of filth and decay pervaded the air.

The marked man covered his nose with his sleeve and asked in a muffled voice, "What happened to those people?"

"Have you ever heard of a Maledixit?" the skinless man asked.

"No."

"It is the darkest part of the human soul. Things happen to us in life that we don't ask for. My father, and mother, and sister are among these bones."

The marked man shook his head, realization coming upon him.

"A Maledixit stole my flesh and left me with this hunger . . . like that wave took everything from you and left you with such feelings of despair. But its energy, the emotions, the pain, the whole experience can be used and contained. That's what I learned, that's what I'm teaching you."

Sara blinked, and the cave faded to blackness.

The dark woman whispered something to Veil, and Veil reached out his hand. The darkness emitting from it stretched across the space between them and took hold of Sara's arm.

Sara tried to pull away, but Veil's shadow held fast, bringing her closer and closer to him.

Rai rushed at Veil, sword raised and blazing, but her sword went through him, not harming him. Her body went through his, and she fell to the floor.

Rodan sent a branch to pierce Veil's heart, but like Rai's body, the branch went through Veil, and he was unharmed.

"Sara, take my hand." Rodan reached out to Sara, and she grabbed his hand.

VASSAL hobbled to the port, his wooden leg making speed impossible.

Many of the ships had sailed away, their crew eager to flee the growing cloud, but one vessel remained. The captain and his crew rushed to release the sails.

"Sir!" Vassal hobbled along the docked ship. "Don't you dare leave this port!"

The captain looked at Vassal like he had gone mad. "I don't know what that thing is, but my crew and I are sailing before it gets any closer."

"You must wait!" Vassal said.

"Wait? Like hell!"

"Please, sir," Vassal said, "until no man nor woman can board your ship, until the chamber and the deck are full."

"I'm not going to endanger my crew."

Bolton came running into port followed by a troop of terrified citizens. Bolton joined Vassal, as the people rushed on board the ship, leaving the captain no time to refuse passengers.

When the ship was full to the brim with passengers, the captain ordered the men to set sail. The ship left the port, people still throwing themselves at its stern. These people fell into the water and swam for the boat.

Bolton ushered the others toward Dustpath and told them to run. The citizens and travelers rushed away from the city toward Dustpath Road.

"We can't save them all," Vassal said.

Bolton turned back to him. "The Stadium."

"What about it?" Vassal asked.

"It has a dome," Bolton said. "It could protect the people."

Bolton led the people to the Stadium. Panicked, some citizens were too frightened to remain in the city, but several others followed him, not knowing what to do as the cloud grew, stretching to the far corners of the city.

The people piled into the stands.

Bolton climbed into the announcer's stand, high above the rows of seating. He pressed the control buttons inside the booth, not knowing which one controlled the dome covering.

The gears turned, and the dome covered the wide space. Soon, the Stadium was closed to the outside. Sunlight peered through the semi-transparent covering.

Bolton exited the Stadium and met up with Vassal.

"How long have they been in there?" Vassal stared at the black cloud.

"Too long for comfort," Bolton said. "These people can only run now. As that cloud grows, they're all in danger. We have to stop it."

Bolton and Vassal made their way to the edge of the dark cloud. Bolton was ahead of Vassal.

"Wait!" Vassal hobbled to meet him. "Stay here, wait for my signal."

"What?" Bolton asked.

"You're our best weapon. Veil won't see it coming if you stay outside the cloud. Trust me."

"Didn't you stab your friends in the back?"

Vassal grabbed the collar of Bolton's shirt. "You want to save these people," he hissed, "then listen to me."

Bolton pulled Vassal's hand away from him. "All right. I'll be waiting for your signal."

As he entered the cloud, Vassal was taken to its center. Sara was in the grasp of Veil's shadow, Rodan's hand in hers. Rai lay in the darkness. Atrus and Pentagon loaded more bullets, after exhausting their first rounds. Farah went in for the attack, but her dagger went through Veil's body. She backed away as the dark woman lashed at her.

Rai managed to stand. "Sara! Your weapon."

Sara glanced down at her arm. Beneath the shadows was the outline of her wrist gun. The Aether was seated in its center.

She aimed at Veil.

"Now!" Rai and Vassal's voices twined into one.

VASSAL'S voice echoed through the cloud. Bolton sent Lightning into the dark mist and hoped he would hit his target.

At the same moment, Sara willed the Aether, and Lightning darted from its body, hitting Veil at the same time.

As the Lightning struck him, Veil's body lunged. The shadow released Sara.

Bolton stared into the darkness with no way of knowing whether his shot hit home. He shook his head and marched into the cloud.

Darkness swallowed him. He sparked Lightning in his hand and, by the glow, searched the darkness.

Someone approached. In his hand, he too was guided by a spark of Lightning.

His light, blond hair was streaked with white, and his blue eyes pierced the darkness. Up ahead, he saw what appeared to be his younger self.

Bolton blinked twice. "Dad?"

"Son?" Benn asked. "It can't be you."

Bolton sighed. "This darkness. It brings out our demons."

"What do you mean?" Benn asked.

"You're my darkness. You left me and my mother to die."

Benn hung his head. "This is my nightmare: to have my son hate me."

"How could it be any other way? Mom's dead because of you." Bolton's hand clenched into a fist.

"They're both dead because of me, wife and son." Benn closed his eyes and disappeared, turning his back on his nightmare.

"Dad? Dad? Coward!" Bolton kneeled and put his head in his hands. He was alone in the darkness. "Coward," he whispered.

THE people shuttered as the darkness spread over the dome and blocked the sunlight.

The darkness crawled over the Chariot. The cloud blackened the windows and shadows thundered at the glass.

"This is incredible," Thatch whispered.

Stannum floated to his side. His glowing eye blinked.

"WE don't need them!" the dark woman screamed.

Veil put his head in his hands and kneeled to the ground. "Forgive me!" His tears leaked through his fingers in thick, black globs, spreading across the ground.

Sara coughed. Smoke filled her lungs. She too, kneeled.

Rodan dropped beside her. "What's wrong?"

Sara put her hand to her throat. She struggled to breathe.

The shadow approached Sara. Rodan shielded her from it as Sara knelt on the ground and gasped for air. But the shadow went through Rodan's body, and he keeled over.

The shadow raised a dark hand, dripping with black ooze and touched Sara's chest. "Feel his despair," the shadow whispered. Her touch left its mark.

The shadow retreated to Veil's side and watched the turmoil that ensued.

Rai faced Vassal. Small, glowing worms emerged from his mouth and eyes and spread across the ground. He walked toward her, and she drew her sword.

"Stay away, monster," Rai said.

"It's me," Vassal pleaded with her.

Rai swung her sword at him, and Vassal raised his hand to shield his face. The blade embedded in his wooden hand, and as Rai swung back her sword, the wood splintered.

Vassal raised his sword to meet her next blow.

"Get up!" the dark woman urged Veil. "Show them the pinnacle of your power, my son. Destroy them!"

Veil screamed. "My father's words from my mother's lips."

"You pulled me from the darkness, my son. You pulled me out to see your victory."

"I pulled you out to comfort me in my sadness," Veil said, "but you're just a shadow, a poor imitation of my mother."

Veil rose, his legs shaking. He put his hand on his mother's head. "You can only bring me pain." He pushed her down into the shadows, and her screams echoed through the cloud.

A path of light emerged.

Lucerna, surrounded by the light that emitted around her, cut through the darkness. She closed her eyes to it. Light flooded toward Veil and washed over him. Light cleared the darkness engulfing the city.

BOLTON searched the misty nothingness before the blinding light tore it down. The ticket booth stood in front of him, but there was no sign of Atrus, Pentagon, or Vassal.

LUCERNA fell to her knees and then to the ground. Pentagon rushed to her side.

Rai dropped her sword.

Sara took a deep breath as she clung to Rodan's arm. Her eyes were distant.

Veil looked around. The darkness that had surrounded him was gone, but it still flooded his heart.

He touched the ground with his hands. His back arched like a cat's as his body twisted and contorted into something inhuman. His bones cracked, were broken, and reformed. He grew, and a suffusion of hair covered his body. His jaw jutted forward and sharp rows of teeth protruded from his extended gums. His scream transformed into a howl. His gray eyes shone beneath the black fur as he stood on all fours.

Rodan lifted his sword from the ground.

Sara stood. Before Rodan could stop her, she approached the beast. "Veil?" Her hand touched the fur on its shoulder. For a moment, there was warmth, and the darkness receded further within him. But he could feel it hastening back to the surface.

The beast lifted its head into the air and growled. It swung its head toward Dustpath, bolted through the market, and left scratches across the marble floor.

Bullets followed him as Atrus tried to get a clear shot. "Damn it!"

"We have to get out of here," Vassal said to Pentagon and Atrus. He tried nodding to Rai, but she would not look his way.

"Come on," Rai said. "We should leave too."

Sara stared into the distance where Veil had escaped. She said nothing. She had a look of despair in her eyes.

"Come on, Sara, let's go," Rai urged, but Sara did not respond. Her eyes were anchored to the street.

Rai grabbed her arm and led her away as she and Farah rushed to Dustpath. Rodan carried the still unconscious Lucerna.

Pentagon, Atrus, and Vassal ran toward the port to meet Bolton.

"Wait," Pentagon said, "we should go back."

"We can't do that," Atrus said.

"We should tell him," Pentagon said.

"It'll only upset him," Vassal said as they approached Bolton.

"What'll upset me?" Bolton asked.

Orka chirped and landed on Bolton's shoulder.

A chariot piloted by Morica guards flew down from its place of safety, far from the shadow. Guards piled out, guns raised.

"That's upsetting," Atrus said.

"You're under arrest by order of the High Council."

"What? We do their bidding, and we're fugitives again?" Atrus asked.

"Atrus, shut up, and use your only real weapon to its advantage," Vassal said.

Atrus swept his hand in front of him, and the pistols flew from the guards' hands and into the water.

"I meant your gun," Vassal said, "but that'll do."

Vassal approached the unarmed guards, and punched one of them in the face. His body slumped to the ground. As the other tried to defend, Vassal swept his wooden leg across the wharf and kicked the man's legs out from under him. His head hit the piling, and he fell unconscious.

Vassal walked to the chariot and turned back to Atrus. "I hope you know how to fly this thing."

63

DESPAIR

RAI and Farah joined Thatch in the control room while Rodan carried Lucerna to the cabin to rest.

Sara had not said a word since the shadow touched her. She had retreated to the hallway outside the door to the roof.

Benn did not return to the Chariot.

"I say we leave him," Rai said. "It's not like he's well-liked here."

"I'm worried about Sara," Farah said. "She hasn't said anything since we've been back, and the way she went up to Veil after he turned into that creature was creepy."

"That shadow," Rai said, "it touched her. If Darkness did that to her then Lucerna might be able to fix it."

"But we don't know when she's going to wake up," Farah said.

"That's true." Thatch sat in his seat.

"Her energy is drained," Rai said. "She will wake when she is stronger."

"What are we going to do about Veil?" Thatch asked.

"Well, we can't let him roam around Mirmina in beast mode," Farah said.

"We'll have to find him." Rai flipped the switch, and the Chariot roared to life. "He's weakened. He probably retreated to a place of safety. A place where he feels he'll be protected."

"Vella City?" Farah asked.

"No," Rai said. "The Council would kill him. Mordecai would especially want him dead. He's an Elemental now and a strong one. My best guess is that he went back to Tosia. He's probably hiding in the Domum Fidei until he gets his strength back. We should go there now."

"Shouldn't we wait until Lucerna wakes up?" Farah asked. "She's our best weapon."

Rai tilted the steering wheel. "Let's hope she wakes up by the time we arrive. We can't hold this off any longer. Every second we wait, Veil is regaining his strength. In his weakened state, we may be able to take him down without Lucerna."

SARA stared at the wall opposite her.

She felt a heaviness in the depths of her being, like she was at the bottom of a well clawing to get out, but the world above that well was cloudy and gray, and she felt an insurmountable despair at the notion of going there. But the bottom of the well was silent and isolating. She could not see the light.

Dread and anxiety filled her, and hope had left. She felt that she didn't have the energy to stand, and an ache rose in her chest and pressure built behind her eyes, but she could not cry.

The world went on without her as the Chariot lifted into the air. She barely felt the jolt as it sailed through the sky.

Night fell, and Rodan knelt beside her as she stared at the steel wall. "Sara? Can you hear me?"

Sara gulped, and her eyes became glassy, but she didn't speak.

"What are you feeling?" Rodan asked.

Silence.

"You should get some rest," he said. "We're going to Tosia. We think Veil might be there, and there's a good chance Lucerna will wake up soon. She might be able to help you when she does."

Sara didn't look at him.

"Come on." Rodan took her arm and helped her to her feet. "You should rest."

She did not resist as Rodan led her to the cabin room and placed her in the bed across from Lucerna's.

He pulled the blankets up to her chin. Sara didn't close her eyes. She stared up at the dark sky through the windows on the ceiling.

Rodan feared she would spend the night staring at the dark clouds, but he didn't know what he could do to help her.

RAI landed the ship in D'arkadia. Rodan met Rai and Farah in the engine room near the hatch door. The door opened.

"You ready?" Rai asked.

Rodan and Farah nodded. They exited the Chariot and walked to the entrance of Tosia.

Sara still rested in the cabin room beside Lucerna. When the Chariot landed, she felt a strange pull. It urged her to rise even though her body willed her not to. She was drawn to Tosia.

Moments after Rodan, Rai, and Farah had entered the village, Sara left the Chariot.

Thatch had not noticed because his eyes were focused on the screen beside his seat. The Aether sensed a great burst of Elemental energy coming from each of the sphere sanctums. This energy grew at a greater rate than when their journey began. Thatch predicted that this energy came from the Protectors. They had to replace the spheres if they wanted to stabilize the situation.

Sara wandered into the village.

Rodan, Farah, and Rai stood outside the Domum Fidei. The darkness Veil had spread through the village lingered, but the inhabitants had fled, leaving the streets blackened and empty.

"Don't let that shadow touch you," Rai said.

"If you see Veil," Rodan said, "use all your energy on him. We'll back you up." Rodan spotted Sara walking to the center of the village. He approached her. Rodan grabbed her shoulders. "Why did you leave the Chariot?"

He turned to Rai and Farah. "We have to get her back to Thatch."

"There's no time," Rai said. "Veil could be in there."

"I could stay with her," Farah said.

"We need you," Rai said. "She might be mute right now, but she's not an imbecile. Tell her to wait here. The sooner we get to Veil, the sooner we can heal her."

Rodan sighed. "Sara, please, don't follow us. Wait here. I promise, we'll be right back."

Rai and Farah turned back to the Domum Fidei. Rodan hesitated, but he followed them. Rai kicked the door in, and they entered. Rodan took one last look at Sara before disappearing into the dwelling.

Sara stared ahead, still feeling the pull. She had not interpreted Rodan's words nor did she realize that he had spoken them. Her mind was like a narrow tunnel filled with haze. Rodan's voice had echoed down that tunnel only to be lost in indistinct whispers.

As if strings were tethered to her soul, she was led to the east side of the village. She stepped upon the sparkling path to the Cliff. She could feel her feet, independent of her, easing her to the edge.

She felt as if she had approached the opening of the well. That she would soon journey into the world with the darkened sky, and somehow that was better than being at the bottom of the well. Somehow that idea was liberating.

She stared into the stormy sky as one foot stepped over the ledge, and without looking down, she stepped into the sky and fell.

64

ON THE JOB

ATRUS sat in the driver's seat. He turned the engine on and steered the chariot through the water. As he pulled back on the steer, the chariot jolted into the air. He eased the steering wheel into the neutral position, and the chariot sailed through the sky.

"Glad you can fly it." Vassal clapped him on the shoulder. "Now we have to find Veil."

"How are we going to do that?" Atrus asked. "Who knows where he's headed, and you saw what he turned into."

Pentagon and Bolton sat in the seats lining the chariot's inner walls.

"He's weak," Pentagon said. "There are tunnels under the Domum Fidei. He would likely take refuge there."

"Are you sure?" Atrus asked.

"It's the best we got," Vassal said. "I can't think of where else he would go."

Bolton leaned his head against the wall and sighed. Orka moved along his shoulder.

"You okay?" Pentagon asked.

Bolton laughed. "I wish I would have never got caught up with you guys."

"It's been a pleasure travelling with you too," Atrus said.

"Look," Bolton said, "I understand you have to clear these charges Morica has on you, but Sara is out there somewhere, and I have to find her."

"Yes," Vassal said. "She's out there somewhere."

"Right, so—"

"So," Vassal said, "we have a problem. We don't have time to drop you off wherever it is you think Sara might have gone. You see, neither of us is a strong Elemental like you, and we have a very limited window of time to kill a very powerful Elemental. So, I suggest you sit tight because this bird's flying all the way to Tosia. If it suits you, you can get off there and travel alone until you happen upon Sara."

Bolton stood face to face with Vassal. "If it wasn't for me, you would have been housed in Lumina City jail when that Elemental terrorized the city. I think you owe me more than a pat on the back and a handshake."

"Where do you want to go?" Atrus asked.

"Elementa," Bolton said.

"We can't do that," Atrus said. "Besides, it would be a waste of your time."

"How would you know that?" Bolton asked.

"We might as well tell him," Pentagon said.

"Tell me what?"

"Bolton, I think maybe you should sit," Pentagon said.

"Just tell me."

"We saw Sara," Atrus said.

"What?" Bolton asked. "In Lumina? Why didn't you tell me when we were there?"

"We met her in the cloud," Pentagon said. "She seemed pretty out of it after the battle, and we had to make a run for it. I'm sorry. We thought it best not to tell you."

Bolton laughed. "So it wouldn't slow you down."

"That's right," Vassal said.

"And you know where she's going?" Bolton asked.

"She's tracking Veil," Vassal said.

"That means there's a good possibility that we'll meet her in Tosia," Pentagon said.

"Or if you prefer," Vassal said. "We could just drop you into the sea."

Atrus landed the small chariot on the coast of the Lake de Somnia. He, Pentagon, Vassal, and Bolton with Orka perched upon his shoulder exited the vessel and headed for Tosia.

They walked through the blackened entryway. As they approached the center of the village, Farah, Rodan, and Rai exited the Domum Fidei.

"Any sign of Veil?" Vassal asked as they approached.

"We searched the whole place," Rai said. "No sign of him."

Orka chirped and flew to Farah's shoulder.

"Orka!" The anxiety lifted from her as she petted and cooed at the little, green bird on her shoulder. "You were here the whole time?"

"No, she was with me." Bolton stepped from behind Vassal.

Farah's eyes widened. "It can't be. Bolton!" She ran to him and put her arms around him.

Bolton hunched over as Farah pulled him down into her embrace.

Once Farah released Bolton, Rodan approached him. His face twisted in shock. He hugged him, clapping him on the shoulder, waiting for reality to set in.

"Where's Sara?" Rai asked.

Rodan drew away from Bolton and looked around for Sara. She was nowhere to be seen.

Bolton left them and searched the village. The others took different directions. Bolton's feet thundered along the glimmering path to the Cliff. He watched as Sara's feet left the ledge and her body fell.

"No!" He jumped. Other thoughts were useless to him. He grabbed her in mid-air and hugged her body to his.

All her despair left as their bodies sailed through the air.

65

THE CREATOR

SARA'S eyes blinked open. She waited for the haze to dissipate, but it never did. Rising to her feet, she looked around.

Had it been a dream?

A dull roar echoed in the distance.

She could see nothing beyond the mist. Reaching out, she fell into the darkness until she touched upon a rocky wall. Her fingers grazed the wall, and she followed it until the ground sloped upward, and the mist cleared.

She journeyed up the steep slope until she could see the sky above the fog. The air was cold. The rocky walls and the stone buildings of Omega Ray rose in the distance.

How did I get here?

The roaring sounded closer and more distinct.

Crossing her arms over her body, Sara made her way through the cold air to the walls of the city. She reached Hephaestus's ruined castle. Stairs led down to the dungeon.

The wind was biting, and the hideous roar grew closer.

Sara climbed down the stairs to take shelter within the vestiges of the ruined castle. As she reached the last step, her foot lighted upon something that clanged against the stone floor.

She looked down.

Upon the final step was Talon's sword. It had never been recovered from the battle three years ago.

Sara reached for the grip and lifted the sword from the ground. It was heavier than Rodan's sword. With great effort, she held the sword and brought it with her into the dungeons. She wanted it to be mounted in Element where it belonged.

Dim light flooded in from the doorway. Sara took a torch from the wall and reached into her canvas bag to find matches. Striking a match, she lit the torch.

She wandered through the dungeons and past the cells. She stopped. On the back wall of a cell, something caught her eye.

She looked again.

It was faint, but she thought she saw something carved into the wall.

She opened the cell door and approached the wall. A faint circle the size of a dinner plate was engraved in the stone. It was divided into four parts.

Her finger traced the circle, and the grooves glowed.

Sara stepped back.

The circle stopped glowing.

She leaned Talon's sword against the adjacent wall and placed the torch on the stone floor. She placed her hands upon the cold stone, and once again, the grooves glowed. Sara could feel her power leaving her.

A crack ran down the wall and cut through the center of the circle. Where the crack formed, the wall began to separate.

Sara staggered back, the energy sapped from her body. She struggled to stand as the walls halted.

Inside the wall, steps led down into darkness.

Sara picked up the torch and Talon's sword. By the light of the torch, she journeyed down the steps behind the wall. The steps led down to a tunnel. The walls were narrow and lined with stone.

The further down she journeyed, the darker the tunnel became until the darkness swallowed the torch's illumination.

A smell wafted through the air. It was a rotten smell that stung Sara's nose. She had never smelled anything like that before.

As Sara turned the corner, the tunnel opened to a chamber also lined in stone. By the dim light of the torch, Sara could see the skeletal remains of rats piled against the wall. Some had their flesh recently picked from the bones.

Sara's torch swept the walls until she spotted something slumped in the corner. It turned around and faced her with flesh rotting from its face.

It was a man. At least, that's what he appeared to be. Sara had seen him before in the darkness.

He stepped into the light, but Sara stepped back.

In that glimpse where the light touched his face, she could see the skin peeling back, showing the sinews beneath. Around one eye, the flesh was rotted, making the eye appear to pop out from his face.

"Who are you, my dear?" it asked. "Are you one of my children? You must be, to have gotten in here."

Sara stepped further back. Her eyes traveled to the pile of rats in the corner.

"He left me no choice. Destan has no love for his father. I've been hungry since he imprisoned me here." He stepped closer to Sara.

"Wait," it said, "you are a child of the sphere. I can sense your power. Water. I gave you that power. I am your god, the only force more powerful than the most treacherous hail storm, the fiercest fire, the mightiest gust of wind, the swiftest flood, the sharpest sting of lightning, the greatest earthquake, or the darkest night. I invested this power, which I obtained in the souls of six others. With flesh, I compensate for my lack of flesh, and with power, I compensate for the loss of my life due to this curse, to my inhuman needs, and to my increasing desire for more than I possess.

"Now, tell me, my child, have you seen great destruction?" Erebus revealed from beneath his cloak a sphere, empty of any essence, waiting to be filled.

"I have." Sara's voice shook. "I have seen destruction worse than any of the elements of nature: the destruction brought upon by selfish greed. This is what truly destroys and turns one soul against another. Trust is broken, hopes are dashed, and lives are thrown carelessly into the flames. The lust for power has sewn its place in the fabric of the human heart, and it seems that nothing can rip that stitch out."

With her last ounce of strength, Sara plunged Talon's sword into his chest. Then, she ran.

"No!" came an inhuman roar. "Don't touch the door!"

Darkness, blacker than the depths of the tunnels, raced along the walls and swept upon Sara like a flood. As it washed over her, everything went black.

66

UNCHAINED SHADOWS

SARA lifted herself from the darkness. The torch had gone out. She crept along the walls of the tunnel until she saw the brighter light of the dungeons above her. She climbed the stairs.

Finding her way back to the crumbled throne room, Sara searched the cold, night air for the creature. She could still see the skin dripping off his face as he clenched the empty sphere in his rotting hand.

She saw her own breath like white mist in the coldness as her feet kicked over the crumbling stone ruins of the forgotten palace.

Staring at the place where Hephaestus fell, she remembered the darkness. The same blackness had swallowed her up in the tunnels beneath the dungeon. The same darkness consumed Veil. She had felt the shadow touch her soul, and it was cold despair.

Thinking of that superior chill, she folded her bare arms across her chest, but they granted little protection from the invisible iciness.

Buildings surrounded the ruined palace dressed in white snow. Their doorknobs frosted over with ice. Clear, icy teeth hung from the undersides of roofs and archways.

And the howl sounded in the distance. It was the sound of the Maledixit prowling the night, reveling in the cold, its heart mourning the friends that fell prey to its hunger. The Maledixit, man at his most basic, had good defense against the winter, its thick fur curling down its back and chest.

As the wind swept her hair across her face, Sara stood among the ruins, frozen, afraid of what was to come in this empty void she had created.

No longer did the warmth of the flames combat the cold. The city was as empty as the sphere Erebus clenched onto for dear life. The darkness was a void, an absence of power, and that void rested in the old monster's soul.

Sara had felt that void envelope her. She could no longer feel the pull of her element, the water rushing against the dam to be free.

When the Water Sphere cracked, she hadn't felt as if something was leaving her. She had only felt that something inside her was being suppressed, caged within her. Now she felt her power leaving, seeping from her like blood from the body. It was not being forced out, but was leaving her because she wanted it to. That thing in the ground had given her that power.

A figure approached in the distance. Searching the ground, she picked up a palm-sized stone, heavy and jagged. The stone once helped hold up the walls of the crumbling palace. It had given power to her enemy and now that power was going to defend her.

She envisioned the rotting flesh and the bony hands of the creature beneath the ground. She imagined the darkness creeping along the ground toward her.

But as the figure got closer, she could make out the blond hair and the scarred face.

Her breathing slowed. The rock fell from Sara's hand.

And her feet moved of their own accord, slowly at first, and then her pace quickened to a run. She could sense her power returning to her, flooding back in like a stream funneling toward a cliff.

She put her arms around Bolton's neck and held him close. "Did I die?" she asked.

Bolton shook his head.

"What happened to you?" Sara asked.

"I looked for you as soon as I woke," Bolton said. "I fell from the cliff with you."

Sara touched his face. The scars had faded along his jawline and cheek, but they left the skin plastered and tough, without pores or softness.

"Fero did some extra damage to me when we fell," he said.

Sara smiled and took refuge in the brightness of his eyes. They reminded her so much of the sea off the coast of the Insula. "You're here. I don't know how, but you're here, and that's all that matters to me right now."

The cold retreated from them, like an injured animal creeping into the comfort of the darkness.

Bolton lifted his head. A figure stood in the distance.

"Who's that?" he asked.

Sara turned around in his arms.

The figure approached them from the mist. He was an old man with a permanent tear running down his face. A red glow followed him wherever he went. His face twisted in a look of despair. "You let him out."

EPILOGUE: MY CHILDREN

DAWN sat upon a satin pillow in her home in Tosia where she, Vuur, Glaciem, and Vjetar had gathered. They had been walled up there since Veil's departure.

There was no need for them to eat. They lived on, whether the pain of hunger tolled or not.

Dawn had been patient as the darkness reveled in dispelling the light. Life had worn down her body, but she could not die. Neither could life abandon Fulgur, Vjetar, Vuur, Glaciem or Destan to the dark peacefulness of death.

They had all felt a change happen a few days ago, shortly after the darkness had taken Tosia. Their shared energies were being drawn into another essence, imprisoned in another sphere. The draining of their powers was weakening them. For once, they could see the walls of their strength. They too had limits.

A knock came to the door.

"Fulgur?" Vjetar asked.

Dawn stood and walked to the door.

They all knew it was not Fulgur. They could not sense his energy that surged like lightning. What they felt was darker.

As the heavy door creaked open, the visitor walked in. He was in the form of a man, with his skin eaten away. His yellowed eyeballs glistened in the dim light. His teeth were still sharp despite the centuries of gnawing on bones.

"I'm home, my children."

Here is a preview of the third volume
of the Elementals Trilogy

THE CREATOR

L. M. PERALTA

Now available in Kindle and paperback

THE walls and ground of Dawn's home where living roots used to grow were now black and dying. The leaves were curling in on themselves and falling to ashes on the floor.

Dawn salvaged some of the herbs before they begun to die. She used them to make tea for her father and brothers.

Dawn's hands shook as she placed the cup of tea in the fleshless hands.

Suddenly, one of the fleshless hands seized her wrist.

"I've missed you." He held onto her spotted hand. He looked around at Vuur, Glaciem, and Vjetar. "I've missed all of you."

He let go of Dawn's wrist.

"Where is your brother, Destan?"

Dawn gulped.

Did he know? Did he know what she and Destan had done?

"Destan has been wandering the earth," Vuur said, "looking for you, Father." His waxy hand rested in his lap.

Erebus touched the burnt side of Vuur's face with his fleshless hand. "He is a good son." There was no sarcasm in his voice because there could be none.

Dawn sat next to Erebus. "How long have you been back, Father?"

"Time rolls by when you are hungry."

"I can get you something." Dawn rose from her seat. Dawn had stopped faking her raspy voice. Now her voice rang out clear, like a young woman's. It seemed unnatural to her weathered form.

"Oh, can you, my dear. Perhaps a little baker's boy or a wandering traveler."

"The town is abandoned," Vjetar said, "and travelers do not pass through often." His sharp blue eyes pierced the darkness.

"Pity."

Glaciem gripped one of his ashy, grayish brown fingers and broke it off with a dull crack. The brown nail fell away. "Here, father."

"I can't eat your frost bit flesh."

Glaciem withdrew the finger and put it in his pocket with his head down.

"Why are you hiding in this hole?" Erebus asked.

When Dawn had touched his face to see him with her sightless eyes, she noted that he was more deteriorated than when she last saw him. Dawn feared that his eye, ungrounded by any flesh, would pop out and fall upon the floor. Eating rats underground had rotted his teeth and increased his need for human flesh.

Dawn still had the nightmares about Dustpath, and the people lining up to eat from the communal stew. She could still smell the rotting intestines of the bodies.

Erebus slammed the small table with his fist. "Why are you hiding here?"

The butter knife clamored to the floor.

A knock came to the door.

Dawn rose from her seat to answer it.

A tall, shadowy form stood in the doorway, but that was all her eyes would allow her to see. Still, she knew it was Fulgur. She could sense his energy.

She moved aside so that he may enter.

"Fulgur, my son," Erebus said, "please sit. We were having tea."

Dawn thought for a moment how absurd it was that they were having tea. After all, they could find no joy in it. They could eat dirt just as well to dissuade their hunger.

Fulgur sat where Dawn had been sitting next to Erebus.

Dawn walked over to the kettle and poured a cup of tea. She tried to hand it to Fulgur, but he refused it.

When was the last time Fulgur had eaten? Dawn wondered. Was he just letting the pings of hunger consume him?

"What have you been doing?" Vjetar asked.

"Amusing myself," Fulgur said.

"With humans," Vuur said.

When their father was gone, they had made a pact not to mess in the affairs of humans. They would watch from afar but never again try to present themselves as gods. Fulgur had gone against that pact.

"Why are you all dressed in rags?" Erebus stared from Dawn's plain robes to Vjetar's tattered gray shirt. "You look like prisoners. Humans should be making you glowing robes with glass beads and gifting you golden necklaces."

Dawn had kept her fine robes and golden necklaces of the past locked away in a chest to remind her of the decadence that killed so many people.

"This is a different world than when you left it, Father," Dawn said.

"I did not leave it," Erebus snapped. "I was imprisoned by one of my sons."

They looked around at each other.

"Destan," he hissed. "He bites the hand that feeds."

Dawn visualized Erebus's arm where the flesh had been pulled away.

Destan used to be his favorite son. Would he give Destan the fatted calf if he returned or would Erebus condemn him?

"You were supposed to keep this world in line for me. Instead you've let the humans take over to rule themselves again?"

Glaciem's head sank towards his lap.

Vjetar stared at the ground, now dying with the great tree.

"They brought this world to shambles the first time," Erebus said, "and I cleaned it up. Now, you have let it go to ruin. I've seen vessels flying. Little machines to replace them. Government. There would be no need for shadow leaders if the people had gods."

Vuur stared into the eyes of his father.

Dawn watched his form.

Fulgur focused on his peeling lips, the blood dripping from the corners of his mouth as if he had just eaten.

"I am the Creator of the Children of Spheres. They must bow before their gods."

Dawn remembered the old days. Humans were their slaves. The Children of the Spheres kept them in line, like sentinels, but they were no less slaves than their ungifted counterparts.

She remembered the first uprising.

The Children of the Spheres armed with their elements attempted to fight against the Keepers. Hundreds of thousands died fighting against their gods.

Dawn had refused to help her father, and Destan hid himself away.

When the battle was done, those who remained cowered in fear.

Erebus celebrated with his children, sad that Destan was not there to join them.

Until one day, Erebus disappeared.

His children didn't look for him, didn't wonder where he had gone. They retired until, over the centuries, the people forgot them.

Dawn didn't want power. She didn't want life. She wanted to sleep, to be restful.

No matter how often she closed her eyes, she could not sleep, could not dream, and could not see anything beyond this world. That was the gift her father had given her.

Now, he wanted to be worshiped again.

Dawn had lived in a semi-calm before this moment. She knew her father didn't trust her. She would refuse to help once again. He said she had more water in her soul than Destan, that her fate was wavering.

"You will show them what we can do," Erebus said. "I will reveal myself to them after they have seen this show of power. Give them time to digest it."

Dawn could sense Fulgur staring at her. She shifted in her seat.

She still felt his lightning rage the day she scorned him.

She had moved the earth in Jetty Verte.

Their lovers' quarrel had inconsequently freed the prisoners in the underground jail and crushed many beneath the falling earth. Power had consumed her that day.

Since then, it had been decades since she had used her element. It stirred inside her, but just as Fulgur refused to eat, Dawn refused to give into releasing the energy.

They sipped their tea in silence.

Dawn could hear no breathing. She had been used to such silence when they were together, but now it was unsettling.

She wondered how long Erebus had been out of his cage.

It would be like her father to settle a few matters behind their backs before coming to them. He no longer trusted his children.

Dawn heard something wet hit the floor, and she wondered if that was a piece of her father's flesh falling from his bones.

They settled into pairs.

Vuur and Vjetar sat in one corner and talked.

Erebus and Fulgur sat together in silence.

Glaciem was reading to Dawn from an old book that she kept. It was the history of Tosia, but it was only a partial history. It told the story of how fate led the people of Dustpath to the Great Tree where they carved their future. It spoke of their vows to live by nature and to never use their elements.

Glaciem had difficulty turning the pages. He could only use his ring finger and thumb because the other fingers had turned stiff and brown. His voice rang out youthful and clear.

Sometimes Dawn imagined they were all young.

She could feel her thinning, brittle hair and the deep wrinkles on her face, but she had never seen herself after her hands left the sphere.

Her father was the only one in the room whose face she had seen, and she could never forget it. The skin on one cheek was rotted away so that the sinews beneath were visible. The flesh around his eyes was starting to rot, and he had several bony fingers where the flesh was almost completely gone.

Dawn looked up from the book.

She was so lost in her thoughts, she had not noticed her father and Fulgur leave. She had not heard the door opening or closing.

Dawn placed a hand on Glaciem's arm. "Is Father still here?" she asked.

"He and Fulgur left moments ago."

Dawn allowed Galciem to read for a little while longer, so as not to draw suspicion. Then, she stood from where she sat.

"Where are you going?"

"I need some fresh air," Dawn said. "Now that my plants have died, this room has become stuffy."

Dawn felt the wall to the door. She sensed her father and brother's energy and followed it to the Cliff of Broken Promise.

Dawn leaned against the tunnel-like walls. Through her dull vision, she could make out two forms on the Cliff. Sensing their energy, she knew it was Erebus and Fulgur.

"Don't you want peace, my son?"

"But I'm afraid to die."

"You have been a good son. You deserve to rest. Will you help me gather them?"

"Yes, father."

From the remnants she had gathered, Dawn could not piece together what her father had meant. Keepers could not be killed. They could not rest. The eternal slumber was denied to them.

Dawn could see their forms move towards the tunnels.

She snaked along the walls until she was out. She walked along the blackened tree branches that made up the pathway. She moved into the center of town where the Domom Fidei was nestled and up the narrow pathway.

If her heart could beat, it would be hammering.

Once she was satisfied she was far enough away not to be suspected, Dawn slowed her pace to a steady stroll.

She was turned around by the shoulder and pushed against the wall.

She felt static.

"Fulgur?"

"It is so nice to hear that voice," he said.

She felt urgent lips pressed against hers.

She slapped him.

Fulgur pressed a hand against her chest and shocked her.

She thought she felt her heart beat again, but only for a moment.

"What were you and Father talking about?" she asked.

"It was between me and him."

"Don't you think we should all know?"

"If you kiss me with passion, I'll tell you."

Dawn glared at him with her sightless eyes.

"I have to go," he said.

"Where?"

"Not where father has sent me."

"You're disobeying him."

"I'm just making a detour," he said. "There is so much to get settled first."

He touched her face. "You are so lucky you held onto the sphere long enough to take your sight, so you can't see what I'm about to do."

ABOUT THE AUTHOR

L. M. PERALTA graduated from the University of New Orleans with a degree in English and holds a law degree from Tulane University. She lives in Louisiana with her husband. She is the author of The Elementals trilogy (*The Elementals, The Council,* and *The Creator*), The Arcadian Steel Sequence (*The Wings of Heaven and Hell, The Seven Archangels of Heaven,* and *The Seven Princes of Hell*), and *United Trace*. She was a finalist for *The Elementals* in the Dante Rossetti Awards 2013 for Young Adult Novels.

Follow L. M. Peralta on Facebook
www.facebook.com/authorlmperalta

Follow L. M. Peralta on Twitter
www.twitter.com/l_m_peralta

For free content, updates, and
behind the scenes information,
visit www.lmperalta.com.

ACKNOWLEDGMENTS

I would like to especially thank my grandmother, Marie Peralta, for without whom my books would go largely unread.

I want to also thank my father, Lorne Peralta, for his tireless efforts.

Also, a special thanks to my family, friends, teachers, and mentors, all of whom have contributed to my character and success. Thank you all.